Love Th

CW01335944

Victoria Lary was born in the ancient city of Omdurman in the Sudan, into a Christian family, although the majority of her education was gained in Muslim schools.

She began her working life at the age of seventeen as an air-hostess in Sudan Airways. During her travels to many countries she met her English husband John, in London, to whom she is greatly indebted for his assistance and moral support.

Victoria started her writing as a hobby to entertain her family, in particular her only son David, who is currently a postgraduate at Cambridge. Since his childhood, he has been one of her most enthusiastic fans, reading her stories with relish.

Love Thy Enemy

Victoria Lary

Spectral Power

First published in 1989 by
Spectral Power
12 Gladeside, Bar Hill
Cambridge CB3 8DY

British Library Cataloguing-in-Publication Data

Lary, Victoria, *1944-*
Love thy enemy,.
I. Title
823'.914 [F]

ISBN 0 9514765 0 5

Typeset by Spectral Power

Artwork by David Cutting Graphics

Printed and bound in Great Britain by
Richard Clay Ltd
Bungay, Suffolk NR35 1ED

Contents

CHAPTER 1

THE BOMB

From the air it looked a beautiful and prosperous land. Its narrow coastline hugged the eastern end of the Mediterranean. The deep blue waters glistened and shone as the sun's rays reflected off their surface. Its mountains rose directly from the sea, with their heads touching the clouds. Lebanon was a jewel in the Arab world, the Switzerland of the Middle East, and people of the neighbouring countries dreamed of travelling there to find refreshment and rest for their souls.

Poets and songwriters enumerated its beauties and described its pleasant landscape. Like a magnet, it attracted so many that it became a centre of recreation, and in this atmosphere trade prospered. Trade in everything, even in money, so the tourist could buy and sell whatever currency he required, from Japanese yen to American dollars, easily and without entering a bank or office, but right on the crowded streets. There was the smell of roasted meat and the sight of smart, young waiters, who stood at the corners of the main shopping areas, to invite, persuade, entice passers-by to enter their well-arranged restaurants and try their mouth-watering dishes at cheap prices.

Lebanon was the centre of education and enlightenment for the Middle East, and students travelled from far and near to seek a place in her celebrated University, staffed with well-known doctors and teachers with world famous reputations.

All these facilities helped Lebanon to rise in splendour, causing the Americans to rush to her shores and mountains for their summer holidays and the Europeans, especially the French, to seek it out as an oasis for pleasure seeking and fun.

In its early years, the population was fairly equally divided between Christians and Muslims, with a Christian president and Muslim prime minister. However, with the wars in the area between Arabs and Jews, the balance became disturbed as thousands of Muslim Palestinians fled to seek shelter in her land.

Syria, a close neighbour, stretched out her hand in support of the Palestinians, which aided in tipping the balance altogether, making the situation unstable for the inhabitants.

Although Lebanon is still attractive from the air, when you touch its land and rub shoulders with her population, you find the story has taken a horrifying change, with divisions worse than that caused by the Berlin Wall. There are three main groups; the Christians, the Muslims and the Druze. Besides these, there are numerous other factions that keep splitting and growing by the day, so making the entire land a living scene of terror, as one no longer knows his friends from his foes. Those who were once good neighbours now aim their weapons towards each other. Children stay close to parents and shelter indoors, while their schooling is interrupted time and time again.

In the midst of all these living tragedies, life continues. Love and weddings, giving birth to children and bringing them up with new hopes and dreams that tomorrow will be better, tomorrow things will change.

George Bishara was a young Lebanese with an attractive wife and three children. They lived in the Christian sector of Beirut. He had named his firstborn daughter, Amal, meaning hope, as he and his wife were hoping for a better and more secure, prosperous life. Amal was now eleven, who with her younger brother of nine and baby sister only two, never left their mother's sight. They felt safe as long as their mama and papa were there, at home. Amal understood that the country was in trouble as she often heard her father and uncles talking in whispers.

"The Muslims are planning it, brother. I am sure they want to finish us off and take our place."

One day she heard her mama saying, with concern showing in her green eyes,

"Let's emigrate to America or Canada."

"Impossible," answered her father in desperation, "from where can we get the money? Business has almost come to a standstill, so we don't even have enough money to cross to Cyprus, let alone go to America."

Amal's little heart quivered, and she felt in danger, so she ran to her father, climbed onto his lap and tightly clutched his hands. She knew that her family was in a crisis and the villains were 'those Muslims'.

Night and darkness were the enemies of Amal and her brother and sister, as things looked worse and sounds turned into nightmares that woke her screaming,

"Papa, the Muslims are coming," or "Mama, there is a bomb outside. Mama, let us run away."

The next evening, the family gathered together again, to talk out their concerns and worries. The children, too, heard the conversation, even though everyone spoke in whispers. Uncle had determination in his voice as he said,

"We must hit back. We will not leave our country for America or anywhere else. This is our home, and this is where we'll stay."

Whilst the conversation continued, many names were mentioned, but one kept coming up - Abu Mansour.

"He's the key man and is building a name for himself among the militia, and planning a bombing campaign, I swear, as I heard this news from reliable sources. He's working in two camps and gathering great support from the Palestinians. In fact, he's been spotted down this road, so be aware, keep your eyes open."

That night was the last night in which Amal saw her parents and brother and sister. On that night she lost her uncles and aunts. She lost everything.

A bomb was left in a parked car outside the block of flats where they lived and exploded with a deafening roar. She heard it and saw her mama dashing to hug her children, but in seconds the roof collapsed and the walls came tumbling down. Blood was mixed with the dust and debris. Amal was lucky to escape unhurt as she was thrown under the table, which saved her life, but her memory was marred forever.

It was so dark, and when she stretched out her little hand to feel her situation, all she could touch were bricks, whose dust was almost choking her. She called out,

"Mama, where are you? Papa, take me away".

But no answer.

Ambulance crews and neighbours came to search for and rescue survivors. Police and soldiers filled the area, digging carefully through the rubble. They eventually reached to where Amal sat under the table, frozen with fear and pale with shock.

A rescuer gently carried her out.

"There, now you're all safe and well. You are a brave girl," he said, trying to comfort the wide-eyed child. "What's your name, honey?"

"Amal. I want Mama."

"We will soon find your mama, so don't cry."

As Amal was taken from the blown-up apartment block that had been her home, she thought in her mind that "Mama, Papa, the baby, and brother will soon be here." She did not take her eyes from the men who were working with speed and care.

"There's Mama," she shouted, but one of the nurses carried her away and tried to cover her eyes.

The ambulance moved from the scene to the hospital, containing a bewildered Amal, who sensed that a great tragedy had struck, especially as her mama and papa had been taken off, covered with white sheets, in another ambulance.

At the hospital, where the nurses were busy caring for the wounded, a doctor examined the child, and softly asked her.

"What is your name, my love?"

"Amal. Will my mama come to this place?"

The doctor looked at the enquiring child. He knew that all of Amal's family had been killed, and the quicker he informed the child, the better, to enable her to adapt to the new way of life. He spoke again, ignoring her question,

"How old are you, Amal?"

"Eleven years. Will Papa be coming to take me away?"

"Amal, you are a big girl, and very brave, so listen to me, and be a good girl as well. Your mama and papa, your brother and sister, have all gone to heaven. They are all resting in peace. So now you be a good girl and show them how you can live and succeed in school, and then they will be very happy."

Amal's life had suddenly changed overnight. No home, not one relative around her. She was just left with terrifying memories. She stayed in the hospital for a few days, but, all the time she kept looking around, searching for someone who resembled Mama, and, when she heard a male voice, she rose, held her hands tightly together against her body and whispered to herself,

"There, maybe Papa is coming to take me to heaven, too."

One morning, the Father from the convent appeared in Amal's ward, accompanied by an elderly nun. The nurse pointed out Amal to them, and, with a kind smile on their lips, they went over to her.

"Aha, Amal," said the Father. "We have come to take you home with us, to a lovely home, where you will have many, many brothers and sisters. I will be your new father and sister Teresa will be your new mother. We promise that we will look after you well."

Amal looked at the Father and then at the new mother. She preferred her own parents, but these seemed kind and gentle, and had come especially for her, to take her away. She smiled a faint smile and asked,

"Are there any bombs near your home?"

The Father smiled and replied,

"We will pray that no bomb will be near our home, and I am sure Jesus will make sure no bomb will be left there, because there are hundreds of little children like you there, and everyone has a little angel to look after him and her, so don't you worry, Amal. Come, let us go and meet the rest of the family."

The Father took one hand and sister Teresa held the other, then they turned round and walked out of the ward. The nurses smiled and waved goodbye to the beautiful child, who now looked a bit more secure as she tightly held onto two hands, those of her new mama and papa.

Amal's new home was different from anything she had ever experienced. There were many children, younger and older than herself. It was like a big school, but they ate together, slept together and worshipped together. She liked her new home and soon made many friends. Sister Teresa kept Amal and the children fully occupied with homework and other tasks.

Every night Amal said a prayer for her parents in the little chapel of the convent. One evening, the Father happened to be there, praying behind the curtain, when Amal walked in to say her nightly prayer. He paused to hear what she would ask the Lord for. She knelt down, raised her hands towards heaven and prayed,

"Lord, thankyou for today. Please look after Mama and Papa, my brother and the baby. Please do not forget to kill the

Muslims and blow them up with a big bomb, because I hate them."

The Father was astonished at this request, and he realised that hate and bitterness was robbing the child of the joy of living, and hindering her progress in adapting to her new life. He coughed slightly to alert her of his presence and then walked out slowly from behind the curtain and went near to her. She glanced up at him and smiled softly. He looked into her eyes and asked her,

"Do you love Jesus, Amal?"

"Yes Father."

"How much do you love him?"

"Very much," she said, while still kneeling on the ground and looking up at the tall figure in front of her.

The Father continued his questions,

"Do you think Jesus loves you, Amal?"

She nodded her head, whilst looking up at her new father, who was trying hard to reach her little heart, and plant in it the seed of love, the pure love of Christ.

"How do you know he does?"

The child stopped and thought for a time. She was young, but had feelings, even if they were hard to explain or express. She knew Mama loved her, because she had always hugged and kissed her, provided her with pretty dresses and cooked her favourite dishes, but now Mama had gone to heaven and she had a new mama. The new mama also loved her, but in a different way. Not many kisses or hugs, as she had so many children to look after, but she provided food and discipline and sometimes strict orders that had to be obeyed immediately. Nevertheless, she could sense inside her that that was evidence of love; but how could she be sure that Jesus loved her? Then, suddenly her eyes widened and brightened as she found an answer,

"I know he loves me," she said, then added, "He is looking after Mama and Papa, and my brother and my baby, too."

The Father replied, quietly and softly,

"That is so, Amal. He is also looking after you right now, and me, and everyone else, because he loves everybody in this world."

"Everyone?" she asked.

"Everyone, including the Muslims and the Jews and everyone. We know that, because he died that we might live," said the tall man.

That was very difficult to understand. She did not speak to the Father, just tried to comprehend in her head how Jesus could love everyone, including those she hated so much, who had killed her family and all her relatives. She continued kneeling on the ground, just looking to the Father, who kept watching her eyes, and understanding her feelings. Then he knelt beside her on the floor, hugged her and asked another question,

"Do you want Jesus to hear your prayer, Amal?"

"Yes Father," she whispered.

"Then you have to obey his wishes, and his wish is very easy. He asked us to love each other, and also to love our enemies. You think of that, Amal. If you want Jesus to listen to you and be with you, you must obey him. I am also speaking about myself, we must all love our enemies and each other. Think about it; just keep thinking about it." Then he rose from the floor, helped her up, and warmly said to her, "Go and have a nice sleep and think of the good things. Alright, my child?"

Amal looked at him, and whispered gently,

"Goodnight, Father."

Then she ran to her bedroom which she shared with ten other girls, who were similar in age and sharing a common experience, that is, all had lost their real parents and had no home of their own.

Amal hated the night and detested darkness. She lay on her bed and covered herself from head to toe with her blankets, then stuck her thumb in her mouth for comfort and shut her eyes, trying to sleep, but was not successful. Every time she closed her eyes, she could see her mother and hear her father. She pulled the sheet from her face and tried to listen to the voices around her. She heard the sound of babies crying,

"That is my baby." That was how she always called her baby sister. Then she thought again, "It can't be my baby, because she's gone to heaven, and Jesus is looking after her."

She heard the voice of the Father ringing in her ears, 'Think about it, Amal. Keep thinking about it.' She found herself wide awake, thinking, 'Love thy enemies, if you want Jesus to listen to you.'

Amal stayed awake, thinking over and over again, "I hate them. I want to kill them." Another part of her little heart kept repeating the Father's words, 'Jesus loves everyone, everyone.' Her tears streamed from her eyes and she found herself praying,

"Jesus, I love you, but I don't know how to love them, as I hate them."

Amal cried herself to sleep and no one was aware of her wet face, except the One who loved everyone.

As soon as morning arrived, the convent buzzed with activity. The strict rules had to be followed to the letter to ease the load of the heavy tasks. The nuns were in charge of the kitchen and prepared the breakfast. Some of the older children made the tables ready, while others fed the little baby orphans, before eating their own meals.

Amal was too young to feed babies yet so was given the assignment of helping some of the others to wash-up in the kitchen after the meal was over. She loved to share in looking after the new home, and looked forward to the task of feeding the babies when she grew a bit older.

After breakfast and the morning prayer, the children went to their different classes, to learn to read and write and add up. They were taught how to sew, cook, clean and polish in the hope that, as soon as they were old enough to do so, they would be able to look after themselves and help their community.

The days passed by swiftly, and Amal grew fast. The memory of the tragedy was pushed to the background of her inner soul, although it all came back to the forefront each time a new group of children joined the big family. The wide open eyes, the shocked faces, the screaming babies; all brought the nightmare right up to the front of her memory.

On those occasions she would try to get close to them, as she understood their feelings. She knew what was in their hearts. She would ask those old enough to speak,

"How did it happen? Did you have a bomb?"

The answer was invariably the same - "A bomb planted by the Muslims killed my mama."

But one day Amal was shocked when one of the new children replied to her question,

"The Christians killed my parents with a bomb."

She looked to the crying girl and said, so positively,

"No, that can't be true, for Christians do not kill, as otherwise Jesus will not hear their prayers, because he said you must love everyone and," then she paused, looking at the Muslim girl, "and he said, 'you must love your enemies, too.'"

Amal opened her arms, hugged the new girl and said to her, "I love you. You're my sister. And don't worry about your parents, they'll be alright. Jesus looks after them, because he loves everyone, everyone in this whole world."

Amal could not sleep that night, for she was thinking. In fact, she had never stopped thinking about the matter since the Father mentioned it to her a few years ago when she was eleven, and now she was fifteen, but was still trying to figure out how she could love her enemy.

"I met one of my enemy's children today, my new sister. She was crying just as I was then, and she is suffering the same as I did, and the cause is the same, a bomb, but this time planted by a Christian."

Amal sat on her bed, with her Bible in her hand. It had become her constant companion in her tragic life.

"I really must think this puzzle over. What is love, anyhow? What is hate?" She found herself answering her thoughts, "Love is to care, to look after someone, anyone." Then the scripture flashed into her head, 'If your enemy is hungry, feed him; if he is thirsty, give him a drink.' She stopped there, thought it over and said to herself, "These are orders, or, perhaps better put, the wishes of Christ." She smiled softly to herself and continued, "I did not find it difficult to love my enemy today. I wonder why? I suppose because I did not realise she was the child of a Muslim, although, even supposing I had, that doesn't change the fact that she's loved by Jesus, and his wish is that I love her, and everyone else, too."

Amal began to comprehend the meaning of the word 'love', and, whenever she read it in the Bible, she pondered on it for quite a long time. She also noticed the word 'hate', but what surprised her was that Jesus recommended a person to hate oneself, so they could love him. "That is amazing," she reasoned to herself. "That makes me my own enemy. How can that be?"

A few more years passed, and Amal grew into a beautiful young woman, capable of looking after babies and attending to sick and ill children. She knew how to cook and clean, to comfort and wipe away tears from the eyes of the victims of hate. The orphanage in the convent was full to the brim with children of Christians and Muslims whose parents had been ripped and torn by bombs that had been placed and planted by hate. With every new case, she felt more confirmed in her mind that the wisest advice ever given to humans were the words of Jesus, 'Love thy enemy'. "How true, for the minute I love my enemy, he is my love, my friend, and no longer my enemy. A true follower of Christ has no enemies, but everyone is a friend."

The time came for Amal to take a crucial decision about her future. She passed her examinations with great success, so now had to go and earn her living and start a new life of her own. The Father and Mother Teresa invited her to the office to discuss her future. The Father looked at her with admiration and greeted her warmly, saying,

"Amal, how lovely to see you growing into a wonderful young woman. It seems as if it was just yesterday when Mother Teresa and I collected you from the hospital and now I can't tell you how proud we are of you and do appreciate your help in running the orphanage."

Amal stood there quietly, with a bashful smile on her face and a bit of fear in her heart, fear of the unknown. She guessed what the meeting was for. "I bet they want me to leave, and where can I go? I know nobody in this big world, except the Father and Mother Teresa and my hundreds of brothers and sisters. Where can I go? It's safe here. No bombs and no hate, we are one big family...."

The Father interrupted her thoughts when he asked her a question. That was his method. He spoke and taught by questions, so that the individual had to find the answers for themself.

"Amal, have you thought about what you would like to do for your future?"

She answered softly,

"I have been thinking about it all the time, Father."

He smiled, and so did Mother Teresa, and they asked together,

"What have you been thinking?"

"I would like to love my enemies," she answered.

The Father and the old nun were struck with astonishment at the strange answer and it took them a few moments to comprehend the meaning of the statement. After a short pause, the Father asked for more details,

"What do you mean, Amal? What are you intending to do?" Then he said to her, "Please, do sit down and explain your thoughts to us."

Amal pulled a chair close to the desk and sat down. Then she spoke slowly and explained herself,

"I have been thinking, ever since the day you asked me to do so, and I have come to one conclusion, and that is that I must love everyone if I want Jesus to be my love. I have no difficulty to love those who love me, but I have found it almost impossible to come to terms with loving my enemies."

The kind parents just kept staring at the young woman, without interrupting her thoughts. They were aware of her background. They understood her feelings and how deeply she had been hurt. They were interested to see the result of her thinking, the thinking of years. They examined her gentle eyes, searching for the answer.

She smiled and said,

"I came to the conclusion recently, when I discovered what is the cause of the problem, the big wall that stands in the way, prohibiting me from loving my enemies. When I discovered it, I felt victorious, because I think I can overcome it; mind you, with difficulty."

Amal noticed that her audience were extremely interested in her having found the obstacle which stood in the way of divine love, for they too were human and had enemies in one form or another. They were keenly interested to see how the Lord had revealed his wisdom to babies, while learned persons missed it all the way.

"I discovered that my biggest enemy is here." She pointed toward her heart while still looking at them. Then, with the same soft smile on her lips, she repeated,

"My worst enemy is inside me. It is my hate that dwells within my soul, because every time I can clearly see the way and the logic of love, this horrible beast raises its ugly head and showers my clear vision with mist, with thoughts of revenge and anger."

The Father's eyes misted with tender tears, as he knew just how true was the young girl's description. He tried to speak in his usual way, by questions,

"How are you going to destroy that ugly beast, Amal?"

"I will never be able to kill the beast alone, Father," she said, without any doubt in her voice. "But thanks to Jesus, who spelt out the way. He managed to kill the ugly beast, and he said, 'I have conquered the enemy, so take heart, for you shall be a conqueror like me, if you manage to walk in the steps I have set for you.'"

The Father glanced at the old nun, smiled gently and asked in his calm voice,

"What are you suggesting, Amal. What are to be your steps, my child?"

She took a deep breath and said,

"I want to go right into my one-time enemy's territory and try to show them the pure love, so they, too, can break free from that ugly beast that robs them from the peace of Christ."

The Father sat erect on his chair, with concern and worry showing clearly in his eyes.

"What do you mean by 'going right into the enemy's territory', Amal? Do you know who are your one-time enemies? You were only eleven when your family was wiped out, so how could you know who killed them?"

"I know exactly who killed them, Father, and I know precisely where they live. I have also decided on the steps I will take."

"Amal," said the old man, as he saw the determination and idealism in the girl's eyes, "I am worried for you, and I will not let you go out of the orphanage with such plans in your head." He looked to Mother Teresa and asked for her help and suggestions, as she was a woman, and maybe she would be able to provide a solution in a different way.

Mother Teresa looked challengingly to Amal and, in her customary direct and firm way, but with concern in her voice, she asked,

"Tell me, Amal, first of all, who killed your family? Don't repeat the sentence, 'the Muslims'. Tell me the individual who killed your family."

The Father sat back on his chair, as he could see the logic of the question. He was interested to hear her answer, as everyone used a blanket cover and then killed innocent people in the process.

Amal looked to the Mother. She must give the precise names of the villains; this was an order and Mother Teresa demanded the right answer, with no messing about and wasting of time allowed. Amal answered quietly,

"Abu Mansour killed my family. He is working in two camps at the same time, as he belongs to the Muslim militia and he supports the Palestinians in their fight against Israel."

The Father nearly jumped out of his skin. His face turned into a white sheet and his hands shook violently. Amal had uttered an unmentionable name and knew exactly where the man lived and with whom he worked. He looked to the nun, who was also looking quite sick and faint.

Abu Mansour, or the father of Mansour, was a devout Muslim supporter of the ayatollahs of Iran. He was fighting to clear Lebanon from all the infidels, who were, according to his fanatical group, any persons who did not belong to their sect; but with priorities. The Christians were first, followed by the Jews, the Druze and then anyone else who dared to challenge or contradict or resist in any way or manner. Abu Mansour and his son were responsible for many murders. They had killed many innocent young families. Mother Teresa had brought up countless children who had been made orphans by Abu Mansour; and Amal was one of them.

The Father did not know what to say or advise. His mind brought back the words of Amal, 'I want to go right into the home of my one-time enemy and show them the pure love of Jesus'. The more he digested those words, the more desperate he became. He felt like giving strict orders, saying, "No way, you cannot leave this place." However, he could not say that, for he was the one who had sown the seed of love in the heart of this child, and now it had become a beautiful tree, full of blossom, with a promising crop of fruit for the glory of God.

Amal looked at her pale and trembling audience. She was surprised to see them so worried, as if they saw the ugly beast which she had just managed to conquer with the help of the pattern that had been left for her and them. She kept staring from one to the other. She needed their advice, but felt and sensed she would not be supported, as they were trying to protect her, just like Peter who, with the best of intentions, tried to protect his Lord. So she prepared herself, "Get behind me, Satan. You are thinking and reasoning like humans and not like God".

At last the Father asked, while controlling his fear,

"How are you planning to show the pure love of Christ, Amal? In that den of lions, vicious lions, and hungry beasts that do not know what mercy or compassion means."

She answered, with calmness and peace,

"I shall conquer them with the good." Then she quoted the words of the pattern which she was trying to exactly follow, "'if your enemy is hungry, feed him; if he is thirsty, give him a drink'."

They both continued looking at her intently, so she added her own words,

"Because such deeds will melt the rocky hearts and make them pliable like clay, then there will be no bombs, no wars, just pure love, divine love."

Those words calmed the Father quite a lot, as he could see that Amal was not idealistic, but practical. She was not going to hammer their rocky hearts with the Bible message but rather let the light of love shine, so her enemies could see the way to peace. The old man smiled and asked the angel of peace who was sitting in front of him,

"What exactly are your plans, then? If both of us can help in any way, we shall support you."

Amal's face brightened up and her eyes sparkled with hope. She had obviously been thinking a great deal and planning the details, for she put her proposal on the table without any hesitation.

"I have been planning to sew a lot of clothes, especially children's ones, and sell some in the market so I can buy more material with the money to make more clothes, and then I will go to the territory of my past enemies and distribute them among the naked and needy. I shall also bake cakes, just like those Mother Teresa bakes for us here, sell some, and take the rest to the hungry ones among my friends."

Then she pleaded,

"If you can only give me the initial cost to start, then I am sure I can finance my project myself. I will do my best to help in the orphanage in the way of nursing or teaching."

She looked to the Father, with her head bowed to one side,

"I beg you, please let me stay here, as I have nowhere to go and I do feel secure with you."

The Father felt uplifted with the plans of peace, so he said in a triumphant voice,

"I am sure we can help Amal, don't you feel so, Mother Teresa? Also, we need Amal in the orphanage, as the children love her."

Mother Teresa nodded her head many times with approval.

Then the Father turned to the delighted Amal and asked her a last question,

"When are you intending to start your project?"

Amal felt good that her road was clear from any obstacles and her fears unfounded, so she answered with confidence,

"As soon as I have some money," she said excitedly. Adding slowly, "It could be as soon as early in the morning, I mean tomorrow morning, if the Lord wishes it."

Amal could not sleep that night, not because of fear, or worry, but because of joy. She had never felt so good. She smiled to herself and said,

"You know what's the matter with you, Amal? You must be in love, and what a unique love!" Then she continued thinking, following the Father's advice to her when she was eleven, 'Keep on thinking of good things', and that habit of thinking had stuck with her ever since. Her thoughts travelled to the one who originated her joy. "I know why my Lord was always joyful. It must be because he was always planning to show love, either towards his friends or his one-time enemies."

She stayed awake, counting the cost of the various items in her head. Although Mother Teresa had many other expenses, she had given her a few Lebanese pounds to help start her project. "It's better that I buy ingredients for the cakes first because I'm sure I can sell those quicker than the dresses, then maybe I'll buy the material the day after."

Amal had never known an endless night like that one. "When will that cock crow?" she said, turning from one side of the bed to the other. In between thoughts she thanked her Lord for opening her eyes to see his love.

At last the morning arrived and she jumped out of bed, singing and humming happy songs of praise. She made her bed, then dashed to help in the kitchen, to prepare breakfast for the very large family. Everything was done in order and with proper arrangement, under the strict supervision of Mother Teresa. When Amal had finished her morning duties she went and reported to the Mother, who smiled and commented,

"Everything done Amal? Properly?"

"Yes Mother, and perfectly. Can I go and do some shopping for my project, please?"

"Of course, but be careful. Think before you dash to do anything."

Amal ran to her room, took her shopping bag and went out into the crowded streets of Beirut. She feared the crowds and hated loud sounds. She disliked the cries of children. For all these things brought to her mind terrifying memories. She was very aware of parked cars; they made her hair stand on end. "I mustn't go near the parked cars," she advised herself.

Everyone watched everyone else on the street. Nobody trusted anybody.

"Why is he staring at me like that?" she thought as she noticed a young man gazing at her. "Maybe he is a Muslim?" Her heart started to beat faster and her breathing quickened. She tried to encourage herself by saying, "And so what, aren't they my new friends? You ugly beast that is living inside me, why are you causing my heart to beat so fast? I am going shopping to show love for them." She found herself humming a song of praise, to remind herself of her peace mission.

Other eyes watched Amal shopping. A few men whispered quietly,

"Beautiful, isn't she. I wonder who she is, Muslim? Christian?"

"I feel she must be a Christian."

"Let's follow and see where she's going to and where she came from."

Amal thought nobody was aware of her in the crowded shopping centre, but she was indeed mistaken, for many were watching, many were following, many were enquiring. She entered the supermarket and bought her flour and sugar and other things, crossing off from her list each item as she went.

"She must be working in a restaurant or something like that," said one of the following eyes as he noticed the organised way she did her shopping and the great amount she bought.

Amal finished her shopping and headed back home, followed by many eyes. Because she had hardly ventured out of the convent much before, nobody yet knew her, so they followed. She entered the orphanage and disappeared into the haven of the pure love, where there were no bombs.

The men spoke with disappointment,

"She's a Christian, buying food for the orphans. I told you I can sense a Christian, especially those who work in places like convents or hospitals. They all have a certain air about them."

Amal worked hard at baking her buns, which she decorated with dried fruits. When she finished she filled her two large wooden trays. Mother Teresa came and inspected the mouth-watering buns and said a word of blessing for Amal, for assistance in selling all her products and doing her good deeds.

Amal left one tray behind to distribute later to her new friends, put the other one on her head and emerged from the orphanage. She walked to a busy street corner where there were many people passing on their way to work or to do their shopping. She had never done any selling before, but felt hopeful that she would have a speedy and successful sale, particularly as she was anxious to take the other tray to her friends whom she had yet to meet.

The passers-by stopped and looked at the attractive buns and especially at the attractive young lady, so they kept buying, and in no time Amal had sold out. She put the empty tray on her head and walked happily home.

The Father was now sure Amal would succeed in her new mission, but he still felt concern, especially when she took the other tray and said,

"I am going to the territory of Abu Mansour."

"Amal," he said, "Let us pray so the angel of the Lord will guard and keep you."

They both shut their eyes and the Father prayed earnestly for her. Then he advised her,

"Don't go into the camp, Amal. Just stay on the edge and distribute your cakes, because you know how dangerous is that area."

She answered calmly,

"Father, do not concern yourself about me, for I am looking forward to meeting these people; to show my Redeemer that I love him and am obeying his wishes."

Then she put her cake-tray on her head and set off for the enemy's territory. She walked speedily, for she just could not wait to arrive soon enough. Her heart experienced the most odd feeling; it was a sort of deep compassion that moved her bowels and brought tears rushing to her eyes. At last she was doing what her Lord had done before when he hurried down from heaven to express his love toward his enemies.

As she approached the camp where the most fanatical Muslims dwelt, her heart speeded up and her feet slowed down. She felt like turning round and returning, but her thoughts told her, "You have come so far, so why do you return? Go ahead, prove that you love by deeds and not by words, and accept the consequences. Be like your Lord, he died while he was extending the hand of love toward his enemies."

Amal had been closely watched and already recognized.

"Well I never. It's the Christian girl who lives in the convent and sells cakes. She's coming to sell cakes in our camp!"

The men watched her from their shacks and shelters. The women stretched out their necks to peep at this Christian girl who was selling cakes. The children heard the whispers and ran into the narrow street to see what she had on the covered tray.

Amal saw the children running towards her, with their eyes and faces covered with flies, their noses running and their hair uncombed. She saw how their clothes were just about hanging round their skinny and unwashed bodies. Their feet were bare, cracked by the cold, and the hard ground. She put her tray down on the ground and uncovered it. The children surrounded her, even crowded on top of her, all speaking at once.

"What do you have there? Do you sell this nice food? How much does it cost? Can you sell it without money?"

Amal smiled sweetly to the children. She had never been asked so many questions in one go. She replied gently and with great pleasure,

"I am selling these cakes without money."

"In that case," said a little boy, "Can I buy one for Mama and Baba, and one for my sister and my baby."

Amal looked at the young boy who was about eleven. "My baby," she thought. "That is what I used to call my sister. We are all just the same, the same feelings, the same love and care for those we love."

Then she said to the boy,

"Here you are, one bun each, but be careful not to drop them. Are you able to carry all of them?" she asked, while filling the little boy's hands.

"I shall put them in my shirt," he said, lifting up his dirty and torn shirt that had one sleeve missing.

Amal placed the buns on the stretched rag, then the lad ran off in great excitement with his bargain, shouting,

"Tislameely". (May you prosper for my sake).

The other children almost broke out into chaos as they, too, desired to buy the lovely cakes without money. Amal raised her voice and commanded in the same manner that Mother Teresa used in the orphanage,

"Quiet now. There is plenty for everyone, so get into line and I shall give to all of you. May the Lord bless and add to it."

The children queued in a very wobbly line, jumping and hopping from one foot to the other, watching the buns on the tray becoming less and less. She smiled and said to them,

"Don't worry. I assure you, you shall all be satisfied with the blessing of the good Lord."

The children received their buns and ran off to their mothers, disappearing in different directions, this one through a hole, that one behind a tin wall, until all were gone, while adult eyes were fixed on her activity. Amal had almost finished the buns as only four remained, so she covered the wooden tray and prepared to return to the convent, but then noticed her first customer, the little boy, running towards her, eating his bun and shouting,

"Don't go yet."

She stopped and waited to see what he desired. While he tried to catch his breath, he spoke and ate his cake at the same time,

"I want to buy some cakes for my neighbour's little boy. He can't come to buy because he is very ill, but he wants to buy some. He also has a sister, his baby."

Amal said to him,

"Alright, open your shirt," and she started to count. "One for the ill boy, one for his baby sister, one for his mama and one for his papa."

The boy said to her, in a matter-of-fact tone of voice,

"He doesn't have a father. The Israelis killed him."

Amal stopped and looked to the boy, sensing the hate and bitterness in his voice, the same feelings she had before she thought about divine love. She asked him,

"What is your name?"

"Muhammad."

"Muhammad, it is very kind of you to care for your neighbour and show love, as it's good to love everyone, isn't it? Because you are kind, I am giving you another bun for yourself."

Muhammad smiled and said his normal sweet word,

"Tislameely".

Then he turned to run to his neighbour, but suddenly stopped and asked the kind young lady,

"Are you coming to sell free cakes tomorrow?"

Amal smiled and replied with great satisfaction in her voice, "If God wishes it, and I am sure He does."

Then she asked him.

"What kind of illness does your friend have?"

"He is very ill. He coughs and vomits and is going to die."

She answered quickly,

"No, he will not die. I will bring some medicine for him tomorrow and you can take it to him."

The Father could not settle for a moment. He kept praying and trembling. His mind imagined all sorts of horrible thoughts but then he pushed them aside and went and stood at the gate as he felt anxious for Amal. He saw her coming in the distance and rushed to meet her. He saw a victorious smile on her lips and a joy that could not be contained in her human vessel as it oozed out and radiated all around her.

"How did it go, Amal? You were very quick."

She answered with a broad smile,

"I have never experienced such happiness in my whole life, and I can see there is a great need for Jesus' love in the camp."

Then she explained to him the details of her experience.

The Father listened and shared her joy. He knew the need was great, but no one dared to venture into that area, as each group's territory in Beirut was a war zone, jealously guarded and fought for, even though its dwellers could be dying.

CHAPTER 2

THE RAID

Amal worked hard, day and night. She worked in the orphanage to pay for her keep, and, as soon as she finished that task, she rushed to work on her love-project. Her buns earned a good income that was immediately exchanged for food, which she made up into parcels; and material, which was sewn into lovely garments. The Father helped by supplying medicine.

Muhammad proved to be her right hand, informing her about the very needy and sick ones. As he graphically put it,

"This one is going to die, very soon he is going to die."

From that Amal would understand it was an emergency, and would provide what help she could, and, as a result, her name spread in the Palestinian camp and Abu Mansour's territory.

The children always awaited her arrival and welcomed her with all their souls but their parents were suspicious of her.

"A Christian spy. No more than an Israeli informer who is trying to get information through the children."

So the children were clearly warned by their parents,

"Don't speak a word to her. She is a spy, a Christian spy. You just take the food and the clothes that she gives you but don't speak, not even a whisper."

Amal noticed the changed atmosphere, how the children were quiet and subdued, trying not to speak but just staring into her soft brown eyes. When they thought she could not hear, they whispered to each other,

"She is a spy, a Christian spy, but she is a nice Christian spy. I like her."

Then they would look at her and smile. Even her right hand was struck with dumbness. He started to say his normal word after receiving some children's books Amal had brought from the orphanage, but then suddenly realised he had spoken, although the strict order was not to speak a word, so all he managed was,

"Tisla...." and then he covered his mouth with his hand and started to laugh.

Abu Mansour felt very uncomfortable with Amal's regular visits and her distributions. He knew how much the children loved her and that her gifts filled a great need, but she was a threat to his camp. He knew exactly who she was, for he was always very careful to take note of his victims and those who survived from among them. He was particularly aware of the victim's children, as they were his most dangerous enemies, for, as soon as they would grow up they would attempt revenge, armed with tremendous hatred and bitterness. So he knew Amal, 'The daughter of George Bishara.' She was the only survivor from a bombing campaign he had undertaken a few years ago, when his son Mansour was sixteen years old.

Abu Mansour held a special meeting with some of his men to discuss the Amal problem. He conducted it in his brother's house as he was one of his greatest supporters, together with his daughter Baha, a brilliant informer, well trained in spying and fighting. In fact, Mansour had trained his cousin so well that she could snipe at Israelis through any convenient hole. She often followed Christian families, found out their names and all necessary details to enable her uncle and father to arrange an ambush to tear them to pieces with bombs.

Abu Mansour summarised his problem,

"Amal is a headache. She is insisting to come here and, although I could many times easily finish her off on the spot, the children adore her and are always surrounding her. I know exactly what is her aim, she is fishing for information to pass on to the Christian militia, so we must think of a way to deal with her. We could kidnap her but then the regular supply of clothes and medicine and books will stop and our children need those badly. So, any suggestions?"

The Muslim fighters sat and discussed the problem. After a while Mansour recommended,

"Amal is the same age as Baha, so why don't we send Baha to befriend her and get information from her about her aims and who she is working with. Then we'll catch two birds with one stone."

"A good idea," agreed everyone. "Let's get information from her. Maybe she's spying for the Israelis as well."

Baha was called to the secret meeting. She was always invited when there was a mission for her to undertake.

"Baha," Abu Mansour said seriously, "you are needed again, as there's no one like you in finding out information. This time your mission is very easy, as it's right outside your door."

Everyone smiled as he continued,

"Amal is our target. She is trying to buy us with cakes and clothes, so only keeps close to the children. I don't need to tell you what to do when she arrives here tomorrow, at her usual time, to empty her bait and then hurry back to the convent."

Baha was excited. She loved to dig up her enemies and catch them out and then hand them over for the slaughter. She was aware that Amal was attractive and always made the boys turn and look at her.

"I will soon uncover your mask, pretty girl, and see what those eyes of yours will tell me tomorrow."

Amal prayed extra hard that day, for she sensed the territory of those she was trying to help was becoming difficult, and the ugly beast who had been knocked unconscious within her was starting to awake.

"I mustn't give up," she said to herself, "This is the time to prove my love, when the going becomes hard and others show me their resentment. I mustn't allow my love to cool down. I will be like my Lord; at least I'll know that I'm winning him."

Amal took her tray of goodies and went to her normal spot.

In no time the children appeared from various shacks and tents and surrounded her as usual, then they started to queue, as they knew they had to do that before receiving anything. Baha saw Amal, so immediately left her home and walked slowly towards her. When the children saw her approaching, they hushed, took their gifts and ran to their homes.

Amal smiled softly to the young lady who stood nearby, looking at her, and said,

"Welcome."

Baha came closer and replied,

"Ahla."

Then she looked at the almost empty tray and asked,

"They look very nice. Who made them?"

Amal smiled bashfully. She picked one up and handed it to her, saying,

"Try one, with good health. I made them."

Baha took the bun and tasted it. Then she said,

"It's very good. Tislam eedik, these must have cost a lot of money."

Amal answered, while looking toward heaven,

"Thanks to God. He provided the money."

Baha fixed her eyes on Amal's. She could see a serene personality, showing through soft, gentle eyes and an open, smiling face. But she was not quite sure of the words, 'for words are easy, an answer like that is only a cover', so she said,

"I suppose the Father gave you the money?"

Amal was delighted to talk to an adult, a girl of similar age to herself. Now she could speak, to make a real friend, so she opened her heart and spoke to the stranger that kept her gaze fixed on her eyes, waiting for the answer.

"God provided me with an income, as I also sell these buns. Then I in turn give it back to him, so it is from God and back to God," she said with a giggle.

Baha had never met a spy like this; she was completely different from those she had informed on before. Her new target was lovable, gentle and very friendly, and quite naive. She repeated Amal's sentence as she found it amusing and strange,

"What? 'From God and back to God?'"

Then they both laughed together. Baha continued her search to uncover what lay beneath the 'mask'.

"Why have you chosen this place instead of a Christian area?"

Amal had wanted to be asked that question for a long time and she was glad to give the answer,

"Because I love the people here, and I want to show my love towards them by my work."

That was a very surprising answer that took Baha aback and let her lose her cool a bit, so she said,

"Do you know who live here? They are all Muslims and have nothing to do with you Christians, so I can't believe you at all."

Amal exactly understood the girl's feelings, so she gently said,

"I know who lives here, but it doesn't make any difference, as I love everybody, everyone on this earth. As far as I'm concerned, I have no enemies, not a single one."

"No enemies? Not one? What about the Israelis? Do you love them, too?"

"Yes, I love everyone because my Lord loves everyone, and he set the example. All I have to do is follow, so I have no

30

enemy at all, not one." Then she paused and said, with a twinkle in her eyes, "I tell a lie, I do have an enemy, but only one."

Baha's blood rose to her head. She thought she knew who that was, "it's Abu Mansour, the one who blew up her family", she thought, so asked impatiently,

"Who is he? Who?"

Amal had anticipated that question, as the Father had asked it before and she knew what the reaction would be, for she experienced that in the orphanage from her adoptive parents, so she said, trying not to grin,

"My enemy is here," and she pointed toward her heart.

Baha opened her mouth but did not speak.

"My enemy is my own hate that dwells within me, but I managed to conquer it, thanks to God." Then Amal told her new friend about "This beast, this very ugly beast, that robbed my joy, because he doesn't know love." She told her how she had managed to overcome it, even though she found it extremely difficult at the beginning. "But now I am free, I am happy, for I'm among my lovers all the time. I fear nothing and I'm very happy, so that's why I'm here, to help you to be happy. It's quite simple, hate yourself, that is, the hate in yourself, and then just love your enemy - you find he suddenly becomes your friend."

Baha stood and listened to this strange talk that Amal believed so strongly and practised so well, as she radiated such happiness and joy. She just stood listening until Amal looked at her watch and said,

"The time runs so fast and Mother Teresa will get anxious. I must go, but I must tell you how wonderful it's been to have this little chat with you. What's your name?"

Baha never gave her name to strangers, but, without realizing it, she said,

"Baha. I live down there."

She pointed to a proper house which stood out from the rest, in contrast to the majority of the dwellings, which were shacks and shelters made of wood and flattened tins or boxes.

Amal smiled and hugged Baha, then ran away, leaving her standing in her place, watching the strange spy disappear down the street. When Amal was out of sight, she turned and went to her home.

Her father and Abu Mansour, as well as her cousins, were all waiting for the information to pour out, but she seemed quiet and subdued.

"What's the matter, Baha? Has she been difficult? You had such a long talk, so tell us from the beginning, as we've waited long enough," said Abu Mansour, alternately laughing and grinning, but at the same time he was keenly interested.

Baha started from the beginning and told her strange story. It produced much laughter and disbelief of motive.

"Don't be deceived, Baha. Do you honestly believe that she loves her enemy?" asked her father.

"Yes, I do."

The assembled men were shocked by the reply, as they always trusted in Baha's judgement and observations, but now she believed in that nonsense. Mansour, who had much admiration for her, said crossly,

"Don't be stupid, you can't believe her just like that, not from only one meeting. You keep asking and seeking, then you'll find another person inside her."

"I know," replied Baha, "She also knows about him. That's her only enemy, an ugly beast who tries to raise his head from time to time, but she knows exactly how to deal with him."

Abu Mansour turned pale and his eyes widened,

"What's that, Baha?" he asked anxiously.

Baha smiled, as he had reacted the same way she did, so she answered, laughing,

"Oh, don't worry, uncle. It's only an ugly old beast that dwells inside her, and also in all of us, that tries to stop us from loving our enemies, but the minute...." and that proved too much to listen to, so Mansour shouted,

"Enough. No more of what she said, Baha. No more of this rubbish, but you just keep close to her for other information that can help our cause; and none of this preaching."

From then on, the two girls met every day after Amal had finished her distribution to the children and the needy. The more they met, the closer they became. Baha started to use a lot of the phraseology which Amal used. She could not help than to be attracted to the gentle and loving ways of Amal. She also began to think about what Amal kept telling her,

"You have to convince yourself. No one can do it for you. You just try it and see how true it is."

Baha spent nights thinking. "It's a vicious circle. We kill them and they kill us, we bomb them and they destroy our homes. It must stop somewhere. I must start with myself, I must try to love my enemy." She stopped to consider her words. "I have many, so many. All those Christians, then those dogs, the Druze, and those pigs, the Jews; how can I ever love people like that?" 'It is easy,' she could hear Amal's words in her head. "Poor Amal, she is making me go mad. All the time, 'love thy enemy, do not kill', but I can't help it, I do like her. She is just lovely, gentle."

It was clear to all, including Abu Mansour, that Amal was a "mobashira", a preacher, and nothing else. They admired her love. It touched their hearts, especially those of the children. The news spread in the camp that Amal was not a Christian spy or an Israeli informer, but a preacher doing good deeds.

The parents lifted the ban from the children, and allowed them to speak with the mobashira, and that they did with enthusiasm. Muhammad even tried to teach Amal how to whistle to warn the camp of danger. He asked her,

"Can you do a grasshopper whistle, Amal?"

"What is that, Muhammad?" she enquired, as she had never heard of it.

"It's like this," and he whistled so low and quiet, just like the sound of a grasshopper. Then he said, "This is when you see an Israeli, so you can get ready to shoot him down. And this," then he whistled slightly differently, "is when you want to mark a Christian so you can plant a bomb."

Amal was distressed and said to Muhammad,

"Why to kill, why not love everyone?"

The boy stopped and looked at her with a surprised look. She then asked him,

"Will you mark me to kill me, Muhammad, for I am a Christian?"

The boy looked straight into her eyes and said, disbelievingly,

"Oh no you are not a Christian, my father said so."

"What do you think I am then?" she asked.

"You are a mobashira," said the boy, as he ran off, laughing and playing.

Abu Mansour and his men kept pestering the Israeli soldiers. They would spy on them to check their movements, then wait for the lonely ones, to shoot at them. They hid and sniped at them, one here and one there, and then hid again.

But no sooner had they done that, than Israel would avenge the death and injury done to her boys. They also had eyes following everyone like everyone else. They knew who were their arch-enemies and where to hit back. They knew who was responsible.

"Abu Mansour and family," said the young officer, preparing for a raid to avenge the death of two boys that Abu Mansour and his son ambushed and shot dead. "They live here," he said, pointing to a spot on the map. "Blow the street, especially this house, for the whole family is worthy of death, girls and all. Baha is their main eyes, so don't let her escape. Mansour must die and also his father. We only hit those who hit us, that's fair. We must protect our boys and our land."

Baha's father was very concerned for his daughter. He described to his brother how she had become so difficult,

"She does not want to co-operate with me. I wanted her to go and spot for me some new Israeli men who came to support the Christian militia, but she openly refused and said, 'Why do we have to kill. Why can't we start to learn to love them?' I could have shot her, my daughter or not."

He stopped to take his breath and then said, sadly,

"The cause of the trouble is Amal. We must stop Amal from seeing her; they spend too much time talking together, and I can see Baha is thinking seriously of taking up this stupid business of showing 'love to thy enemy'."

Abu Mansour spoke consolingly,

"Don't take it to heart, man. I will speak to Mansour, to arrange to keep her away when Amal comes to the camp, because if you resist with force, it will only make her more determined. Let us just separate them gently. Mansour will soon work on her. Leave it to me."

The agreement was put into effect, and Baha was invited out by Mansour to go to this place and that each time when Amal was due at the camp.

Amal missed her friend,

"I wonder if she is ill?" she asked herself. "I must go and ask her mother after I finish, for I have not seen her for days."

Amal kept looking towards the house of Baha, wishing for her to come and see her, but no sign, so she finished quickly, put her empty tray on her head and walked straight to the house.

She did not need to knock on the door, because, as soon as she approached the house, the door opened and there stood Baha's mother, with a faint smile on her lips.

"Is Baha in, please?"

"No, she went out, but do come in for a minute or two."

Amal entered and the woman shut the door behind them.

"Come into the inner room, Amal."

She went in, looking around her as she did so, and saw that the house was full of wooden boxes and crates. She guessed they were full of weapons and explosives, which made her feel very uncomfortable and want to run away, but she could not, especially as the woman was looking at her, with the same faint smile on her face.

Amal said,

"I just wanted to enquire if Baha is alright, as I've not seen her for some days."

"She's very well," replied the woman, "and is most probably enjoying herself with her cousin."

Then she quickly asked Amal,

"How is business going? Still selling well?"

Amal smiled and responded,

"The more I give, the more I receive to give."

The woman laughed and said,

"I know. 'From God and back to God'. Baha told us that, and it's very nice. We are all using these words of yours but they upset Baha's father a lot, so we try not to say them in front of him."

She went off to make a drink for Amal. After a few minutes she came back with a cup of tea, which she placed on the big table in the centre of the room. Amal put her tray down on the floor and started to drink her tea. The woman kept looking at her; she could see why her daughter was so closely attached to Amal. 'Such a gentle personality, and kind eyes. Just as innocent as a child, nothing in her mind except love for all,' she thought to herself.

Suddenly she jumped to her feet,

"Amal, hurry up. The Israelis are coming."

Amal heard the warning whistle that the little boy had tried to teach her. She jumped to her feet and looked around. Her heart thumped so loudly and she started to sweat; she felt panicky.

"Where shall we hide?" she asked, looking to the woman, who immediately hurried in the direction of the kitchen. Before Amal had chance to follow there was a loud roar from a low flying plane as it passed over the house, so she threw herself under the big table.

Then a mighty explosion hit the building and the walls came crashing down. She heard Baha's mother scream and then silence, except for the last few bricks tumbling down. Amal felt sick, she vomited, and could see her mother crying and dashing to hug her children.

"Take me away," she cried out loudly. Then she screamed, "Pa, take me away from here."

The Israelis filled the area, dragging out of the houses everyone who was still alive. They were shouting and shooting in the air, following the path of the plane, and picking up anyone who was left of their enemies, to carry them off to Israel as prisoners. They heard Amal screaming, "Take me away, Pa", so came towards her. In no time they removed the debris, and there they were, face to face with their enemy,

"She's the cause of all the trouble, pull her to the convoy," shouted a young officer.

Amal was pulled and dragged, as her legs felt like water from the shock, then she was pushed and herded like an animal into the jeep and knocked on the head with the butt of a gun. She was terrified and bewildered and her pale white face gazed at two young soldiers who looked at her with emotionless eyes, then said in Arabic,

"Down, head down."

She did as they ordered. She tried to think, but her head felt fuzzy and faint. She did not know where she was - in the past or the present. "Are they going to take me to hospital?" she wondered, for that was what happened when her enemies blew-up her family, but now a new type of enemy had blown-up her new friend. She thought of the convent,

"The orphanage," she said. "The Father and Mother Teresa will get worried." She raised her head, forgetting about the orders.

"Down," shouted the angry soldier, "or you'll have the hood."

"That might be a good idea," said the other one, in Hebrew, to his friend. "She's the informer, keep her eyes covered."

A black hood was drawn out from the side of the jeep and put over Amal's head. She felt claustrophobic and suffocating. She felt like screaming her head off, when she suddenly remembered something, 'Why are you so panicky, my soul. Hope in the Lord, and he will look after you'. That was her favourite tune that she used to hum whenever she was fearful.

"Of course, silly girl," she said to herself, "You are among your friends. Don't you know you have no enemies, not one in this big world, so why are you acting as if you are in the midst of enemies? These are poor boys, too, Israelis or not, so you just love them. Right now, love them." She smiled under her hood, and no one saw her soft smile, except those who created love and joy. "I must keep that ugly beast in check, for I feel his roar inside me." Then she pleaded, "Help me, Lord, to conquer my hate."

The two soldiers heard her muttering, so they hit her on the head and shouted,

"Shut up, no sound."

Abu Mansour and his son survived the raid and came to count their losses after the Israelis left. Baha lost both of her parents and one of her brothers was taken off as a prisoner. Mansour and his father discovered that the mobashira had also been taken prisoner. Other people had died in the area. Baha was beyond comforting as she left her mother alive and, by the time she returned from an enjoyable hour with her cousin, her life had been turned upside down. She felt like killing herself. She was so bitter that she could taste the bitterness on her tongue. She did not speak a word, she just sat on top of the rubble that had been her home, and cried.

Om Mansour and her family came to raise her from the ground, saying,

"This is life, Baha, and this is our share in this life, but one day we shall win and wipe those Jews from the face of the ground. We shall."

Baha just sat speechless, thinking. 'Just keep thinking' was what she heard in her ears, and that brought forth a tiny smile in the midst of tears. Her aunt thought that what she had just said had brought a ray of hope to her niece's lips, so she said,

"That's much better to see you smiling than crying. You just mark my words, we'll kill every single Jew, all of them."

Baha spoke quietly,

"Actually it was Amal who made me smile. In fact, she always makes me smile, for she says such funny things, poor girl. I wonder what she's doing now, as she told me that she loves everyone, including the Israelis. Now she has the whole country to love."

Mansour and his parents laughed at the ridiculous idea of 'loving thy enemy'.

The Father and the old nun soon received the news, as there were so many eyes who saw what happened and passed the news along in whispers from one to the other until it reached the orphanage.

"Amal has been bundled into a jeep and taken by the Jews to Israel, from where there is no return."

The old man and the nun went into the chapel and knelt down, and prayed and prayed for Amal. Their tears fell and made little puddles on the floor in front of them, but they kept praying.

"Help her, Lord. She loves you and is doing your will by loving those whom you said we should love. Help her to love."

The Father stayed on the floor for quite a while just meditating, until a small smile broke on his lips. Mother Teresa also found herself smiling and wondering what was in his mind to cause that smile. Then he said,

"Amal worked so hard to go and show love in her enemy's territory, now she has been transported free to another kind of enemy, to take the love of Christ there."

The nun nodded her head sadly.

He continued, with confidence and faith, "She will succeed, as long as she keeps the ugly beast in check."

They both smiled and somehow felt comforted, as they realized that Amal would be alright.

The convoy of jeeps and army vehicles eventually stopped after what seemed like a lifetime's journey to Amal. She was so cramped, her neck was aching from bending down and her legs were numb. She wished she could be rid of the black hood that kept her in the dark, as she hated darkness. She could hear men speaking in a strange tongue, of which she could not understand a single word. After a few moments she was ordered with a harsh command,

"Get down, quick."

She managed to feel the edge of the vehicle, then lowered her feet, while hanging onto the jeep. The two boys that were with her hurried her up.

"Move, quick."

They then put handcuffs on her wrists and ankles and lifted her into another much larger vehicle, like a room. She could not see anything, but she knew it was big, because when they pushed her in, she rolled quite a distance. She wriggled towards the side, to support herself against an upright. Then it was loaded with boxes and boxes. She huddled at the side, listening to the thumping of the heavy boxes. After that was finished, two soldiers climbed up and sat on the seats in the rear, the engine started and she began to move.

"Oh no," she dreaded in her soul, "not another journey. For how long, O my God, for how long?"

The convoy of booty and prisoners were carried across to Israel by road.

"It must be night now," thought Amal, for she could hear her guard snoring, and the air was quite cold. She was too, as she only had a light dress on, what she called her 'Palestinian dress', that she had made especially to wear when she visited the camp, to match the dresses of the other girls there. She told herself, "It's better that you also go to sleep, and do not worry about tomorrow, for tomorrow will have its own anxieties. Today's evils are quite sufficient."

Amal dropped off into such a deep sleep that she did not awake until she heard loud voices laughing and speaking in the new, strange language.

"Shalom. Boker tov."

"We must be in Israel now," she thought. She found herself trembling, for she had heard a lot of stories about Israel, the enemies' land. About the dreadful prisons and those who died whilst there. Her stomach felt sick, especially as she had been without food for quite a while now. Then she comforted herself, "You think of good things, as the Father always advised, and do not think horrible thoughts." She paused to find some good thoughts, but, "I can't seem to find any," and her tears started to roll down her cheeks, wetting her black hood. Then she said, while sobbing, "This land is the homeland of my Lord, he who taught me to love, who loved me whilst I was still his enemy." That made her feel good and the thought cheered her a lot. "It is good to be here, in the same land that my Lord walked in, taught in and died in." Her heart fluttered with joy; just the thought of being in the same place made her feel so close to him. "He is as real as this land I'm in, so I'm very lucky, and happy, too."

A voice broke into her thoughts and ordered,

"Down you come."

She moved on her bottom until she reached the location of the voice. She felt the edge of the vehicle, and because it was quite high from the ground, the men held her arms and assisted her down and then marched her to a building. She walked at their speed. "Lucky they undid my feet," she thought. "At least I can walk."

It was a large prison, full of Palestinian and Arab terrorists. The walls were high and the cells small and cramped, with no furniture except for a mat on the ground. The two men took her into an office, an interrogation room. She could hear the voices of some men there, all speaking in Hebrew. From time to time, she heard a few words in English, which she partially understood but could hardly speak, as her native tongue was Arabic, although she also spoke French.

The chief, who was sitting behind the desk, ordered the guard, in Hebrew,

"Take off her mask and let's see our dangerous informer who's killed so many of our boys." He had papers in front of him and knew for sure that she was Baha and no other. She was badly wanted by the Israeli forces and was now about to be revealed.

The men removed Amal's hood and all stared into her face.

She smiled softly, relieved that she could see the light at last, and whispered,

"Shukran." (Thankyou).

"Polite, uh?" said the officer to the others in the room, while still looking at her eyes, which were a gentle, soft brown, and red from crying. He continued, "You can't believe appearances, or words. All these Arabs that come here smile sweetly and speak politely and, the minute you turn round, they stick a knife in your back."

40

The other men just kept looking at the pleasant face, the calm personality. Then the senior officer continued talking to the others in Hebrew.

"We'll soon illustrate my point that you can't trust them; that they're liars, murderers, evil enemies of God."

He looked to Amal and asked her, in Arabic,

"Your name?"

"Amal," she calmly answered.

He banged the table with his hand and said to them,

"You see. Can you believe it? Amal! Amal! She is just sort of trying to provoke. Amal!" (Amal was also the name of a Lebanese militia group fighting Israel).

The men looked at the girl with great suspicion. They could imagine how she could act so calmly, as, to be an effective informer, she had to be a good actor and brilliant deceiver. So the officer said to his subordinates,

"I will predict what her second answer will be. I am going to ask her a question and she will reply that she was just visiting her own house."

Then, while the rest concentrated on the girl's eyes, he asked,

"Do you live in the camp of Abu Mansour?"

"No, I was just visiting."

The men laughed and looked with admiration to the officer for his astuteness. He lost his temper and shouted,

"You lying Arab. I'm going to teach you how to speak the truth. We have plenty of tools that will turn the crooked into a straight line, but, before I take that line with you, I'm going to ask one more question. If you lie to me, I'll rub your tongue in it."

Amal looked at the man, surprised. "Why can't he believe me? I never told him a lie, I have no need to," she thought to herself. She waited for the next question, wondering that if telling her name was considered a lie, how would the answer to a difficult question be received.

"Tell me, what has happened to our two boys that disappeared in your camp a month ago?"

"Boys?" she enquired. "What two boys? I have never heard about them or seen them."

"Liar. Murderer." he screamed, banging on the table. "You had better go and think about it, and concentrate, inside the hood, and tomorrow I want you to tell me where those boys are or you shall rot in this prison."

The guard put the hood back over Amal's head, causing her to struggle a bit, so one of the men gave her a hard slap on the face, and then she was taken to a lonely cell to think about it.

As she sat on the floor, she could hear wailing and sobbing and, from time to time, screaming. She recognized some of the words and told herself, "They're Arabs. I think they've been beaten and most probably nobody believed them and it's my turn tomorrow. I wonder who are the two boys they asked me about? I don't know them, perhaps if I did I could have helped them." She felt very insecure and frightened and could feel her cheek burning from the slap, which made her start to sob and cry.

"I must stop this crying. I have been advised to think." She felt the ugly beast kicking inside her. "How dare he call me a liar and a murderer." Her heart resented the man and the thought brought the slap back to mind, "Stupid man, why did he slap me like that?" The beast was fully awake inside her now and she found herself biting her lips and becoming angry. She noticed this and felt upset with herself.

"Amal, what are you doing? Those horrible feelings of hate. The beast is awake. Knock him down quick, as you are losing your inner peace." She began to think and reason with herself. "Amal, control that lower nature, the world of hate inside you. Follow the pattern, see what your Lord did and you just copy. Don't lose your grip." She thought, "My Lord walked this road before me; when they questioned him, he answered, but they didn't believe, so what did he do?" she asked herself and then answered her own question. "He calmly surrendered without getting angry, like a sheep being taken to the slaughter. It's just the same with these people, they questioned me, but did not believe my answer. If nothing can make them believe, why should I worry? I will keep calm and quiet and, whatever happens, let it be."

Amal settled down and felt like a hero. She had controlled her hate and was looking forward to loving this different enemy. She was almost excited. At that moment the cell door opened and the guard entered with a piece of bread and a glass of water. That was her first meal since she had been captured in Baha's house. He undid the handcuffs and removed the hood so she could eat. She smiled softly, and said in a gentle voice,

"Shukran jezeela." (Thankyou very much).

The guard stood silent and emotionless, as if he had neither heard her voice nor seen her smile. She ate and drank and very appreciatively thanked him again as if she had had a banquet, instead of a piece of bread.

The guard felt a strange feeling in himself towards the Arab girl. "Strange girl," he said to himself, still looking at her soft eyes and open, friendly face. He put her hood and handcuffs back on, then went out, locking the door behind him.

The time came for Amal to meet the officer as promised. She was marched by her guard to his office and she stood herself facing the right direction. He commanded that the hood be lifted. The other men were standing in the same places as on the previous day, wearing their little skull-caps and observing her in the same way as before. The officer seemed busy and he had no time to waste, so he straight away asked,

"Name?"

"Amal," she calmly replied.

The man just glanced at his friends and continued,

"What happened to our boys? Tell me. They are young boys, the same age like you and their parents are in anguish; one of them is an only child. Why did you have to kill them? Why did you have to kidnap them, they were minding their own business? Why did you snipe at them?"

Amal stood quietly and listened, her heart moved, her compassion stirred, but she kept quiet, she had nothing to say. She knew exactly how those parents were feeling. "I didn't kill them," she said in her heart, I only know how to love. I did not snipe at anyone, I love everyone." She kept the words in her heart, as she knew it would be a waste of time to justify herself, or to deny, so she kept quiet, although her eyes talked compassion, and her face expressed gentleness and understanding.

The men looked and waited. "She is a very strange Arab," they puzzled inside themselves. Her calmness inspired calmness, so they kept looking at her, waiting for words, but no words were uttered. Then the officer interrupted the silence and threatened her again,

"I can see you are determined to rot in this place. I have the time of the world. You can stay in your cell for a week, or a month or a year, until you make up your mind to speak the truth."

Amal looked at the guard, waiting for her hood to be put back on. She had become accustomed to the routine. The officer nodded to the man who placed the hood in position and took the girl back to her cell.

Amal sat on her mat and felt quite relieved. "How amazing," she thought, "Jesus' pattern is a perfect one to copy. The officer was not too upset today, he didn't shout at me like yesterday. Now I only have to rot for a week before I see him for the next appointment." She stopped to consider the situation. "A week in this darkness and loneliness! It will drive me mad. I hate darkness, but...." and she thought of the good side, "At least there are no bombs here, that is one blessing."

She had the time of the world to think, so she thought. "Why do I have to rot? There's no need for that, as the Pattern, the one I am following, stayed forty days and nights in loneliness. He did not rot, he spoke to his father, he meditated on good things and conquered the opposer at the end of the trials; so I will do the same. I shall talk to my God, I shall sing for him, I shall meditate on good thoughts, and I will succeed with his help, without doubt."

Amal felt good, very good, and extremely happy. She meditated a great deal and prayed continually, for her enemies and everyone else. Then she sang, sweetly and softly, her favourite Psalms that always imparted strength and courage. She sang to her own tunes and made music by rattling the chains on her hands and clashing them together. She felt happy and uplifted.

The guard outside was very surprised as he was accustomed to hear wailing, cursing and prayers of vengeance, but not singing, not from people in that state. "She is either mad or innocent," he said to himself, then added, "or a very good actor." He strolled from one end of the corridor and settled himself down outside Amal's cell to listen to the beautiful singing of happy songs, although he could not quite understand the words as the voice was soft, and muffled because of the hood.

The week passed and the officer had the report from the guard about the condition of the prisoners, those who refused to co-operate and tell the truth.

"What about Baha?" the officer asked the guard.

"She is alright, adoni."

The officer looked at him with a surprised look,

"What do you mean, 'she is alright'?"

"She is very happy and I think she is enjoying her own company, as she's singing all the time. She has a sweet voice, too."

The officer was somewhat disturbed by the report, so he enquired further,

"What kind of songs? Love songs?"

"I can't tell exactly, adoni," he answered. "My Arabic is not that good and the sound is muffled because of the hood."

"Take the hood away, and call me when you hear her next time. Maybe the songs can tell us something about her."

The guard obeyed the order and removed the hood the following meal-time. Amal was delighted and thanked him very much, wishing him blessings and a long life. He just looked at her without any expression or feelings, as if she was not there.

"I wish he would answer me. I don't know why I bother to talk to him so nicely," she thought. Then she brought the pattern to mind, "Of course I'll bother. What is the good if I only speak to those who greet me, I will also speak to those who don't. I must also be grateful," she told herself, "my black hood has been lifted away, maybe they have believed me at last."

Amal was indeed now very happy, so after she had her bread and water, she determined to sing some joyful psalms to celebrate the occasion. No sooner had she started than the guard ran to the office,

"Adoni," he said excitedly, "She has started singing, nice and loud, and quite good."

The officer immediately left his desk and the work he was doing and walked fast with the guard until they both stopped to listen outside her cell. The guard obviously enjoyed the singing, for he started tapping his hands on his gun, in time with the rhythm. The officer was not quite sure what to make of it and said, to the enquiring eyes of the guard,

"Blessed be the Name, she is singing one of the Psalms!"

Then he slowly walked back to his office, where he spoke to his subordinates about his puzzle.

"I think we have a very difficult case with us," he said.

The other two men lifted their eyes from their work, looking at him enquiringly.

"This girl, Baha, is acting her part perfectly. She is singing Psalms. I think she's either trying to confuse us or gain our favour. Whatever her reason, she is insisting to play it cool, so we must rub her nose in it and that will soon make her toe the line."

He pressed the call-button for the guard, who came immediately.

"Moshe, take Baha to the lavatory and make sure that she does not come out from there until they are perfect. If she resists, you know what to do, as my patience is fast running out with this pretence."

Moshe opened the cell door and Amal smiled sweetly, saying, "Ahla."

The guard ignored her greeting, as usual, and firmly said,

"You have to do some work, and I warn you, it will have to be done perfectly or your nose will be rubbed in it."

That was so far the best piece of news that Amal had heard in the prison, as she had been sat there for a week, without any work or love-project, so she felt like work. "Any work will suit me fine," she said to herself and stood up from the mat. Moshe undid her handcuffs and feet, stuck his gun in her back and marched behind her.

"Straight ahead," he ordered.

She almost walked with joy and was not worried about the gun stuck in her back. "I am not afraid of what man does to me," she said to herself, with a smile on her lips.

Moshe stopped near a little storeroom where brooms, scrubbing brushes, buckets and other cleaning items were kept. He ordered again,

"Take a bucket and brush, and that mop, quick."

She obeyed. She knew how to clean, so picked up other items while she was about it; cleaning powder and a duster, and smiled to the guard, saying,

"I might need these as well."

"I wonder how long it will take for her to lose this eagerness," Moshe laughed to himself, as he marched her towards a lavatory block from which emanated a smell that worsened with every step they took.

Amal knew where she was going to clean. "What a dreadful smell," she said to her heart. "I've never liked it, but I'll soon transform it into perfection," and she looked at the cleaning powder, for she would need the whole tinful to get rid of such an odour. She remembered when she had been assigned to clean the lavatories in the orphanage and how Mother Teresa advised, 'The quicker you deal with it, the quicker you finish it'. "That's good advice, I must get on with it as quickly as I can." She hurried toward the building, much to the amazement of Moshe, but then hesitated at the door as the smell knocked her back.

Moshe shouted,

"Get in and clean it properly, or you'll have your nose rubbed in it."

Amal put her bucket down, undid the top button of her prison shirt, stuck her nose inside and re-buttoned it. "That makes a good mask," she said. Then she picked up her cleaning tools and entered, while Moshe stood outside. He hated to go near those filthy rooms, but when he had a difficult prisoner like Baha he often had to take them there many times, as it usually encouraged them to confess quickly.

Amal stepped in and found the floor covered with human excrement, as the prisoners tried to avoid walking right in to the proper place because of the defilement, so everyone would choose an unfouled area but, by the day's end, the place was impossible. Adding to all that, water and urine flooded the floor, and there was even mess all over the walls.

"How filthy," said Amal, wondering where to start. She felt very sick but said, to encourage herself, "Whatever you do, you do it whole-heartedly to God and not to people. Quick Amal, the sooner you start, the quicker you finish."

She started in the washing area, cleaning and mopping and scrubbing the tiles. Then she gradually worked her way into the interior, not leaving a spot of dirt or mess. She slowly became accustomed to the smell which was progressively going as the cleaning powder won the battle. Whenever she felt exhausted, she would return to where she had just cleaned and stand to admire it. "It's very good, almost as clean as the convent."

Moshe waited outside for a long time; for a whole hour. He was used to seeing the prisoners emerging after only a few minutes, when he would quickly enter to see if it was clean. If not, he would literally rub their noses in it and tell them,

"It's your own fault. You were warned to clean it properly. You fouled it, so you clean it." But with this actor, "What is she up to in there?" he asked himself, whilst trying to work up the courage to enter. Eventually his curiosity won and he walked in, calling out,

"Where are you? Sleeping on the job?"

But he was stopped at the entrance by the sparkling tiles he had never noticed before. Then he saw the glittering washbasins and clean floor. "What has she been doing?" he wondered, as he looked through a doorway and saw more shining tiles and smelt only the cleaning powder. "This is what I call magic. I'll have to use these toilets next time, as they're cleaner than our's."

Amal appeared with her broom and scrubbing brush from one of the cubicles, her nose still buried inside her shirt, and said to him,

"Tomorrow will be quicker. Only half the time."

Moshe had nothing to say, he just stood, looking at the soft brown eyes that smiled gently, waiting to hear his verdict, but he said nothing. For sure, there was not a speck of dirt for him to rub her nose in, so he ordered her,

"Off you go. Back to your cell."

Amal marched in front of the guard, first to the little store where she left her cleaning gear and then to her cell, where Moshe locked her in and then he hurried off to give his report.

"Well, Moshe?" enquired the officer, with interest.

"Adoni, that girl is unnatural, not human. Maybe if you come and have a look yourself at the lavatories, you will understand what I mean."

The officer stood immediately and they sped towards the toilets.

"They are better than in a first class hotel," commented the surprised officer as he inspected the rooms. Moshe smiled and said,

"She said, 'Tomorrow will be quicker. Only half the time'."

Amal slept so sweetly and deeply, as she was tired from her hard work. She had a good and relaxed conscience, as she felt she had done a bit toward her love-project. However, her officer and guards were in a dilemma with her. They knew for sure that she was Baha, as she had been dragged from the house of Abu Mansour's brother, and she fitted the description of Baha - the black hair, brown eyes and style of dress. Even her own brother, who had been captured at the same time, had told them that his parents and sister were in the house when the raid happened. They knew that the bodies of the parents were found and that the only survivor was Baha, a dangerous informer who had personally shared many times in kidnapping and bombing Israeli soldiers. But they could not understand why she was a very hard worker, showing great tenderness and love.

"Maybe the shock altered her thinking," suggested one of the officers. Anyway, whatever treatment they tried, the result was always the same, so they came to the conclusion that, 'we will mark her with an 'alef' (the first letter in the Hebrew alphabet) armband, to warn every Israeli who sees her that she is a potentially dangerous prisoner, although, as she is an excellent worker, she can do useful work in the prison.'

Abu Mansour and his son, picking up the pieces after the raid, became more determined than ever to take revenge and kill any Israeli they could possibly find. Baha had never been the same since she had befriended Amal, and now, after she had lost her parents, she could see the sense of her words. Mansour was becoming very impatient with her, for, although he loved her and intended to marry her, he found she was gradually driving him mad. He complained bitterly to his father,

"Baha doesn't want to co-operate with me. She just keeps speaking like the mobashira, saying, 'Don't kill, why not just try to love your enemies? We must start somewhere and it'll work, as the minute you love your enemy he is your friend'. It just makes me sick."

"Don't be too impatient, Mansour," he said to his son, repeating the words he had recently said to his brother. He was, though, worried about Baha's behaviour, so he said, "I will speak to her later and see if I can convince her to carry on with her duties. We need her help more than ever now, as I heard that Jonathan is back in Lebanon, which means that another raid is on its way."

Baha was now living with her uncle, Abu Mansour, and her kind aunt, Om Mansour, who tried her utmost to replace her mother for her. That evening, when the militia gathered together to discuss their plans, they sat drinking tea and eating salted nuts in Abu Mansour's house.

"Baha," her name was called from the men's quarters.

She knew what that meant; her uncle wanted her to go and spy. "I am not going," she said to herself. "I must conquer that ugly beast; as Amal said, I can only do it for myself. I have lost everything. I have lost my mother and my real friend that showed her love by her work, so I have nothing to lose. I must try to do some kind of work that will make me happy, as she was, a 'Project of Love', or something like that."

"Baha, are you coming?" her uncle's irritated voice called.

Baha walked slowly until she stood at the door of the room.

"Come in, girl. What has possessed you these last few days? I can't understand you, Baha. Does the blood of your parents mean nothing to you? Don't you know we're in a holy war against those God hates, so why do you behave like an infidel?"

Baha stood at the door, looking at her uncle and saying not a word. Mansour looked at her and ordered,

"Come in and shut the door, and do as you are told; immediately."

Baha entered and shut the door, but she was boiling and felt humiliated in front of all those men. "Amal, what shall I do?" she called in her heart. 'You can only change yourself, as everyone just has authority on himself alone. So you try to love your enemy; it works, then you will be the happiest person in all the world.' She could hear Amal's words going round and round in her head.

"Baha, my eyes, my sweet eyes," said Abu Mansour, softly and beggingly. "We need you badly. You know we recently killed three Israelis? Well, Jonathan, the man who led the last raid, is back in Lebanon. You know how to collect information. You don't have to kill, no, nor to kidnap, but just to go and enquire from your girl friends, just to help us a bit, so we can prepare ourselves."

Baha stood in the middle of the room, looking at the ground to avoid everybody's eyes. The men waited for her reply, but Baha just stood like a wax dummy, staring at the floor.

"Baha," said her uncle, in a threatening tone of voice, "If you are not going to co-operate with us, I shall throw you out of my house, and then let us see who will look after you and protect you from your enemies, as you are wanted by so many. The Christian militias are after you, and the Israelis want you urgently, so, are you going to help us and yourself? If not, you can leave this house immediately, and we will have nothing to do with you, ... forever."

Baha's heart trembled, she felt very insecure and her tears rushed to her eyes. "True, I have not one single person to turn to, besides my uncle, and it's also true that I have hundreds of enemies," she said to her broken soul. Then she remembered the words that had influenced her so much and said them out loud, with a soft smile on her lips,

"I have no enemies, not one enemy in this big world." Then she giggled, just like her friend, Amal, as that statement always produced laughter.

Abu Mansour lost his temper, his hands shook and his face turned red with anger. He shouted so loud that the seventh neighbour heard his roar.

"Baha, get out, you infidel, you traitor. Your blood is mahdour." (Permissible to be shed).

Baha turned round and quickly walked out, shutting the door behind her. Then she ran into the street, her tears blinding her vision, and just kept running. Now she had no friends, only enemies, especially as her uncle had denounced her and lifted the sacredness of her blood. She wondered if she had done the right thing as she speedily approached the crowded streets.

"I don't know Jesus much, except as our Lord Eesa, the prophet of peace, and I only know one sentence of his, 'Love thy enemy', that changed my thinking and my life. I don't know how to think or what to do or where to go. There are so many people here in this crowded place, but I am lonely, I am alone. Where can I spend the night? Not in the street, for sure, that will be very dangerous. Those girl friends of mine are not real friends, and even if I go to them they will soon discover my real identity, and then I will be in even greater difficulties than now."

She kept looking round. She was worried that every person behind her was spying on her or going to harm her. Every loud call or laughter seemed as if it was directed at her. She speeded up a little, then slowed to look around, to see which would be the best route to take.

She came to the junction where Amal used to sell her cakes to finance her love-project. She found her feet following the road which led to the orphanage, and her eyes anxiously looking up for the high walls of the convent and the big gates that Amal walked through so many times. 'I must hurry, or Mother Teresa will get anxious', she could hear Amal saying every time they had a long chat and happy time together. "I wonder if Mother Teresa will take me into her home? I don't think so," she answered herself. "You are a Muslim and known to belong to a Muslim militia."

Baha stopped outside the convent, looking at the imposing gates. "I must try. If they refuse me shelter, they refuse me, but I must at least try." Then, with shaking hands and shivering knees, she tapped at the gate.

The Father happened to be walking round the yard in the convent, where the orphanage was situated, when he heard the soft tapping on the gate. His heart jumped, as the tap sounded just like Amal's. He looked at his watch,

"This is about the time when Amal usually returns from her love-project," he thought and ran to open the gate, but froze in his place when he saw the figure of a girl who closely resembled Amal. She was standing looking at him with her soft brown eyes and a tender smile on her lips.

"Yes, my daughter. Who are you, and what do you want?" he asked at last.

"I am Baha, Father," she said in a quivering voice, "Amal's friend. Can I sleep in your home for just tonight, please?"

The Father knew about Baha, as Amal used to tell him about her; of how the seed of love for Jesus was growing in her heart, but he was not so convinced, as he also knew who Baha was, the one who had informed about so many Christian families and caused their deaths. He stood thinking for a time, looking to the girl, "I wonder if she is here to carry news about the orphans, or is she in need? Why only for one night?" Then he thought, "At least I must let her in and enquire from her about the reason." Then he said to her,

"Come in, my daughter. We can talk inside, rather than stand here at the gate."

Baha felt relieved, at least she was inside with the gate securely shut behind her. The Father took her into his office and called for Mother Teresa, as she had more experience than him in dealing with girls' problems. Shortly afterwards she entered the office and her mouth dropped open as, for a moment, she thought she saw Amal, but then the Father introduced his visitor,

"Baha, Amal's friend."

Mother Teresa smiled and looked to the Father for more information about the cause of the visit.

"Baha is asking if it is possible for her to spend just one night with us in the orphanage?"

Baha opened her heart and told her story to the understanding old man and the nun. Then, in a manner similar to Amal's, she said,

"If you can have me only for tonight, then, in the morning, insha-allah, (God willing) I will think of something, like.. ah.." and she hesitated, as she could not think of any love-project. She looked to the old man, "Unless you have some ideas?"

Mother Teresa spoke with tenderness,

"You can stay the night, Baha, and a bit longer, until the Lord will find a solution for you."

Then the Father added another piece of advice,

"You just keep thinking of good things, and ask the loving God to help you, for he does love everyone."

Mother Teresa took Baha to the kitchen and found for her some bread and white cheese and olives. The girl ate her fill and gratefully said to the old nun,

"Tislameely, may God extend your life."

Then Mother Teresa took her to the room where Amal used to sleep. When they entered they found the other young girls laying on their beds, busy doing their homework.

"This is Amal's friend," she announced to them. "She will be staying here with us for a little while."

The girls smiled and welcomed the stranger, then jumped up to prepare a place for her to sleep.

The Father and the old nun spent a long time thinking about how they could help Baha. They knew her life was in danger, as she had so many enemies, amongst her own people, as well as many others seeking revenge.

"We can't let her go outside the orphanage," said the Father, with concern, "as she will either be straight away shot or kidnapped. We must keep her here, maybe to work in the orphanage or help in the kitchen, or something."

Mother Teresa sat silent, just thinking, and every time the Father made a suggestion, she just nodded her head without speaking. The Father knew he had not yet hit upon the right idea.

Then she said,

"I wonder if Baha would like to be a nurse? Some of our nuns train nurses and then she could earn her living independently from us and live in the residential quarters of the hospital, away from those seeking her life. At the same time, she can carry on her love-project towards all humans."

The Father jumped from his seat, ran to Mother Teresa, and, taking her hand in his, said, with delight in his eyes,

"You are an angel, a real angel of mercy. I feel that's a very good idea, so let's sort out the possibilities with Mother Margarita, the senior nurse."

Mansour and his father and the others in the meeting gradually cooled their tempers. They never thought Baha would take them at their word and actually leave for good, because they knew she had nowhere to go and was aware of all her enemies.

"She will go around for a few hours, see some of her girl friends and come back, regretting what she has done," said Abu Mansour, "and waters will then return to their former courses."

The others agreed and continued with their planning, especially on how to gather news from their many sources, about Jonathan and the other Israelis.

"We can't count on Baha," said Mansour. "She seems to be fixed on this new idea of 'love thy enemy', so we'd better appoint another person quickly, as we've no time to lose."

The hours passed slowly for Abu Mansour and his son. Mansour loved Baha, and felt bad to have seen her thrown out like that, so said to his father,

"You shouldn't have been so hard and harsh. Look, now it's very late, and there's no sign of her."

Abu Mansour felt bad, too, and regretted the rash decision he took in anger, but he justified his action by saying,

"She is rebellious. I gave her plenty of time to co-operate. Anyhow, let her learn who are actually her friends, who really love and care for her."

Mansour could not settle down to sleep, so walked around the Palestinian camp and then out into the main city streets, which were now quite deserted, except for those just returning from night clubs and restaurants.

"Baha," he whispered, "Why did you have to do that? Don't you know I love you, so why have you deserted me for an ideal that is impossible to keep or practise. I love you, but I hate them and them and them. I'll kill them, I'll destroy my enemy to the finish."

He found himself banging his feet hard on the ground, to the point that he attracted the attention of some passers-by. He felt insecure and heavy hearted. He had never known himself to be so unhappy, so embittered, as on this night.

"Baha," he called, with his tears streaming, "Come back, and do as you wish."

Baha hardly slept that night, either, but kept thinking, "I feel safe here, and free. These people are poor but happy. The girls sleeping with me are loving and kind, although they have passed through much misery and many nightmares. If only I could stay here for good and leave all that hate and bitterness far behind." She thought hard, but could not find a solution to her problem. "I must leave it to God," she advised herself. "He is bound to find an answer, a happy answer." She found herself smiling, as if someone had lifted a heavy burden from her shoulders. Then she shut her eyes and slept peacefully until the morning bell aroused the big family to another day's activity.

The Father and Mother Teresa came to her while she was still with her new room mates. They smiled warmly to her.

"Did you have a good sleep?" enquired the aged man.

"Yes thankyou. I managed to sleep after a long time." Then she smiled and added, "I have been thinking a lot."

"Have you had any ideas?" asked the Father, continuing his questions.

"No, my mind just went blank, so in the end I left it with God to think of an idea, and I went to sleep."

The Father and the nun laughed, and he said,

"I am glad to inform you that God thought of an idea and it is now up to you as to whether you accept or refuse it."

Baha accepted. She floated on top of the world from such a delightful idea and joined the nursing school that same day, mixing in with Christian girls, as well as those from other religions, but she did not notice any difference between them, because they were all lovely humans. "I love everyone, everyone," she said to herself with a broad smile. "I wish you were here, Amal, so you could share my happiness, as you are the one who showed me this beautiful way of love. I am laughing, while you are in a horrible prison."

Jonathan was a young Israeli who was born and brought up in England. His prosperous parents had him educated at a public school, and from there he went to university. Whilst there, he was invited by fellow Israeli students to join them, and return to the land of his ancestors. After graduation he did so, and enlisted in the army, to defend his people from their enemies.

"Our enemies are many and abundant," said an old army officer to the young generation of fighters. "Our enemies are people who dwell all around us; they want to wipe us from the face of the ground that our God promised us. Our enemies are living among us, our enemies are everywhere."

Jonathan hated the enemies, no matter who they were or where they were. His hate helped him to fight with determination. 'To protect our land, our people. No tolerance, no talk. Just wipe out any enemy in sight.' That was his policy, which helped make him a rising star in the army. When the enemy kept nibbling at the soldiers like angry bees, he had devised and directed a few very successful raids in retaliation. His method was simple,

"They shot at us first, they provoked us, so we wipe the whole area clean. Whatever street our enemy lives in, we will destroy, and flatten the houses to the ground, so they must know we are not joking. We mean business, fair business."

Jonathan had gone to Lebanon to take revenge for the lives of the three Israelis who had just been killed by Abu Mansour and his men, and he was now giving instructions to the carefully chosen squad who would make the attack.

"Although Abu Mansour and his son escaped from our last attack, and we cut his family in half, he's still up to his games. So, we are here to answer him. He lives here," and Jonathan pointed to a spot on the huge wall-map. "This time we are only interested in these few houses, our enemy's houses. We'll wipe them clear to the ground. We will knock them out of existence, raze them completely."

Abu Mansour and his family were informed by their many eyes about the inevitable raid, so they evacuated their houses and hid among their men. They were only just in time to escape, because Jonathan's men left their houses flattened to the ground, but, as with any raid, a few casualties resulted, causing more unhappy families, more orphans, more fuel for vicious hate.

After the cycle was complete, Jonathan returned to his army hostel in Israel, to train other officers to repeat it all over again.

In Lebanon and other places, Abu Mansour and his men were picking up the pieces, reorganizing themselves and planning for revenge as well as new attacks. More money was needed to buy weapons to maintain the hate cycle, and that money had to be obtained by any means or method, including drugs, crime and terrorism. The beautiful valleys of Lebanon became fields of opium poppies, to produce drugs that would be sold all over Europe and America, to reduce humans to misery.

"It's for a good cause," said Abu Mansour, discussing new plantation plans. "Anyhow, Europe is made up of Christian countries and we hate them, too, as they're infidels. They should be Muslims and then they could be our brothers, but, as they're not, let them go mad. They don't have brains, anyhow."

CHAPTER 3

A NEW NAME, A NEW HOPE

Amal became used to her new home. She realized her stay there was going to be a very long one, since, as the prison officer told her, "You can stay here to rot. I have the time of the world, so it doesn't matter to me."

She found joy in whatever work she did, because as far as she was concerned, all her work was toward her pure and divine love-project, all done to God, so she put her soul into it and performed her best. Whenever the beast dwelling in her started to kick, she would encourage herself by saying, "Only the very best will do for my lovers and friends."

She was moved from her solitary confinement to an ordinary prison ward where she met other Arab girls who had all been captured taking part in one kind of terrorist act or another. All were full of determination to continue the struggle as soon as they were freed. Amal found herself mothering everybody in her ward, nursing the sick, encouraging the depressed and wiping away the tears of sadness. She tried to help by planting the seed of love.

"You must just try this method of love. I guarantee you that it works. I know because I've tried it and been so happy ever since. You just try it, love everyone with the same type of love, without any partiality, and you will find yourself among friends. It's up to you, whether to make them your friend or enemy; after all, you're the one who has to live with yourself, and that's what matters. So, kill that beast, the world of self love, and love others instead, and you will feel a hero, a conqueror, who has overpowered the impossible enemy."

The other women prisoners found Amal a strange person, although a lovable one, who would do anything for everyone. Her gentle eyes and friendly face were enough to soothe the grief of the soul. The officer assigned her to the kitchen, as she worked hard and quickly. She could even make an appetizing dish out of a plain loaf of bread, just by the thoughtful way she arranged it on the tray.

Mordecai was in charge of the army hostel where Jonathan lived. Being a training centre, it was full of young soldiers, both men and women. It had an international feel about it as its residents were from Israel and all corners of the world, drawn together by one aim, namely, 'to protect our people from our enemies'. They were prepared to sacrifice their comfort and homes to be ready, at an instant's notice, to go and fight the foe.

Each one would speak his own language, besides Hebrew, and this would enhance the cosmopolitan atmosphere in the hostel. There was Mark, boisterous and full of life, who spoke with a heavy American accent. He and Jonathan were good friends, as they both spoke English, which they understood better than their newly-learnt Hebrew. Adding to that, they were of similar age and looking forward to a secure future in which to raise their families. They spent most of their free time together, listening to Western music and reading books.

Mordecai had a kind, elderly woman called Dahaba, to assist him in looking after the hostel. She did the cooking for the boys and girls, helped by some part-time workers who cleaned and washed the laundry. One day she was taken ill, and sent a message to Mordecai, regretfully informing him she would not be able to work anymore, having suffered a slight stroke. Mordecai did not know whether he was coming or going and said to Dahaba's son, who had brought him the message,

"What am I going to do now? Just when the hostel is full and Jonathan is here, which means the training school will be open, which means more cooking, more work. How am I going to do everything, or even find someone at such short notice?"

Mordecai had to think quickly, as he needed an alternative by dinnertime. He looked at his watch,

"Still morning. The beds and cleaning will have to be left, as the main thing is to prepare dinner for the boys by seven o'clock." He went to the kitchen and found baskets on the tables, full of vegetables, fruit and meat. "What am I going to do, where can I start? Why do you have to be ill just now, Dahaba? Couldn't you wait for a week or two?" He started to panic. "I can't do it, I just can't do it, the boys can go hungry today."

Then he thought of his friend, the governor of the Arabs' prison. "Ah," he said, as his eyes brightened with a ray of hope, "I'll give Dudu a ring, he's bound to help me."

Mordecai ran to the office and rang his friend,

"Oh, Dudu, boker tov. I'm glad I found you, because I'm in dreadful trouble, an emergency. Dahaba, my cook, has been taken ill. Can you help me and send me anyone from your team until I can obtain a replacement?"

David could feel that Mordecai was in a crisis. He thought for a moment and then explained how he could not dispense with any of his team, for all were needed.

"Help me, Dudu. I beg you, anyone, only for a day or two?" begged the most anxious Mordecai.

"Well, I'm sorry to say I can't, as Jonathan has just brought us so many new prisoners of war, but...," the officer hesitated as an idea came into his head, and lifted Mordecai's spirit. "I have a good cook that I can dispense with, but you will have to come and collect. I can't send her as she's an Alef prisoner. Come to my office first, then I can explain the problem, and, if you want her, that's fine, otherwise, don't worry."

"I'll come straight away, she'll do, Alef or otherwise. I'll come directly." Mordecai put the receiver down and ran to his army jeep.

David quickly explained his problem to Mordecai,

"This informer is insisting to call herself Amal, while we're certain she's Baha, a first class informer and murderer of many of our boys. However, she's very strange, as she is happy and joyful, a good worker for whom nothing is too much for her. I've tried all my most severe treatments on her, but they just proved to be like water off a duck's back. You're welcome to have her for a few days, until you find an alternative, but keep your eyes on her. She has the band on her sleeve to warn everybody to be aware of her activity, but, other than that, I don't know what to suggest."

Mordecai smiled and said,

"I'll keep my eyes open and warn the boys to do the same, but let me see her before deciding. I urgently need someone to cook the dinner, at least for today."

The officer pressed his bell and the guard appeared a few moments later.

"Get me Baha from the kitchen. Quickly," he ordered.

The guard hurried away and found Amal cleaning and scrubbing the floor, while she hummed a song in a low tone. He stood in front of her, so she lifted her head and smiled.

"Ahla," she greeted him.

"Up. You're wanted in the office. Hurry up."

Amal's stomach felt sick, as she knew from experience what happened when she went to the office. "Oh no," she called to her Lord. "Help me, my Lord. Just when I thought life was getting a bit easier, and now he is calling me. I don't think I can take anymore." She felt fearful, as the road seemed to be without an end, stretching so far ahead of her. Then she reminded herself, "Love throws fear outside; there is no fear in true love, so why are you acting as if you have no faith. No one will be tempted beyond what he can bear, so maybe the Lord knows you can bear a little more burden." She felt comforted by the good thoughts that came to her mind, so smiled and hurried with the guard.

They entered the office. She saw Mordecai standing near the desk, obviously in a hurry, as he kept looking at his watch and impatiently tapping the desk with his fingers. He fixed his eyes on her, searching for information. The officer asked her,

"Name?" That was his usual question before announcing the next punishment.

"Amal." She answered calmly.

The officer looked at Mordecai, then said to the prisoner,

"Well, I hate the name Amal, which you seem delighted to use."

Mordecai spoke to his friend in Hebrew,

"The boys will be most offended to hear a name like that in the hostel, as they want to forget about Lebanon and Amal and all the others, so we must change her name, at least while she is with me."

The officer looked at Amal, trying to fit her with a new name. Both men stared at her, and the guard also joined in, all looking at her, just like parents who would study their newborn child in order to choose a suitable name for him or her.

Mordecai smiled and said to David,

"Natanya would be a good name. She has a lovely face and kind eyes. Anyhow, she is Natanya to me."

The men laughed, for the name meant, 'Yah, the Lord, has given.'

The officer spoke to Amal, trying to be harsh, but he was definitely in a happy mood,

"I have two things to say to you. First, from today your name is Natanya, not Amal or any other name. I hate that name you have chosen for yourself, and so does everyone else here.

"Second, you have been promoted. As you've worked hard and diligently in the prison, you're going to work in a hostel."

Amal smiled and said to the officer, with delight in her eyes,

"Shukran gezeela." (Thankyou very much). Then she looked to Mordecai, who also had a smile on his face.

The officer then added,

"Be aware, any misbehaviour, or trouble in any way, and you will be punished severely. You are still a prisoner, just remember that fact."

Natanya left with Mordecai, still dressed in her prison uniform. She had no possessions, so no case to pack, nothing besides what she wore. Just a few personal items which she kept in a carrier bag. Mordecai sat her beside him in the jeep, to keep his eyes on her and her movements. He thought to himself, "She looks so young, I wonder if she can cook for an army?" He drove at great speed, as the morning was over and the cooking had yet to be started. "If I'm really stuck, then the boys will just have to eat bread and cheese for today."

Natanya was also thinking and far away in her thoughts. "I like my new name, as it indicates they've accepted me as a friend, and not an enemy anymore." She felt good and joyful. She thanked her God who had not allowed her to be tempted beyond what she could bear. She watched the countryside, the beautiful landscape, and the speeding cars and buses which were rushing with them along the road. She glanced to Mordecai from time to time. "He looks very friendly and fatherly. I wonder if he minds me to talk with him?" she asked herself, and found herself automatically speaking with him,

"A beautiful land, isn't it?"

Mordecai nearly answered her kindly, but remembered she was an enemy, so spoke gruffly,

"No talk, don't speak. You are not free, you are a prisoner."

Natanya felt sad, her tears rushed to her eyes. "Why? What have I done to him or any of these people?" These thoughts provided the right nourishment for the beast dwelling inside her. "No, Natanya," she said to her new self. "You have just been promoted and given a new name, so that means new hope in your relations with these people. You must rejoice at the progress, because you know it will take a long time and great effort, but it does work, in the end."

Mordecai drove the jeep right up to the hostel, stopped and jumped down. Natanya also jumped out, shutting the door behind her.

"Come quick, we have a lot of work to do," he said, leading the way into the building. They kept pace, side by side. He was almost running, so Natanya followed. They entered the kitchen. Mordecai pointed to the pile of dishes which had been used for breakfast, to the baskets full of food, and then to his watch.

"Food must be ready to serve by seven, so you only have a few hours."

Natanya smiled sweetly at the flustered man, who spoke her language very brokenly and full of mistakes, although he expressed himself well. She remembered the times that the nuns had to face such work, especially when one of the team was ill or not available. She also remembered the way they used to calm each other, 'A big mountain will soon be level ground before you.' So she said to Mordecai,

"This mountain will soon be level ground before you, so don't worry."

He looked at her, for he was familiar with that quotation, but had forgotten exactly where he had heard it, especially as he was not very religious.

Natanya headed for the sink and speedily washed up, as she could not work with mess. "It wastes good time," she told herself. Then she investigated the contents of the baskets, while Mordecai followed her from one to the other, hopping and fussing about, doing nothing. She asked him,

"How many are going to have dinner?"

"Forty, at least forty. It could be more or it could be less."

Now she knew how much to cook and set to work. She started her Psalm singing, for that was how she timed herself, as well as praising her God. She told herself, "This is a real project of love, for my Lord many times prepared food for thousands, so I love to prepare food for tens of my friends."

The mountain of jobs soon became a small hill and so Mordecai relaxed a bit, amazed at the organized way Natanya worked. "She must have done this work before. Perhaps she was employed in a hotel or restaurant?" he wondered to himself.

Before long all was prepared and the cooking filled the air with a homely, appetizing aroma. Natanya asked him another question,

"Where do you serve the dinner?"

"We put the bread and salad bowls on the tables there." He pointed beyond the kitchen serving counter to the dining hall, which had five rows of tables, each sufficient for about twelve persons. "Then the boys will take a tray and plate from that table and bring them to us so we can fill them from those big pots on the warming slab."

Natanya understood the idea and prepared the tables, assisted by Mordecai. She arranged the salad most attractively in the bowls and placed the salt and pepper with thought and care, as if a king was about to partake of the meal, and not tired, hungry soldiers that had been on hard training. She filled some of the jugs with soft drinks and others with cold water. When everything was just right, she stood and admired her work; then asked Mordecai,

"Do you like it?"

He forgot the fact that she was an enemy, so smiled and said to her,

"The boys will like it."

Mordecai felt excited as he waited for the boys to come, for he knew they would have a surprise, because, although Dahaba was a good cook, lately her cooking had deteriorated and the boys found it difficult to eat the food, as it never looked appetizing or tasted good. "That will stop them moaning, especially Mark, as he never likes anyone's cooking, except his mother's," laughed Mordecai to himself.

Natanya had her big pots all ready with the various items, waiting for the boys to come and try her cooking. Mordecai opened the dining room doors and the stream of hungry souls came in slowly, as they were tired, and anticipated the usual disappointment with the food. But this time the aroma was completely different.

"Smells good," said Mark to Jonathan.

"Yes, hopefully it will taste as good," he answered with a doubting look on his face.

Each one took his tray from the table near where Natanya was standing ready to serve. At first they did not notice her, as they were puzzling at the way each tray had a napkin neatly laid on it.

Then Jonathan lifted his eyes and saw the figure of the serving girl. She looked familiar and he knew he had seen her somewhere before. He stared into her gentle, smiling face, and then his eyes caught sight of her armband with its big letter 'alef'. "Oh, I know. She's an Arab, a dangerous enemy." He was surprised to see her there, but that was not his problem. "Mordecai knows what he's doing, so it's not my business," he said, while still looking at Natanya with cool, examining eyes, full of distrust.

Mark was next in the queue. He also saw the gentle, smiling face and the armband and took heed of the silent warning, and so did every boy and girl. They marked their enemy who had just cooked their dinner and served them with a smile.

The diners sat admiring their well-arranged tables.

"It's a first class service for a change," remarked one of the girls, smiling to her friend.

"This is incredible," said Mark. "It tastes good, almost like my mother's cooking. What's happening here? Do you know?" he asked.

"No," replied Jonathan, "but I'll find out from Mordecai as soon as I have a chance. Look at him, with a big smile. He's usually rushing everywhere, fussing, but today he really looks happy." Then Jonathan looked around at the happy company of diners. "In fact, everyone looks very happy," he added.

Natanya surveyed her well satisfied friends, and her heart rejoiced. "I really cannot comprehend this marvellous love. Imagine it, I'm in the midst of Israeli fighters, but I feel I could even sacrifice myself if the need arose, just to see them happy," she thought. "I can see now what my Lord meant when he said it's a new kind of love, like his; how wonderful. I can't express my gratitude enough, for his showing me this unique way of pure love."

Mordecai noticed the boy's plates were wiped clean, so he went to see if there was extra in the pots.

"If anyone wants more, there is still food left," said Natanya, with her gentle look.

Mordecai clapped his hands and announced,

"If you need more, there is plenty left."

Immediately a number of boys rushed up with their empty plates, including Mark, which indeed surprised Mordecai, for he always brought back some of his food, untouched.

Mordecai stood at the end of the hall and clapped his hands again for attention, before the soldiers disappeared to their rooms. Everyone hushed and looked at him.

"I am sorry to announce to you that our cook, Dahaba, won't be coming anymore."

This caused laughter, and some whispering, which Mordecai ignored, as he guessed what they were talking about. He continued,

"Well, poor Dahaba had a stroke this morning, and I had great difficulty to arrange for an alternative at such short notice."

Natanya could not understand a single word, so she started collecting the pots to take them to the sink to wash up, while Mordecai gave his speech.

"Our temporary new cook is an Arab prisoner, as you have already noticed, but she has a favourable report of good behaviour and hard work. Her name to us is Natanya. What I want to tell you all is this, keep your eyes on her. If you see any unusual behaviour or movement, report it, or you can act personally. She will only be here for a few days, so just keep on your guard."

The young girls and boys stood up, gathered their plates and put them on their trays, then left them in a pile on the table. After that, they went to their rooms, very tired but well satisfied. Natanya cleared up and washed the plates, counting as she went. "The Lord satisfied fifty people with good things," she commented to herself.

Now Mordecai had the problem of finding somewhere for Natanya to sleep, so he strolled around the hostel, seeking to find a suitable place. "Where shall I put her? It must be somewhere that I can keep my eyes on her." At last he found what he sought, a little room, more like a large cupboard, next to the kitchen and opposite his own room. It was a storeroom for the clean laundry, with shelves all round from floor to ceiling. There were no windows, and the only openings were two air vents, one above the door and the other in the outside wall, facing the street. "This is a very good room," thought Mordecai. "It's just large enough for a camp bed, and well located so I can keep an eye on her. Jonathan's room is at the end of the passage, so he and Mark can also watch her." He prepared the little room for its new occupant and then gave his instructions to the very tired girl.

"You will sleep here. I want you up and ready by five in the morning to prepare breakfast."

Natanya nodded her head. She entered her room and looked around. "It's a laundry store," she said in an undertone. "But it doesn't matter what it is, as long as it's my own room." She stood by the end of her bed, thinking. "This is the first time I have ever had a room of my own, as I shared with my brother and sister when we were children, with others at the orphanage and with the prisoners in the prison, except for my time in that lonely cell, which I shall not count. Here I have my own room, shared with the laundry."

She closed her door, changed, and sat on the bed to pray, thanking her God for providing this promotion. Then she lay down and stretched out her hands to see how far the shelves were from the bed. "I can't stretch my hands fully," she said, "but at least I am well tucked in here and no fear of any bombs, not with all these young soldiers around me."

She slept very lightly, aware of all the movement around her. She heard the cars and passers-by, as well as the footsteps of the patrolling night-guards, as her head was near the street wall. She could also hear the sound of talking and laughter in the corridor. After a time, she dozed off into a deep sleep, but awoke early, not wanting to oversleep in the morning; so she was up and ready when she heard the hurried steps of Mordecai approaching her little room. He tapped on the door and opened it at the same time.

"Natanya," he said. "Good, you are ready. We go straight to the kitchen."

They walked this time, not running like the day before. He gave his instructions, "Eggs, yogurt, cheese and some cucumber. We put the food on the tables and serve a lot of tea and coffee."

Natanya prepared the breakfast with tender love and thought, just like a loving mother would do for her family. "Eggs," she thought. "He didn't say how he likes them cooked." She wanted to ask him but changed her mind. "I think I will boil some, fry some, and scramble some, so the boys will have a choice."

Mordecai noticed she was preparing the eggs in a number of different ways. "She's going to thoroughly spoil the boys, and ruin them." He shrugged his shoulders and said to himself, "I don't care, as long as the boys are happy, and she does the work."

Natanya set the tables just like the day before, so attractively, but this time with the white cheese and yogurt. The cucumber was sliced and made into beautiful patterns with green and black olives for decoration. Mordecai looked at the tables, then at her and smiled. She said to him,

"When everyone has sat down, I will bring the eggs, so they can have them nice and hot."

He nodded. She knew he appreciated her work, but as she was a prisoner, it would be difficult for him to say 'thankyou' or 'well done'. She smiled softly to herself as one of Jesus' parables came to mind, and she thought, "What I have done is my duty, and nothing extraordinary to be thanked for."

The room filled with the young soldiers, who greeted Mordecai but did not seem to notice Natanya. "Everyone ignores me as if I am not here," and her heart resented that, but she immediately rebuked herself and said, "I wish you would stop thinking of yourself like this. Forget about you and put everyone else above yourself."

Natanya and Mordecai served breakfast. The boys and girls glanced at their new cook, who gave them a choice of eggs and made a good start to their day. They noticed how she watched their cups and plates, and, as soon as they were empty, she rushed and brought more. They felt good and well looked after.

Jonathan almost said 'thankyou' once, as he was brought up to be courteous, but he caught himself just in time, "You can't say thankyou to your enemy," he told himself.

After breakfast was over and Natanya had cleared up the kitchen, assisted by Mordecai, he spoke to her in his usual business-like way.

"We have a lot of work to do. The beds have to be made and the rooms cleaned, as they were not done yesterday."

Then he led the way and Natanya followed.

All the rooms were shared. Some had up to eight beds and a few only two. Clothes and very dusty boots scattered all over the place were a common sight in most rooms, although the girl's rooms were a bit tidier than the rest.

"This will not do," said Natanya to herself, looking at one of the boy's rooms, as she recalled the words of the nun in the orphanage, 'an untidy room means an untidy mind, and who wants that?'"

Mordecai stood watching Natanya while she sorted the mess. "What amazes me," he thought, "is the strange way she works; like magic, as if there's an invisible power behind her hands."

She stripped each bed and changed it, then folded the clothes neatly and put them in their wardrobes. She stacked the books and papers, and placed the dusty boots on the lower shelves. When she had finished the room, she turned to Mordecai, who was still watching her, and said,

"Very dirty," pointing to some boots. "I will polish them later, when I've finished cleaning."

"No Natanya," he objected. "That's going too far."

"I'll do it quickly. It will make the boys feel good."

He did not know what to say to that, he just looked at his watch and tapped it to indicate that time was running. Natanya won by the end of the day, as she finished the cleaning of the rooms and the polishing of the boots, besides producing another exciting meal. It was a changed group which came to the hostel at the end of the day, as they were looking forward to another good meal, just like the one they had enjoyed the day before, but they did not let their heart's desire to be known, except for Mark.

"I wonder what she has cooked for us today?" he remarked to Jonathan, as he rubbed his stomach.

Jonathan laughed and said,

"You'll have to watch your figure. Two full plates everyday won't do you any good!"

"I have to make up for the last six months. I've hardly eaten a proper meal, with Dahaba's style of cooking."

The boys usually had a shower before the evening meal, to clean and cool their aching bodies from the severe training and hard exercises which they had undergone. They headed for their rooms, to collect a clean change of clothes and dump the dirty ones. When they entered, they noticed a complete revelation.

"The place has been cleaned," said Jonathan, looking at the transformed room, the perfectly made bed. Mark stood looking at his side of the room and noticed how his clothes, that he had thrown all over his bed that morning, were now tidy on the shelf.

Then he caught sight of the shining boots. He had never polished them before, as he did not believe in wasting time and effort. "Those are not my boots, for a start," he thought, so he said to Jonathan,

"Whoever cleaned this room, mixed up the boots." Then he picked up the polished boots and said, "Are they yours?"

"No," answered Jonathan, and he picked up his own shiny boots, with a smile of puzzlement on his face, just like a child who has discovered a surprise hidden in his room. "Look at mine, lovely and clean. I shall look forward to wear them tomorrow."

Every boy and girl was thrilled with the results of the love-project. They had their showers and came promptly to the dining room, drawn by the inviting aroma of the cooking and the delightful surprise they had all just received, which made the hostel a home, a real home.

David phoned his friend Mordecai in the evening, to enquire about the prisoner's behaviour.

"She is wonderful," said Mordecai, gratefully. "The best thing that ever happened to this hostel. She cooks beautifully, she has taken the place over as if it's her own home, and she even polished the boys' boots, to make them feel good!"

David laughed and replied,

"I know she's like that. She did great things here in the prison. I think she's mad."

"No, I feel she is unnatural, but not mad. I think she just loves people, everyone. Strange to say, but I notice she goes out of her way to make others happy; she does things she has no need to do. For example, in the morning...." and Mordecai went on to relate the story in detail, concluding, "If not for that band on her sleeve, you would think she is one of us."

Everyone relied on Natanya, but no one ever said a word of appreciation. Everyone noticed her love that was clearly shown by her deeds, yet none called her gently. She became used to hearing her name shouted from one side of the hostel to the other. It was not that they wished to be nasty, but that was the way one should talk to their enemy. There was no need to shout, but that was the way they always spoke to their enemies, for somehow, although they looked human, in reality they were not quite so, whether male or female. There was no sense or logic to that viewpoint, but that is actuality.

Natanya knew why they shouted and treated her as they did. "It is not them, it's that ugly world of lower nature that dwells in everyone. It must be destroyed so they, too, can be conquerors, and triumph over an entire world of hate."

Baha progressed well in her nursing course, working diligently for long hours, as the hospital stayed full of casualties, mostly the victims of hate. She nursed so many who had been injured by bombs and explosions. She had patients from all religions, but that never concerned her. "They're all humans, and that's all I'm interested in. God loves all humans, as he created us in his image, and it's that image which I want to nurse and help." Baha told herself this every time new casualties were brought in.

Abu Mansour and his son became very frustrated, because whenever they sniped at the Israelis, Jonathan and his troops would retaliate and flatten a few more houses, so gradually depleting their resources. As they urgently needed more weapons, Abu Mansour made a tour of the Arab countries, to collect money and contributions for the Jihad. Some contributed generously, supplying money and weapons, whilst others hesitated, but they soon capitulated when they realized they would be marked, and attacked as traitors and supporters of America, or even worse, as the tail of Zionists, the biggest insult with which to label any Arab state.

He went as far as Iran, and returned home with great support, and agreements to supply money and weapons. He re-organized his group, as he had Iranian officers coming to train his men to use the new weapons, which they were anxiously awaiting. At the same time, he had other problems besides Israel.

Every day a new group of fighters would appear on the scene, gathering men around them and showing their strength by blowing up each other and their common enemies. Mansour had to watch the Christian militias, the Druze and the endless new parties, so his men were sectioned into small bands, who were sent in different directions, to follow and annihilate their opponents.

The consignment of weapons arrived and a great celebration was planned.

"This is enough to blow up all the Jews!" said the celebrating Abu Mansour to his men. "We must plan carefully, and not say a word or whisper about our treasures, otherwise we'll have Jonathan descend upon us and wipe the lot to the ground."

The weapons were quickly distributed in various directions, and a rigorous training programme started to enable the men to effectively use their new, up-to-date tools of destruction.

Mansour discovered where his cousin, Baha, was working and admired her immensely. "She has great courage to stand up for what she believes," he told himself. "It's a pity her beliefs are not the same as mine, because we could have established so much together." He sat thinking thoughtfully of his lovely Baha, feeling sorry for himself. "No one can ever take her place, for she does things so conscientiously. The times she worked all day to bring us information ready to use. If only she was with me now, she could have gathered what all these useless eyes have collected in their whole lives." He sighed and said, "Well, at least she chose a good job. I've always admired the nurses whom they call angels of mercy, and now my Baha is one of those angels." Then he smiled softly, "'Love thy enemy' is what Amal taught her and that's what she's trying to do. I detest the thought." He jumped to his feet, ready to train some of the men in using their new weapons.

Natanya was allowed to move freely around the hostel, as everyone knew her well and trusted her. She never disappointed the boys and girls regarding meals or keeping a clean and comfortable home. They became accustomed to her soft smile and gentle brown eyes. She did not speak a word of Hebrew, so lived in her own world, which was sometimes very lonely. This made her wish to talk a little to someone, but only Mordecai knew some Arabic, and no one spoke French. She could understand some English, in fact, she noticed she could almost comprehend Jonathan and Mark when they conversed together. But nobody spoke to her; she was there to work, not to speak, as Mordecai many times reminded her when she talked for any length.

She became well acquainted with the personalities of those living in the hostel. She noticed how Jonathan was very different from Mark. He was quiet and polite; he never shouted her name or spoke gruffly, he just did not speak to her at all. On the other hand, she found Mark 'easy come, easy go', only centred on himself and not caring about anyone else. She became familiar with the individuality of everyone in the large family that she lived with and served, but no one bothered about her, for she was the enemy.

Mordecai asked his friend David if it was possible to keep Natanya for good. "At least she is more useful here than stuck in one of the cells," he told his friend one day during a telephone conversation.

"Remember," said David, "she is a prisoner."

"I know, Dudu, but please, forget about her for a time and let me get the use of her skills and service."

David agreed, and the arrangement was made that Natanya would stay there as long as the need existed; otherwise she would return to the prison.

Natanya followed her usual routine that day. She felt good and happy as she went to the kitchen to prepare dinner. Everything went well, it being done with love. It was almost time for dinner and the tables were spread with bowls of salad and baskets of bread, while the hot main course was on a low heat, ready to be served on time.

Jonathan had his shower and changed ready for the evening meal, then went to the common room to sit and read for a while. Mark, as usual, took off his shirt, and threw it on the bed, then emptied the contents of his pockets onto the crumpled shirt, including his bulging wallet, which he was prone to overload. He picked up his towel and a clean set of clothes and left to have his shower, leaving the room door wide open.

Mordecai happened to pass by on his way to the kitchen and noticed the door wide open, so put his head in to have a word or two with the boys. He found no one in, but saw the untidy bed with the wallet on top. "Stupid boy," he said to himself. "Leaving his wallet like that, with the door wide open. I'll take it and give him a lesson, so he will not be careless again like this." He picked it up, put it in his pocket and left to do his work.

Mark had a shower and returned to his room to finish dressing. He noticed the wallet had disappeared. "Funny," he said to himself, "I left it just there, so where has it gone?" He lifted his dirty shirt and the other items he had thrown onto the bed, but it was nowhere to be seen. "This is the biggest tragedy of my life. All my money, a whole month's salary, and my documents and other papers. Who could have taken it?" He searched all around the floor and under the beds, while wondering who would have stolen his wallet. "I know, it must be Natanya. She is the only one who enters the rooms to clean. I bet she saw it and took it, the thief, the dirty Arab."

Then he shouted her name so loud that most of those in the hostel heard his yell, including Jonathan, who cocked his ears to hear what was happening.

"Natanya, come here at once."

Natanya smiled to herself, "Oh Mark, what's up now? I am in the middle of my work; can't you wait?" But she left her stirring spoon and ran to Mark's room. When she reached the door, she stood there, enquiring with her eyes. She saw Mark half-dressed and looking extremely angry.

"Where is my wallet?" he shouted in English.

"Wallet? Wallet?" repeated Natanya, not quite understanding the meaning of the word.

"My money, girl. My money was here. Where has it gone?"

"I did not take it," she answered in English.

"You took it; bring it back," shouted the angry young man.

Natanya started to shake from the shock. Her colour disappeared and she felt very frightened, as Mark was certainly furious. She froze in her place, staring at him with wide and frightened eyes. He tightened his lips and walked toward her, grabbed hold of her collar and shouted furiously,

"Give it back to me immediately, or I'll kill you."

Hearing the shouting, Jonathan picked up his book and returned to the room, to investigate the problem caused by Natanya. He arrived to find Mark still gripping the pale girl by the collar, so asked him,

"What's the matter?"

"This thieving Arab has stolen my wallet. It has all my salary and other valuables in it, as well as some important documents," replied Mark almost crying, while he shook her by the neck.

Jonathan was shocked. He felt very upset and disappointed. "I wondered when she would do something like that," he thought as he looked at her frightened eyes. He walked slowly toward her and Mark, and said to his friend,

"Leave her to me, Mark. I shall soon encourage her to speak. These people don't respond to questions, they need force."

Jonathan held Natanya by the neck and looked straight into her eyes and she could see how much he despised her from the look on his face. Then he spoke firmly and clearly,

"Give him his money."

"I didn't take it," she replied, swallowing her saliva.

"You did, return it straight away."

Natanya knew they would not believe her, just as they did not believe her name. "What is the use to deny; let them do what they like with me," she thought, and stood shaking, while Jonathan waited, before he let her talk by his method.

He waited a little longer, then held her with the left hand, lifted his right hand and slapped her so hard in the face that she felt her teeth rattle. She nearly bit her tongue. Her tears dashed to her eyes as she stood staring into the eyes of one who despised her so much. She knew he was about to strike her on the other cheek when Mordecai walked in. "Oh no," she trembled, "now the three of them will beat me to death." She looked at Mordecai, talking and pleading with her eyes, "I did not take any money." But no words escaped her lips.

Mordecai saw Jonathan holding Natanya's neck, and a very angry Mark looking on, so he stood at the door and enquired,

"What's all the noise for, boys?"

Jonathan answered his question, with loathing in his voice,

"She stole his wallet, with all his salary and other valuables in it."

Then he waited to see his reaction. Mark, too, stood looking to the father figure, and Natanya begged for mercy with her frightened eyes.

Mordecai pulled the wallet from his picket, and asked, while looking at Mark,

"You mean this?"

Mark nodded his head.

"Well, you're a careless boy. Anyone could have walked in and taken your wallet. I hope that will teach you a lesson."

Then he handed it over to Mark, who smiled and said,

"Thanks a lot, Mordecai."

Mordecai left the room and hurried to the kitchen. Natanya looked at Jonathan who was still gripping her collar, and then to Mark. He smiled and said,

"That saved you just in time. You're lucky."

Then she looked to Jonathan's eyes. They seemed to be a bit misty. He regretted his hasty and unfair action, and wanted to say "I'm sorry", but could not bring himself to do so. He just kept looking at the waiting eyes. Then he slowly withdrew his hand from her neck, although he continued his gaze.

"Natanya."

Another call for her, this time from the kitchen. Mordecai was becoming flustered; it was time to serve dinner. Natanya hesitated, wanting to hear the word 'sorry' from Jonathan, but no chance of that, so she turned and left the room, back to the kitchen.

She kept choking from her sobbing, very unhappy and disappointed, as she realised that the polite, quiet young Jonathan was also controlled by the ugly beast within him. She took her stirring spoon, lifted the lid and gave a gentle stir, but her mind and heart were aching beyond belief. "Why do I have to bother?" she asked her heart. "Till when will I have to bear with these insolent people?"

The beast was kicking hard inside her, stirring her hate and bringing her to the boil, just like the dinner she was stirring. "Natanya," she said, "I feel that hate I managed to conquer is rising." She stirred some more. Her tears dropped warmly onto her cheeks, so she wiped her face with her sleeves before they dripped into the pot. "Cool yourself, Natanya," she whispered. "The road is narrow and full of hardship. You have travelled so far so well; why do you have to stop and turn round now. Go ahead. Please, try again." The beast inside responded, loud and clear, "No, no, I've had enough. I must kill myself, I must die. There is nothing left for me in this big world. Look where my love has brought me - I loved those who killed my family, and what did I gain from that love? Unfair imprisonment."

Although Mordecai saw how hurt Natanya was, he pretended nothing had happened. He opened the door of the dining room and the young soldiers started to enter. They picked up their plates from the neat pile and stood in front of Natanya for her to fill them. But when they saw her red face they knew she was not her usual happy self. She did not lift her eyes to greet them, as was her custom, as she was in the midst of a fierce battle being fought in her heart.

She loaded the serving spoon and started to fill the plate in front of her, as she continued to look down. Then she took roasted potatoes and put them on the plate, while being fully occupied in the battle. "Why Natanya? Why are you treating this poor person in front of you like this, just because Jonathan has upset you?" She lifted her eyes and saw it was one of the local Israeli boys who was standing there, looking at her sad eyes. "He looks a pitiful boy," she thought. "Young and hungry. Why upset his feelings?" She found herself smiling softly to him, and he smiled back and left, followed by another and another.

Jonathan felt so angry with himself. "Unfair, unjust," the words kept going round and round in his head. "Coward, lacking moral stamina; why couldn't you say sorry? I can't, she is my enemy." A big battle raged inside Jonathan. "How can I go and take from her hand the food which she cooks with care and thought, when I have just struck her face so cruelly, while she is innocent, a hundred percent innocent. How can I go and eat?"

Mark interrupted the thoughtful and unhappy Jonathan by saying,
"Come on, Johnny. Why the glums? You shouldn't take it to heart. After all, she's only an Arab, an alef enemy, so let's hurry and have our meal."
"I don't feel like seeing her, nor do I feel like eating."
"Oh boy, you're too sensitive." Then he paused to find some good logic to make an excuse for the conscience. "Look at it this way, Jonathan," he said. "That slap will serve as a lesson for next time, if she had it in her mind to pick any property from us."
Jonathan looked at Mark. He could see that was nonsense reasoning, but did not feel like arguing or talking, so he stood up and they both left for the dining room.

Mark advanced, took his tray and plate and pushed it along the counter. Natanya had now cooled down quite a bit, as she was winning the battle again, but at that moment, she happened to lift her eyes and saw him. She quickly averted her gaze and filled his plate with the various appetizing foods, prepared especially to make the boys happy. Mark's presence caused the beast to suddenly kick so hard that her heart felt on fire. "I wish I hadn't lifted my eyes, as now I feel worse than ever."

Jonathan placed his tray in front of her. His heart, too, was in a turmoil. He was upset with himself, because he could not say, "I'm sorry."

Natanya knew who was standing in front of her, but did not look at him in case she lost her temper. Then she might lose her grip of the beast and the whole battle. She filled his plate and forced herself to give him an extra spoonful of his favourite dish.

Jonathan noticed that and stood for a while, looking at her sad face. "Now's your chance. Please say sorry. Look, she gave you an extra spoonful, so please, say that word; it's only one word." He breathed rapidly, but just could not say sorry to his enemy, although his eyes said hundreds of 'sorry's', all to no avail, as Natanya insisted not to look at him. He hesitated for a while, then took his tray and went to sit down.

Those who were sitting with Jonathan at the table noticed his unhappiness. They had heard Mark shouting and gathered there was a problem, with Natanya in the middle, as her name had been shouted out earlier on. She had obviously been crying and still looked very unhappy. They were curious to know the reason and one of the girls asked Mark directly,

"What's the problem? What was all that shouting for?"

Mark glanced to Jonathan. He wished that question had not been asked when Jonathan had only just cooled down a little.

"Oh, that's alright," he said. "Mordecai played a trick on me. A small misunderstanding, that's all."

Jonathan could not sleep that night as he spent the time thinking, sorting out his feelings, his logic and his reasonings. He asked himself question after question, in an endeavour to reach the root of the problem. Common sense told him that the solution was simple. Natanya had been accused of stealing, as the evidence pointed the finger at her, so she was punished. However, she was then vindicated as being innocent, beyond any shadow of doubt, so common sense and justice demanded that she be declared innocent, and compensated for the injustice, at least with the word 'sorry'. "So why can't you say that?" he asked himself. "She is my enemy," he said. "But that is no reason for practising injustice. She is a human, isn't she? Hm.... that is a very difficult question to answer, so it must be the root of the problem," he concluded. "Now the question I must answer for myself is this - is my enemy a human, or less than human?" Jonathan turned from one side to the other, battling with his conscience. He came to the right decision, but it was up to him to put it into action.

Natanya, too, spent much of the night not sleeping; crying for a while and reasoning for a while. She was very concerned, as she told herself, "I thought a great deal of myself today. That's not a good sign. I should be out and everyone else in. Why can't I follow the Pattern exactly? When he was slapped on the face many times, did he feel sorry for himself? In fact, when he was impaled as a criminal, did he shut his compassion from those who were killing him? Did he?" She demanded an answer from her common sense. Then she answered humbly, "He prayed for them and said, "Please Father, forgive them, as they don't understand what they're doing."

Natanya immediately sat up in bed and started to follow the Pattern. She prayed sincerely for Jonathan and Mark. "Forgive them please, Father. Help them to see your love and conquer their hate." With those words she felt as if a heavy burden had just been lifted from her shoulders, and so lay down and drifted into a restful sleep.

Jonathan arose early, extra early, the next morning. He wanted to put his decision into action; he wished to see Natanya, to tell her how sorry he was. "She will serve us tea and coffee at our table. I must tell her, I must." He was looking forward to seeing her, to right the wrong, so was ready in good time, feeling butterflies fluttering in his stomach, just as if he was entering an important examination. Would he pass the impossible exam? If he overcame his prejudice, then he would be a conqueror.

Natanya was back to her gentle smile and soft brown eyes, waiting upon the young family, watching their cups and bread baskets, to refill them.

Jonathan looked at her whilst she served the others and saw that her cheek was badly bruised. He was cut to the heart. "Poor girl," he muttered to himself. "I am dreadfully sorry, please forgive me."

Natanya noticed that his cup was empty, so quickly came to him with her coffee jug and asked,

"Coffee?"

His tongue stuck in his mouth, his hands trembled, "Say it right now." He looked at her eyes. She was waiting, looking at him. She noticed his shaking hands and felt her compassion moved towards him. "Poor boy," she thought. "He's not well." She poured the coffee for him, even though he did not answer her, and said, with a tender, motherly look,

"It is good coffee."

Then she moved away to serve others.

"You're a failure, Jonathan," he rebuked himself. "You failed the test. No sorry, no please, no thankyou. You're an utter failure."

From that day Jonathan was extra quiet. He thought a great deal and watched Natanya carefully, admiring her tender care, regardless of the treatment she received. "That's what you call strength," he told himself. "It's very easy to shoot and kill, but it's impossible to show love to your enemy. I failed the test in even saying a single word, but she shows love, pure love, to those who killed her parents, then mistreat her and slap her in the face."

Jonathan continued to train the boys all the while he stayed in the hostel. They had lectures and films in the classroom and practical training out in the field. They would be assigned different drills, but, no matter what they practised it had the same effect on them. They would return to the hostel worn out and aching from running, crawling through tunnels and under bushes, dragging heavy weights and wearing their full combat gear.

Jonathan felt sapped of energy, as he had to set the lead by running and climbing ahead of the trainees. He found himself panting and out of breath. He was disgusted with himself. "I have become a useless man," he said, trying to stir himself into action. "I mustn't give in to myself, otherwise I'll be good for nothing and I must set a fine lead in front of these boys. It's my own fault, anyhow, as if I'd said sorry to Natanya, I would have slept better, but since that cruel slap I gave her, I've never been able to sleep." He ignored his aching body and pressed on, climbing, crawling and running, until he felt like dying. He kept looking at his watch as he desired to cool his body with a shower, to refresh himself.

The drill finished and the boys returned to their hostel, sweating and panting, carrying their guns and the loads on their backs. Jonathan took his clean clothes and had a cool shower. He felt better, but still ached all over.

The dining room door opened and everyone dashed in, looking forward to a lovely surprise from Natanya, as she always managed to produce delightful dishes to please her friends. Jonathan dragged himself along and managed to pick up his tray and plate and push it along the serving line. Natanya looked at him and smiled gently. He just stared back, too tired to stand or smile.

He sat next to Mark, at his usual table, and stared at his plate, attractively filled with appetizing food.

"Hey, Jonathan." Mark gave him a nudge with his elbow. "Come on, eat up and stop daydreaming. It's really delicious. I do confess this time that Natanya has excelled my mother's cooking."

Jonathan picked up his fork and tasted a little, but as his head throbbed and he ached all over, he could not eat much. He had his cup of coffee and left the dining room early.

Natanya watched him leave. "Why has he brought his food back and left early," she asked herself. "He's hardly eaten any. Maybe he didn't like it, or perhaps I upset him because of Mark's money, because since then he has changed a lot, and now doesn't even look at me, except with that strange stare." Then she shrugged her shoulders and said, "I can only do my best. I personally have forgiven him and I shall pray for him to find joy, the joy that comes from the pure love."

Jonathan had a lot of paper work to do and reports to prepare after dinner. Although he felt like going straight to bed, he did not want to give in to himself, so went to his office. He sat down, pulled out his various files and trays and tried to write his reports. His eyes kept watering but he ignored his tormented body, to prove to himself that he was the boss over his feelings, because he just could not forgive himself for his failure.

He finished what he had to do and dragged his feet to his room. He took off his shirt and laid it on the chair, and just managed to pull off his trousers and slide into bed. Then his body started to take revenge on him. It throbbed and ached from head to toe, shivering and shaking.

Mark came in, took one look at him and exclaimed,

"You look terrible, kid. Why didn't you say earlier on that you're ill? It's too late to call a doctor at this hour."

Jonathan had no energy to answer or worry. His throat was dry and sore, and that made him keep coughing. Mark got into his bed and winked to his friend as he drew the sheet over his head, saying,

"Make sure to keep those germs over your side, as I don't fancy an attack of flu; there's so much to do." Then he turned toward the wall, away from Jonathan's direction, and a muffled "goodnight" came from beneath the pillow.

Natanya went to bed and prayed for Jonathan and for all she knew, by name. She always mentioned Baha in her petitions to God, as she wondered what had happened to her after she was taken from Lebanon. She pulled the cover over her body and tried to sleep, but found she was disturbed by a coughing she could hear which came from down the passage. She kept listening to identify who was so uncomfortable. A few seconds later there was another cough, another clearing of the throat.

"Who is so ill?" she asked, sitting up in bed and listening. She remembered the day when she was assigned as a night nurse in the orphanage, how she used to patrol the rooms of the ill children, testing their temperature with the back of her hand. How she was taught by the nuns to identify the illness in a primitive but always successful way, and then to relieve the various pains.

"That sounds like Jonathan," she exclaimed, jumping from her bed and opening the door a tiny slit to listen. She noticed that his room light was on. "That is Jonathan, for sure," she said. She returned to her bed and pulled the sheet over herself. She thought, and listened to the continuous cough. "Poor boy, he must be in agony and his throat on fire." The beast dwelling within her offered its thoughts, "Let him suffer, it serves him right as he acts so unfeelingly, so he can have a bit of his own medicine."

She pushed the cover away from her and rebuked the unkind thought, "Get behind me, Satan. You're always trying to hinder me from doing what is right and lovable. Remember what the Father used to advise you," she reminded herself. "'Think of good things', so why can't you be like the perfect image of God and show mercy to all without partiality?" She jumped out of bed, put on her prison shirt and trousers, and stood behind the door, listening.

Jonathan tossed and turned. No matter which side he lay on, it was unbearable, as his conscience started to torment him. "This is justice, the Almighty is paying me back for my unjust act," he thought, turning to the other side, then over onto his back. "However will this night pass? I feel like dying, and don't even have the energy to get myself a glass of water." He thought of his mother, "Mother, I wish you were here. The times you sat by my bed for the whole night to comfort me and ease my pain."

Natanya could not stay any longer behind her door, so she quietly walked to Jonathan's room, tapped gently on the door and then waited. Jonathan was not quite sure if he heard a tap or if it was just a hallucination from his fever. Natanya turned the handle and stood by the opened door, looking tenderly at him, just like a nursing mother towards her child.

Jonathan could not believe his eyes. "Natanya," he said in his heart, trying to raise his head. All he managed to do was stare at the angelic creature who stood at the door, waiting for permission to enter.

"Jonathan," she said softly in her limited English, as she went towards him. "You are not well?"

He just looked at her eyes.

"I know," she said in her heart, "you will not answer me, Jonathan, but I shall look after you and be like my heavenly Father, who cares for the good and the evil alike." She touched his forehead with the back of her hand.

"Very hot," she said quietly, as she could see Mark was asleep, or trying to sleep. "I get you hot drink. You will feel good. I also bring oil; is good, it make you feel good."

Then she turned quickly and went to the kitchen.

Mark uncovered his head and smiled to Jonathan,

"Let's hope she can make you feel good."

Then he covered his head again.

Natanya boiled some water. She cut a lemon, squeezed the juice from half into a cup with a spoonful of honey and added the slices, after which she poured in the boiling water. 'The best medicine for a sore throat', was what Mother Teresa always said.

Then she poured olive oil into another cup and stirred in a teaspoonful of salt. This was her embrocation to help ease the aching muscles and induce the body to sweat and naturally relieve the fever. She put her two cups on a tray and returned to Jonathan.

He had managed to support himself on the pillows, ready to welcome any drink or remedy for his agonizing aches and pains.

Natanya entered with the tray in her hands and handed the drink to Jonathan.

"Drink," she said, just as she used to order the children in the orphanage.

He sipped a little but it was very hot.

"Hot?" she asked. "Okay, drink it later. I rub the oil now. Is good, you will feel good."

Jonathan surrendered to his nurse, as he noticed she was determined to nurse him regardless of what he said or did not say. While he watched, she put her fingers in the cup of oil and started to gently rub his shoulders, and then his throat and arms, dipping her fingers into the oil from time to time. After rubbing for a time, she said,

"In a minute you sweat, then you feel good."

All the while Jonathan was thinking and watching the strange enemy. "So gentle, so caring, just like my own mother; how can this be? Only a few days ago I slapped her face." He then looked at her face and could still see the faint mark of his slap. He felt like touching her cheek and apologizing, but instead he just continued in his thinking, silently admiring his enemy.

"I do the back now," she informed him, and immediately helped him to turn over onto his stomach. Then she massaged his aching muscles.

"She knows exactly where it hurts the most and eases the pain away. Natanya, who are you, please?" But that question was in his head and he never managed to bring it to his lips.

She finished her massaging and put the cup on the tray, then handed Jonathan his drink, saying,

"Now you can drink."

He took it from her hand and managed a grateful smile. She noticed his faint smile and felt victorious. "I am winning my enemy," she told herself the good news. Then she said to Jonathan,

"Now I go and pray, and you will be good in the morning, insha-allah."

With that, she turned and went to the kitchen, leaving Jonathan drinking his pleasant and welcome drink.

He emptied his cup and started to sweat, just as his nurse predicted. The ache had eased greatly and he felt so peaceful. He smiled, "I bet that is Natanya's prayer. I think she has forgiven me." Then he said a little prayer before he turned off his light, "Thankyou, Lord, for Natanya." His throat had stopped irritating and he soon dropped off to sleep.

Natanya lay on her bed after an entreaty for her new friend, all the while listening for any coughs coming from Jonathan's direction. "Oh good, he is feeling better. Now I can go to sleep, restful and happy."

The first thing she did in the morning was make another cup of the healing drink; hot water, honey and sliced lemon. She tapped gently on his door, wondering if he would answer or ignore her. She was about to turn the handle when she heard,

"Come in, please."

That was the best sentence she had heard since arriving in Israel. "Thankyou, my Lord," she said, looking up to heaven as she entered.

"Feeling good?" she enquired with a soft smile on her lips, as she looked at her patient. She touched his forehead with the back of her hand. "Good," she exclaimed. "Not hot anymore."

Jonathan smiled and accepted the cup from her hand, and very quietly said,

"Thanks."

He did not want Mark to hear him say 'thankyou' to an Arab prisoner, a first class enemy, because that was just not done, as enemies were not considered humans, but rather hated creatures that caused death to the young soldiers of Israel.

Natanya was on top of the world, as she could see Jonathan conquering his hate. "He was smiling, he was happy. All these are the signs of a winner; of a brave person who is managing to overcome the ugly beast dwelling inside us." She remembered Baha, and the great time they had together, talking about the divine love. "I wonder if Jonathan will be able to see his way to the road of this perfect love? What a victory that will be for our God."

CHAPTER 4

FOR MEMORY

Abu Mansour and his men were now well-trained and fully equipped to face Israel. They had rockets capable of crossing over to Israel and causing great damage to the small villages scattered around near the border.

"We will plan carefully," said Abu Mansour to Mansour and the top young fighters. "Our main supplies will be hidden in the camp, but we'll take a few rockets into the bush for tests, and fire them at Israel. At the same time, we'll continue to snipe at individual Israelis, so we'll torment them from all sides."

The men could not wait to start firing their rockets across the border, because, as Mansour said,

"The Israelis are our enemies, and our enemies are the enemies of Allah, so their blood is permissible to be shed and trodden on."

Abu Mansour chose his site carefully. They set up the rocket and launched it by remote control, then immediately disappeared from the district, because they knew for sure that Israel would send her planes and flatten the area to the ground. They were soon back in their territory, acting as if nothing had happened. They turned on their radio to discover where their rocket had landed and how many it had managed to blow-up.

While the announcer of Israel's Arabic broadcasting service spoke, the delighted Abu Mansour and his family surrounded the transistor radio, listening.

"A rocket hit a nursery school this morning, killing twenty children. The Prime Minister pledged to avenge every drop of blood of those innocent dead...."

"Good," shouted Mansour. "Twenty less Israelis to fight in future."

His father felt uneasy, as he well knew that threat would soon be translated into action.

"Come on, Mansour. We've no time to waste, as we must personally go and see from which direction the retaliation will come, so we can distract the Israelis' attention from our weapons stores, otherwise, if our ammunition is hit, that will be our greatest tragedy."

So they organized rocket attacks from various areas, far from their main hiding places, in an endeavour to fool the Israelis. Explosion followed explosion, and the circle of hate began to spread as each blast brought casualties, resulting in embittered relatives swearing and vowing to hit back. Many local Christians were hit, as they were relying on Israel for protection and, at the same time, Israel depended on them for information and assistance in finding their enemies.

The hospitals started to overflow with injured and badly burned people. Baha sighed and said to one of her nursing friends,

"What a waste of life! If only everyone would love their enemies, then these human tragedies would never happen."

Her friend shrugged her shoulders and sadly replied,

"You're wishing for the impossible. That will never happen. Nobody will love their enemies."

"It isn't impossible," she replied with conviction. "I know someone who managed to love her enemy, and when I say love, I mean real love, that nothing in this world can stop." Then she smiled as she remembered her dear friend, and added, "Except the ugly beast that lives inside us, but even that can be conquered, and then a person finds himself free from hate and love of self, absolutely free to love everyone else except oneself."

The other girl looked at Baha's soft, gentle eyes and her mouth dropped open. Then she enquired,

"Are you feeling alright, Baha?"

"Of course I'm alright. I'll tell you more about these things later, but now let's attempt to bind up the wounds that have been caused by this ugly hate."

Jonathan and his team were called back to active duty to avenge the children's blood. Feelings ran high as great repulsion built up and the happy hostel atmosphere turned into one of hate and revenge. Natanya noticed that the eyes of those whom she was caring for were watching her, staring at her with detestation.

"What's going on now?" she asked herself.

The radio was on very loud, but as it was in Hebrew, she had no clue as to the cause of the horrible atmosphere. She noticed the boys were packing their combat gear and loading it onto army vehicles, which then left the hostel. "Oh no," her heart sank into her stomach. "I think there is a war going on." Her worry was increased when she realised that the fighters roaring overhead were more frequent than usual. Natanya felt anxious and trapped. She loved everyone, whether they were in Lebanon or Israel. She was helpless. "What can I do? How can I stop them?" She looked around her. Everyone had become so cold toward her, as she represented the enemy. Her prison uniform, her armband, they were all reminders to those boys of the ugly facts.

"O, my Father, help me," she lifted her eyes toward heaven. "I beg you to help me, to help them to see your love. I entreat you to open their eyes to see the fruits of the pure love."

She rushed to Jonathan's room.

"Jonathan has started to understand the joyful road, maybe he might listen to me," she said, with concern in her eyes and face. She tapped on his door with shaking hands. He recognized her gentle tap, but was in no mood to answer or be worried about her, so continued his packing. Then he noticed the door handle move. "How dare she...." but before he had finished his thought, she was in and softly approaching him, looking at the cold eyes staring at her.

He saw tenderness and kindness in her soft brown eyes. Those were the same eyes that had watched over him when he was suffering in his illness. "How can I push her away? She has been too good to me. I must control my hate." He just stood looking at her in deadly silence.

"Jonathan," she interrupted the quietness, and looked him straight in the eyes. "You going to Lebanon?"

He felt very tense. "She is Abu Mansour's relative," he thought. "What's her business. They've just killed twenty innocent children, so how dare she even ask."

"Jonathan," she said, with sadness in her voice. "I shall pray that you will come safe."

He put down the item which was in his hand and stood scrutinizing the strange enemy who would pray for his safety, while she was aware he was about to go and blow her people to pieces.

"I will pray hard," she continued, watching him with eyes that started to fill with emotion and tears. "I will pray that no one will be killed, no one will be hurt."

Then she looked desperately around her, searching for something, something to give to Jonathan as a token of her sincerity and divine love. She put her hands in her pockets, but all she found there was some used tissue paper. She put it back and looked at herself. Suddenly her eyes shone with delight as she had a brilliant idea, triggered by her long, plaited black hair.

Jonathan stood watching, wondering what was the matter with her. He wanted to finish his packing as he was in a tremendous hurry, but this enemy was holding him up. He could not stop her or order her to go out, because he could feel her power, a different power and strength that he could not resist or stop. He tried to figure it out for himself, but could not put his finger on it to identify it.

Natanya saw the penknife chained to Jonathan's belt. She looked at him bashfully, stretched out her hand and pulled it from his pocket. She held her long, plaited hair, cut five inches off the end, then returned the knife to his pocket. She handed him her hair and said,

"This is for a..a..," and she tried to find the English word to express her thought, but her limited vocabulary failed her, so she said it in Arabic, "This is for zikra," which meant memory.

Jonathan understood the word, as it sounded similar in Hebrew, so he quietly said,

"Memory."

She smiled, nodded her head and repeated,

"For memory. Everytime you see this hair, you remember I will be praying that no one will be killed."

Jonathan took the hank of hair and held it in his hand, but fixed his eyes on the tender face.

Natanya then begged, saying,

"Just one more thing, please Jonathan, then I shall go."

He stood to see what that was, with interest.

She continued,

"Love your enemy."

She saw his face change. He was shocked and surprised. So she added, with an understanding voice,

"Try to love your enemy, then you will be very happy."

She smiled sweetly and squeezed his arm, then left the room, shutting the door behind her.

Jonathan stood frozen in his place, holding the piece of hair in his hand, and staring at the door. Natanya's last sentence was ringing in his ears.

'Just one more thing, then I shall go. Love your enemy.'

"I've heard those words before," he said, still staring at the shut door and holding the piece of plaited black hair in his hand. "In fact, I'm sure I remember them from school; was it Shakespeare who said them, or maybe it was one of the ancient Greeks?" Jonathan had never attended religious instruction classes at school in England, where Christianity was taught, as his parents requested his exemption to attend Jewish classes.

Suddenly he remembered, "Of course, that quotation was from Jesus of Nazareth. 'Love thy enemy'." He laughed in his heart at the ridiculousness of the statement, but, nevertheless, it did stick in his mind. He put Natanya's hair in his right shirt pocket, where he kept a piece of paper containing a prayer for safety, given to him by his mother. He hurriedly finished packing his bag and rushed to the waiting vehicle.

Before Jonathan could undertake any attack of revenge, he had to work with others in seeking to identify which of his country's many enemies was responsible, as they had a clear policy of only hitting back at those who start trouble. The experts searched through the rubble at the destroyed infant school and found some remains of the death-dealing rocket. They carried their find to the Centre, located near the Lebanese border, where all information was gathered and analysed. The Israeli agents in Lebanon, who gleaned their information from different sources, also sent their news there.

Jonathan had to study all the information carefully and then propose a plan which would be offered to the team of officers for discussion. After that, it would require approval by the government, before being put into action. He went to his quiet and comfortable office where he spread out the pieces of the jigsaw puzzle, and started to create a picture from them. "All the facts point to Abu Mansour's faction," was the conclusion he began to draw from the picture that was forming in front of him. "The weapons which he is using are up-to-date and of recent manufacture. That means he has received a fresh supply of such destructive rockets; in other words, this is only the tip of the iceberg."

Every time Jonathan inserted a new piece into the picture, he became more concerned about the evolving scene. "What mystifies me," he wondered, holding another piece of the puzzle in his hand, "is why did they attack all these different streets?" He stood and spread a very large scale map on the conference table, placing markers on each attacked street. He pondered for a long time, endeavouring to discover the reason behind the attacks. "Some are Christians, but that's not surprising," he said. "There must be another reason."

Mordecai informed Natanya that there was no need to cook much food as most of the soldiers had left for a tour of duty. This left her with only half the residents in the hostel and spare time on her hands, so she started spring-cleaning the rooms, to occupy her anxious mind. She prayed unceasingly in her heart. "Help Jonathan, Father. Uncover his eyes to see your love. I beg you, my God, to protect all your children, the work of your hands. Help us all to love each other, so wars will end forever." She hummed a few Psalms to herself, but her mind kept going back to Jonathan, as she knew how he dealt with his enemies, for she had personally experienced one of his raids. "Poor Baha," she thought. "If Jonathan makes a raid in Abu Mansour's territory, they will all be wiped out." She remembered the children that used to buy her free cakes. "Muhammad and his baby, and all those beautiful children, they are bound to get hurt."

Jonathan was still puzzling over the map. "Oh, I can see the reason," he exclaimed. "He's trying to divert our attention from this area," and he encircled a large zone with his pencil. "I can guess why." Now he had the full picture in front of him. He had identified his enemy and weighed him carefully, together with his strengths and supports, so it was time to draw the plan of revenge.

Before he prepared any plan he always read the prayer on the piece of paper in his pocket, so he undid the button and reached for his prayer. He felt the soft hair and was puzzled for a moment as he had forgotten about what had happened earlier on in the day, having been so busy. He pulled out the two items.

"Natanya," he remembered, then smiled, looking at the shiny, black plait. His mind could see the soft, tender eyes, full of compassion and feeling. He could hear her words, 'This is for memory.' "Natanya," he called her name quietly, while stroking the soft hair with his finger and recalling her words again, 'For memory. Everytime you see this hair, you remember I will be praying that no one will be killed. I shall pray hard.' He continued smiling, contemplating the hair that brought back the memory of the strange prisoner, the gentle nurse.

The recollections kept pouring in.

'Love thy enemy.'

Jonathan quickly returned the hair to his pocket. "I can't love my enemy, I will wipe him from the surface of the ground."

He read the prayer that his mother had written for him and taken to the Western Wall in Jerusalem for added guarantee of being heard by the Almighty. He paid extra attention to his Mother's prayer as he noticed the similarity between the two prayers. 'May the God of Israel keep you safe and guard you from all harm.' 'I shall pray that you will come safe, that no one will be killed, no one will be hurt.' He found himself thinking, "Natanya is praying for me, and everyone else, while my mother only prayed for me."

'Love thy enemy.'

The quotation kept going round and round in his head, and every time it marked a deeper groove in his soul. "How can I love him, when he is busy killing my people?" he asked, looking at the circle he had marked on the map. He felt the urge to pull the piece of hair from his pocket. "Natanya," he pleaded, "please leave me alone. You are controlling me, let me go free."

He paused, meditating and looking at the shiny, soft hair, then corrected his sentence, "It's not Natanya who is controlling me, but her words, the quotation she used." He continued to follow his logic, "She obviously believes it, although she is a Muslim. I heard this maxim before, but it had no effect on me. Natanya heard it just the same as me, but she put it into action and what I see in front of my eyes is a token of that strange love."

Jonathan gazed far into his memory. "Now I can see why she always works beyond her call of duty. Now I understand why she forgave me for my cruel slap." His memory recalled her very last words, 'Try to love your enemy, then you will be very happy.' "Yes, I can say that about her, she always has a happy and friendly face. She is always smiling."

Jonathan carefully replaced the precious prayer and the token of the strange love in their resting place and began to formulate a plan to avenge the blood of the innocent children, with the sincere desire to strive to be understanding and caring for human lives, no matter whose they were.

The night advanced, while Jonathan sat alone in the silence of the small hours, carefully arranging his plan. "I'm really only interested in destroying the weapons and preventing any more rocket attacks. If I attain that without human losses, then I'll have achieved a very successful mission." He held his pocket with his right hand and entreated, "Natanya, keep praying. I am trying hard."

Natanya kept tossing and turning. The sleep fled from her eyes. "I can't sleep while others are suffering," she said. "Poor Jonathan must be anxious. I bet he can't sleep, either." She knelt on her bed, and prayed and petitioned for peace, for God to find a peaceful solution. "I know you can, my Father," she implored. "I know, because you have already shown us how to achieve the victory, although it's impossible for us to find the way, unless you open our eyes to see."

Jonathan's eyes brightened as he suddenly had a brilliant idea. "If we have a very noisy raid, with supersonic bangs from low flying aircraft, but without bombing the area, then we can frighten them out and swamp the camp with tanks and armoured vehicles, while having air-cover for extra protection." He breathed a sigh of relief and smiled. "That way, we can gather all the weapons and anything else they have in mind to use against us."

The task was easy now, as he only had to finalise the exact details of the raid and calculate the team size required. He stood up, very exhausted, but quite excited, as he had never attempted such a raid before, for his policy was predictable, 'Wipe out, flatten them to the ground.' He only had a few hours before morning would dawn. He yawned and said, "If the others agree to my plan without objections, than I'll know that the hand of Ha-shem is with me, and Natanya's prayer answered."

The meeting of the top officers began. They sat around the conference table, with the map open on it and a scale model of their target area, showing in colour the terrain and main buildings. They all looked forward to hearing from their master-brain, as he had never had any unsuccessful raids since he joined the fighting.

Jonathan stood calm and relaxed, with confidence shining from his eyes. He explained to them about the discovery he made from the jigsaw puzzle picture he had reconstructed. They all listened intently to every word he said. Then he continued,

"This time our aim is a little different. It's to actually get hold of their missiles, otherwise, we'll end up receiving more of them. There must also be countless other weapons and explosives filling their stores. My plan is this...." Jonathan detailed his strategy, after which he looked at his team and asked,

"How do you feel about it? If you don't approve, then please advise."

Then he stood watching them, waiting for their opinions. The officers looked at each other. They saw it was a complete change of style, yet at the same time, they followed the logic behind the plan, agreeing with the reasons Jonathan had just explained. They all nodded their heads in approval.

One commented,

"It's much better to gather all these weapons without destroying them, then Israel can use them in fighting back, with their own weapons."

Jonathan felt relieved. He knew he would succeed and said to his men,

"Now we can inform the minister, and, as soon as he approves it, we shall start to put it into action."

The minister agreed at once to the plan.

"It's very good, and original thinking," he commended Jonathan, and added. "Of course, it will take longer and cost us more, but, if you manage to capture all those weapons, that will be a tremendous victory. Good luck and may the True God be with you all, and bring you back in peace."

Jonathan set the time for the raid, then, leaving some of the team in Israel, he crossed the border to the headquarters in Lebanon, to lead the attack from the ground.

A tremor of fear spread among Abu Mansour and his fighters when they heard the news from the many eyes which, day and night, watched the Israelis' movements in Lebanon.

"Jonathan has arrived," he said, with terror clearly showing in his eyes.

"I know," replied Mansour, "but I think it will be impossible for him to know where we are."

"I wouldn't be so sure, Mansour. These pigs have the demons to tell them everything."

"Father!" said Mansour, surprised at his father's low spirits. "What's the matter? Aren't our rockets our main treasures? Well, we've hidden them all over the place, so even if he raids one of our stores, we have others full. So just let's watch, as he'll most probably attack our old hiding places. Cheer up, we've already killed twenty of them, and that's a nice figure to cheer anybody."

Jonathan spent the day in Lebanon, organizing and preparing his team for the raid early the next morning. He sat down for a few minutes by himself, to rest and eat his sandwiches. His mind thought of Natanya. He looked at his watch and remarked, "Of course, they will be having their dinner now in the hostel; the good cooking of Natanya, while I'm eating a half-dry sandwich."

Just the thought of Natanya made his heart move. He noticed that peculiar feeling inside him again. "I must watch it," he advised himself. "She's only a prisoner." He ate some more of his sandwiches, seeing in his mind's vision Natanya's soft brown eyes looking at him. "But a special prisoner, an angel of love, a strange type of love, that nothing can stand in its way." He continued in his thoughts, ignoring his own advice. "I don't care who she is, a prisoner or an Arab, it makes no difference. She is a human, a very pleasant human." He touched his shirt pocket and smiled, "Amazing how I can feel her right next to my heart. I wonder if she is thinking of me, as I am of her?" He sat daydreaming, forgetting all about the world outside him, just dreaming of the pleasant world of peace and tenderness that was associated with Natanya. "I must give her something in return," he told himself, "as so far, I am receiving all the time, her care, her prayers, her tokens of concern, but I've given nothing in return, not so much as a word." There was a tap on the door that immediately awoke him from his dreams.

"Come in," he called out.

Mark entered, carrying news and information for him from Israel.

"Everything is on schedule," said Mark, ending his news, "Everyone is ready. The best of luck." Then he added, "Any message from here?"

"Just waiting for time to pass," said Jonathan, wanting to enquire about Natanya, although he could not bring himself to do it, so he asked, "How is everyone in the hostel?"

"The same," he replied. "Mordecai is a bit under the weather, and the boys are subdued. You know the tension when there's a mission of revenge in the air."

"Yes, I know the feeling, but there's no need for concern. Everything rests in the hands of our God, and I'm sure He is with our mission," he said, with a smile on his lips.

Mark put his papers and documents into his wallet and rose to leave. He noticed Jonathan seemed anxious or wanted to say something, so paused for a while, watching him. Jonathan smiled and indirectly asked about Natanya, avoiding Mark's eyes,

"Is Natanya mothering everyone as usual?"

Mark smiled and pointed to his boots.

"They're getting shinier every day," he said, then added, "She seems to me to be a bit depressed, or preoccupied. I suppose that's not surprising under the circumstances."

Jonathan looked anxiously about him, to find something to send to her, as he desired to reassure her that he had tried, and that her prayers had been answered. Mark interrupted him by asking,

"Is there anything worrying you?"

"Not really, it's just this raid you know we have tomorrow; and anything could happen," he said, glancing down at his open necked shirt and spotting his star of David medallion. He immediately started to take it off as he continued speaking to Mark.

"This golden medallion is very precious to me and I don't want to lose it, under any circumstances." Then he paused, looking at the very understanding Mark, and added, "Would you do me a favour, please, and give it to Natanya to keep for me until I return, Im Yirtseh ha-Shem (God willing), as she is very conscientious and careful."

"Of course, no trouble. I shall make sure she looks after it well, or else!" he replied, with a big grin on his face.

Jonathan felt relieved and happy he had managed to send something in return to the one of whom he thought a lot.

Natanya had just finished preparing the tables for the morning's breakfast, before she went to bed, when Mark appeared in the dining room.

"So this is where you are hiding," he said.

She stopped and looked at him, enquiring with her eyes.

He spoke, while taking the medallion from his wallet,

"Jonathan wants you to keep this. Don't go and lose it."

Natanya's face brightened and she smiled with delight, thinking that Jonathan had sent her a present.

"Very nice," she said, looking at the golden star.

Mark noticed her expression and understood what was in her mind, so he raised his voice and said, to make his point clear,

"Not for you."

He spelt out his order,

"You only keep, KEEP. When Jonathan will come, he will have it back. Keep and do not lose it."

Natanya understood the instruction, so she repeated the new word she had just learnt,

"Keep, keep, not to lose it."

Then she smiled sweetly, unbuttoned the top pocket of her prison shirt, and carefully put the medallion in, buttoning it up afterwards, while Mark stood watching her. She said to him, pointing to her pocket,

"I keep it here."

Natanya went to her bed, doubly thrilled. First, because Jonathan was well and must be thinking of her, and second, that he was trusting her to look after his gold medallion. "I know why he gave it to me, to keep," she thought, admiring the shining star of gold. "Because he wants to tell me he can trust me, and doesn't believe I'm an Arab thief. I will look after it with my own eyes."

She lay on her stomach for a long time, looking at the medallion and thinking good thoughts. "He is the best of the boys in the hostel," she thought, "because he doesn't shout, and he listens to me whenever I speak to him, even though he never says much but only gives that stare. Never mind, I remember that Baha used to stare at me like that, but later we became the best of friends. I am sure Jonathan will eventually become a good friend of mine."

Natanya said a lot of prayers while she held the treasure in her hand, then she put it underneath her pillow, still gripping it tightly, in case someone would attempt to steal it. After that, she dropped off into a happy sleep.

Abu Mansour had an anxious night. It was the fourth night since they had blown up the nursery school and the second since Jonathan had arrived in Lebanon. He spoke to his son, who was wide awake, watching and listening for any sounds of warning from their eyes that were spread everywhere near the Christian and Israeli sectors of Lebanon.

"I wonder why Jonathan is dragging it out for so long? He's not his usual speedy self, as he would have performed his attack by now, yet this is the fourth night."

"It's a good omen, Father," said Mansour. "I told you before that this time we fixed him. He most probably doesn't know where to start."

"No, I don't think so. He's very cunning and most likely planning horrible things for us."

"What do you mean by horrible things?"

"Wiping out the entire area, as the news came to me earlier that many ships have arrived from Israel and unloaded tanks and other things."

"Father," said Mansour, "why are you so anxious this time? We have done these attacks many times, yet the best one of them all results in your nerve giving way. Why?"

"I just do not trust Jonathan. Since he came to this place, we have never had any peace."

Jonathan was up before the sun rose and in contact with his team in Israel. They, too, were up and ready to start on time.

Abu Mansour's men were hiding in various locations, to spot any manoeuvres by the Israelis. They saw tanks and armoured vehicles heading towards the forbidden secret area of Abu Mansour, so immediately sent the warning alarm, the grasshopper sound, which each group, in turn, passed on to the next post.

Abu Mansour and his son sprang into action.

"They're coming in our direction. Just where we don't want them to be!"

"Let's move the rockets," suggested Mansour.

"Don't be stupid. If we move them at this time, they'll spot us, kill us and take our weapons. We'll leave them in their places and let's hope they'll change their direction."

But the grasshopper warnings were becoming louder and more frequent.

"They're so close. We're trapped. Cursed be you, Jonathan," said the most frustrated Abu Mansour.

His son determinedly said to him,

"We'll fight back to the death. Let's dig ourselves in and be ready for them," and he sent a signal to the waiting fighters, who immediately positioned themselves, ready to fight the approaching army.

Suddenly a loud roar burst on them from the sky.

"Oh no, they're raiding us from above as well," shouted Mansour as the supersonic planes filled the sky with eardrum shattering sounds that caused the hearts of the bravest fighters to quiver within them.

"I told you that Jonathan was up to trouble. Now we're surrounded from all directions and the whole area will be wiped out in seconds."

The aircraft flew lower and lower, almost touching the buildings and throwing the entire camp into confusion, as they could not distinguish between the sonic bangs and real explosions. Adding to that, the tanks and armoured vehicles started to shoot, pointing their guns up into the air and down at the ground.

"We must evacuate the area quickly, and forget about fighting back, as they've swamped the place," said Abu Mansour, running off in one direction, while his son ran in another, to sound the alarm to the people to flee.

A high flying plane monitored the situation and reported the picture to Jonathan - "the enemy are fleeing to the south."

More fighters were sent to increase the air cover as the area was quickly evacuated by the escaping militia. The army followed after them, carefully checking the suspect houses with their sophisticated detection equipment. All the while the planes kept roaring and banging above them.

It was now just a matter of an easy house to house search for weapons, led by Jonathan.

"One of the stores," he reported. "We need the trucks to advance close by for loading."

The team worked hard, transporting the matériel of destruction, still in its original boxes. The quantity seemed endless, as crates and crates of ammunition were loaded.

"Our first rocket found in the sixth house," Jonathan reported.

The whole area became like a colony of ants, as each soldier carried and loaded, while others returned to hump more loads.

As soon as the trucks were filled with weapons, they left for the Israeli base, while others arrived to take their places.

"Imagine it," said Jonathan to his assistant. "All these destructive tools were meant for us. What a horrifying thought, it makes you shudder."

Documents were also found, as well as many American dollars, to pay the fighters and finance the terrorists to kill and spread the hate.

The raid was over in just a few hours, during which time the territory of Abu Mansour was emptied of all its weapons, but no destruction took place of any dwellings, except for a few that had obviously been used as factories for manufacturing explosives and assembling weapons. No one was killed or injured, on either side.

Jonathan returned to the base to recover from his exhaustion, before crossing back to Israel. He found a message waiting for him.

"Congratulations. Celebrations are awaiting you at the Centre. Signed, Defence Minister."

He felt good and very happy that no one had been killed or hurt, and then realized he had never experienced that feeling before. "It's because no one was killed," he said to himself, as he sat in the chair, drinking a glass of cold lemonade. "I do owe so much to Natanya." Then he put his fingers into his pocket and pulled out her soft black hair. "Thankyou, Natanya, for praying so much for me. I'll look forward to seeing you soon," he said, as if she was standing in front of him. Then he lifted his hands towards heaven and thanked his God for answering the prayers of two wonderful people, "My mother and my friend Natanya."

He returned his piece of treasured hair to its home and left the office. He stood for a while, watching the boys busily unloading the endless boxes collected during the raid. They smiled at him with admiration and he smiled back, with joy radiating from his soul.

A big celebration was waiting for Jonathan and his successful team of fighters when they arrived the next day at the Centre. The minister was there in person to welcome him back. They hugged, shook hands, and walked together to the spread tables. The minister sat Jonathan at the head of the top table and then gave a welcoming speech.

"I just want to congratulate all of you for an excellent performance, well planned, well thought-out and well rewarded. Of course, it is too soon yet to tell how much we have gained from our enemies, but, from the number of trucks that have been off-loaded onto our ships, it must be estimated in the millions."

The officers and men clapped, laughed and congratulated themselves. The minister then continued,

"I have pleasure in announcing to you that Jonathan is promoted from today to Major-General, as he has proved without any shadow of a doubt his great abilities and talents in leadership, and shrewd judgement in assessing the enemy."

He turned to his right and looked at Jonathan,

"Israel is proud of you. I wish you a very happy and prosperous future."

Then he sat down, deafened by the cheering and singing of the soldiers.

Mark felt quite annoyed in himself. "We all worked hard, we all fought and endangered our lives, so why all the fuss over Jonathan?" From that moment on he started to resent his close friend. "We're the same age and both university graduates. It isn't fair, he has been elevated so high and now the gap between us is even greater. Why? Why him and not me?"

Mordecai hurried to the kitchen in a state of great excitement.

"Natanya, we need more food as the boys are coming home this evening. I have just had a call from Jonathan."

Natanya almost jumped from joy.

"That is good," she said with a big smile, then asked,

"Anyone hurt?"

"No one hurt, no one killed. Not a single one."

Natanya lifted her hands to heaven, and tears of joy flowed down her cheeks.

Mordecai stood smiling at her and said to himself, "I will never understand this girl. Even if I live to be a hundred years old, I will never understand her."

Jonathan went to shop for presents and gifts, to share his joy with his friends in the hostel. He bought presents for Mark and Mordecai and others, but the most important gift of all was for Natanya. "What shall I get for her?" he thought, looking at the multitude of items on display. "What do girls like?"

He did not have any sisters, only brothers. He noticed a few lady customers in the shop with him. "They are both wearing earrings, and what else? Oh yes, rings on their fingers. I think a ring will make a lovely present for Natanya."

Jonathan hurried into a nearby jewellers, after having a brief look at the window display. The shopkeeper approached and greeted him in English,

"What can I do for you, sir?"

"I would like to buy a little present for my girlfriend."

"Any particular item in mind?" asked the man.

"I think a ring would be a good idea."

The man nodded his head in approval.

"Yes, I have an endless variety, all made with Israeli diamonds."

He opened a glass cabinet and brought out a good selection of rings. Jonathan picked a dainty one with a small cluster of diamonds. The jeweller smiled at him, and said,

"That will make a lovely engagement ring."

Jonathan looked at the man with his usual stare, and said quietly,

"I think I'll buy it as a little present."

Natanya was working hard in the kitchen when Jonathan arrived at the hostel, but she knew he was back, as she could hear the cheering and laughter and his name from everyone's lips.

"I'm glad they all returned safely and no one was killed, not my friend Baha, nor the little children. I am very happy," she said, while hurrying to finish the cooking.

Jonathan gave Mordecai his present, then the other boys.

After that, he returned to his room to give Mark his gift. He handed it to him and gratefully said,

"Thanks a lot for your help, Mark. I do appreciate what you have done."

Mark took the well wrapped present, and muttered quietly, "Thanks."

"What's the matter?" enquired Jonathan, with concern.

"I'm tired and worn out," burst Mark. "I don't know how many times I risked my life, and what do I get for it?" he complained.

"I see," replied Jonathan calmly. "I think you need a good sleep and a few days off, away from all the tension, then you'll feel on top of the world. But I do understand your feelings, as I always feel dreadful after a raid, although, I must confess that this time I felt entirely different. I suppose because I was not alone."

Mark gave him a funny look and asked,

"Ya, not alone? Then who was with you?"

Jonathan regretted his sentence, but, as he had landed himself in the problem, he tried to explain himself.

"I had other people praying for me, so I didn't feel alone. I felt God was with me."

"I see, we are becoming religious now as well!"

Jonathan stopped the conversation and thought no more about the discussion or Mark's attitude, as he put it down to nerves and fatigue.

Dinner was late, but no one minded, as everyone was in a celebratory mood. Jonathan walked to the dining room, looking forward to seeing Natanya, for he had missed her gentle smile and tender, soft eyes. He took his tray as usual and followed the line, watching the very busy Natanya. She lifted her face, and their eyes met.

"Jonathan," she said, smiling. "It is good to see you again."

He smiled, but his tongue stuck in his mouth as usual; he just stared at her eyes. She knew him well by now, so was very pleased to see his smile. Then she loaded his plate with all the goodies, while he still watched her happy face.

"Thanks," he said, as he picked up the tray and left for his table.

After dinner, he delayed himself, looking for an opportunity to see her alone, to give her his little present. "I'll come later," he said to himself. "Nobody seems to want to move today."

He left for his room, to unpack his equipment.

"My favourite job," he said to Mark, who sat in a chair, reading a novel. "I hate packing, but I delight in putting things back in their proper places."

Mark made a muffled remark, but Jonathan understood. He was not in the mood to talk.

Jonathan left his door open so he could catch Natanya when she came back to her room. "At last," he breathed, and jumped up, feeling his pocket to make sure the present was still there. She had nearly reached her room when he called her,

"Natanya."

She stopped and turned towards him. He put his hand in his pocket and withdrew the attractively wrapped box, complete with a pretty bow, and handed it to her. She was not going to make the same mistake again that she had done with the medallion, so she asked,

"Keep?"

"Yes, you can keep it, Natanya."

She smiled and put it in her trouser pocket. Jonathan stood looking at her. After a moment he said softly,

"Thankyou for everything, Natanya."

She smiled and lifted her hand to heaven, saying,

"Thanks to God."

Then she turned round and entered her room, feeling good and proud that Jonathan was entrusting her with his valuables.

Abu Mansour and his men returned to their territory to examine the damage. They were surprised to see the buildings still standing, except for their factories.

"What happened to them?" he asked those around him. Then he entered the storerooms where they kept their treasures and discovered the tragedy.

"They have emptied the place!" he cried, his hands trembling. "They haven't left behind so much as one bullet. The thieves. The vipers."

Mansour went to check the rest of their stores, and he nearly fainted.

"They have ruined us, Father, absolutely and completely. The rockets, the ammunition, even the dollars. They've stolen the lot!"

Abu Mansour sat on the ground, mourning their great loss. He shook his head in sorrow, and said to his son,

"Now you can see their plan. They didn't destroy the houses, so they could rob their contents." Then he raised his hands to heaven and swore,

"If I don't finish you Jonathan, I'll be cursed. I vow to Allah to follow you to the end of the world and get rid of you."

The families returned to their homes. The women were very grateful their houses were still in one piece after all that had happened, but all the men were weeping, in mourning.

Om Mansour tried to comfort her husband and son but they were inconsolable, even refusing to drink. She said to them,

"You shouldn't be like this. Can't you see the bright side? We could all be dead now and our homes heaps of rubble, but only the weapons have gone. You can always replace weapons, but you can never replace life."

The men could see the logic of Om Mansour, but at the same time, their tragedy was so great and their losses extensive, that it would take them a long time to gather such power again.

Jonathan enjoyed his few weeks off after the successful raid. He had a number of friends and relatives visit him in the hostel and Natanya obliged by making coffee and soft drinks for them.

One afternoon, he had another three guests, an elderly couple and their beautiful, blond young daughter. Mordecai went to Natanya and informed her that three coffees were required for the Major-General's friends. She made the coffee and took it to Jonathan's friends in the common room. She noticed the girl was beautiful, and how Jonathan was joking with her and enjoying himself. The three guests took the coffee, but none thanked her. She saw Mark sitting nearby, watching the television. She glanced again at the girl, and left. No one acknowledged her, or even seemed aware of her presence.

She went to the kitchen feeling hurt and depressed. "Jonathan can talk very well to others, but he finds it difficult to speak to me," she thought. Her lower nature started to awaken within her, the ugly beast of self-love. "Till when shall I act as a servant, till when shall I serve for nothing?" and she felt tears dashing to her eyes. She noticed her behaviour and awakened herself, "You silly girl, why do you resent the beautiful girl? What is wrong if Jonathan has a nice girl to love and marry? Remember, you are only a prisoner. Your love is different from other loves; remember when the Father asked you about your future, what answer did you give him?" She recalled the memory of her past, and heard herself repeating what she told the old man and the nun, "I would like to go and love my enemies."

She smiled to herself and said, "Well, your wishes have been fulfilled. You have been to Abu Mansour's territory and you loved them. Then you were transported here and have continued loving your enemies in Israel. You love for the sake of the pure love, and should not demand any reward and nor should you have any ulterior motive. Did not the Pattern you are following love all humans for the sake of it? He never waited for a thankyou." She felt better after her soliloquy, for it enabled her to take a grip on herself.

Mark was aware that Jonathan had a soft place in his heart for Natanya, as many times he saw him staring at her for ages. He also noticed how Natanya glanced at the pretty girl when she came with the coffee. He jumped from his chair and rushed to the kitchen, where he saw Natanya preparing for dinner.

"Natanya," he smiled, drawing close to her. "Did you see that beautiful girl with Jonathan?"

Natanya looked at him, wondering why he should ask her such a question.

He continued, "She is Jonathan's love. Soon they will get married."

Natanya responded,

"Good. She is very nice, very beautiful."

"You are nice, too," he said.

She turned away from him, and continued with her work, ignoring his remark.

He left her and returned to the common room, feeling deflated and resenting the way she had just ignored him. "What an insolent Arab," he fumed, looking at the television but seeing nothing, as if he was in a trance. "She should consider herself privileged that I spoke to her." He was becoming more bitter by the minute. "I bet if Jonathan spoke to her, she would be all smiles, of course. But I don't count, I'm a nobody, even the Arab prisoner turned her nose away from me." He glanced at the laughing company with Jonathan, talking nearby, "It isn't fair, he has everything going for him. All the girls laugh at his jokes...."

At that moment Jonathan turned round and saw Mark looking at his guests, and rather bored.

"Mark," he called to him. "Come and join us, as you're not watching the television."

He smiled and sprang from his seat, walked across to the young girl and shook her hand.

"This is Mark, one of my close friends. He shares my room and delivers my news. Excellent chap," Jonathan said, smiling, as Mark shook hands with the elderly couple.

Mark sat down and kept quiet at first, listening to the old man telling about an incident that happened to him, but he soon took over the conversation, telling hair-raising accounts about his experiences in the army. His throat became dry from all the talking, which made him desire a drink, so he asked his audience,

"Would you like another coffee?"

"Yes please," they all said together.

"That was a lovely cup of coffee we had just now," said the old lady in a good English accent.

Mark turned his head toward the kitchen and shouted at the top of his voice,

"Natanya. Come at once."

The company smiled, although the old lady quietly muttered to herself, "Oh dear!" Jonathan looked at Mark, as he felt hurt at the way he called the gentle Natanya.

She heard his call, but was determined to follow the Pattern to the dot, "My love is divine, not from this world. Nothing can stop or hinder my love, not shouting nor death," she said to herself, and hurried to Jonathan's party.

Everyone turned round to have a look at the girl who bore the lovely name Natanya, who made beautiful cups of coffee and had just been shouted at as a worthless dog. She had a lovely soft smile on her lips and tender, kind eyes that spotted the empty coffee cups, so, before anyone could speak, she looked first to the pretty girl, then to the old couple and asked,

"Coffee?"

They all nodded, except Jonathan, who felt hurt for her.

"Jonathan," she said. "Coffee? Is good."

He looked at her gentle eyes and nodded.

Natanya felt good in herself, that she had conquered again. "I feel happy now as nothing can upset me, when I have the right kind of love."

She brought their coffee, said "Thankyou" for them and left, to go to her own world of happiness. She sang one of her victory Psalms, as she felt like celebrating a victory over an ugly beast.

Jonathan was kept very busy because his promotion had added more work and responsibility for him, and much of his time was now spent away from the hostel, in the Centre near the border. Whenever he was home and saw Natanya, he looked carefully for his ring, but never once did he see her wearing it. "Why, I wonder?" he asked himself, every time she served him coffee at the breakfast table. "Maybe she didn't like it; or perhaps she doesn't like me." Thoughts like that always made him anxious.

He found he could not push Natanya from his mind. The more he thought of her, the more he watched her; the more he observed her behaviour and attitude, the more he admired her. "I've never met a girl like her in my whole life and sometimes I feel she isn't human, as she doesn't act as humans do. I wish I could talk to her, to get to know her better, but somehow, everytime I try, I fail."

Jonathan turned over onto his other side, trying to sleep, but Natanya would not leave his mind. "Anyhow," he told himself, trying to find the root of his concern, "why am I so preoccupied about her? Perhaps it's because she has a certain magnetic power that pulls the heart to her, and, after that, it's impossible to get free from her pleasant grip." He paused in his thoughts, then added, "But I don't desire to escape her grip, in fact, I wish I could draw closer." He could see numerous obstacles in front of him which prevented him drawing closer to Natanya. "She is my enemy." Then he smiled to himself, "Well, enemy in name only, but that's a big hurdle. Then she's a prisoner, an alef prisoner, and I can't puzzle out how that can be, but I know I personally pulled her out from under the table during that raid." Jonathan stopped at that point, as the puzzle was just too difficult to work out, even for an officer with his abilities.

CHAPTER 5

"THERE ARE MANY BOMBS OUTSIDE"

Abu Mansour and his men attempted to build their broken strength again after Jonathan had shattered it to the ground. They were more determined than ever to fight, but not yet, as they had hardly any weapons left. He would have to go around his suppliers, to rebuild his power, but the road was very difficult, so he thought it would be a good idea to have a secret meeting with his men to discuss the problem.

One Friday evening, after prayers in the local mosque, all the chief fighters of Abu Mansour met in his secret hide-out. The men sat on chairs around a table, on which were jugs of fruit juice and small plates piled high with salted nuts and sweets. Mansour sat opposite his rather depressed father, who opened their meeting by saying,

"We are born to struggle, but, at the end of it, we shall free the holy lands from the Zionists. Our main concern at the moment is how to obtain more weapons and money. We need funds badly, as we can't fight without weapons, and we can't get weapons without money. I'm going to take a trip round the friendly Arab countries, but my mission won't be easy, and I'm not looking forward to it."

The men nodded their heads. They too seemed very depressed and despondent. Mansour sat with his elbows on the table and his head resting on his hands, looking at the sad faces around him.

Abu Mansour then asked them,

"I would welcome any good ideas of how to get money, and, when I say money, I mean lots of it, to replace what Jonathan stole from us."

Two of the young mujaheddin offered their services and put it to Abu Mansour in simple words,

"We will hijack an American plane, so we can ask for millions of dollars in ransom."

Then they looked at Abu Mansour for his response, then to Mansour. Their leader swung slowly from side to side, thinking carefully about their offer, looking at them from time to time, then staring at the pile of salted nuts on the plates. After a long pause he spoke,

"I don't think it will work, for lately no one has been willing to pay any ransom, and you'll just end up in jail somewhere, or be killed, and that will be a waste of resources for us, as we need every single man of you."

The two young men sat back on their chairs, ready to hear what other suggestions the rest would offer.

Another tough and strong fighter said,

"Nothing beats direct robbery. We can soon organize a bank raid in one of the European capitals, say Paris, and pick up hundreds of thousands in one day. Of course, we would have to carry it out carefully."

Abu Mansour found this offer more interesting, so it took him even longer to open his mouth, but Mansour interrupted his father's long pause by saying,

"What's the use of getting money or buying weapons, and then Jonathan takes them to Israel in a few hours?"

His father sat leaning on the table, looking at his son challenging him.

"Okay Mansour, you tell me what to do? How are we going to fight? Give me a suggestion, one suggestion."

Mansour rubbed his chin with his hand and kept quiet for a few moments, then said,

"We only need to get rid of Jonathan, then we've won the battle."

The men smiled and Abu Mansour swayed faster from side to side, with a grin on his face, and said,

"I agree, but how are you going to finish him? It's easy to dream, but not so easy to face reality."

Mansour smiled, with his eyes sparkling, as he had an idea.

"A good idea," he said to the men.

They all drew their heads closer around the table to listen to the new ray of hope that the zealous Mansour was bringing them.

"It's no good considering even trying to touch Jonathan in Lebanon, for he's a coward, always surrounded by arms and tanks, but, if we get him when he isn't aware of us, then we can kill him as easily as killing a fly."

The men were now building up to great excitement, and each filled his hands with nuts and started to chew, as they felt this was a really good suggestion.

Abu Mansour asked,
"Where can we find him alone?"

"Easy," answered Mansour. "Very easy. In his own country, in Israel. I guarantee you, he will not have even one guard around him, then we can shoot him, or blow him up, or even stab him. He's the brain behind all the raids, and especially now they have promoted him, he can do anything he likes whenever he wants to."

Then he looked round at the men and banged on the table, "Jonathan must die!"

"How are you going to Israel?" asked Abu Mansour, after a long pause.

"I will not go personally, but we'll arrange for our brothers to finish him off. Then it will be the time to get money and weapons."

The men wanted more details so they could carry out their mission.

"We shall go to Jordan and collaborate with our men there. After all, we are supporting the Palestinians to get rid of one of their main enemies."

The following day father and son left for Jordan to organize the new campaign.

"We mustn't be in a hurry," advised Mansour, "because we only have one chance and no possibility of a repeat, so we shall take our time, plan carefully and then attack."

They met their friends in Jordan and put the idea to them for discussion. Everyone agreed that it was the best thing to do, as Jonathan's name was also frequently mentioned by the men in Jordan.

Badrawi was a Palestinian, born in Jordan, who regularly crossed over to Israel for trade. He would not arouse any suspicions as he had a special pass and was known in Israel as a Jordanian trader. He had many friends in Israel and often met with them in Jerusalem. Some of them were strong supporters of Abu Mansour's party.

"I will talk to my friends," he said to Abu Mansour. "I'll first ask them to find out where Jonathan is living, and then we can arrange the matter from there. It will take time, but we must be patient."

He communicated with his friends, who loved the idea and promised a speedy report. Numerous eyes spread out in different directions in Israel, searching for Jonathan. A few days later the report arrived, 'He lives in a very quiet army hostel. A lot of his men also stay with him in the same place.' Badrawi took the reports to Abu Mansour and his son.

"That's wonderful," exclaimed Mansour. "Then we'll catch ten birds with one stone!"

Badrawi corrected him,

"Forty to fifty birds with one stone."

The men laughed and celebrated their find, and then put their heads together to draw up their plan.

Badrawi was the expert, as he knew Israel very well, having been all over the place with his friends from Jerusalem, Hebron and Nablus, as well as touring up and down on business.

Abu Mansour asked him for his ideas first.

"Our problem is very huge, as the hostel is located in an Israeli area and any of our people would easily be spotted. You know how the Jews are very careful and suspicious of everybody and everything."

The men were absorbed in his conversation and he went on to give them some idea of how cautious they were.

"For example," he said, gesturing with his hands, "in almost every open area and bus stop you find posters hanging, warning people to keep their eyes open, and they do, from little child to the aged woman. They are all watching."

Mansour sighed with frustration. Badrawi looked at him and said,

"We just have to draw our plan with this information in mind. If we face the challenge carefully, I can't see why we should fail."

They stayed up until late at night, discussing the problem, and came to the decision to go around the hostel and its neighbouring streets, to survey every foot of the ground and record it all. Then they would meet again for further discussions.

Jonathan and his team were enjoying a period of peace, as Abu Mansour's faction had stopped their nibbling of Israeli soldiers to enable them to concentrate on their arch-enemy, Jonathan, who now worked mainly at the Centre, controlling matters from there and arranging his plans for the future.

"Natanya has completely changed my thinking," he thought to himself, as he studied some reports and other papers. "I feel that this new method of disarming is far superior to the 'wipe out completely' method. It has worked perfectly so far, and not so much as a whisper from Abu Mansour. Most probably he is regathering his forces again. Anyhow, I shall worry about that when it comes."

Badrawi chose a team of fair skinned Palestinians and two sympathetic Frenchmen, to carry out a survey of the Jewish area. The very highly paid Frenchmen hired a car and booked into a hotel near the hostel. They took their cameras and toured the district, frequently losing their way and stopping to ask passersby for directions. As most of the locals spoke English and hardly any French, they were directed to several large shops, to enquire there, as nobody was able to help them. On their way to the various locations, they took photographs of buildings and the landscape. Thus every tree, bush, building and feature was recorded and photographed.

When the French tourists arrived in Jordan, Badrawi gathered the report from them and the others and took it to the waiting leaders. Mansour became so excited when he saw the progress.

"It's a pleasant area," he told his friends. "While we are living in a slum, Jonathan is enjoying a paradise, but not for long, as we are getting closer, and his end is fast approaching."

The men put their photographs together and constructed a huge picture of the area, showing the shops, main roads and side streets.

"Now we have to monitor this area day and night for weeks, so we will know all the comings and goings and be able to slip in and out without being spotted," said Badrawi.

That was an even harder task than the previous one. More men were recruited, some working as fruit and vegetable sellers, to carefully watch the hostel and surrounding area for twenty-four hours a day, working in shifts.

Abu Mansour and his son waited for days, chewing their nails, as the information slowly trickled in. Mansour said to his father,

"Even if it takes a complete year, we shall wait, but our celebration will be great when we have blown up him and his team. Now we just have to learn to be patient." Then he smiled and added, "Have you heard about the waiting game?"

As he spoke those words they brought Baha to his mind and he started daydreaming about her. "I remember the time Baha talked to me about the waiting game and even threatened that she might try it on me." His memory recalled the pleasant picture of Baha, and also dragged behind it the shattered dreams. "What a great pity, what a tragedy," his heart mourned. "The times I gazed into her beautiful eyes, dreaming of the happy future we would have together." He sighed so deeply and sadly that even his father heard him.

"Who was just telling me to be patient?" he asked, with a grin on his face. "You lift your head up and think of those hard workers monitoring that den of wolves."

Mansour looked to his father, rested his head between his hands, and continued in his daydreaming. "We were almost at the point of getting married, when Amal appeared on the scene," and he squeezed his eyes shut, as if to keep Amal far from his dreams. But the harder he pushed her from his mind, the more she came in, with her soft smile and tray full of free cakes, into his memory's territory. He could see the children running toward her, excited and joyful. He could see her gently bending down, talking to the children and hugging them. "Amal," he whispered deep in his soul. "Why did you have to come and separate me from my love with your words? Why did you have to teach them to my love?" he asked with regret. "You kept convincing and brainwashing her all the time, 'Love thy enemy, don't kill', why? why?"

Amal stood there in his memory, "Strange girl!" he said. "But I must admit you are very brave, very loving. Nothing could stop you from loving your enemies, but at the end of it you drew my love away from me and made her as strange as you are, to the point that she almost looks remarkably similar. Her eyes and her smile, they are just the same, and her words and conversation became centred on one subject, the new love."

Mansour lifted his head high up, as if to obtain a closer look, when Amal gradually dimmed from his sight and disappeared in the mist of his thoughts.

Abu Mansour's men kept busy in Lebanon, planting home made bombs in the Christian militia's sector of the city. Although the amount of explosive material was small, the damage was extensive.

The Christians felt hemmed in by the different Muslim groups, and, since the Israelis last successful raid, they had received more than the normal amount of destruction. Their leaders sent the whisper to their members and they gathered secretly to discuss their problems. That was how evenings and nights were spent in Beirut. Various groups would gather together, in secret, to plan revenge or search for ideas for attacks. Each group sincerely believed they had God's support, and, for that reason, they were prepared to sacrifice their lives to fulfil their aims. The Christian militia met behind closed doors and shut windows, whispering and discussing the same old subject, which had become a part of every Lebanese.

"Brothers, we can't take any more. Our homes are in ruins, our families are blown asunder. We must hit back, we must take revenge."

Another senior member contributed his part to the meeting,

"It's not fair, Libya supports Abu Mansour's party with thousands of dollars, to convert the entire country to Islam. We are a free nation, a free people. We have chosen Christianity, so why should they force us to compromise our principles? We must seek help, we must find support."

Feelings were becoming inflamed and temperatures rising, hate was prospering and animosity growing, until one of the leaders silenced the group by waving his hands up and down, like a traffic policeman.

"Calm down, calm down," he said, and they became quiet.

Then he continued,

"We must send for Jonathan. We are acting as a buffer for them, so they ought to help us, they must take revenge on our behalf. We must send for their help. Abu Mansour has Libya and other countries supporting him, so we must have Israel to support us, it's only fair. Someone has to give us a hand, and I think we must send right away."

A short while later, Jonathan arrived secretly in Lebanon, to look into the request of the militia. They had prepared their case well, giving many reasons why he should do something, so the wisdom of Solomon was needed to negotiate and compromise. All the cards were laid ready on the table, as time was valuable, and life was always in the balance, as the slightest tip here or there meant a few more lives would topple to the ground and be snuffed by death.

"Since your last raid," said the old man, "your troops are okay and we are the ones taking the battering, so you must take revenge on our behalf. You have the planes and the expertise. You must aid us. We rely on you."

Jonathan had to explain the policy of his government and the seriousness of the situation.

"We can't," he emphasised. "We can't undertake a raid on your behalf, as our policy is clear; we only hit back at those who hit our boys. So, no way, but...." and then the hard bargaining started.

The hours of the night ticked away, yet, even in the silence of the night, ears were attentive and the eyes were looking and searching. Each one was gathering information for his own group, his own men. Though the streets were empty, there were eyes behind curtains, watching; ears close to walls, straining to pick up any sound, any piece of information.

The meeting eventually came to a close, after much hard work, and the treaty was agreed.

Concluded Jonathan,

"We will support you financially and with medical aid. We will take your injured men to hospital in Tel Aviv; but we can't fight for you, although we will train your men, so you can fight your own battles."

After the secret meeting, Jonathan disappeared to his own land, tired and depressed. The problem was too big for him to solve, it was too great for any one else to loosen its entanglements, except by applying the simple remedy that Natanya quoted. "If only it was possible to 'love thy enemy', then this problem would be solved, but that's just an impossible dream," thought Jonathan. "They are Christians, and find it difficult to put it into action, but Natanya, though she is a Muslim, practises it. It's one of those riddles that life imposes on us from time to time. I know, deep in me, that it does work, as I tried it on a very limited scale and it did produce happiness."

Abu Mansour's teams brought their monitoring reports to Badrawi. A meeting was held to study the details.

"It's like a busy hive," said Mansour. "There's a full schedule, for almost twenty-four hours," he exclaimed, looking at the figures in front of him.

"Ah yes, but this is where our planning and ingenious thinking will show itself at its best," said Abu Mansour. "Let's arrange our figures hour by hour, and then make a scale for each day, to find out which is the quietest hour, and which is the busiest time. Then we do the same for the whole week and, after that we'll be able to decide the time for the attack."

The men started with Friday, as they were Muslims and that was their holy day. They had a card for each hour, on which was written the number of cars and people that passed the hostel. They started at 1 a.m. and Mansour announced,

"Fifty cars, twenty people and one patrol of the hostel guard." Then he laid the card on the table and read out for the next hour.

"Two a.m. Thirty cars, five persons, no patrol."

Each hour of the day was laid on the table. They all stood and studied the figures to discover the quietest hour.

"Three a.m. is not bad," said Abu Mansour. "Only five cars, one person and no patrol."

"Ah," interrupted Badrawi, "you look at the following Friday, and all the figures are upsidedown."

The men looked at the card in his hand.

"Fifteen cars, twenty five people."

"Maybe there was a party or some celebration going on," said Mansour, wiping the sweat from his forehead. He felt hot, as the room was a small one and every door and window was shut on the six men who were hard at work, studying their figures.

"Maybe," answered Badrawi, "but what I am trying to say is this, we can't rely too much on these figures, as you only need just one party like that, which suddenly turns up at the wrong time, and our men will be shot on the spot."

"That's not the way we should face this problem," advised Abu Mansour. "We will just find the quietest hour and then send our men to concentrate on that. However, let's continue with these figures, as we've only done one day so far and look at the time, soon the dawn will break."

"Saturday," announced Abu Mansour, scrutinizing the cards. "Worse than Friday. More patrols, more delivery vehicles, a few buses, but the best hour of the day is 4 a.m."

Badrawi, who was holding two cards in his hand, and waving them like a fan to cool his face, looked to Abu Mansour and said,

"Not according to these figures. One has 2 a.m. and the other 3 a.m."

Abu Mansour ignored his remarks and said,

"Sunday next."

Their task proved to be very complicated and difficult, and they spent a few days in just arranging their figures. They eventually came to the conclusion that they needed more monitoring of the hours between two and four a.m. every day, to enable them to reach the best hour for the execution. All this work was absorbing more money than they had available, so Abu Mansour interrupted his stay in Jordan to visit a few of his supporters to request more funds.

Jonathan spent a considerable time in Israel, as there was no incident against the troops in Lebanon. He felt very pleased with the situation, as it meant he could spend his time in training the young fighters in a more relaxed way.

"It's great fun," he explained to the young men, "when you play this game, as nobody gets hurt. We'll divide into two groups, who will alternate. One team will be the enemy and the other is our army, who will plan carefully in how to overcome the enemy without any casualties."

Then he asked for volunteers for the first enemy team and stood waiting for a response.

"Come on, it's only a game."

But they all stood there, smiling at him, for no one wanted to be the enemy.

"If that's the case," he said, "we'll choose the teams by lots." He took a coin from his pocket and said, "Line up and each one pick up the coin after I shake it. The head is us, the tail is the enemy."

The teams were chosen and Jonathan stood in front of his men and repeated the principle.

"This is only a game and the winner is the team that takes the greatest spoil of weapons and other valuables without any casualties." He looked at his enthusiastic men and commanded,

"We start now."

The hours passed swiftly, while the young men enjoyed their game immensely. At the end of the day they lined up for their commander's verdict, as he had been supervising their plans, manoeuvres and attacks.

Jonathan was amazed at the ways the soldiers overcame their enemies, using ingenious methods to paralyse the opposing side, without injuries. He saw the happy, smiling faces in front of him, waiting to hear the result of the battle. Before announcing his verdict, he asked them a question,

"Tell me, did you enjoy the battles you've just fought?"

They all raised their arms and guns and shouted,

"Tremendously."

"Well," he declared, "you impressed me to the limit."

Then he gave the result,

"Mission of disabling the enemy without casualties was fought successfully. A complete victory for both teams."

The men shouted and hugged each other, congratulating themselves. Then they picked up their loads and started filling the army vehicles, ready to return to their hostel, hungry and looking forward to enjoy another of Natanya's delicious meals.

"Jonathan's a super trainer," said the boys, as they discussed the day's events amongst themselves. "He knows how to turn fighting into a real joy."

After a refreshing shower, Jonathan sat in his room, trying to read for a few minutes before dinner, but he found himself daydreaming. "It's lovely to come back home, to a clean, well kept room." He looked around. "Everything is in its place, clean and sparkling. Boots, shirts, books, everything neatly in its place." He took a deep breath, "That beautiful smell coming down the passage from the kitchen. All these things make this hostel a happy home, a haven of happiness." He turned back to his book, but his eyes looked through the page to a far distant dream. "The hostel has changed into a pleasant home, since Natanya's arrival. She is a wonderful girl, a gentle creature. Nothing is too much for her," and he smiled as he heard in his head her most used word in her limited vocabulary, 'This is good, it make you feel good.'

Mark entered the room and saw Jonathan with a smile on his face.

"A good book?" he enquired, looking at the contented young man.

"Not bad," came the reply, then he added, "We had a wonderful time today, as no one lost the battle, all were winners!"

Mark looked at his friend with envious eyes, as a sentence like that turned him green, so he changed the subject immediately.

"The dining room is open and I'm starving. Let's hurry before the queue builds up."

Jonathan put his book down and stood up, took a comb from his pocket and combed his hair.

"It's alright! It doesn't need any combing," commented Mark, looking at the smart officer.

Jonathan blushed. He did not want anybody to discover his heart's desire, or his feelings toward the girl that controlled his thinking.

The first thing Jonathan looked at when Natanya filled his plate was her fingers. "No sign of my ring," he thought, and his heart ached so much, but when he looked at her face, she smiled softly to him and added another spoon for good measure. "She always gives me an extra serving, so maybe there's another reason for not wearing the ring." He smiled back and quietly said,

"Thanks."

Abu Mansour disappeared for a few weeks, then returned to Jordan with tremendous support, as he had assured his friends that the end was in sight for the brain behind all the raids into Lebanon. The monitoring results were ready and waiting for him, so no time was wasted, but a secret meeting held the same night he returned.

Monday was found to be the least busy day of the week, according to the figures, with the best time being between two and three in the morning.

"That's one headache out of the way," said Abu Mansour to the others, while he looked at the card. "Now we have to decide about the next problem. What type of explosive shall we use?"

The men suggested different methods, but Mansour's was preferred.

"Time bombs," he remarked. "We can plant a number of them around the hostel and set them to give ourselves ample time to disappear from the area, before the explosions take place and they set up road blocks to delay our escape."

The men agreed.

"How long shall we allow ourselves?" asked Badrawi.

"Ten minutes," said Mansour.

"Oh no, that hardly gives us any time. Suppose we get interrupted for one reason or another. I think we should allow ourselves more than that, but we can decide later."

"How many bombs do you feel are needed to wipe the hostel from the face of the earth?" asked Abu Mansour, rubbing his chin.

"Six big ones would be enough," said Badrawi. "Two each along the length of the hostel and one along the width. But," he spoke with anxiety in his voice, "we must practise many, many times before the actual day, otherwise, I'm sure we'll get nervous, and that will be our end."

The men took the photographs of the hostel and began to construct a model, to enable their partisans to practise planting the bombs without mistakes.

"But what if we're disturbed?" asked Abu Mansour. "We must have in mind some hiding places for the men to run to until they can resume their work."

Mansour looked at the ground around the hostel.

"We have a few trees, where they can hide in their shadow, plus there's a bus shelter on the east side which can be used."

Then he thought for a long time, and added, "We need someone to watch the end of each road and send a signal whenever a car or people appear."

Badrawi nodded his head, thinking, gazing far beyond the wall that was facing him, then he advised,

"I feel it will be a good idea if we can choose the winter months, because then the wind will be blowing quite strongly and cover the sound of our steps, plus it should encourage the people to stay at home."

"That's good advice," said Abu Mansour, patting Badrawi on the shoulder. "We can now concentrate on training our boys and timing them, until they can play their part in their sleep. After that, we shall meet again in order to finalize the plan."

Jonathan and his team were excelling in the new method of fighting, which was given the title, 'Disarming Without Casualties'. It was extremely hard work and tasking for the brain, but the boys continued to improve by the day. Many of them spent their nights thinking of ways of disarming the opposing team, so they would not waste any time in the following day's battle. Mark noticed the atmosphere in the hostel, how the young fighters admired their leader and talked about him as 'a great man' and 'a super trainer'.

"It's not fair," he moaned to himself. "All of them love him, and no one bothers about me. In fact, the situation is worse since his promotion and now they feel he is the Messiah himself." Mark felt his heart bleeding. "No one wants to talk now, as the new excuse is, 'Sorry, we're busy, we have a battle tomorrow. It's crucial, so much armour and surrounded by enemies. Sorry Mark, after the battle we'll have more time.' Now this hostel has become a horrible place, except for Natanya's cooking," He smiled to himself as he added, "and her lovely smile."

It was after ten at night, and Jonathan was struggling to go to sleep, but someone did not want to free his mind. He begged and entreated, as he turned from one side to the other, "Natanya, please go away and let me sleep."

Mark had his nose buried in a spy novel and was too engrossed in it to notice his friend's agony.

"Take a firm grip on your heart, man," said he, in an effort to sort out his problem. "Let us weigh the matter on a scale, and use logic, just to prove that you must wipe Natanya from your memory."

He turned to face the wall, away from Mark, so he could concentrate on convincing his heart against his infatuation with the strange girl. "Imagine you have a balance with its two pans. On one we will put all the points for having these ridiculous feelings, and on the other we shall put the logic against the situation, and the result will be that Natanya must go from that soft place you have arranged for her."

"Let's start with the negative points," said Jonathan, mentally counting the points in his head. "One, she is an Arab, two, an enemy, three, a Muslim, four, an alef prisoner, five, a..a.." Here he stopped as he tried to find more points but could not. "Oh well, those are quite enough," and then he remembered something else. "Of course, five, your parents will one hundred percent oppose any marriage proposal." At this he held his head with his hands, as he could just imagine the shock to his parents if he ever announced to them,

"'Mother, I'm in love with my alef enemy'. That will give her a heart attack on the spot."

Jonathan could see that it was obvious the scales were tipped against Natanya, but he had to be fair and try to balance them.

"Right, you can see, even before we consider the positive side, that the answer is 'No' for Natanya."

"I am waiting," his heart cried. "She.... she is strange to describe. One, gentle, two, kind, three, caring, four, a good cook, five, a lovely nurse, six, a devout woman who prays a lot and has her prayers answered. Seven, I love her." He paused as his heart retained the thoughts of the gentle girl and refused to let them pass away. "You are blind, of course. You're looking at her through rose tinted glasses. You need another opinion besides your own, so you can look at the problem from a balanced angle."

He turned towards Mark, who was still engrossed in his story. "I'll ask Mark," he said, lifting himself up and resting on the pillow.

"Mark," he called.

"Uha," he answered, resenting the interruption and keeping his eyes on his line in the book.

"I'd be very grateful to have your opinion, please, on a matter of concern to me."

Mark removed the book from in front of his eyes and laid it down on his chest, to look at Jonathan enquiringly. "I can guess what he wants my opinion on," he thought. "It will be about tomorrow's battle, 'Disarming Without Casualties'."

There was a soft smile on Jonathan's lips, as he felt bashful to ask about such a subject, but he arranged his thoughts and said,

"I am making a report about Natanya and would appreciate it very much if you could tell me about your feelings and observations regarding her."

That was an unexpected question for Mark, although he was aware that Jonathan, being head of the hostel, often had to write reports about staff members and residents. He put his book aside and sat up in bed, while he rested his chin on his hands and thought hard, trying to summarize his feelings and observations about Natanya. After a long pause, he said,

"She is not bad," then added more observations, while Jonathan stared into his eyes and scrutinized his expressions, as he was so anxious to know how the others felt about her. "To me," he said, "she is an Arab, a prisoner, an alef prisoner who can't be trusted. Although she is a good cook and...." he hesitated, as he felt embarrassed to describe her beautiful eyes and soft smile. Jonathan wanted to hear the rest of the sentence, so he asked,

"And what?"

"Well, she is good looking and quite likeable, and she has a certain pull, difficult to explain."

Jonathan sighed, as he knew exactly what that pull felt like, but he did not interrupt his friend.

"You can't put your finger on the source of that strong pull, but it's a sort of magnet that keeps a person attracted to her." He glanced at Jonathan and noticed he was dreaming, so he quickly advised, "I think we should watch her. She is, after all, an alef prisoner, very dangerous."

Jonathan sat on his bed, resting his head in his cupped hands, thinking. He was in a great dilemma, as Mark had come to the same conclusion as himself about the strange girl. He too, was affected by her pull, but, at the same time, was aware of her history.

"I have found her very difficult to assess," said Jonathan, after a long pause. "On the one hand, she is an alef enemy, yet, on the other, she is the best of friends."

Mark smiled and warned,

"That's the problem. I think she's a good actor and trying to get close to us and then, when the opportunity arises, she will pass all the information she has learnt on to her people."

Jonathan's mind was now becoming anxious, as he could see the correctness of his friend's view.

"Of course," he thought. "My heart is blinding me from her origin. I know who she is, and I mustn't forget her real name, Baha; she isn't really Natanya. But," and another thought came to the forefront of his mind, "what about the care she showed to me when I was so ill? She did ease my pain, even at that late hour of the night, when she could easily have not bothered."

Then he voiced his thoughts aloud to Mark, who sat erect, with a worried look in his eyes. The situation seemed desperate to him because he was affected by the novel he was reading.

"But she is so caring. When I was ill that night, she did everything possible to ease my pain."

"That's it," said Mark excitedly. "Can't you see the plot, man?"

Jonathan's heart was now thumping furiously, as he knew it had made him so blind that he could not even see the vaguest outline of a plot, so he asked Mark,

"Please tell me, as I am too stupid, and my brain doesn't see anything."

"From all the boys here," Mark carried on explaining, "you are the target of that girl. Remember, she is Mansour's girlfriend. They have been seen together many times in various cafes and restaurants in Lebanon, holding hands and looking into each other's eyes, plotting together."

"Yes, I completely forgot Mansour," said Jonathan, rubbing his forehead. "I know the report. Of course she will be very much interested in me, to gather more information for her beloved cousin. Yes, I can see the plot. I can see it very plainly." Then he pushed the sheet away from himself and started to dress.

"Where are you going?" asked Mark.

"I'm going to phone Dudu, right away. That prisoner should never have been sent here, and she is endangering everyone in the hostel."

"Can't you wait until the morning, as it's almost eleven?"

"No, I can't. It's my responsibility to protect our boys, and how such a mistake could have happened in the first place, I just can't understand."

Mark saw how angry Jonathan was, but could not see the need of worrying the man at that hour, so he picked up his book to continue the story.

"Mark," said Jonathan, before he left the room. "Thankyou very much. I do appreciate your help. Good thinking."

Jonathan went to his office and sat at his desk, feeling a failure, and hot with anger, disappointment and regret. He found David's home number, but sat for a while, staring at the phone, as he tried to organize his thoughts, to find a way out of the mess in which he found himself. "Of course," he said, "Mansour is her love. That's why she never once wore my ring, as she is remaining loyal and faithful to him." He was shaking with anger at himself. "How stupid I was to let my heart go like that. How foolish to be overtaken by her charms." He undid his shirt pocket and snatched out the piece of hair, to throw it in the wastepaper basket. But the moment he touched and looked at it, he could only see her soft brown eyes and hear her gentle words,

'For memory. Every time you see this, I will pray for you.'

He stared at the shiny, soft black hair, and could not throw it away. He just kept looking at it and talking to the soft brown eyes. "Why Natanya?" he asked with sadness. "Why did you have to deceive me, why do you act? 'Love your enemy'," he could hear her voice. "Yes, I can see why you quoted that to me, you wanted to safeguard your love, but why did you have to ruin my heart in the process? 'I shall pray that no one will be hurt'. Oh Natanya, I love you, I love you." Then he replaced the hair in his pocket and dialled the number. The phone rang for a while and then a sleepy voice came from the other end,

"Hello."

"Is that Dudu?"

"Yes. Who is speaking?"

"Jonathan. I'm sorry to get you out of bed at this hour, but it's urgent."

"Jonathan," replied David, surprised and anxious, "I didn't know you have been to Lebanon?" He anticipated that a fresh batch of Arab prisoners were arriving unexpectedly, because he was accustomed to receive a number of them every time Jonathan returned from Lebanon.

"No, I haven't. I am phoning about a prisoner we have with us. Natanya."

"Oh no, don't tell me that something has gone wrong?" said a very worried David.

"Not yet, but I want to know why you sent a person like her here, while you know she is a very dangerous enemy?"

David tried, with difficulty, to explain himself.

"Jonathan, I will explain the whole situation, but please, try to understand me. I know I shouldn't have let her out of the prison, in fact, since she came to you, my heart has never let me rest in peace and that is why I keep phoning Mordecai, to enquire about her behaviour, and he assures me that she is wonderful." Then he paused, and continued, "You see, my dear, it is one of those situations when you do something without knowing why."

Jonathan kept quiet, listening.

"Are you with me?" the anxious man asked.

"Yes, do continue. I'm listening."

"I don't know what came over me to suggest Baha on that day when your cook was taken ill and Mordecai phoned for help. I suppose it was because she fitted the description of what he wanted, as he said he was in a mess, with the boys soon wanting their meal and the place upsidedown. He asked me to help him, and the only one who could sort out all his problems was Natanya, as she could turn chaos into order in no time at all.

126

That is where I made my mistake, I forgot about her real person." Then he took his breath and asked, "Would you like me to have her back, as I can arrange that first thing tomorrow?"

"I'll have to speak to Mordecai first," answered Jonathan, "before I take any decision, as the damage has already been done. It's no good shutting the door after the horse has bolted, as she already knows a great deal about us, the hostel and me."

"I am very sorry, Jonathan. I only tried to help. I know I was wrong in taking that decision, but I just did."

"What happened, happened, Dudu. My concern now is that we never let her go back to Lebanon, under any circumstances, because she will inform on us, especially as Mansour is her boyfriend and cousin. She must stay a prisoner here for good."

"Well, I promise that, as soon as the morning comes, I shall enter that order in her file, that under no circumstances shall she be freed. All I can suggest now is that you keep your eyes on her, and tell the others to do the same, but, even that has its problems."

"What do you mean?" enquired Jonathan.

"Well, if I can illustrate what I mean by what happened to Moshe, our guard. I ordered him to watch her carefully, every movement she made. Well," said David, laughing, "he went and got himself hooked on her. She's a very strange girl, as the more you watch her, the more you get to like her. She is like a drug, like heroin, and our Moshe definitely suffered withdrawal symptoms for weeks after she left us. In fact, only this morning he asked me when she would be coming back to the prison. She has something about her, very difficult to explain, but it's ...." and before he had finished his statement, Jonathan did so for him.

"It's like a pull, a magnet."

"That's right. Have you found that?"

"That was an expression used by Mark to describe her, just a few minutes ago, and that is what makes the problem so enormous. Anyhow, no need for you to worry much about her. I shall talk to Mordecai and also warn the boys, in case they get hooked on her, and I will let you know about my decision. Im Yirtseh ha-Shem."

Jonathan put down the receiver and looked at his watch; he had been talking about Natanya for one hour. He rubbed his tired and anxious eyes. "So," he said to his heart, "what can you see from the result of weighing this girl that you keep holding so tight?" He found his hand reaching to his pocket for her hair.

127

He rested it on his hand, admiring it, and smiled to himself. His heart whispered, "I can't help it, I need her and I love her. I confess, I am addicted to her, and it can't be helped."

He dragged his feet in the direction of his room, and on the way he paused near her door for a moment. "Fast asleep," he said. Then he walked into his room and found a sleeping Mark, with his book fallen on the floor. "Lucky boy, fast asleep too. I wish I could sleep like that, but it serves me right, I should have kept my eyes open, or, in this case, shut. But now it's too late, I'll have to spend the rest of my life under her grip."

Jonathan was now more than ever aware about Natanya's movements and very concerned about her activities, so, when he heard her open her door and walk along the passage to the kitchen, he said to himself, "She could easily do a lot of harm, early in the morning like this, while the boys are still asleep. It's so dangerous." He jumped up and opened his door to see where she was going and nearly bumped into her. She smiled sweetly and said,

"Good morning."

He just stood, staring into her eyes as he used to, without a word or any expression on his face. She was puzzled but continued to the kitchen, to prepare breakfast. "Why did Jonathan look at me like that, as if I am nothing, or a piece of rubbish?" The big, ugly beast started to move inside her, making her feel hot and agitated. "How strange," she said to herself. "I have just spent most of the night praying for him and others, that they may see the pure love of our God, but I can't understand why humans don't respond to such love."

Jonathan hurriedly dressed and went to catch Mordecai before he left for the kitchen.

"Boker tov," he said, with surprise on his face.

"Boker tov, Mordecai. I just wanted to have a quick word with you before the breakfast. I will wait for you in my office."

"Anything wrong, Jonathan?" he enquired with anxious eyes, looking to his visitor.

"Nothing wrong yet, but I want to talk to you about Natanya."

"Natanya?" he repeated. "What has she done? Anything wrong?"

Then he pulled out a chair and said,

"Please sit down Jonathan. We can talk here, right now. I will shut the door, so no one will interrupt. Now, what has she done?"

Jonathan sat down and said,

"Don't worry, Mordecai. I said nothing has happened yet, but I am worried about what is going to happen. Don't forget that Natanya was an informer, and her relatives are fighting us at this moment and planning our destruction. I phoned Dudu last night, and he suggested that we can send her back."

Mordecai held his head between his hands and shook it from side to side, objecting.

"Take Natanya back to the prison? Why? Why do you want to take my Natanya? What will I do? No. No. No."

Then he looked at Jonathan with anger and despair.

"Why do you want to do that to me? Why take my daughter from me?" And a few tears rushed from his eyes.

Jonathan was shocked at the response and words of Mordecai.

"Oh no," he said in his heart. "He's got hooked too, very badly hooked."

"Please," pleaded the old man, holding his hands together, "don't take my daughter away from me."

"What do you mean, your daughter?" asked Jonathan, staring into the tearful eyes of Mordecai.

"Well, we have adopted each other and are both feeling good for it."

"Feeling good?" Jonathan repeated to himself. "Those are Natanya's words." He asked again,

"What do you mean, Mordecai? It seems to me you have forgotten that Natanya is our enemy?"

"Enemy maybe, to you, but to me she is my daughter. She is not my enemy."

Jonathan could see a big problem forming in front of him, so he looked to the sad eyes for an explanation.

"I will tell you everything," said Mordecai. "And please, you must try to understand, even if it seems strange to you."

Jonathan nodded his head, still concentrating on Mordecai's expressions and words.

"I know Natanya is an alef enemy, so I watched her very carefully, and I even tried to trick her many times, to see who she is, but every time I liked her even more, and one day, something happened on the anniversary of my Esther's funeral. You know my Esther died in a car accident, just two years after her mother's death. Well, I was feeling very unhappy, very sad, and I tried to keep myself busy in the kitchen, but I felt so miserable, that I went and stood in front of the window, just staring into my unhappy past. I didn't know that Natanya was watching me, as she was right on the other side of the kitchen, preparing the meal. In fact, I was not even aware myself that I was crying, but she was, and came and stood quietly by my side. I did not see her or feel her presence; I don't know how she walked so gently."

The old man stopped to dry his tears, while Jonathan quietly listened and understood the man's feelings.

"Well," continued Mordecai, still rubbing his hands together, "it happened that I turned my head away from the window, and there, right next to me, stood Natanya, staring at me, with tears rolling down her cheeks. I didn't know what to say or do. She stretched out her hand and dried my tears from my face with her bare hand, then she wiped away her own and asked me, 'You are not happy?' I nodded, and she said to me, 'I will pray, then you feel good'."

Mordecai spoke with a soft smile as he cherished her loving thoughts.

"Then she asked me, 'Why are you crying?' I told her that my only daughter and child was dead, so she said to me, 'I understand. Your daughter is alright. I will pray for you.' Then she smiled and said, 'I will be your daughter and you be my father, as I have no father and cry a lot, too, so now we can have each other'."

Mordecai smiled gently and said to Jonathan,

"You see, since that day, we have adopted each other. When we are alone, she calls me Pa, but when anyone else is around, she calls me by my name." Then Mordecai begged again, "Please, don't take her from me, she is the only one I have, the only relative I've got."

Jonathan felt very touched, and his heart was moved toward her, so he said to the waiting man,

"I do understand your feelings, and I hope you also understand my problem. We must keep our eyes open. She can stay here, but you must keep on guard. The other point I want to tell you is this, under no circumstances should she be returned to Lebanon, or set free, as she knows so much about us."

"I agree, we will never let her go from here, never let her go. I promise to keep my eyes open on her all the time." Then he looked at the clock. "Oh dear, look at the time," he said to Jonathan. "Breakfast will be late now and there's all that work in the kitchen."

Jonathan smiled and said,

"No need to worry, Natanya is in the kitchen. She can sort out the mess in no time."

The warning was passed to everyone in the hostel.

"Watch Natanya carefully, and don't forget she's an enemy".

Mordecai rushed into the kitchen, where he saw that his daughter had prepared everything ready, and was just waiting for the boys to arrive as everyone seemed late that morning. She asked him softly,

"Did you have a good sleep?"

"Yes Natanya," he said gruffly, then added, "Don't ask too many questions."

She looked at him very surprised, and asked herself, "What has happened to everyone today? First Jonathan ignored me, and now my own father tells me to keep quiet. What have I done to deserve all this?" "It is all a waste of time," repeated the voice of lower nature. "It is all a waste of time, what's the use of working hard to try making others happy. They will kick you and tread on you and ignore your love." The tears started to rush to her eyes, but the other part of her that always tried to control the ugly beast spoke out loud and clear, "Get a grip on that hate and selfishness, before it goes out of control. Do not get tired of doing the good, because you shall reap wonderful fruits at the harvest time. Don't think of yourself all the time, but rather think of the Pattern and how he reacted; he never got tired, no matter how hard the road was in front of him." She felt ashamed of herself and prayed for help to enable her to reflect the light of love.

The young fighters arrived to have their breakfast and all looked at her with cold eyes and watched her carefully.

"Something must have happened," she thought while she served the coffee. "Maybe more trouble in Lebanon, as I can feel the atmosphere is full of hate and distrust."

A few days passed and no change took place, except with Mark, whose shouting and bossing were becoming intolerable, so Natanya kept herself busy, praying in her heart and singing some of her Psalms to charge her thoughts with love and understanding.

Abu Mansour met with his group to finalize the last stage of their plan. The men were tense with excitement and nerves, all at the same time. Badrawi spoke first, to inform them about the progress and all sat in rapt attention, following his every word.

"We have constructed imaginary buildings," he told them, "with the same measurements as the hostel area, and we placed stones to represent the hiding places. Our boys gradually improved their speed of planting the dummies, until they reached the fantastic rate of ten minutes to plant and set the six bombs."

Abu Mansour was delighted, then Badrawi continued.

"We interrupted the procedure many times, but everything went just right. At the same time, our team toured round the hostel, to get the feel of the place, and they are very confident they will be able to carry out the mission with ease. We have two teams, working in opposite directions at the same time. One team will go down the east side from north to south and plant their last bomb on the south side, while the other team will go up the west side from the south, finishing up along the north wall. We have arranged for watchmen to cover the main roads from all directions, and also for waiting cars to pick up the teams immediately they finish and then take them from the area, so that, in a matter of five minutes, they will be parked in a secure place, where they can stay until it's safe to continue their journey the following day."

"That's just wonderful," said Mansour. "We'll reward the team generously. I'll make sure everyone has a few months holiday in Europe, to rest from all their hard work."

Then Abu Mansour said, checking his list,

"We have almost prepared everything, I think. Oh yes, what about the bombs, are they all ready?"

"Yes," answered Badrawi. "All ready to be planted on Monday, starting at two a.m., and they will be establishing their purpose at three a.m., in three days time, insha-allah."

"I can't believe that our plan is almost ready," remarked Mansour, "as we've been sweating for months, and now it's only another three days to wait until Jonathan and all his teams have their end, for ever."

"Just let us hope he doesn't go on holiday!" said Abu Mansour, laughing.

"You always say the wrong thing Father, just to ruin my nerves," said Mansour, angrily.

Abu Mansour concluded the meeting by standing and giving a speech.

"Our dear brothers, we would love to be with you in Israel, to fight the enemy face to face, but, as we can't be with you in person, Mansour and I shall spend Sunday in fasting and prayer on your behalf, so Allah will give you the victory against those kofar (infidels). We shall win and a place will be prepared for us in the paradise. So fight with all your strength, and if you die, then happy are you, as you will be assigned to the seventh heaven, where Say-yidoona (our master) Muhammad is, and what an honour that will be."

Natanya was washing up the dinner plates, singing to herself, as she felt lonely and depressed. She sang for a time, then stopped to think for a while. "If I only knew what has happened to everyone. Mordecai doesn't speak to me anymore and Jonathan has stopped his 'thankyou' and returned to that strange stare of his, and I do feel very lonely." Her mind went to the convent. "They would just be finishing their prayers now. I used to love singing those songs with the other children on Sunday evenings; it was just lovely." She stopped her washing and gazed into the distance, through the window of her kitchen, and saw the guard patrolling round the yard. It was wintry weather, and the cold wind was blowing swiftly, driving in front of it the fallen autumn leaves. "I hate darkness and the roar of the wind. It's better that I hurry up and go to my room, as it's small and warm, and very cosy. Then I can talk properly to my Heavenly Father."

Jonathan went to bed early, as he felt unhappy and depressed. "I hate winter and the sound of the roaring wind," he said. "It reminds me of those horrible nights in Lebanon, when we used to sit and wait for hours for our enemy, cold and anxious. When you couldn't see anything, and the sound of the leaves being driven by the wind sounded like a marching army." He felt so uneasy. "I wish I knew what is inside Natanya's heart. She seems so lonely and sad, and when I saw her eyes today, they looked to me as if she had been crying. I wish I knew where I stand with her, as I do love her, but am not sure of her motives. I just can't figure out her thinking, as she is so pleasant, kind and understanding, yet, at the same time, she is Baha. Of that I am sure, because I was the one who dragged her out from her own home, otherwise, I could say it was an error."

Mordecai felt tearful and could not sleep. "I wish Jonathan had never given these new orders about how to treat Natanya, because I can't see any fault in her. I am just breaking her heart, as she many times came to talk to me, even calling me Pa, and I pushed her away. Why? She is my daughter. Why can't we accept her as she is, and when she behaves differently, then we can punish her." He turned onto his other side, as his conscience was hurting him. "I was very happy with her and we were getting so close, just like Esther and I used to be. Why can't people leave me alone?"

Natanya turned off her light and jumped into bed, where she did her routine checking. "Jonathan's medallion, and the little box." She touched each with her hand to make sure they were still there. "I must keep, not lose it," and she repeated Mark's sentence as it had dug a deep groove in her brain.
"I can pray now," she said, and prayed for everybody.
"Father, help me to reflect your love, please. The going is so hard, and I feel worn out. Do help me to be a reflection of your son." Then she prayed by name for everyone she knew. "Mordecai, he feels very unhappy. Please, make him forget his sadness and see your goodness that you create afresh every morning. And Jonathan...." and she prayed for all those who were with her in the hostel. Then she travelled in her thoughts to Lebanon and prayed for Baha, Abu Mansour and his son, "I beg you, Holy Father, let them see your love, so they can love their enemies and enjoy the happiness that comes from love."

The time ticked by slowly, as Abu Mansour sat on his prayer mat with Mansour, fasting and praying, and feeling extremely anxious for their men. He said to his son,
"It's almost two, so they must be in the area by now."
"Pray," responded Mansour. "Now is the time to pray. May the angel of Allah be with them, and help them to blow those pigs out of the world."

The team were smoking heavily to calm their nerves, while they waited in their cars until the right moment arrived.

"I hate waiting like this," said Hassan. "I would rather get on with it and finish. My stomach feels very upset, not because I'm frightened, but I'm worried in case things go wrong."

"We don't talk about things going wrong," answered Hamid, his hands shaking from anxiety. "We have Allah with us, and the prayers of Abu Mansour and his son, so, just let us watch for the signal."

Jonathan tossed and turned on his bed. "Natanya, please get out of my mind. I am dreadfully tired and must go to sleep as it's nearly two o'clock. My head is almost bursting from thinking, and I'm on the point of going mad." He could not shake the girl from his mind, no matter how he tried. "I must go to the office and do something, as I feel awful." Then he changed his mind. "Better not, as I'll disturb Mark and worry the guard unnecessarily. I must pray for help." Then he turned toward Jerusalem and prayed, "Ha Elohim, I beg your help. Please direct my steps, as I love my enemy, Natanya, but I can't trust her as she is known to be a killer of your people Israel. Open my eyes to see through her; is she really as she appears, or is she acting? I trust you will guide me. Amen." He felt restful in his heart and laid down, dozing gradually.

Natanya could not sleep. She hated the sound of the wind as it reminded her of unhappy occasions in her childhood. She remembered the times that she ran to her mother's room crying, "Mama, the Muslims are outside, they want to blow us up." She smiled and told herself, "Well, that is impossible here. No one will be outside except the leaves, blown by the wind." She turned onto her side, saying to herself, "I wish Mama was here, then I could run to her room, as I feel very frightened tonight, although I don't know why, and I am shaking, for no reason." She tried to encourage herself, "I think it's because I'm just very tired, and also because the boys have not been feeling in a good mood these last few days. I must think of something good so I can send myself to sleep." She thought for a moment as she endeavoured to find a good subject to dwell on and noticed that she was holding Jonathan's medallion. "That is a good subject, as I have won Jonathan's trust. Once he thought I was an Arab thief, but now he has made me his treasure keeper."

Abu Mansour's watchmen were waiting for the patrols to appear and do their rounds before they could start their mission.

"We can't chance it," said Ahmed. "I hope they hurry up and do their patrolling. They should have done it minutes ago. The more they hang about, the worse they make it for us."

"Just be patient," Saaid advised, not even daring to blink. "I suppose, if need be, we could postpone it until tomorrow."

"Oh no, I couldn't stand this tension for two days running. We will plant them tonight, no matter what happens," said Ahmed, concentrating on the road toward the hostel.

The guard patrolled around the yard inside the hostel. They marched up and down, then stood in front of the passage that led to Natanya's room and watched her door, as they all had the order, "Watch her movements. Any suspicious move and don't hesitate to use force." That was Jonathan's command and that was what the guards were concentrating on. They stood at the end of the passage, chatting to each other, and then took another stroll. Menachem looked at the time and said to Aaron,

"I suppose we'd better do our patrol outside and get it over with. I do hate nights like this, when it's so windy and dark."

Aaron responded without any enthusiasm,

"We've never yet found anybody outside, so I can't see the sense of patrolling round the hostel. After all, it's a Jewish site and no Arab would ever dare come near here."

"I agree, but orders are orders, so let's get on with it, and then we can discuss some of the points we have in mind for our coming battle, as we must beat them this time."

"Great, let's march away," said Aaron, parading through the gate.

"Blessed be Allah," quietly cheered Ahmed. "At last they have appeared." He rubbed his hands with excitement. "We don't have long left, but at least we can start as soon as they disappear inside."

Aaron and Menachem marched with a steady, but fast step, looking carefully around them. There was nothing in sight, except a few parked cars in the distance, but not a soul to be seen, or a moving vehicle.

"Deadly silent," said Aaron, "except for the whistle of the wind."

They stopped for a moment, watching the swaying trees in the direction of the parked cars.

"Oh no," exclaimed Hassan, lowering his head. "They've both stopped and are looking in our direction."

"Shush, we're too far away to be recognized, and it's very dark. Just let's keep our heads down."

Natanya tried her best to think of good things, but she had run out of thoughts and was still shaking, unable to sleep. "An eternal night," she said, desperately. "If only I had my Bible with me, I could read myself to sleep." She lifted her head as she could hear footsteps. "Ah, the guards are patrolling. I can recognize their steps, so that means there is nothing to fear," she said, trying to calm herself. "I must try to sleep now, when they are outside, protecting me with all the others in the hostel. If I don't sleep now, I'll never sleep tonight."

The guards marched slowly, as if they were searching around for something.

"So many leaves. Someone could easily hide bombs among them," said Menachem, kicking the leaves with his boots.

"You've given me an idea," said Aaron. "We can use the leaves to hide our spoil which we'll gather from the enemy in the next battle. We can heap them, like this," and he pushed a few of them into a heap with his boots, then stood back and admired it in the light of his torch.

"Yes, that looks very natural. Good thinking."

They continued their patrol and eventually reached the gate, where they stood talking.

"The time is running fast, and those stupid men don't want to go in," said Ahmed, chewing his nails. "We hardly have any time left for us."

"It doesn't matter too much, we only need a few minutes to plant the bombs."

"Yes, but suppose we have an interruption; then we will really be in trouble." Ahmed cursed the two soldiers in his frustration, "Cursed be your mother. Go in!"

The guards walked in, discussing their plans for the coming game, as they strolled around the hostel. They automatically halted outside the passage and glanced at the shut door of Natanya's room.

Jonathan was half asleep, especially as Mark was snoring so loudly and disturbing him. "This is my worst night ever. I just can't wait for the morning to come," he muttered dozily.

The signal was raised, by one flash from the torch. The two cars moved off slowly and quietly, carrying the execution crews in opposite directions along parallel streets to the hostel. The doors opened quietly, and two men emerged from each car, carrying their parcels. The cars then quietly continued down each road.

The first bombs were quickly placed and set, and the teams gently whistled to their captain to announce their achievement. They swiftly moved along the sides of the hostel and placed the second set, adjusted the clocks and then covered the bombs with the fallen leaves. They were on their way to the third and last location, when the watchman shone two flashes of light, indicating that a car was entering the street. The men rushed and hid in their prearranged hiding places.

A car passed by, and then another came from the opposite direction. The crew could not move from their hideout until they heard the grasshopper whistle or saw the flashlight signal. Although it was chilly and a strong wind was blowing, whistling through the trees, the men were sweating, as every second was like an hour.

"What's the matter with him?" whispered Hassan to his friend. "Why no signal. We have already set the time and we'll soon be trapped in the midst of all this mess."

Hamid replied, with his teeth knocking and chattering,

"I think we'll just have to leave the job half done and run when we reach our time, as we need ten minutes to get away safely. But we still have five minutes to spare."

A minute passed, then footsteps approached near to where the men were hiding. Their hearts were beating fast and their breathing quickened, but they kept perfectly quiet. The watchman was in a state of near panic as he saw the figures of two men drawing near one of the hiding places.

"They've had it," he said, biting his lips. "The men have stopped near them."

Abu Mansour and Mansour were in agony.

"What's the time, Mansour?"

"Quarter past two. I think they must be finished by now, unless they've had some interruption. I'll be relieved when three o'clock comes, as this waiting seems to be stretching on for ever. Let's concentrate on prayer, as they will need it with those people."

Natanya managed to calm down and shut her eyes. She was very tired and exhausted from nerves and fear. But her eyes opened slightly whenever a gust of wind blew, as her sleep was very light and she was always aware of any movement or noise around her.

The two men were on their way home from a nightclub, staggering and stumbling, well intoxicated. They dallied by the bus shelter, where Hassan and his friend were hiding behind its wall, then gradually moved down the road, stopping from time to time and looking towards the hostel. Eventually they turned into a side street and disappeared.

"Thanks to God," sighed Ahmed, raising his torch.

The execution crews jumped swiftly into action as the time was running fast. Two of the men had a difficult spot, right near the hostel's gate. The other team had their location just outside Natanya's room.

Hassan reached his last location and whistled softly to indicate that his bomb was about to be set.

Natanya half opened her eyes, as her ears picked up the sound of the whistle. "That sounds just like the whistle Muhammad tried to teach me." Her mind brought back the memory of Muhammad, "And you can whistle like this.... when you are planting a bomb to blow your enemies." She lifted her head from the pillow and turned toward the wall of the street. "Don't be stupid Amal; I mean Natanya. It's only the wind; you are just imagining things."

She thought she heard footsteps outside her room. "I'm certain there are people outside," she whispered to herself and started trembling like a leaf in the blowing wind. Her heart was almost jumping out of her breast. She tried to swallow her saliva, but her throat was too dry. Then she heard soft voices speaking in Arabic.

"Al hamdo lil-lah, khal-las de achir wahada (Thanks to God, this is the last one). Let us run, as we only have a few minutes to escape from here."

Then the footsteps rapidly faded as the men hurried away.

She jumped from her bed, saying to herself, "I must tell the guard there are many bombs outside and there's only a few minutes left!"

She tried to pick up her shirt, but was trembling too much to pick up anything, so she left her prison pyjamas on, opened the door and sped down the passage, passing Jonathan's room. He heard her door open, so lifted his head to listen carefully and heard her gentle footsteps hurry past his door.

"Oh no," he said, "that's Natanya. What's she doing out of her room at this hour of the night?" Then he remembered his prayer before he went to sleep. "Thankyou God. You answered my prayer very quickly to show me she's an informer, an enemy."

He jumped out of bed and speedily put his clothes on, to follow her.

The guard was on the other side of the yard when he turned round and spotted Natanya. He shouted out at the top of his voice,

"Stop, or I'll shoot you."

As soon as Jonathan heard the guard, he sprinted down the passage into the yard, where he saw Natanya running towards them, screaming,

"Bombs, quick, bombs!"

The guard lifted his gun and was just about to fire because she ignored his order, when Jonathan shouted to him, so he lowered it again, as he caught up with her and roughly grabbed her wrist, pulling her close and looking into her frightened brown eyes. She noticed his stare, the same as when he slapped her for the money she never stole. She repeated the warning,

"Hurry Jonathan, there are bombs."

"Bombs?" he enquired, with mockery in his voice and distrust in his eyes. "Where are these bombs?"

"Outside. Hurry, no time."

She felt desperate, knowing he was about to slap her face, which made her fear of the bombs momentarily disappear, but then her anxiety returned, as she was certain the whole place was in danger and there was no time to waste. She looked him right in the eyes and ordered him with all her power,

"Go out and look for them now. Go out, Jonathan!"

A faint smile appeared on his lips. "What an actor and a liar. She's been interrupted from whatever she was about to do, and now she is giving me orders," were the thoughts going round his mind, while feeling her shaking hands and direct gaze.

"Go out, Jonathan!" she screamed in his face.

He replied, with a grin on his lips,

"You're a very good actor, Natanya, but two can play this game, and I'll show you how I do it."

He turned to the guards,

"Let's raise the bomb alarm. The drill will do everyone good, and we can have our game at the same time."

Then he pushed the shaking girl to the wall and commanded,

"You face that wall, and put your hands up. If you dare to move, Aaron will shoot you."

Natanya lifted her hands up and Aaron stood behind her, holding his gun at her back. The wind was blowing hard and whistling, while she shivered from the cold and the shock of the whole situation. "At least he is doing something about it," she reasoned, trying to calm herself. "I just can't understand the human race. I am only trying to warn everybody, so they don't get hurt, but they treat me as an enemy."

Jonathan gave instructions to Aaron,

"Don't let her move. She is very dangerous, and when the game is over, I shall deal with her. But now let us concentrate on the bomb drill."

Then he blew his whistle, to warn that there was a battle on, and the hostel was surrounded by enemies. The alarm bells were deafening, and in no time everyone had jumped out of bed and headed in their pre-arranged direction. Those whom Jonathan was training donned their gear as speedily as an eagle swooping onto its prey. The others rushed towards the bomb shelter, situated in the centre of the yard. Some of the girls wrapped themselves with their blankets, as they knew from experience that the drill would last for quite a time, and that particular night was the wrong night for such an exercise.

Nearly everyone had to pass by the passage where Natanya was being held, with the gun at her back and her hands above her head as she faced the wall.

"Oh my God!" exclaimed everyone who passed by her. "It's not a drill, it's a real emergency and Natanya is at the centre of it. How horrifying to have an enemy sleeping right in our midst."

Mordecai was terrified and his face turned as white as a sheet. "Oh no, that is just impossible! Not my daughter, she can't betray her father?" He tried to calm himself. "I suppose I should never have got involved with her in the first place, but she is so kind, so caring. I can't believe she is acting." He shook his head in disbelief, although the evidence told everyone that she was behind the problem. "Well, I do admire our Jonathan," he said to himself. "How he managed to uncover her intentions just a few days before she actually performed her evil deed."

The same remarks were made by others, and, when Mark heard them, he felt very pleased with himself, and declared loudly and clearly to everybody,

"It wasn't Jonathan who uncovered her plot, as I warned him just a few nights ago."

"Did you?" they asked with surprise.

"Yes. Go and ask him. In fact, he couldn't see her real person and admitted to me that he was stupid and blind not to see anything wrong in her."

"You are a genius," said one of the girl soldiers with admiration. "But how did you find out, as she is very pleasant and kind, always gentle and happy? How did you discover her real person?"

"Well, I am very experienced in reading people's personalities, so it didn't take me long to draw the whole plan she had in her head."

The twenty members of Jonathan's team stood around him to receive their instructions and assignments before they left on their mission.

"We only have a few minutes," he said, repeating Natanya's words, "and there are bombs all around the place, so go out and search with the utmost care. Any bomb you find is to be reported to me immediately. We'll be divided into the same groups as yesterday, as it's too urgent to reassign the teams now. One team will start from the gate and then take the east side, round to the north. I'll join the team searching the other way, after I've covered the rest of the south side, from the gate."

Aaron felt left out of the game, as he was a member of the team.

"You're the only one of the whole team who has an enemy to guard, so your part is more important than all the others. When the game's over, we'll punish our enemy severely," said Jonathan.

Then he commanded,

"Start now."

The two groups saluted and rushed outside, holding their torches and long metal detectors.

Although only a few minutes had so far passed since the bomb alarm was raised, the whole hostel had been disturbed, all the rooms emptied and the search teams deployed outside, working hard, and enjoying the challenge of the game. The only one who was really anxious was Natanya, and she kept her eyes shut tight in anticipation of hearing an explosion at any moment. As her hands became numb and tired, she rested them on her head.

"Hands up!" shouted Aaron, pushing the gun in her back.

She felt lonely and desperate. "Pray, Natanya," she told herself. "Don't resent the treatment and waste valuable time in self pity, as life is in danger." She lifted up her eyes and prayed, "I beg you, Father, to forgive them, as they do not know what they are doing." She paused after she said those words. "How strange," she thought, "my redeemer passed through the same situation in the past. He tried to show love and save life, but nobody believed his motive or recognized his love. I can feel how he must have felt on that day." Her thoughts pictured the loving redeemer, with his hands nailed to the stake. "It must have been an agony," she said, squeezing her hands as she imagined the nails piercing through, fastening them to the cross. "He did that for me, and for everyone, so they can see the pure love, the redeeming love, and his wish is to show that same love to others, with no resentment, no wall of hate. Yes, he died so we can live."

She shut her eyes and prayed, "Father, help them to find the bombs and don't let anyone get hurt. Help Jonathan. Please my Lord, open his eyes, as only the living can find and praise you." She felt a warm feeling inside her, of love and affection, peace and serenity.

Abu Mansour and his son had their ears glued to the radio.

"This will be the best way of instantly receiving the latest news," he said to Mansour.

"That's if they managed to plant the bombs alright," answered Mansour, holding his head from the pressure.

"At any rate, they must be out of the area by now, because soon the milk delivery and other traders will be starting."

"Father, I can't take any more pressures. I don't care if the traders are about to come or not, they know they have to plant those bombs today, as they will never be able to repeat this night again," answered Mansour, his face pale from the tension, and the whole day's fast with his father.

Jonathan was angry with himself and boiling inside his chest. "She's made a fool out of me. 'Bombs, many bombs', what a story! I'm glad I prayed to my God last night and he uncovered her to me so clearly. Bombs! The guards have just been outside, and there is not a single person or vehicle; only the howling wind and the leaves." He kicked the leaves with his boot and stamped on the ground as he said, "I will punish you, Baha."

He paused for a moment, "But what I can't understand is what was she trying to do outside her room at this hour?" He shone his torch on the leaves as he thought. "Why, Natanya? Why two personalities? One, an angelic person, tender and loving, and the other a deadly cunning serpent, a murderer." He kicked another pile of leaves. "She had the audacity to order me, 'Go out, now'. What a girl! What an actor! If I did not know the in's and out's about her, I could have believed her eyes. Now the entire hostel has been disturbed. The poor boys, searching around at this time of night, in such weather, it's just not fair."

He stopped, looking around. "I can't call them back, as they are eager to play the game; but you wait, girl, I'll let you pay for the discomfort of all these people."

Menachem was very excited about the exercise, as he told his companion,

"It's funny, we've just patrolled this area, and we thought how the leaves would make a natural covering for bombs. You just look at them, they're all neatly piled and heaped by the wind. Maybe Jonathan used them to hide the bombs, so I think we should concentrate our attention on every pile we find and then I bet you we'll win this battle."

Jonathan was staring at the ground, although his mind was thinking of the strange girl that he loved and detested at the same time. Suddenly he noticed that the leaves had been disturbed just a few feet away from him. He stopped and shone his torch around where he was standing and said, "These leaves have been moved by someone."

He carefully poked around his feet with his detector and heard a faint beep. "I wonder what that is?" he muttered, as his heart speeded up. His hands trembled slightly as he pointed his detector closer to a pile just a few feet from the hostel wall and the beeping grew louder. He followed it and gently removed the pile of leaves and then froze for a moment, as he found himself looking at a parcel.

"Oh no! Oh my God, is it...?"

He felt too shocked to mention the fearful word. He drew closer and heard the bomb ticking.

"It is a bomb! Natanya is right, and I have wasted so much time." 'Many bombs around', he could hear her words. He picked up his walkie-talkie and sent an urgent message to the Centre,

"Help urgently needed. We are surrounded by bombs. Lay road-blocks immediately around the entire area."

Then he sent another message to the police. No sooner had he finished that than Menachem radioed in his first find,

"We've found our first bomb, but it's set, so we're defusing it."

Jonathan immediately contacted the whole team and warned them,

"This is a real battle. It's not a game."

He had never before felt so desperate in his whole life, and tried hard to think clearly. He next sent a message to the rest of the boys and girls, telling them to come out and help in the search, as they only had a few minutes, according to the time set on the two bombs found so far, which they were defusing, and he did not know how many were still around. The other team sent details of their find,

"We've found a big bomb, which we're defusing. There's only a short time left, as it's set for three a.m."

The army quickly and efficiently laid road-blocks and sent bomb disposal experts to the hostel. The police also despatched a team of experts, with tools and equipment. The local hospital was alerted and ambulances sent. The whole hostel area became a hive of activity; people, vehicles, alarms and flashing lights. The army set up flood lighting to help the searchers in their work.

Abu Mansour's team had just left the area and safely hidden themselves when the road-blocks were erected. They hurriedly switched on their radio, to hear what had happened to their bombs, because, as far as they knew, their plan had been successful so far, except for the small delay.

"I doubt if they will find those bombs," said Hamid, smiling for the first time that day.

"I wouldn't be so sure, Hamid," replied Hassan. "These people are like cats, they have nine lives and you just can't get rid of them easily."

"Well, they only have a few minutes before the bombs go off and there's no way they can discover them all, as no one was around, and the guard was not aware of us, so I think we can congratulate ourselves right now."

Jonathan and his team were now aided by dozens of others, who worked so hard that the sweat ran down their faces, as they wasted not a second in their hunt. While the wind howled and whistled, a senior officer asked him,

"How many bombs have you found so far?"

"Five altogether, all the same size and design and with the same time setting. My great anxiety is that I don't know how many are still hidden around the place, so I think we'll have to move everyone away in a few minutes time, in case we missed any, because we don't want any casualties."

"You and your team are doing marvellously, Jonathan," remarked the old man. "Don't worry, we can use our bomb robots to comb the immediate vicinity around the hostel and then extend our search to the adjacent areas later."

Aaron was still inside, watching the great activity shared in by everyone else except himself, and he felt very disappointed. He could hear the bells and sirens and see the lights, and there he was, with the boring job of holding Natanya against the wall with his gun. Suddenly she interrupted his thoughts.

"Aaron," she said, with her hands still above her head. "Tell Jonathan there is a bomb outside my room. That is the last one, no more bombs after that, so they do not need to waste any more time searching."

He immediately lifted his walkie-talkie and repeated Natanya's words to Jonathan.

"Natanya says there's a bomb outside her room, and no more after that. It's the last one."

"Thankyou Aaron, we'll search there immediately," replied the anxious and weary man.

He ran with two of his men, who were now very experienced in recognizing the heaps of leaves.

"There, a fresh pile of leaves!" he exclaimed, as he pointed his detector at it. It started to beep. "Let's deal very carefully with this one, as time's running out," said Jonathan, squatting next to the parcel he had just uncovered. The perspiration poured down his forehead as he carefully defused the deadly device.

The senior officer ordered everyone to move away from the hostel area for the next few minutes, in case there were more bombs still hidden.

Jonathan carefully cut the vital connecting wire and noticed he had but two minutes to spare as he finished. Then the three of them ran away from the wall. He had covered a few metres, when he stopped and turned round, looking at the hostel. His heart almost stopped.

"Oh no," he shouted in dismay. "Aaron and Natanya are trapped inside!" He grabbed his walkie-talkie and shouted with all his strength, "Aaron. Run to the shelter and make sure Natanya is with you. You only have one and a half minutes before the place might be blown down. Run quick, and look after Natanya."

Natanya heard the loud call, too. Aaron seized her hand and they ran towards the shelter in the centre of the yard.

"Can't you run?" he screamed, as he was terrified and Natanya was slowing him down, as she had no shoes on, and the pebbles on the ground were hurting and pricking her feet. They entered the cluttered bomb shelter, for the girls had left their blankets and other items they had brought with them, when they rushed out to help in the search. Natanya looked around the room and asked,

"There is no table?"

Aaron stared at her, perplexed by her strange question. She noticed his surprised face, so explained,

"Tables are good for hiding from bombs. I know they are very good." Then she burst out giggling, as she could not help laughing at the expression on his face.

"What a strange girl, everyone is panicking and she is so calm that she can even joke in a serious situation like this," he thought, looking at her soft brown eyes and happy face.

Jonathan began to shake while the seconds ticked slowly by, as he anticipated a huge explosion at any second.

"I should have searched that far corner," he exclaimed, covering his mouth with his hand.

"You've done your best, lad," said the officer, patting him on the shoulder to encourage him. Then he added, "Your guardian angel must be camping around you, as the damage which would have been done by the bombs found so far could have killed everyone here ten times over."

Jonathan looked at the officer and gazed into his eyes, then said, with worry and anxiety in his voice,

"I know, but I am always taking him for granted." He paused before continuing, "My angel actually camps with us in the hostel." He touched his top pocket, to feel the piece of hair, and added, "My angel is next to my heart and is always asking God on my behalf."

The officer laughed and gave him another strong pat on the arm and said,

"That's the spirit I like to see in my young fighters."

Then both raised their left arms to watch the seconds tick by. The seconds hand moved over the set time, but everyone continued to peer at their watches, as they stood at a safe distance from the threatened buildings.

When a minute beyond the set execution time had passed, Jonathan raised his two hands and cheered. Then the entire assembly of soldiers, police and others raised their voices and cheered and praised the God who had saved their lives from certain calamity. When Aaron and Natanya heard the cheering, they too lifted their hands towards heaven and cheered. Aaron almost hugged his prisoner from joy, but noticed himself just in time, and moved back from her.

"Now our work is about to start," said Jonathan to the officer. "We have to analyse the situation to discover from where the bombs came, who planted them, and how they managed to perform such a perfect plan right in the heart of Israel, without anyone being aware of their activity, except my angel."

He turned towards the hostel and said,

148

"I have an important duty that I must deal with before I do anything else." Then he ran inside the gate.

Abu Mansour and his son were waiting beside the radio at their base in Jordan, impatient for the news. Badrawi and the execution crew sat round the table in their hiding place, also listening to the radio.

"What's happened?" asked Hassan. "Not a word so far about the hostel. Do you think they found the bombs?"

"I'm not sure, but my heart is very anxious," replied Hamid. "Maybe we should have checked the setting carefully, as I have a feeling that maybe we didn't connect the wires right."

"Don't be stupid, man. Of course we did, the clock was ticking in each parcel, so there was nothing wrong with our wiring. The problem is that Jonathan's in that place, and has a nose like a dog. He can sniff explosives from a mile away."

Badrawi lifted his hand to silence the worried men.

"Shush, it's the news," he announced.

They all hushed.

"This is the Voice of Israel broadcasting from Jerusalem. Here is the news. A state of emergency has been declared as a group of terrorists successfully planted a great number of time bombs around a large army hostel. The local team of officers, helped by the army and the police, succeeded in defusing all the bombs. Road blocks have been set up to...."

Badrawi hit the radio set with his hand, sending it flying across the room, still continuing with the news. Hamid collapsed onto the table, while Hassan held his stomach and declared to the rest of the team,

"I'm going to be sick!"

Jonathan ran through the gate and headed for the bomb shelter. He halted at the door, and saw Natanya sitting on the floor, next to her guard. They both lifted their heads together and saw Jonathan standing at the head of the stairs, looking tired and hot, with his top shirt buttons undone, to cool himself down. Aaron jumped up immediately and smiled sheepishly, as his captain had found him sitting down on the job. Natanya stood, watching the tired figure, and felt deeply sorry. Jonathan interrupted the silence, while looking at Aaron.

"Thankyou very much Aaron, for looking after Natanya, and also for contacting me about the last bomb, because we just managed to defuse it in time. We would never have found it otherwise, and it would have caused a lot of damage, plus both of your lives."

Then he turned to Natanya and continued,

"You come with me, Natanya. I would like to talk to you in the office."

She looked at him with concern, as she hated the word office, because it meant interrogation and punishment. She walked out of the room just a few steps ahead of him as he turned to Aaron and said,

"Aaron, you can go and join the others, for you did miss a lot of fun."

He saluted with delight and charged toward the gates.

The icy wind was still blowing, and Natanya felt cold as she only had her light pyjamas on, so she held her arms around herself to keep warm, as she marched in the direction of the passage.

"Go and put on some warm clothes and shoes," said Jonathan, gently. "I'll wait for you in the office." Then he left her and went to his office.

"Why does he want to see me in the office?" she asked, anxiously. "Maybe he thinks I planted the bombs." She felt so shaky as she shut her door and began to take off her pyjamas. She could still hear the crowd outside, the sirens, the shouting and the laughter. "Oh my Lord, what is he going to do to me? Maybe he will send me back to the prison, and then I'll be back where I started; no progress. It's all just a waste of time."

Her tears streamed down her cheeks as she felt depressed. "I have done my best to love my enemy, but the problem is that my enemy does not want to see my love or my works. They just don't believe me." She put on her prison shirt, with the band around the sleeve having a big letter 'alef', whose meaning was still unknown to her. Her thoughts wandered to Abu Mansour's camp. "I remember these same feelings of depression when I was doing my love project at the camp. I had almost given up when I met Baha, and we became the best of friends. I won her, and helped her to see the road of love, which brought her happiness and joy."

Feeling encouraged by these thoughts, she put on her sandals and left for the office.

Jonathan sat at his desk, waiting for the angel. He heard her footsteps approaching, then her gentle tap on the door.

"Come in, please," he called out.

She entered, pale and anxious, and stood by the door, looking at him. He rose immediately, as if a senior officer or hero had just walked in.

"Please come in, Natanya, and close the door behind you."

She did so and walked across to his desk, standing opposite him.

"I am very sorry for the way I treated you today, and every day, since you came here. Please forgive me."

Natanya could not believe her ears and her mouth opened slightly from the surprise, as she looked at the officer who had threatened her with great punishment only an hour ago.

Jonathan repeated his request.

"Will you forgive me, please, Natanya?"

A soft smile broke on her lips and she said,

"I am not upset with you."

He understood she did not hold any bad feelings against him, so he continued,

"I want to say thankyou very much for what you have done today, and for all the hard work and care which you have shown to everyone here. I also thank you on behalf of all the boys and girls in the hostel, and on behalf of the country."

"That's just incredible," thought the surprised Natanya in her heart. "How could that ever be? It just shows you, never jump to conclusions too quickly," she told herself.

Jonathan watched her expressions and waited for her answer before he continued.

She raised her hands toward heaven and said,

"Thanks to God. He opened our eyes and ears, so no one could get hurt. My God let me hear the men outside my room, saying in Arabic, 'This is the last bomb and we only have a few minutes to get away'." Then she shrugged her shoulders and modestly said, "I did nothing, nothing at all."

Jonathan looked at her in amazement at the way she answered his question, as he just could not puzzle her out. "This girl isn't natural," he thought, while looking at her open, friendly face, and gentle brown eyes. Then he sounded his puzzlement aloud.

"What I can't understand," he said, "is how you can do so much for your enemy. You almost sacrificed your life today, as Aaron was about to shoot you when you ran towards him, ignoring his warning. I had told him to shoot you if he saw you acting suspiciously; so how can you go so far for the sake of your enemy?"

She looked at him a bit hurt, and said with emphasis,

"You are not my enemy. No one here is my enemy. I have no enemies anywhere."

Jonathan's heart disappeared into his stomach. He was so anxious, and immediately asked,

"Who are you then? A Jewess?"

"No," she calmly replied. "I am Christian."

Then she proceeded to explain, in her very limited English,

"I have many reasons to love you all. First, because you are the relatives of my Redeemer, for he loved you and came to show us all how to love each other. But even if you are not his relative, I still have to love you, because he said, 'Love thy enemy', and he is right, because the moment I love my enemy, he is no longer an enemy, but my love."

Jonathan stood staring at the strange girl. "So, she is not a Muslim, but a Christian, believing in our relative. I see," he thought and pondered, "so Baha became a Christian. What a strange event, what a queer world! I can't figure it out." Then he spoke his thoughts out loud.

"I killed both of your parents in one day, dragged you out from underneath the table, and brought you here as a prisoner, yet you still find room in your heart to love us?"

Natanya could see the puzzlement in his eyes and face as he thought hard. "Exactly like Baha; she was so surprised when I told her I was in the camp to love everybody, and she found it difficult to comprehend. Now Jonathan is also baffled, even though the answer is so simple." She smiled softly before she expressed her thoughts in words, shaking her head gently.

"You did not kill Mama and Papa. They died a long time ago."

She paused and brought to mind the dreadful memory of that night, as her eyes stared far beyond the wall of the room into the distant past, her hands trembling and her soft eyes clouding with tears. Jonathan stood looking at the sad eyes, but he kept quiet, waiting until she had overcome her emotions. She looked at him and could see how he was listening to her with understanding. She had hardly spoken in detail before about her parents, although she desired to, but there had been no one to confide in, except her heavenly friends, but somehow she felt she

152

could tell Jonathan, as he never interrupted. She wiped her eyes with her hands, smiled sadly and continued,

"A big bomb was put outside our house by the Muslim militia, and I lost all, all, my baby, my brother, all. I ran under the table and was alone. That is a long time now. Then I had a new father, and Mother Teresa. I have so many brothers and sisters, all alone, too. Bombs killed their mamas and papas. We all cried a lot and hated a lot, but I also think a lot, all night I think. The Father said I must think good things. At first I think bad things and pray a lot, to go and kill my enemy. The Father said that Jesus will not hear me because he loves everyone, including his enemy, and he died so they can live. That is why he has no enemy." She paused and giggled, as she could see the logic of the statement, and how it sounded ridiculous at the same time.

Jonathan found her experiences fascinating and tried hard to follow her pattern of thinking, as he also had enemies whom he hated, it being impossible to love them. As she had overcome the obstacles, then hopefully he could copy her pattern.

"I spent the night thinking, and then I found my enemy, the real one."

Jonathan's eyes widened. She covered her mouth to hide her smile, as she could not help but laugh at the reaction this sentence always produced in those who heard it. "The Father and Mother Teresa were shocked, Baha almost fainted, and now Jonathan is really frightened."

Jonathan stood staring at the very strange and interesting girl, not bothered by the sounds and activity which was taking place outside. She pointed to herself and said,

"I found my enemy here, inside."

Then she attempted to explain, using many gestures to illustrate her point, as her English was limited.

"This enemy is I, a very big I, that, when I want to love, I, this one," she pointed to her heart, "say 'no'. But thanks to God, after a long time thinking, I can love my enemy. It is very easy. Then I went to the camp to tell everyone that I love them, I forgave them, and I was there when you came."

Jonathan held the desk with his hand to steady himself, as he realised he had been afflicting an innocent person all the time. "I have just written very strong words against her," he thought, while still staring at her. "I gave a strict warning so everyone would watch her. Oh, my God, what am I going to do? I love her even the more."

Natanya stood watching her new friend in whom she had just confided, and waited to hear his verdict.

"If I let this information out, she will be released immediately and returned to Lebanon. Then I will lose the best friend I've ever had, in fact, more than a friend. So I must keep these facts to myself and never let one word out of this room."

He paused as he attempted to justify his proposed action with his conscience and his heart. "I am sure God sent her here to show us a new way of love, and I shall make sure she is well compensated for what she has suffered. I'll be everything to her. The main thing is that she must stay here with me; I need her."

At last Jonathan opened his mouth and thoughtfully said,

"I'll try to comprehend what you have said, Natanya, and I will think seriously about this conversation. Also, may I say again, thankyou very much for everything."

A smile broke on his lips, then he stretched out his hand and shook her's firmly. She smiled sweetly and said,

"Yes, do think, think all the time. It is good to think, because then you will find the way."

Then she turned round and left the office, leaving him still standing by his desk, watching her.

Jonathan sat down, his head going round and round, numb from the information he had just received. "What a divine love!" he said, holding his head between his hands. "No obstacles, barriers, or even death can stand in its way. A Christian orphan, going to the camp of murderers to show them love, and call them friends. She did the same to us, yet I struck her in the face and ill-treated her; but today is the last day of such behaviour and, from now on, she will be the heroine of this hostel, and the queen of my heart!"

The door opened suddenly and the senior officer entered.

"Oh, there you are," he said, walking towards him. "Did you deal with your urgent work?

"By the way, the boys have finished combing the area and found nothing else. All the bombs have been sent to the Centre for investigation."

Then he paused as he noticed Jonathan, with his head between his hands, looking shocked and pale.

"You don't look well, but I suppose it isn't surprising after all we've passed through."

Jonathan stood, and started to move away from his desk, saying,

"I must talk to everyone before we leave for the Centre, as I must thank and commend them for all their hard work and tell them about the girl that did so much to save our lives, while willingly sacrificing her own."

"Who is she?" asked the old man, with interest.

"Natanya, the Arab prisoner we have from Lebanon. She is the one who raised the alarm."

Abu Mansour and his son heard the news on their radio. Mansour was heart-broken, he just sat down and wept and sobbed like a little child.

"After all that hard work, all the training, all the planning, and not one bomb exploded!"

"Never mind, Mansour, we will continue our struggle. We'll think of other methods and other ways. I suppose we can consider it a victory in one way as all our men are safe, and we had no casualties among them."

"Yes, but it seems you have forgotten that Jonathan will be planning revenge on us soon, as he will study every piece of those bombs, and raid us again."

Abu Mansour was unhappy and desperate himself, but he put on a brave front and said to his son,

"Get up, Mansour. We will win one day. We'll wipe them from the face of the ground, and deliver the Holy Land from their grip. So, let's go back to Lebanon and start a new campaign, as I feel there's nothing better than the individual sniping, one here and one there, and they soon mount up."

CHAPTER 6

KIDNAPPED

Jonathan stood in front of a full audience, to summarise the events of the night that had turned the hostel upside down, and brought the area to a halt. His shirt was still half open and his eyes red and tired, like most of the others, for hardly anyone had slept that night, and the morning sun was now just rising above the horizon.

"We must bless our God, who has saved our lives this day from a great calamity. I'm sure you're feeling the same as me; happy for the great salvation, but sad and horrified at the dreadful plan that was designed to kill innocent people, peacefully sleeping in their beds. However, I must share with you a ray of hope, a pleasant thought that brightens the way and refreshes the heart."

Everyone, including the senior man, listened with interest to the young officer. Mordecai was sitting at the back of the hall, full of mixed feelings, as he, like the rest of those present, did not know exactly what had happened. "Is Natanya an enemy or a friend, a true daughter of mine, or a traitor?" he wondered.

Jonathan continued,

"Thanks to our God, who gave us a friend in Natanya."

At this, everyone looked at each other in surprise, yet, at the same time, it was not unexpected.

"All of us are indebted to her for our lives, including me."

Then he explained how she had defied the guard to sound the warning.

"From this day on I want all of us to treat Natanya as a friend. No more bossing and shouting, for she has proved beyond doubt that she is a brave, unselfish and loving girl. I also want to commend you all for your clear thinking and diligent, hard work."

He stopped for a few seconds to allow his audience to quieten down a little, then, with a smile in his eyes, he said,

"No doubt you would like to know how many bombs were planted and who found them?"

At this they all cheered and raised their hands.

"Well, our team found all of them, six in number, and they were enough to destroy the hostel many times over. We are also very grateful for the assistance given us by the army and police, as they offered us substantial help and moral support."

The atmosphere in the hostel was one of celebration for the whole day as no one felt like working, and did not, except Jonathan, who had to leave with the senior officer for the Centre, to finish the job. Mordecai spent the day rushing around, happy and bubbling with joy, telling everyone he met,

"I knew Natanya is an excellent girl. I personally brought her here from the prison because I could see she is wonderful!"

Mark had mixed feelings about the Arab girl.

"You can't be too careful," he said to a group of soldiers. "You just think of it, she had to raise the alarm because her life was in danger, for if those bombs had gone off, she would have been shredded to pieces, especially as one of them was right next to her room. It was self-preservation, not an act of heroism."

"I disagree," said Aaron. "She's a very brave girl. I stood guarding her for the whole time, and she was so calm, even having a good sense of humour, in the midst of such a dreadful situation." He looked to the others with a soft smile, then finished his observation by saying, "I like her, very much."

Natanya was the most satisfied person in the hostel, singing to herself as she prepared the meals. She paused from time to time, to look out of her kitchen windows, as the hostel was a centre of great attention for the entire day, with army and official vehicles coming and going, uniformed officers touring around, looking everywhere and discussing the previous night's events, with excitement one minute and anger the next, then bursting out in laughter, with hands and eyes lifted towards heaven, offering thanks for the miracle.

"I am so happy today," she said in her heart. "At last I have found someone to talk to, someone who can share my thoughts. I sensed from the beginning that Jonathan is different, as he doesn't shout and is very sincere." She felt her pockets, one with each hand. "I will look after his treasures and pray for him, so he can have a happy life with his love, the beautiful girl." She found herself thinking about her own future. "I wonder what will happen to me?" she asked, as she peeled the potatoes. "How long will I stay here? I suppose it doesn't make any difference anyhow, as I have no family or home to go to in Lebanon, except the orphanage, of course. I wonder if the Father will take me in, if Jonathan releases me?" She stood washing the vegetables while deep in thought about her future. "Poor Mordecai, he is my Papa, my Israeli pa. If I leave...."

"Natanya," interrupted the cheerful Mordecai, coming towards her. "I want to tell you how proud I feel about you." He hugged her, while she looked at him with a smile on her face and said,

"I didn't do anything, Pa. I am proud of my God."

"I know, but God uses nice people like my Natanya. Everyone is so happy, so excited. Look," he said, pointing to the yard, "all these people are happy. It's very good."

Jonathan worked with the experts all day, analysing the information they had discovered, so enabling them to build up a picture of those responsible for the bomb plot. After many hours hard work he said to his co-workers, with regret in his voice,

"It's my fault those murderers were able to escape. I could have easily caught them, but I'm a stupid man."

The senior officer heard his remarks and objected,

"I do wish you wouldn't belittle your efforts all the time. You're seeking perfection, lad, and, I'm telling you now, you're almost achieving it." Then he went on to prove his point.

"You and your team found and defused six devastating bombs, in the most difficult weather conditions, with leaves covering the ground, which made the situation impossible, and in a very limited time. So what else do you want to achieve?"

Jonathan lifted his eyes towards the old man and kept quiet, as he could not reveal his secret, even though he wished to give the credit where it was due.

The officers sat round the table, with Jonathan standing at its head, to summarise their findings.

"These bombs have come from Jordan and are made from American materials, similar to those supplied to Jordan for their defence. That means the head of the plot has free access to Israel from Jordan, most probably a trader, an Arab trader. At the same time, this trader was working with Abu Mansour, for I noticed a slip of paper with the trade mark of the Muslim militia on it, a sword inside a crescent, representing the holy war against Israel. That means Abu Mansour should be in Jordan right now, which is why we've had hardly any attacks in Lebanon recently."

The officers looked round at each other, then at the tired and weary man.

"The first thing I suggest is this," he continued. "We must tighten up security at the border with Jordan. Secondly, we must clear the leaves from around all military installations and hostels, in fact, from all important buildings, especially those housing a lot of people. Another immediate precaution is to increase patrols, but the great problem is to be aware of Abu Mansour's next move."

The men nodded their heads in agreement.

"He'll be very disappointed and angry, and will take revenge on our boys with bitterness and severity, so we must warn our men to keep their eyes open, and to avoid the areas where they could be easily trapped or sniped at."

Then he held his head with his hand and said,

"I'm too tired to think properly, but I hope to sit down and think more clearly after a good night's rest." He smiled and added, "I hope, Im Yirtseh ha-Shem."

Jonathan was driven back to the hostel by one of his friends. He was looking forward to a refreshing shower and a glance at his angel. "It's been such a peculiar day," he thought, looking out through his window, as the car sped along the road. "So much has happened, so many revelations. The problem now is how to deal with all this information."

"I bet you're ready to go to bed, Jonathan," said Peres, awakening him from his thoughts.

"Yes, I am looking forward to it, but whether I shall be able to sleep is quite questionable."

"Surely you can sleep tonight, as you will have so many guards around, that there's no need for any worries about the outside."

"True, my only problem is...." and then he stopped in mid sentence, as he was about to repeat Natanya's words, 'the big I'.

"What is the problem?" asked Peres, curiously.

"I find my brain is very active at nights, and I think a lot."

"You'll just have to order yourself to sleep, Jonathan," advised Peres.

"I'll try," he said, bringing the conversation to a halt.

At the hostel, Jonathan enquired from his room mate about the day's happenings.

"It's been such a long day, so much has happened, so many people going in and out for the whole day, that now I feel quite exhausted, and I want nothing except to go to bed and have an uninterrupted night."

"You mean you don't want to eat?" asked Jonathan, pulling his friend's leg.

"Oh well, I mean after my meal, of course."

"How is Natanya?"

"She's been very happy. Everyone has made so much fuss of her, especially Mordecai. I don't know how many times he's told me how he feels about her."

"Yes," said Jonathan, wanting to know more. "How does he feel about her?"

"Very proud. But I feel very anxious," added Mark.

"What for?"

"I feel we are now in danger from Natanya."

"Don't feel that way, Mark," said Jonathan, understanding his friend's anxiety. "She's a very remarkable girl."

"I don't feel so. What she did today was only self-preservation."

"No Mark, she was almost shot; but, at any rate, let us take her as she is. She has been wonderful to all of us, and we must repay kindness with kindness, that is justice. No more suspicions and no more distrust. I personally like her, very much."

"Oh no, not you as well," said Mark, turning away.

"Who else said that?" enquired Jonathan, feeling a bit jealous.

"Aaron. He's absolutely hooked on her."

Jonathan felt very anxious and worried. "She's mine, I loved her first. I must let her know before somebody else gets involved with her."

Mark noticed him staring into the distance and guessed what was in his mind.

"Wakey, wakey," he called to Jonathan. "No need for all that gloom. What will you do if I tell you what the other boys said about her? Natanya is their hero for today, but they will soon calm down and forget all about her, and then we'll return to the bossing and shouting."

The dining room was opened by Mordecai, who was in a very good mood, joking and shaking hands with the boys and girls.

Jonathan had a big hug and a few friendly slaps on the arm, but he was watching the boys, as his heart was full of concern.

"Where is Aaron?" he asked himself, looking around. "Ah, there he is, enjoying himself with the rest of the team. I shouldn't feel so anxious," he counselled himself. "In fact, I should feel proud, like Mordecai, and share Natanya with the others. She is our hero for today, and mine alone forever."

He pushed his tray along the counter, looking at his angel.

"Jonathan," said Natanya with delight. "You tired?"

"Tired, but happy," he answered, smiling.

She smiled and filled his plates, added two extra spoons and said,

"This is good. You like it."

The meal was tasty and delicious, especially as everyone was hungry and the atmosphere good. Mordecai announced that there was plenty of food left if anyone desired more. Aaron was the first to stand and take his plate for a refill. Jonathan watched him carefully, begging in his heart, "Please Aaron, leave my Natanya alone." He wanted to go and hear what was being said, but Natanya had already piled his plate with so much. "Stupid boy," he thought. "She must love you; can't you see she gave you two extra servings. You mustn't feel so jealous." Nevertheless, he continued to watch Aaron smiling and talking to her, and her smiling and speaking in return.

Everyone went to bed early that night. Natanya was very tired and worn out, but feeling on top of the world. She prayed, and thanked her God for what he had done, just when she thought she had wasted her efforts. She thanked Him especially for Jonathan, her new friend. "I do believe," she said in her prayer, "that your words are truth, and happy is the person who believes in them, as they will always establish their purpose."

Jonathan went to his bed, exhausted; and anxious to solve his many problems. "First of all I must think of a way to make Natanya my own." He started to plan. "I must introduce her to my parents, very tactfully, otherwise, if I make the slightest wrong move, they'll put a full stop to it." He arranged his thoughts on how he would broach the subject with them. "I'll write a letter first thing in the morning, God willing, and just mention her in passing, telling them about what she did today, and see how they react to that." Then he thought a bit further, "But what if she doesn't love me? She's never worn my ring. I wonder why? There must be a good reason; maybe she lost it and is afraid to tell me. That could easily happen to anyone." He settled down with that reason. "I must go to sleep, otherwise I'll be good for nothing in the morning. I need a fresh mind to think." He smiled to himself, "After all, my angel advised me to think a lot to find the way." He closed his eyes and went into a deep sleep.

Abu Mansour and his son left Jordan for home, in grief and mourning. They felt defeated, and were filled with bitterness, hate and unhappiness.

"I don't know how to face everyone," said Abu Mansour, as they sat on board the plane. "They have been idle for all these months so we can have Jonathan in the hostel, to finish him. I just can't understand why Allah did not answer our prayer."

Mansour kept silent, as he felt very despondent.

"I feel very bad to meet your mother, for she was so proud of us, and hoped so much we would succeed, but now we're returning, sad, defeated and absolute failures."

"Father," exclaimed Mansour in desperation. "If you speak any more words like that, I swear I'll go and commit suicide. I want to forget about Jonathan and Israel, the Israelis and everyone."

The plane landed at Beirut airport and the two men were met by some of their comrades.

"Welcome back home," said Shakir. "I can't tell you how much we missed you and your leadership. We felt so lost, just like sheep without their shepherd."

"It's been a very hard and trying time," said Abu Mansour. "We worked so hard, and all for nothing."

"It doesn't matter," Shakir said, consolingly. "At least none of our boys got hurt, plus you gave them a terrifying night. That night must have cost the Israelis a lot of money, as the news report said that most of the army was camping all night around the hostel, searching." Then he added, "I feel we did defeat the Israelis, because they didn't catch our team."

"Don't you believe it, Shakir," said Abu Mansour. "They're already making life as hot as hell on the border, so that Badrawi has had to cancel his trips for the coming months, as he was sure they were closely following him."

Om Mansour and her daughters prepared a small celebration for her husband and son, and invited the militia leaders. She was so delighted to see her men again after such a long time. She hugged her son and greeted her husband, saying,

"It's so wonderful to see you back. I've never been so lonely and unhappy as I've been this time."

"Unfortunately," said Abu Mansour, "we have no good news for you."

"To see you both is the best good news. Now we can celebrate together, because our boys are all safe and well."

Mansour sat thinking about life in general, and Baha in particular, while the men were eating and discussing the plot and what took place in Jordan. He thought of his unfulfilled dreams. "What is life?" he asked himself. "Just to live wandering from one country to another, planning to kill and destroy, while the real life passes by. My beautiful Baha, I used to love to talk to her, confide in her, and just speak for hours. Now she has gone and left me, and I have ended up a defeated man, a failure. I've lost my love and lost my battle."

"Mansour!" shouted Shakir. "What's happened to you, man? Is this a strange situation? Aren't we struggling all the time? You shouldn't feel so bad, as tomorrow will be different, tomorrow we'll have a new hope rise with the sun."

The word 'hope' brought Amal to his mind, it being the same word. Now there was a 'new amal'. A smile broke on his lips and all the men cheered when they saw it, but none guessed what was in his mind. Out of the blue he said,

"I must go and visit Baha in the hospital tomorrow."

The men hushed and Abu Mansour looked away.

"She's my cousin, and I've missed her a lot. I must go and talk to her."

"If it will make you happy," said his father, "then go and see her by all means, but I have a feeling she will upset you even more, and what a miserable life we'll have for a few weeks."

Mansour cheered up as the new hope brought a ray of joy. "At least the subject will be different," he thought. "She will be telling me all over again about love, the pure love. But at least it's a lovely subject and she will cheer me no end, with her happy face and thrilling smile."

The little celebration ended in the small hours of the morning, as there was so much to talk about and relate. Mansour had just a few hours sleep, before it was time to meet Baha. As soon as he awoke, he started to worry himself sick about how she would treat him. "I wonder if she will talk to me?" Then he advised himself, "The best thing is to stay off the subject of killing and enemies, and just keep the conversation on our past dreams, and remind her of her promises to me. Mind you, I do feel ashamed of myself, as I didn't buy her any presents from Jordan. I was so concerned to get rid of Jonathan, that I even forgot my manners."

He bathed himself and got ready, spending quite a long time looking at himself in the mirror, to make sure that, after such a long time, he was smart enough to meet his love. He went to the city centre and bought her some presents. His heart was anxious about her reaction, but at the same time he was extremely excited.

He bought a bouquet of flowers, then headed for the hospital. His heart started to beat faster, and his stomach felt agitated, as he entered the reception and enquired about Baha, 'the nurse'.

"Who are you?" asked the receptionist.

"I am Mansour, her cousin," he replied, holding the flowers in one hand and the parcels of presents in the other.

She looked at him distrustfully, as she knew Baha had come from the orphanage and was now living in the hospital residential home, so she said to him,

"Please sit down in the waiting room, and I'll enquire about her for you."

He thanked her and sat down on a chair in the hall outside the reception room. She rang the ward where Baha was working and asked her,

"Do you know someone with the name of Mansour?"

"Oh yes!" said Baha excitedly. "He's my cousin, and a close friend as well."

"He is in the hall here, waiting for you with flowers and presents. He's a very good looking man, too."

"I'll come straight away and see him," she said. "I'm free for the next half an hour."

She ran straight to the washroom, where she combed her hair and powdered her face. Then she ran to meet her long lost friend, forgetting all the bad feelings. As soon as she walked in, he jumped up from his seat, his face shining with delight. He wanted to hug her, so put the flowers and presents on the seat and embraced her.

"Baha, the light of my eyes, I can't tell you how much I have missed you, and how much time I've spent thinking of you."

164

Her face glowed with joy to see him, and her eyes misted with tears. She answered him with a big smile,

"Funny, last night I dreamt that you came to see me, and now my dream has come true."

He picked up the flowers and handed them to her, looking at her soft brown eyes. She smelt them and said,

"Tislamly, but honestly, you shouldn't have gone to all this trouble."

"What trouble, my dear heart? This is just a little reminder to tell you how much I love you." Then he picked up the parcels and gave them to her.

"Mansour, you are a boy! What is all this for?"

"I told you Baha, I need you and I want you. Please do come back to our house, then we'll get married and fulfil our dreams that we used to share together."

She looked at him and paused for a while, then she turned around and said,

"Let's go and sit in that corner; then we can talk in comfort."

They walked together and sat next to each other. She put her flowers and presents down on the adjacent chair, and smiled to the waiting eyes. Then she said,

"Mansour, you know what happened that day, when my uncle threw me out and declared that my blood is 'mahdour'. So how can I go back?"

"My beautiful Baha, he didn't mean it, and he is very sorry. I'll do anything to protect you, my love, so please come back."

"I am very happy here, Mansour. The atmosphere is different, and, although we see the most horrifying cases of injured and ill people, I feel I am doing something constructive. I'm helping to heal the broken-hearted and bind wounds, so how can I go back to an atmosphere of hate, and planning to kill all the time?"

He looked at her gentle face, thinking of her sincere words, as those thoughts had also crossed his mind; but,

"What do you suggest I do then, my only one?"

"I recommend the advice that Amal gave me, because, I swear by God, it does work. I never used to be happy, but I was always a slave of fear and burdened with the heavy load of hate, and then I tried Amal's advice, 'Love thy enemy'. It was very difficult at the start, I know that, but the minute you experience it, you really feel happy, a hero, because you've been able to conquer the ugly beast."

Mansour interrupted her and said,

165

"Please Baha, don't preach to me. Amal was quite enough, and she caused all my trouble."

"No Mansour. Amal brought a new hope to us in the camp, and she demonstrated it by her work. You remember her love-project; just to show us that it's possible to love the enemy."

"Baha," Mansour said with exasperation, "before I came here, I promised myself that I'd keep away from the subject of enemies and killing, as I understand your views. I only came to ask you to come back, so we can share our life together, so you can be beside me all the time. I do promise you that you can keep your views, and practise your love-project, but I must fight my enemy, because it's Allah's wish to do so."

"I am sorry, Mansour," said Baha with regret. "I love you very much, and think of you all the time, but I also love everybody else, no matter who they are, Muslim, Christian or Jew. If any one should come to me for help, I would do my very best to help them. Even if it was an injured Israeli, I'd look after him."

Mansour's face turned red with anger, and he sarcastically asked,

"Would you look after Jonathan if he came to you?"

"Of course," she answered without any hesitation. "He is just a human. What difference does it make? I have no enemies, not one in the whole world."

Mansour stood up and turned to leave, before he lost his temper.

"Don't go yet, Mansour. Please stay for a little while."

"No Baha, we have nothing in common. Better you live your own life and I will live mine."

"Please don't say that. We have a lot in common, except one point, which is love of our enemies. But Mansour, I promise I'll wait for you, no matter how long it takes, until the day when you find this type of love, and then we'll get married, and have everything in common."

He turned away and walked outside the room, leaving her watching him with sadness. She picked up her flowers and presents, and went back to her ward, despondent and heavy-hearted.

Mansour went home, disappointed and more frustrated than ever. He sat alone in his room, avoiding everybody. His father noticed his gloom and knew the reason behind it, but his mother was quite surprised.

"Mansour," she called, "what happened? You left as happy as a lark and now you are so miserable. Where have you been and who did you meet?"

Mansour sat quiet, looking at the pattern on the carpet and ignoring her.

"Did you meet any Israelis?" she asked.

"No," answered Abu Mansour. "I advised him not to go out, but he insisted, so now we have to put up with this misery for weeks."

Om Mansour looked from one to the other, wanting to help and ease the pain of her son.

"Where did he go? Can't anyone feel for me?" she anxiously asked.

"He went to see Baha, and I guess she is still loving her enemies!" said a grinning Abu Mansour, looking at his wife.

"Baha!!" she repeated, with surprise, as she knew about the prohibition. At the same time, she was keenly interested to know how Baha was doing, as she missed her.

"How is she?" she asked Mansour, walking over to him and sitting down at his side, waiting for the information. "How is she, Mansour?"

Mansour stood up and shouted his answer,

"I do not want to know about her, nor do I desire to hear her name again in this house. As far as I'm concerned, she is dead forever, so please don't mention her anymore." Then he stalked out of the house.

Jonathan was now putting Natanya's advice into practise and thinking all the time, trying to find a method of solving the unsolvable problem he had on his hands. "How can I induce Abu Mansour and his people to stop fighting us?" He wondered, and searched for hours in the silence of the nights. "How can one get through to these people that we only want to live in peace in our land, without this waste of time in fighting, and training to fight and kill? I personally would like to get married, raise a family, and live happily with my angel, who has shown me a new way of dealing with hate, but how can I convince the Arabs, or anyone else who wants to annihilate us, of that fact?"

He pondered about how Natanya was able to love her enemies, no matter who they were. "She demonstrated her love by work, her care and kindness. She got rid of her worst enemy, the 'big I', as she called it." A gentle smile appeared on his lips,

"I think I'm on the way to conquer my enemy and I'll teach the team a new way to overcome, too. But my immediate problem is how to convince my own parents to accept Natanya, as so far there's been no reply to my letter."

The burden of his conscience was dragging him down. "She could be released from here right away, but I can't let that happen, no matter what the cost. I'll compensate her for all the hardship she has suffered and ensure that everyone knows what a unique woman she is, but I must tell her about my feelings and intentions, before someone else does so." He started to worry, as he knew how popular she had become since the bombs' episode. "Aaron watches her all the time now. He is a lovable boy, friendly and thoughtful, and their personalities do match. If his heart gets involved with her, that will be my biggest tragedy ever." His heart ached so much, as he saw how trapped he was. "If only I could speak to her alone, but there is no privacy in the hostel. I can't take her out, and whenever I see her, my tongue has the habit of sticking to the roof of my mouth. I really must try next time, and tell her in black and white that I love her, and will be the happiest man in the world if she will marry me, or at least wait for me, until I can think of a way out of the problem."

The Sabbath was the most boring day of the week for the residents. Even the food was plain, no matter how Natanya tried to make it look attractive on the tables. The usual meal was salad, cheese, yogurt and an abundance of bread; nothing hot, as work was not allowed. The boys usually spent the time in the common room, reading or watching television. Some went to the local synagogue, but the majority sat yawning or moaning, until the day was over.

Natanya noticed how nobody looked forward for 'Shabbat'. "That's not right," she thought, at noon one Friday, as she prepared the meal for the beginning of Shabbat. "This day should be the best of all days, a day of joy, when our Heavenly Father gets all the praise. It was an exhilarating day for my Redeemer, as he made a lot of people happy then, because God created the Sabbath to make people joyful and share his joy."

She stopped for a while to think of a way to make Saturday a special day. "I think a special treat, say like a nice iced cake, will give a feeling of celebration." She liked the idea. "Then, if I make potato pie, like we used to have in the orphanage on

Sundays, that will look very appetizing. If I hurry up, I can do all this cooking now, before three o'clock, and the boys will have a good surprise for tomorrow." She put down her knife and ran to find Mordecai.

She found him sitting in his office, dozing.

"Mordecai," she called softly to awaken him.

"What's wrong now, Natanya?" he asked, giving her a worried look, as he felt he could not bear another bout of excitement like the previous month's bomb scare.

"Nothing wrong," she said, looking at him with a smile covering her face. "Tomorrow is Shabbat."

"I know tomorrow is Shabbat," he said, giving her a puzzled look.

"I want to make the boys cakes and other things, so they feel good."

He was surprised at her answer, but pleased at the same time. So he smiled and said,

"No work on Shabbat, Natanya, no work at all. Everything has to be finished by four today. You know the rule."

"I know," she said. "I make it now, only take a few hours. I used to do a lot of cooking. It take no time, but it make everybody feel good."

He rose from his chair and went near to her, saying,

"Natanya, the boys are here to learn how to fight, not to have a party."

She felt sad and disappointed, so said with pleading eyes,

"God make Shabbat for us to learn how to love, and to be happy. I do everything now. No work after four," she repeated.

Then she waited for his answer, looking at him with her soft, gentle eyes.

He thought, while watching her, "It's good to give the boys a surprise. It will make them happy." So he said,

"Okay, but you must finish on time, otherwise I'll be very upset."

"Good." She smiled and hurried toward the door, then stopped.

"One more thing," she said.

He began to get agitated, not knowing what else she was going to ask for.

"Can you write, in Hebrew, 'Happy Shabbat'?"

A big smile filled his face. He withdrew his pen from his pocket and wrote in big clear letters on a piece of paper, 'Shabbat Shalom', and gave it to her.

"Thankyou," she said, and ran to the kitchen.

She sang all the while as she prepared her food.

"This is a real love-project," she told herself. "I love to make everyone happy, then they can see the love of God."

She baked the cakes and prepared the meal for the following day.

"I'll hide it from everybody, then tomorrow, God willing, I'll set the tables and watch everyone's faces."

She prepared the icing, and while she waited for the cakes to cool down, she finished her cooking for the evening. The sink was now overflowing with dirty dishes and bowls.

"I'll do that last, because I must finish icing the cakes before anyone comes," she told herself.

Mordecai went to see what his daughter was up to, as time was progressing, and the smell of baking filled the entire building. He entered to see the slabs of cake, one for each table, and Natanya busy, carefully copying the Hebrew lettering.

"Ha," he said, with satisfaction. "That looks very good."

She lifted her eyes and smiled, then bent down again, to concentrate on her decorating, saying,

"As soon as I've finished, I'll hide everything, so no one can see them."

"Yes, we mustn't let anyone see," said Mordecai, feeling excited himself, and he inspected the cupboards, to find room to secrete their surprises.

"I'll put some here, Natanya," he shouted.

She nodded her head approvingly, so he came and took the decorated slabs and put them away. He looked at his watch and then saw the big pile of dishes and other cooking utensils. "I hate washing-up," he said, "and I don't think she will be able to finish all that on time." Then he sounded aloud his fear,

"Natanya, no time left, and all that washing must be cleared before Shabbat starts."

"I know," she answered calmly. "We have a lot of time."

As he was becoming so agitated, he thought the best thing would be to leave her alone.

The young fighters returned early to the hostel on Fridays, so they could bath themselves and prepare for the Sabbath.

"Lovely smell of cooking," said Mark to one of the girls. "Better we eat as much as we can today, because I hate salad," he said to the laughing girl.

"Yes, I agree Mark. Cheese and salad isn't my favourite food either."

Aaron passed by the kitchen and became aware of the wonderful odour of baking, so he opened the door and stood there, looking for the source of the appetizing smell. Natanya was just closing the cupboard door, after hiding her last item of food. She looked at him and smiled, thinking, "Thanks to God, I hid it just in time."

Aaron saw the pile of washing and thought, "Poor girl, she is running late today. I'll go and give her a hand." So he entered and shut the door behind him, disappearing from view just as Jonathan came into the passage.

"Oh no, I must stop him," he said, speeding his steps towards the kitchen door. Then he stood still, as he could hear conversation.

"Natanya, you have so much washing to be done, and soon Shabbat will start."

"I know, I late," she answered in English, as that was the language everyone used when they communicated with her.

"I'll help you wash-up, as we don't want Mordecai to get upset."

She smiled, and said in appreciation,

"You are very kind."

"I am not kind, Natanya," he replied, rolling up his sleeves. "You have been a good friend to me. You helped me first, so I will help you, too."

"I helped you?" she asked with surprise.

"Yes, you told me where the last bomb was planted, and our team won the battle, for the first time in months. We found four, and the others only found two." Then he stopped and looked at her,

"Natanya, let us make an agreement that we will be good friends like this, forever."

Jonathan grasped the handle to open the door, "Please my God, keep Natanya for me; you know I have loved her for such a long time now."

Aaron continued, before Jonathan had gathered his courage to interrupt,

"Give me your right hand."

She did so, with fascination oozing from her eyes.

"Now we face Jerusalem, as God dwells in Zion."

Then he bowed his head and she did the same.

"O you God of Israel, you be a witness today to this agreement, that Natanya and myself shall be good friends, just like Jonathan and King David; so that, whenever we need help in any way, we shall come to each other's assistance. And may this friendship last forever, and nothing sever it, not even death."

Natanya's tears dropped from her eyes, as she had never anticipated to win such a friend, with an oath. So she prayerfully said,

"Amen, amen, amen."

Jonathan also repeated, "Amen, may it be so."

Then he moved from the door and went to his room, relieved and happy. "I shall honour Aaron, as he is my love's eternal friend."

Dinner was served at one o'clock on Saturday, it being a holiday. Mordecai and Natanya were so excited, like little children who were hiding something thrilling from their parents.

"Natanya, we will shut the dining room door and lay the tables, so when the boys come, they will think it is boiled eggs and salad as usual. Then we can see their faces!" he said, rubbing his hands. They set the tables together, arranging the pies and cakes, and, of course, the salad.

Jonathan sat with Mark and others, chatting to pass the time.

"I think Shabbat is the most boring day of the week," moaned Mark bitterly.

"You should rest and refresh yourself," commented Jonathan. "We work hard enough the rest of the week, so why can't you enjoy it, and stop moaning?"

"I don't mind the rest, it's the salad and yogurt that I don't like," he said, looking to the others for support.

"What about Natanya?" asked Jonathan. "She slaves hard all the week in that kitchen, so bear a thought for her."

Mordecai opened the door and stood there, to welcome the boys and girls, and trying hard to hide his grin. Natanya stood at the other end of the room, next to the table where all the big pots of tea and coffee were lined up. Nobody seemed anxious to come for their dinner, but at last Mordecai announced,

"They are coming, Natanya."

She giggled with delight and had a quick glance at the beautifully laid tables.

"Shabbat Shalom," said the first group of young men to Mordecai, as they entered, wearing their skull caps.

"Shabbat Shalom," he replied, slapping their shoulders, and having a big smile on his face.

They walked towards their table, at first not noticing anything unusual, but then they stopped. Natanya glanced at Mordecai, who was covering his mouth with his hand to hide his large smile.

"What's this ?" they asked, looking at the bedecked table, then at the cake, decorated with blue writing on the white icing. 'Shabbat Shalom' they read together and laughed, looking at Mordecai, but he was just welcoming the next group.

Jonathan and his friends walked in, feeling that the room was full of excitement and laughter, but not realising the cause, so they just crossed over to their table as usual. Jonathan looked to where Natanya was standing, and he raised his hand in greeting, with a soft smile on his lips. She was looking extremely happy and trying to cover her face.

"What's happening here today?" he wondered to himself.

"Look at the table, kid," said Mark with delight, attracting his attention. "We have a party!"

Jonathan looked at the appetizing pies, then he read the writing, 'Shabbat Shalom'. He lifted his eyes to catch Mordecai, feeling so touched and pleased at the tender thought, so he called out,

"Come here, Mordecai. You are wonderful."

Mordecai stood next to him with a beaming smile.

"With every passing day you are making this hostel into a beautiful home."

Mordecai shrugged his shoulders and said,

"Not me."

"Who then? Did some of the parents bring these cakes?" enquired Jonathan, as the Hebrew writing looked professionally done.

Mordecai laughed and said,

"No. You are getting very bad in your guessing."

Then, still laughing, he whispered to the puzzled major-general,

"It is Natanya. She said that God created the Sabbath to make people feel good, so she did all this yesterday, to make the boys feel good today."

Jonathan turned to Natanya, but she was busy pouring out coffee for the diners.

The hostel had never experienced such a Shabbat before. Everyone felt like celebrating and some of the boys started to sing after the dinner was over, clapping their hands as they sang some of the popular Shabbat songs. Mordecai went and stood next to Natanya and whispered,

"The boys are feeling very good."

She nodded and said,

"Yes, and I feel very good, too."

Jonathan stood up and clapped his hands for attention. The company hushed.

"I am sure we all want to thank Natanya and Mordecai for making such a treat for us, so now I suggest that we go to the common room and have a good sing-song, to praise our God, who has made all our hearts to feel good."

Everyone clapped and then rushed to the common room.

Natanya stood beside the counter, well satisfied that her love-project had successfully achieved its purpose. Jonathan went up to her, looked at her happy face and said.

"You come with us too, Natanya, and I will teach you how to sing in Hebrew. Then we can sing together for our God."

She looked at him with delight, then glanced at the tables and said,

"I come in a minute. I just do this work."

"No, leave this work, just for today. Now we shall sing and dance, and the work will be done later."

In the common room the happy company were busy preparing to sing. Some were tuning their musical instruments, while others were arranging the chairs. They all looked to Jonathan to choose the first song, so he chose the popular Psalm, "Look, how good and how pleasant it is for brothers to dwell together in unity." Mordecai acted as a conductor, waving his hands for a while. Then he clapped in time with the rhythm for a while, and the next moment he forgot all about his conducting and joined the others in their dancing.

Jonathan sat on one side, to teach Natanya a few lines, so she could join the others.

"It is very easy," he said to her. "You will be able to pick it up in no time. Just look at my lips, and say after me, 'Hinei ma tov o ma-naaim, shevet achim gam yachad'. That means, 'Look, how good and how pleasant it is for brothers to dwell together in unity'."

Natanya smiled with excitement and said,

"I know, I sing that in Arabic; is very good."

"That's good, now we can sing it in Hebrew. Are you ready? Say after me, 'Hinei ma tov'."

Natanya repeated it after him, carefully watching his lips to get the correct pronunciation. She moved from his side, as she was twisting her head so much, and sat in front of him on the floor, so she could watch him better.

"Now you say it alone," he said, just like a good teacher.

She repeated the first verse with perfect pronunciation.

He laughed with delight and commended her,

"You are very good, Natanya. Soon you will speak Hebrew better than me!"

They laughed together, as they enjoyed every moment of the lesson.

The boys and girls started their second song, with everyone having a great time. Mark looked around and noticed Jonathan, with Natanya sitting so near to him. "I see, we are sitting so close, all by ourselves," he said to himself, feeling left out as usual. "Of course, she is somebody now, and he must take the best. He got the promotion, he received the fame, and now he is working himself in with Natanya. I can't leave him alone with her, so I'll go and join them." And he slowly crept across to them.

"Now we can do the second line. You say after me, 'Shevet achim gam yachad'."

Natanya repeated the sentence, so perfectly, so sweetly.

Mark sat on the settee next to Jonathan, who was not even aware of his presence. Soon Mark was absorbed in the lesson, as it was fascinating to see the Arab girl in front of them speaking the words of the song and then singing it. Mark laughed and said,

"That's very good Natanya. You're a very clever girl."

"No," she replied, with modesty. "Jonathan a good a..a.." but she could not find the word, so Mark came to her aid.

"Teacher."

"Yes, good teacher. I feel happy," she said, smiling.

"Now we'll go and sing this song to the others and dance. That will give them a good surprise!" said Jonathan, laughing.

"Yes, we go now," said Natanya, like a little child, with Jonathan holding one hand and Mark the other, to teach her the first steps of the dance.

Mark shouted to everyone to be quiet as he had an announcement to make. The assembly hushed.

"Natanya is going to sing a song for us," he said, still holding her hand, while Jonathan held the other, ready for the dance. "After the first verse, we can all join in."

The boys and girls clapped, thinking Natanya was going to sing in Arabic. Mordecai stood in front of the trio, to conduct the song. Natanya was overjoyed, because she was about to praise her God in the language that Jesus used. Mordecai lifted his hand up, looking very serious, while the audience was in complete silence.

"Hinei ma tov o ma-naaim, shevet achim gam yachad," sang Natanya in a beautiful voice, full of sincere feelings.

Mordecai looked at her with astonishment, then to the surprised audience. In the second verse, Mark and Jonathan joined in, and suddenly the whole assembly burst into song, jumping to their feet and dancing.

The time flew swiftly by, as no one wanted to stop, so they sang and danced, with one song being followed by another. All the while, Jonathan stayed close by Natanya.

"I'll teach you more songs next Shabbat," he quietly said to her, looking at her happy, gentle eyes.

"That is very good," she said, appreciatively. "I will make more cakes and good things, so we will all feel good."

He wanted to tell her about his feelings towards her, but the words stuck in his throat, and the problem was made worse by Mark, who acted as their shadow.

"Natanya," said Mark in his loud, boisterous voice, "I'll teach you more songs next Shabbat."

She smiled and said,

"Jonathan said he will teach me."

He looked to Jonathan and then her smiling face.

"Alright, we can both teach you."

Jonathan laughed and quoted the proverb.

"Too many cooks spoil the broth, don't you think so?"

Mordecai looked at the time and rushed to Natanya, pointing at his watch,

"Natanya, so much work and no time. All the tables still haven't been cleared, and...." but, before he had finished his list, Jonathan interrupted him.

"Leave the tables for me. I'll show you how they will be cleared in a few minutes, and you and Natanya can stand and watch." Then he clapped his hands. Everyone stopped and directed their attention to him.

"We have a little game to play before we end this most enjoyable Shabbat."

The boys and girls clapped to indicate their agreement.

"It's a race between our two teams. The winner is the one who clears the most tables without cas...." and he nearly said casualties, but quickly changed it to, "without any breakages."

The teams formed two lines and marched to the dining room, followed by the rest who would watch the match. Natanya looked at Jonathan with a big smile and excited eyes.

"Aaron is in my team," she said to him.

"He is in my team, too," he replied, with affection in his voice, and quietly, so no one else could hear him.

"Ready?" he called out.

They all saluted.

"Okay, we start .... NOW."

The teams rushed to the tables, speedily gathering the plates and cutlery, whilst trying to avoid knocking into each other, as they juggled with their piles of plates and cups and saucers. Natanya's eyes were on Aaron all the time. He piled up a large number of plates and tried to balance them as he sped toward the kitchen. The excitement was building up in the observers, as different ones shouted support to their room mates or personal friends. Natanya knew Aaron would soon have an accident and lose the race, because his pile was becoming more wobbly by the second. She glanced at Jonathan and then ran towards Aaron as the shouting and cheering became deafening. She kept pace with him, with her hands stretched out to support the pile before it collapsed. Aaron saw her at his side, so he lowered his hands and she quickly picked a third of his pile from him, and they ran together to the kitchen. They deposited their load on the work-surface and ran back to the dining room, but the tables had all been cleared. Both teams then stood to hear who was the winner. Jonathan declared the result.

"Three tables out of five were cleared by team 'A'."

The audience clapped and cheered the winning team. Jonathan raised his hand for silence and continued,

"But," everyone hushed to hear what was coming next, "but both teams had no cas.... I mean breakages. Team 'A' had an extra member to assist, which helped it to win. So, to be fair, I declare the result a draw."

A great shout of joy resounded round the room, and then everyone returned to their rooms after a most exhilarating Shabbat.

That evening the conversation of the residents was centred on one subject, "What a wonderful Shabbat! What a great time!"

Mark repeated the sentence to his room mate, but in his own words.

"With all honesty I can say that I've never enjoyed myself like I have today. I wouldn't mind if we could stay the whole twenty-four hours, celebrating like this."

Jonathan responded with a beaming smile on his face,

"The same here!" and he pointed to his heart. "We sang and danced the whole time, praising our God, for he is good, and his loving-kindness will endure forever. Now we have to wait for a whole week, before we can have a repeat."

"Do you think Natanya will make special food again for us for the next Shabbat?" asked Mark, curiously.

"We'll have to wait and see," replied Jonathan, keeping his angel's promise to himself.

Mordecai was happy and relaxed, as his work had been done in a few minutes. He was also feeling proud of his daughter and he whispered to her, though there was no one else besides them in the kitchen,

"Natanya, shall we make another party for the boys next Shabbat?"

"Of course, Pa," she said, with excitement in her eyes, "But we shall start early on Friday, then I can do better food."

After her prayers, Natanya checked Jonathan's treasures, then she lay down to sleep, with a happy heart and the new songs she had learnt going round and round in her head. "This is the best day I've ever had in my life. It's good to sing praises together." Her mind kept repeating the happy time. "Jonathan is a really good teacher; I like him. He is the best friend I have here, besides Aaron, and both are sweet in their different ways."

Jonathan lay on his bed, dreaming, still feeling the tingling sensation in his being from the memorable day. "I'm sure we'll be in eternal bliss together. Just to be so close to her and watch her eyes was enough to make my heart happy," he thought, recalling every little word she said, and each enchanting smile. "I can never imagine another girl like my angel. She's the best of them all, and I love her more than ever." Then the problem came to his mind, "I'll do my best to prepare just one sentence for next Shabbat, and I must say it. I will just tell her, 'Natanya, I love you'. That is all I have to say and it won't take any time, but at least she will know what I hold for her in my heart." As soon as he had decided on that, he turned toward the wall and dropped off to sleep.

The training continued to progress daily, with Jonathan placing the emphasis on thinking of ways to remove the tools of destruction.

"It could be in a plan," he said to his young fighters, "or even in a thought. For example, we must know how our enemy thinks, as then we can go directly to deal with the root of the problem. In other words, we can outwit him, but, at the same time, we must respect life and do our best to avoid spilling blood, as our aim is to destroy weapons, and not people."

Shabbat was fast approaching and anticipation building up.

"Only one day to go until Shabbat," said one of the girls to Mark. "Then we'll have a great time."

"I'm looking forward to one of Natanya's specialities."

"Honestly Mark," remarked his girl friend. "You only ever think of one thing, and that's your stomach!"

"Oh no I don't. You're wrong there. I do think of other things, too, you know."

"Oh yes," said the girl, looking at him unbelievingly. "Such as what?"

"I'm not telling you, as you belittled me."

She nudged him with her elbow and carried on with her work.

The celebration of the second Sabbath proved to be surpassingly successful, as Mordecai helped Natanya to start early, and prepare well in advance, so there was no pile of washing-up or anxiety about time. Jonathan kept his promise, and taught Natanya more Psalms, but the shadow never left them alone for the entire period. He felt like ordering him to go away, but realised that would be unwise, knowing how Mark thought. "It's better I keep quiet," he told himself. "I'll have to think of a game to keep him occupied for the next Shabbat."

Natanya noticed Mark staring at her with a strange look. "I don't like Mark," she said to herself, turning her head away from him."

"Hey, Natanya," he said. "Come on, I'll teach you a new dance."

"I danced a lot. No more dance for today," she said firmly.

Jonathan looked at her face, then looked examiningly at Mark, and spoke to him in Hebrew,

"I think we'd better give Natanya a bit of a rest. We must have got on her nerves."

"I don't think that's the reason, but she is getting too big for her boots."

"Let's drop these type of words Mark. I find them upsetting."

Mark turned his head away, resenting Natanya's answer and Jonathan's support for her. "If that Jonathan had wanted to teach her a new dance, she would have jumped at it, because HE is the boss."

Aaron noticed that Natanya was watching him with interest as he played his flute. So, after he had finished his tune, he went over and asked her,

"Do you like it, Natanya?"

"Yes," she said. "You clever."

"Not really," he replied, looking to the two boys who were listening to the conversation. "I made many mistakes tonight."

"Mistakes?" she queried, "I hear no mistakes. It is very good, I like it."

"Thankyou," he said, blushing. "Would you like me to teach you how to play?"

"Yes please," she answered gratefully.

Jonathan stood up and said,

"Right, you have your lesson on the flute, and we'll go and join the others, so you can have some peace." Then he winked at Mark.

Mark was surprised that Jonathan did not mind Aaron to be alone with Natanya. "I do find this kid strange," he thought. "One moment he gives the impression that she belongs to him alone, and, when Aaron offers to give her a lesson, he stands up and leaves, as if she means nothing to him." He continued to watch Jonathan closely, but noticed that he never once turned round to see what the pair were doing. "I think Jonathan is an unselfish man," he concluded. "Although I resent him, nevertheless I admire his qualities."

Mark found himself thinking about Natanya. "She's attractive, and cute; in fact, quite sweet. I really fancy her." His conscience spoke, "Be aware, she is innocent, like a little child; keep away from her. She trusts and cares for everybody; why do you think of such things?" He turned round and saw her giggling, enjoying her lesson. "What's wrong in loving her?" he told his conscience. "There's nothing wrong in loving her, if she is your wife." "Oh no, I will never marry an Arab, especially a prisoner, as that will bring my dignity down. Imagine my friends and relatives enquiring, 'Who is she?' and I say, 'An Arab prisoner, a Muslim'. Oh no, no way will I consider marriage."

Shabbat over, the company left to carry out their duties and start work, feeling refreshed and upbuilt by the spiritual songs and happy dances, that impelled even King David to perform in front of the ark of his God. The only disturbed mind was Mark's, as his fleshly desire was corrupting his clean conscience.

Jonathan missed his opportunity to tell Natanya his sentence, so he promised himself as usual, "Next Shabbat I hope, God willing, I will speak to her." Then he recalled Natanya's reply to Mark. "He must have done something to upset her, as she has never spoken in that manner before. I bet he was up to mischief." This thought made him feel anxious and concerned. "I must speak to her tomorrow. I can't leave it till next week, in case something happens." Then he asked himself, "But what could happen? I am worrying myself unnecessarily. I felt anxious about Aaron, but he is Natanya's best friend, and now I am concerned about Mark. I shouldn't feel this way about my brothers, after all, Mark is my friend and we share the same room. He always behaves in this way, boisterous, thinking of his food, and feeling sorry for himself, but otherwise, he does work hard and afterwards regrets his rash decisions. That's why he doesn't progress in the army." Jonathan convinced himself that all was well, rebuked his suspicious mind, and replaced the bad thoughts with happy ones, which soon sent him to sleep.

The wrong desire was now growing in Mark's heart, as he encouraged it and stayed awake at night, thinking of how he could achieve it. "The best time will be when Jonathan goes away, but it could be ages before he returns to Lebanon," he thought. "The other difficulty is Natanya herself. She always avoids me and moves away whenever I go near to her. And so what? I will compel her, frighten her, and if she refuses me, I shall use force. Who does she think she is?" He turned in his bed, planning. "I wonder who are on guard tonight?" he asked himself. "Oh yes, I remember, Aaron and Menachem, the formidable pair. It's better I don't attempt anything tonight, not with Aaron around, as he loves her too, and will kill me if he finds out."

However, the poisonous tree continued to grow, inflaming the young man's passion. "I know, I'll go to Natanya's room as soon as the pair of them go for their patrol, which is now much more frequent, as that's the new rule since the bombs were found; so that's that sorted out. Now Mordecai is my next headache, as he always leaves his door slightly open, to keep his eyes on her." He stopped and considered that obstacle. "He's getting quite old and will be deep in his sleep. Nothing will get him up, not even if a bomb drops next to him."

Jonathan was thinking and planning about how he could move the barriers that stood in his way, preventing him from marrying the girl he loved. "I'm surprised my parents have completely ignored Natanya, as they haven't even mentioned one word about her, but I feel my conscience is clear. I am happy to marry her, for she has proved her love for God by her works, and God chose her to deliver our lives by her unique love. To me she is in the same category as Rahab and Ruth, who became King David's ancestors. If my parents oppose the idea, I shall go ahead and marry her anyway." He interrupted his thoughts for a moment, as he noticed that Mark was unsettled. "I wonder what's the matter with him tonight? He usually goes to sleep as soon as his head touches the pillow, but he's tossing and turning all the time." He thought for a while, as he concentrated on Mark's movements. "Anyway, it's not my business. Maybe he is in love like me?" He suddenly stopped and his heart fluttered. "With whom, I wonder? I don't think he cares much about Natanya, for he told me he doesn't trust her and is not really bothered much about her."

Mark was determined to carry out his plan, as he had managed to silence his conscience. He now waited patiently for Jonathan to go to sleep, but, every time he thought he was asleep, he would suddenly turn. "For heaven's sake, go to sleep kid!" he said to himself in frustration. "I know what he's planning, another of his battles, 'disarming without casualties'. It's become part of his vocabulary. Even when the teams were clearing the tables, the casualties were mentioned twice."

He was paying attention to the movements of the guards, so he heard them leave the hostel. "That's good, that's one obstacle out of the way, and I know Mordecai will be asleep now as it's after one. Natanya will also be asleep, so I can take her by surprise, and, if she resists, I'll threaten her with my gun. Jonathan seems to have calmed down at last, and I think he's gone to sleep, so I can slip out quietly now."

Mark crept out of his bed and put on his trousers, then picked up his pistol and slipped it in his back pocket. His heart was beating so fast he could hardly breathe. He hesitated, "I mustn't do this, it's foolishness and a dangerous step. If anything goes wrong, I'll lose everything." His inflamed passion and lower nature urged him on. "Don't be a coward. You're almost there and then you will have your desire fulfilled. She's only an Arab anyhow, and has killed many of our boys and informed on them, so why care about her feelings? I am more worthy of her body than Mansour." He opened the door very quietly and slipped out of the room, watching Jonathan all the while. Then he shut the door behind him and tiptoed down the passage.

Jonathan was aware of Mark leaving the room. "Poor boy, he must have a stomach upset. I think he's on his way to the toilet," he said, remembering the day he suffered in agony with the flu. "Natanya did ease my pain and really made me feel good. I wonder if she will sense Mark's suffering and make him feel good, too? Anyhow, if she doesn't, I am sure she wouldn't mind me asking for her help, because she's a wonderful nurse, and her hand has such a healing touch."

Natanya had so much to thank her God for, so her prayer became longer and longer. She had many happy songs going round and round in her head and found it so pleasurable to speak to her heavenly Father, to enumerate his goodness. As she started to doze off to sleep, she heard the sound of marching feet outside her wall. "Ah," she thought, "Aaron is patrolling outside. He is my friend forever." She lifted her head and prayed for him and Menachem. "Father, please guard them and protect them from any harm. Open their eyes to see if there is any bomb outside." Then she laid back and shut her eyes as she drifted into sleep, but her subconscious was aware of every movement around her. She heard a door open along the corridor. "I wonder who that is? There is the office, and Jonathan and Mark's room at the end of the passage." She raised her head to listen carefully. "Maybe it's Jonathan working hard in the office," she thought, listening. "No, I don't think that is Jonathan, as he walks steadily and with confidence, and these are very slow and hesitant, the footsteps of a thief." Her heart speeded up, "He must have stolen something from the office; maybe he is one of Abu Mansour's men." The steps came nearer to her door, then stopped. "Oh help me, my God. I think the thief is coming to steal the linen." She sat up on her bed, ready to confront the intruder. The door handle moved slowly.

"Who is there?" she called, with quickening breath.

The door opened and the light from the corridor brought Mark into focus.

"Mark!" she said with horror, her eyes now wide with surprise and shock. "Go away, Mark!"

"Shush, stupid girl," he said, as he quickly entered and shut the door behind him.

Jonathan lifted his head, as he was sure he heard Natanya's voice.

"Go away, Mark."

He heard it again, as she raised her voice.

"Natanya!" exclaimed Jonathan and he shot from his bed, insulting himself as he quickly slipped on his trousers. "Stupid me, always blind, and I end up too late to help!" He rushed out without his shirt and ran towards her room, from where he could hear her muffled voice.

"No! Go away!"

"Stop shouting, or I'll kill you, I have a gun with me. Let me love you, Natanya; why do you hate me so much?" said Mark, as he muffled her mouth and tried to stop her from kicking him and pushing him away with all her strength.

The door opened and the tall figure of Jonathan stood there, shocked and angry, but well in control of his anger.

"Mark!" ordered the firm voice. "Get out of that bed immediately!"

Mark removed his hand from Natanya's mouth and looked with hate and anger to the man who had frustrated his plan.

"Why can't you keep your nose out of my affairs?"

"How dare you touch Natanya, you dirty dog!"

Mark felt himself boiling, as those words summarized him, and touched a very sore point.

"You call me a dirty dog for the sake of this Arab? I'll let you pay dearly for those words!" said Mark, reaching to his back pocket.

"You are a dirty, filthy, dog!" repeated Jonathan, still standing in the doorway, with his bare chest an easy target for Mark's pistol.

Natanya saw Mark pulling his gun and panicked, as she realized Jonathan was not aware of Mark's intention, so she threw herself on top of his back, shouting,

"Don't kill! Don't kill!"

Jonathan moved immediately and rushed to overpower the angry, raging man, and attempted to wrest the gun from his hand.

Mordecai imagined he was having a nightmare as he heard the sounds of shouting and struggling. He lifted his head and looked at the slit opening of his door to Natanya's room, and saw through her wide open door, two men, wrestling on her bed.

"Oh no! What's going on in there?" he cried, as he quickly jumped up, and, still in his pyjamas, rushed across to her room.

"Jonathan! Mark!" he exclaimed, glancing at the desperate and frightened girl who stood beside her bed, shivering and shaking.

"Stop that at once," he shouted. "What are you doing here, anyway?" he asked, with shock and horror in his eyes.

Jonathan finally managed to take the gun away from Mark, and then he stood up and answered the old man,

"Mark attempted to shoot me."

"Mark!" gasped the shaken man.

"He insulted me first; he called me a dirty dog," said Mark, justifying himself.

Mordecai looked back to Jonathan, enquiring with his eyes for the reason behind such an insult.

"He attempted to rape Natanya," said Jonathan, trying to control his anger.

The old man looked at his daughter, and then to the two men. He felt disturbed and spoke in Hebrew,

"Don't let us fight and argue in front of Natanya, as she's already had enough of a terrifying experience. Mark, you come with me to my room and we'll talk there about what's happened." Then he looked with shame to Jonathan. "I am sorry. I was fast asleep, never anticipating that such a thing would ever take place in Israel."

"I don't want anybody to hear about what has happened," said Jonathan, "as Natanya will be so vulnerable. She trusted us, and we have betrayed that trust."

"I agree," said Mordecai. "Not a whisper will be mentioned."

Then he left the room with Mark. Jonathan stood for a moment, looking at the pale and shaken girl, feeling ashamed and sad, angry and disappointed, yet at the same time, with respect and admiration. She watched his sorrowful eyes as she stood beside her bed, holding her hands to her heart.

"I am very sorry, Natanya," he said, with great regret in his voice.

"Sorry?" she asked.

"Yes, I am the one to blame for what happened to you tonight, but I'll make sure it won't happen again."

She shook her head and said,

"You didn't do bad things. I say thankyou a lot for helping me."

He left the room, shut the door carefully after him, and headed for his office. At that moment, Aaron walked in from his patrol and saw Jonathan walking away from Natanya's room, without any shirt. "What's going on here?" he asked himself, and walked straight to Jonathan. He could see he looked angry, so enquired,

"Anything wrong?"

"A tragedy has just been averted, Aaron."

"Is Natanya alright?" asked Aaron, anxiously.

"Yes, the problem is not Natanya, but Mark."

"Why? What's he up to?"

"He tried to rape her."

"What a dirty dog! I'll kill him!"

"No Aaron," said Jonathan. "We don't want any casualties, and I'm the one to deal with him. I only told you this information because I know you are both good friends and she needs your protection, especially as she is as innocent as a child. We must keep our eyes on her, to safeguard her from the whims and desires of the boys. So, for her sake, don't speak to anyone about this matter."

"Of course not," replied Aaron, feeling hot, and his spirit burning within him. "How dare he even think of such a vile thing!" he thought, trying to control himself before Menachem returned to the hostel. He found his hands trembling from rage. "I've never liked Mark, as he lives just for himself, and always talks about how great he is, and now he thought he could corrupt such an innocent person like Natanya. I'm glad Jonathan found him out." He marched round the yard to vent his anger and sort out his thoughts. "Jonathan is a super chief, and a wise observer. How he gathered that we are good friends, I just can't work out...."

"Aaron," called Menachem with astonishment, "what's going on? I saw Mordecai's light on, and Mark in there, talking with him. Then I noticed the office light, and Jonathan without his top on, looking very upset in there. What's happened in just a few minutes?"

"Tragedies can happen in a few minutes," replied Aaron. "Don't you remember that time when we had just walked in from a patrol, having seen nothing, and then the whole army was here a few minutes later?"

"That's what I mean, are there any enemies around?" continued Menachem, with fear in his voice.

"I asked Jonathan, but he assures me that he's in charge, and we are not needed, except to carry on with our duty. So we had better leave them to deal with whatever happened. What does worry me though," he added, "is how do you identify an enemy?"

Menachem thought for a moment, as the question puzzled him,

"What do you mean?" he asked.

"Well, sometimes an enemy can turn out to be the best of friends, and one whom you think is a friend can be your worst enemy. As both friends and enemies are humans, how can we tell which is which?"

"Have you been reading your books of wisdom again, Aaron?" asked the smiling man. Then he turned round and marched off in the opposite direction.

Mordecai asked Mark to sit down and explain his problem to him.

"Consider me like your own father," said Mordecai to calm Mark down.

"There's nothing to say," said Mark. "I like Natanya and desire her so much that I wanted to share my love with her. What's wrong with that?"

"How can you speak like that, Mark?" asked the old man. "There's a great deal wrong with that. We can't go through life doing what we desire regardless of any consideration for others. We are an elevated people because of our high ethics and divine principles. These morals make us human, not mere animals that are driven by debased passion. The other point is this, how could you dream to defile an angel like Natanya? Didn't she almost sacrifice her life to save all of us, so how could you hurt a person like her?"

Mark kept quiet, feeling very ashamed and unhappy.

"Well, I can understand your feelings toward Natanya, but why did you want to shoot Jonathan? He is your friend and our general, who works so hard to protect us and ensure we are all well cared for, so how could you lift your hand against him? Aren't our lives already in danger from our enemies, so how could you attempt to kill your own brother like that?"

"I didn't mean to kill him, but he called me a dirty dog."

"Do you blame him?" asked Mordecai. "In fact, I felt like calling you that, because what you've done is repulsive."

"I am very sorry, Mordecai. I do regret what happened and I wish it had never taken place. I know I've done wrong, please forgive me."

"I think Jonathan and Natanya are the ones from whom you should beg forgiveness," said the old man.

"Jonathan will kill me if I go and see him," said Mark anxiously. Then he added, "And I can't face Natanya anymore, as I let myself down and I feel bad about the whole matter."

Mordecai stood and said,

"I'll go and explain the situation to Jonathan. He is an understanding man." Then he left.

Jonathan was shaking with rage and indignation. He could see her frightened eyes and pale face standing in front of him. "My dear one, I am sorry, I caused all your trouble. I brought you out of your country, frightening the life out of you, while you were working hard to teach people to love and live in peace. Then when you arrived here, your life was one long chain of hardship, but you bore that load in your gentle heart without any resentment, and, as your reward for all that pure love and care, that debased animal had the audacity to enter your room and climb into your clean bed."

He bit his fingernails as he tried to think of a way to solve the problem. "Mark must go. I can't leave him here as he's a wild ass, having no control over his passions." He could hear Natanya's voice, 'Don't kill', ringing in his ears. "How could he do that to me? My own friend drawing his gun to kill me, while the one who is supposed to be my enemy, delivered me from his hand." He pulled out Mark's records and had just started to go through them when Mordecai tapped on the door and entered.

"Please sit down, Mordecai," he said, while continuing to leaf through the file.

"Jonathan," said the fatherly figure.

He lifted his eyes and looked to Mordecai.

"Please listen to me. I must put to you Mark's side and explain the situation from his point of view, before you take any decision about him."

"I have made my decision, Mordecai, and nothing can change it. Mark must leave this hostel in the morning and I do not want to deal with him anymore. Nevertheless, you can put his side if you wish."

Mordecai rubbed his forehead in anxiety and said,

"It will be a great pity if your friendship is severed because of Natanya."

Jonathan kept quiet, staring at the old man.

"You see, Jonathan," he explained, "Mark is a reckless man. He rushes into things and then afterwards sits regretting them.

189

He's very sorry for what he's done, and seeks your forgiveness and Natanya's. Well, I am sure Natanya will forgive him, for she never bears any resentment."

Jonathan knew that statement was right, "I smacked her face and she nursed me. I treated her with harshness whilst she tried to save our lives," he thought in his heart.

"What took place," he continued, "happened because Natanya is a very lovable person. She has a pleasant, gentle spirit, that causes anyone who sees her to instantly fall in love with her, whether they are male or female; because her heart is spacious, having a unique and pure, unselfish love that has no ulterior motive, except the good of others. Mark got attracted to that divine love, but as he only thinks physically, he tried to express his love in that debased way. He knows he is wrong and deeply regrets what has happened."

Jonathan was silent for a few moments, then he commented,

"I can understand that, but what I can't comprehend is the way he pulled the gun on me, while I stood defenceless in front of him, as I never dreamed that my own friend would kill me just like that. In fact, if Natanya hadn't jumped on top of him and thrown him off balance, I would be dead now."

"I know, my dear, that is regrettable, but if I may say this, he didn't mean to do that but he resented the fact that you insulted him in front of Natanya, and he was deeply injured, and as his predictable personality tells us, he rushed to avenge his hurt feelings with the gun. I know he's made a great mistake, but please, forgive him. He wants to come and see you to express his regret. Do accept him."

After a long pause, Jonathan said,

"You can call him, please. I want to talk to him about his future, anyhow."

Mordecai jumped up and went to call Mark.

Jonathan had now cooled down, and could see the situation in its proper perspective. "I will not put what happened in his file, for that would completely ruin his future, but, at the same time, he has to pay for his mistake."

Mordecai re-entered the room with Mark trailing a few steps behind him. Jonathan lifted his eyes and asked both of them to sit down.

"I am very sorry," apologised Mark. "I don't know what came over me, but I let my feelings run out of control."

"I accept your apology. However, it is my responsibility to protect the residents of this hostel, and Natanya is the most vulnerable person here, as she is a stranger and a prisoner. I also have to protect the other girls that reside here with us. So I will not harm your future by reporting what happened tonight, as I know we're all human and make mistakes many times, but I must transfer you from here. Tomorrow you can go to Beer Sheva army hostel. It's a pleasant place and then you shall be far away from the sources that have caused your stumbling. You will be away from me, because I'm certain that the cause of your pulling that gun was not the words of insult but reasons much deeper than that. So then I will not be around to irritate you nor will you have Natanya to arouse your feelings."

Mark felt relieved, as Jonathan had dealt mercifully with him. He knew in his heart that the cause of his hate was the resentment that had been building up, and a new page would do him a world of good, plus he dreaded to see Natanya again. He stood and stretched out his hand to Jonathan. Jonathan stood up too, and with a faint smile on his lips, shook his brother's hand.

"Thanks, Jonathan," he said. "You're very kind, and I do appreciate your help. I'll miss this hostel very much, but you're right, I need to begin a new page. I've learnt so much these last few weeks. Natanya's behaviour has taught me a lot, and your benevolence has impressed in my mind a pleasant memory."

After Jonathan shut the door, Natanya stood beside her bed for a while, as she was afraid to go back to it. She trembled and shook for a long time, listening to the footsteps that kept passing by her room. She knew Jonathan and Mordecai were very upset and were dealing with the problem. She felt sorry for Mark, as she said to herself, "He is the most to be pitied, as he surrendered to the ugly beast that dwells inside him. He missed the pure love that would enable him to think of others, and let lower nature rule him, robbing him the joy of a clean conscience. I'll pray for him, so he can see the way of the true love."

She looked at her bed. "How funny," she thought, "I even hate the thought of a defiled bed. I am so grateful to my God, who let Jonathan hear my shout, otherwise I really would have lost the most precious possession I have, and that is my purity which I'm reserving for my future husband, whoever he may be."

In Lebanon the activity of Abu Mansour and his son was reorganized. Mansour pushed Baha out of his mind and dedicated himself wholly to the struggle.

"We'll fight face to face," he said to his father. "We will select devout Muslims to go directly to the Israelis and our other enemies, and make sure they blow them up by meeting face to face. Of course, we will die with them, but that doesn't matter, as we must use every possible means to destroy our enemies."

He had set himself a difficult task, as to sacrifice one's own life was the hardest decision to take. Mansour had to set the lead and lecture his team daily, working on their conscience until they could actually look to death as the highest pleasure.

Abu Mansour made another trip around his friends abroad, gathering more weapons and money, while his son programmed the brains of his volunteers. Most of his hopeful executioners were young men and women, who had offered themselves to die with the enemy.

As soon as Mansour was confident enough, two members of the team went on the first mission of the campaign. This was to drive a car, full of explosives, directly into the target, the home of a Christian militia leader, which was also used as the centre for their activities and training.

Fahid and Nawal were in their late teens, children of great supporters of Abu Mansour and the Islamic Jihad. Before the young boy and girl started their last trip through the streets of Beirut, their parents and friends gathered to celebrate with them the beginning of their journey to paradise, as everyone believed they were on their way to heaven, to sit at the right hand of Allah. Mansour gave one of his most moving speeches, that stirred the hearts of all those who had gathered to support them, and he concluded,

"Alas, the lot chose Fahid and Nawal to start us on this wonderful road to deliverance, but we will follow their footsteps later."

Fahid took the driving seat, with Nawal sitting beside him to watch the road and traffic, as the car would be speeding, and they must avoid any accident if they were to successfully accomplish their mission. At last they entered the street of their target and Fahid jammed the accelerator to the floor while Nawal called the directions,

"It's clear, press the horn. We're nearly there.... HIT."

The car struck the house with a tremendous impact, causing a great explosion, which sent pieces of masonry flying for hundreds of metres. There was silence for a few moments, as the sudden shock stunned everybody, but when the enormity of what they saw with their horrified eyes had sunk in, of shattered bodies of passers-by landing from the air and the general carnage; then the place turned into chaos, with screaming women and howling children, and men shouting as they gathered momentum to organize a rescue.

Fahid and Nawal died instantly; there was nothing left of their bodies to gather or identify. Ambulances and police arrived, digging and clearing, listening for sounds or any faint cries to guide them to rescue any buried people. Abu Mansour's eyes mingled with the crowd and rescuers to gather information to assess the success of the mission. A few minutes later a car stopped and the leader of the Christian militia emerged, looking pale but grateful to be alive.

"I can't thank my God enough," he told those who stood around him. "Lucky there was nobody at home today, otherwise the whole family and friends would have been blown to pieces." Then he looked around to see the bodies that had so far been laid out by the roadside and neatly covered, and asked, "How many died?"

"At least twenty persons," replied the officer. "Mainly innocent men and women who were just passing by in life's daily routine."

Gradually the picture emerged.

"There was this black car, driven by a young man, and there was a girl with him. They were speeding at about two hundred kilometres an hour or more," said an excited and shocked woman, as she described to the police what she saw. "They nearly knocked me over as they drove directly into the building. It's just madness, absolute lunacy!"

The story was repeated by so many, as they described the details and filled in the missing pieces of the picture.

Abu Mansour, his son, the parents and other leaders of the movement listened to the informers. The mothers of the dead youths began to weep and wail.

"They are in heaven right now," said Abu Mansour to comfort them. "So why do you weep? It's a day to celebrate."

Fahid's mother answered him, sobbing,

"I would celebrate if they had established what they sacrificed their young lives for, but it ended that they died with other innocent people, and some of them were Muslims, too. It's just a waste of life."

Mansour felt unhappy and depressed. "It seems that whatever we do is a waste of time, a waste of effort, and a waste of life," he thought, watching the grieving parents and the sombre gathering.

"We mustn't speak like this," said Abu Mansour. "This time we missed, next time we will hit. How could any of us here predict they would all have the day off?" he asked. "So, it happened we hit on the wrong day, the day which we chose with care from all the days of the year. How could we ever know they would be out?"

After a few days Mansour recovered from his depression, and advised his team,

"I feel we had better go back to our sniping, it's the most successful method. At the same time, we can be ready to die with the enemy if the opportunity presents itself, as I can't see the sense of killing ourselves unnecessarily."

The favourite road for the snipers was the one the Israelis used from Israel to Lebanon because it twisted and turned and had trees and bushes scattered all around to provide good shelter for the snipers. They usually dug themselves in on high ground on the hillsides, behind sandbags, and watched the Israeli army convoys with their powerful telescopes. Whenever it was possible, they would ambush a vehicle and blow it up, but they had to act with the utmost care, for the convoy usually had air cover, which meant that any mistake or error would be dealt with immediately.

Early one morning, Mansour and his men were lying in wait for their enemy to pass by, when a fleet of fighters screamed past overhead, shattering the peace of the dawn.

"They're on their way," he announced to his men, telling them to prepare themselves. Each adjusted his telescope and aimed his long range weapon. After a while an army convoy appeared on the horizon, so they concentrated on their targets.

"They're mainly Red Cross vehicles," said Mansour. "Maybe Jonathan is building a hospital for the infidels."

The other men laughed.

"They're crawling extra slowly today," Shakouri commented.

"I bet you they're carrying weapons to support the Christian militia and are pretending it's medicine," responded Mansour.

Then he pointed his gun at the biggest vehicle and pressed the trigger. All the men ran from behind their sandbags and hid in the caves on the hillside, watching. They saw the vehicle thrown into the air and the rest of the convoy stop. The fighter aircraft swooped down close to the ground and dropped bombs onto the area around the telescopes.

The hit vehicle was carrying a prefabricated operating theatre, equipped with the latest medical equipment, and was being sent to the Red Cross as part of an agreement between Israel and the Christian militia. The driver and his companion were injured and their comrades rushed to give them first aid as the rest made a protecting wall for them with their vehicles.

"Blessed be Ha-shem (the Divine Name)," said one of the drivers. "The injury could have been worse, but one of the walls collapsed and saved their lives."

Shortly afterwards a helicopter hovered overhead, to pick up the two injured men and take them to Tel Aviv for emergency treatment. Soon the two stretchers were lifted up and disappeared inside the aircraft, which then flew away to Israel. The damaged vehicle was taken in tow and the convoy continued its journey, with one important room damaged beyond repair.

Jonathan noticed how Natanya was keeping herself away from everybody since the incident with Mark. She was aware of the danger that could suddenly flare up because of passion, and because the majority of the residents were young men, she kept her distance. "Mark did scare her, and now she's lost her trust in us," said Jonathan to himself, looking at her one morning while she was serving the breakfast. "If I say my sentence to her, I'm certain she'll scream. So it's better I keep it to myself, until she returns to normal."

The phone rang with an urgent message from the Centre for Jonathan. He stood with haste, leaving his breakfast half eaten, and ran to the office.

"Jonathan," said the senior officer, Victor, in an anxious voice. "Two of our boys have just been injured on their way to Lebanon, and we've lost the operating theatre. The animals hit it, even though it was clearly marked as Red Cross."

"I can't understand the mentality of these people," said the angry and sad Jonathan. "I'll pack my bag and we'll see what we can do." Then he replaced the receiver and rushed to organize his team.

They also left their breakfasts and dashed to pack, after which they departed for the Centre. Jonathan felt uneasy and desperately unhappy. "I hate to leave Natanya, and I feel disturbed for one reason or another." He called for Mordecai.

"I'm leaving for Lebanon, Mordecai," he said anxiously. "I want you to guard Natanya with all your power, as I do not want a repetition of what Mark did."

"Of course not," said the old man, looking at the worried eyes. "You leave her to me. In fact, I'll leave my door wide open, so no one will dare to come near her. Please don't concern yourself, and may you have a good trip."

Jonathan then rushed off and found Aaron, who was feeling left out, as he had not been selected to go with the rest of the team.

"Aaron," he called, "I want to have a word with you." Aaron stared at the sad face. "As you have gathered, we have a mission on our hands, and you will be playing the main role in it."

"Me!" he exclaimed in surprise.

"Yes, you," repeated Jonathan, patting him on the shoulder. "I have left you here to guard Natanya for me." Aaron gazed questioningly into Jonathan's eyes. "I only trust you, Aaron, out of all the boys. So please, look after her for me, as she means so much to me."

Aaron smiled and understood what Jonathan meant.

"I promise to guard her all the time; no one will touch her."

Jonathan smiled, and stood looking at Aaron. He wanted to speak to him about his heavy heart, and tell him about the true identity of Natanya, but the time was passing rapidly and he had to go and pack his bag. Aaron noticed the worry and anxiety in Jonathan's eyes. "I have a feeling he is worrying in case some tragedy might happen, and he wants me to take care of Natanya if he dies," he thought.

"Jonathan," he said with understanding. "I'll look after Natanya, as one of my own family. She will be a sister to me."

"May Ha Elohim bless you, you have lifted a great load from my shoulders." Then he hugged him and ran to his room.

Natanya saw everyone hurrying around and the boys leaving. "Oh no, they are going to Lebanon again. When will it all end?" she sighed. "More raids, more casualties, and now they are all my close friends, here and in Lebanon. Why can't everyone see the way of love?" she asked in desperation, as she put down Jonathan's half-empty breakfast plate. "Poor Jonathan, he is very kind and is trying hard to understand. I'll miss him so much when he goes as he always looks after me and will not allow the boys to come near me. Now I will be left all alone." Then she rebuked herself, "I shouldn't think of myself. After all, when did my Lord leave me alone? I must go and see him before he goes, to remind him to love his enemies and not kill, and tell him that I'll be praying for him even more."

Jonathan was hurrying as fast as he could in order to finish his packing. "I must speak to Natanya before I go. She must share my...." and he heard a soft tap on his door. His heart jumped, as he knew who was standing there.

"Come in, please," he called, trying to control his breathing. She entered and shut the door behind her, then walked toward Jonathan, looking at him.

"You going to Lebanon?" she asked, with sadness in her voice and anxiety in her eyes.

"Yes," he replied.

"Why?" she asked.

He understood that she meant why did he have to go to war and fight, so answered her question.

"Because it is my duty. Because I have to. I must go and help my people."

"I be very sad," she said, looking at his packed bag lying on the bed.

"I am sad too, Natanya, but don't worry, I have asked Mordecai to look after you. I also spoke to Aaron, to make sure you will be well looked after."

She felt touched to the heart at his concern and care towards her. She smiled sadly and said,

"I will pray for you, hard, and pray for everyone, that no one will die." Then she turned round to leave, as she felt her tears rushing to her eyes, although she did not know why. "He seems sad and anxious," she said to herself as she reached for the door.

"Natanya," he called. She turned and saw him with an anxious look all over his face. She walked back to him, enquiring with her eyes. He hesitated to speak, as he found that the sentence had disappeared somewhere inside him. "I must say something before she thinks I am mad. Oh, I know, I'll ask her about the present that she never wears."

"Natanya," he enquired. "Where is the little box I gave to you?"

"To keep?" she asked.

"Yes."

She smiled to herself. "I am glad he will take back the little box, because it's difficult to hide. Then I'll only have the medallion." She looked at him as she put her hand in her trouser pocket and withdrew the box, well wrapped in a white piece of cloth. She unwrapped it and the box appeared, still in its original wrapping. She handed it over to him. He was shocked and hurt to discover that the box had never been opened.

"You didn't even open it!" he said with disappointment, looking at her eyes.

"Open?" she queried, with a puzzled look. "You said I keep."

"Yes Natanya, I did say it is for you to keep, as it's a present. I bought it specially for you, to say thankyou for everything, and for your prayers for me."

"Keep.... for me?" she repeated. "I mistake." Then she covered her mouth with her hands and started giggling, as she realized she had misunderstood the word.

Jonathan stood watching her, still holding the box in his hand.

"I open now," she said, taking the box from his hand. As she unwrapped it, she laughed softly and kept repeating, "Keep for me." Then the box was open and the diamond ring sparkled. Her mouth dropped in surprise and her eyes shone with delight.

"Is very good. Tislamly, is really good." She put it on her left hand finger and looked at his eyes. "Thankyou a lot." Next she put her hand into her top pocket and drew out the medallion, and placed it around her neck, laughing, "For me to keep!! I keep for so long in the pocket."

Jonathan could hold himself no longer. He firmly took hold of her arms and said, smiling,

"You are very sweet, Natanya." She looked at his eyes, which were bearing so much love and affection for her.

198

"Natanya," he said softly, "I love you, very much."

She stepped back and her face changed, as she exclaimed in a shocked voice,

"Jonathan!"

"Please Natanya, don't take me wrong. We will get married when I come back from Lebanon, God willing. Then I'll marry you."

"Marry?" she repeated, even more surprised than ever, and took another step, backing away from him. "You can't marry two!" she said, with suspicious eyes.

"What do you mean, 'marry two'? I'm not married."

"You going to marry soon, the beautiful girl."

"Beautiful girl?" he enquired. "I don't know any other girl," he said, looking at her.

"I saw her," she said, pointing to her eyes.

"You saw her?"

"Yes," she said, with positiveness. "She came here. She is very beautiful. I pray every night for you to be happy."

That was a riddle for him. He rubbed his chin with his hand as he thought hard, attempting to discover the girl who kept him out of Natanya's heart. "I have so many visitors coming and going all the time, so how am I going to find the 'beautiful girl'. I don't know any beautiful girl, except the one I love, my angel." He shook his head.

She tried to jog his memory.

"Mark said you love her, and you marry very soon."

"Mark?" he repeated. "That would explain everything." Then he said to himself, "Now who came to see me when Mark was here? Oh yes, I remember." His face brightened, and he asked Natanya, "I know. Was she a blonde girl?"

She nodded.

"She's my cousin, like a sister to me. I have no sisters and we used to live next door to each other when we were in England, and we're just like brother and sister.... Mark is a liar."

She continued to look at him, and believed him.

He went on,

"I have been thinking for a long time that we could be very happy together, just you and me.... Will you marry me, Natanya?"

She thought for a while, as she considered the many obstacles. Then she looked at him and asked,

"How? We too different. You Israeli and I am Arab, you are Jew and I am Christian. I am a prisoner."

"That's no problem," he said, drawing closer to her. "In the history of our people, many Israelis married excellent women from other nations, like Rahab and Ruth, besides others, and I know everyone speaks only good about you. And about religion, we both worship the same God and we sang his praises together on Shabbat. Jesus is one of our relatives, you told me that, and I like his wisdom, in fact, I do my best to practise it, just as you do. When I return from Lebanon, I'll think of a way to take you from this state you are in, but the main question is, will you wait for me, Natanya?"

She stopped and thought, her eyes gazing far away. "How amazing the truthfulness of Jesus' words, that he will give his followers fathers and mothers, brothers and sisters, and joy, because I believed in his teaching and showed love to my enemies. He gave me a father in Mordecai, a brother in Aaron, and a very precious friend in Jonathan, who is now seeking to be one unit with me."

Jonathan waited patiently for her reply. He hated to hurry her up but the time was passing.

"Will you wait for me, my love?" he repeated.

She looked at his eyes and smiled softly, nodding her head.

"I wait for you, Jonathan."

He felt relieved and a happy smile filled his face.

"I am sure we will be extremely happy. I'll teach you more songs and new dances. We can go to England for our honeymoon, where my family have a big house, and then you can meet my parents."

"She smiled and replied,

"I will pray that our dreams come true, and that you come back safe." Then she sighed, as she well knew the bitterness that comes from hate, and did not wish her love to lose his joy. She looked at him with pleading eyes,

"Jonathan, love your enemy."

He held her in his arms and embraced her.

"I do love my one-time enemy, I love you, my darling." He felt like staying forever, holding her so close to his heart, but was already late. "Natanya," he said, "I must go now, but you think of good things, and I will be thinking of you. When I come back, we'll sit together and think of how we can love our enemies."

She nodded and repeated,

"I will pray that our dreams come true. I will think hard."

Then he touched her soft cheek with his finger as he said, "I'll not say goodbye, because you are with me all the time. See," he said, taking the piece of soft black hair from his pocket, "you are next to my heart. I love you."

She smiled and touched her ring, and with both hands she held the medallion which was hanging round her neck. He laughed, took his bag and ran without turning his head, for he wanted the memory of the beautiful smile to be the last impression on his mind.

Natanya stood at the door, watching her fiance, as he got into the waiting vehicle. The moment his foot left the ground, the driver accelerated out of the hostel in haste, leaving behind smoke and a small cloud of disturbed dust. "May our dreams come true, and may our heavenly Father keep you and guard you for me, my dear love," she prayed as she stood watching. She was suddenly awakened from her dreams by Mordecai.

"Where have you been, Natanya?" he asked. "The dining room has not yet been cleared and there is so much work to do in the kitchen."

She looked at him with a big, happy smile covering her face.

"Mordecai," she said, as if she had not heard any of his words. "Look!" and she stuck her hand out, with its sparkling jewel, and then held out the star of David in the other hand.

"Oooh, who gave you these?" he enquired, looking at her happy eyes.

"Jonathan," she replied. "They are for me to keep."

Mordecai looked at her with a tender, fatherly look in his eyes. He understood the meaning of the presents, so he said to her,

"Jonathan is a very good boy."

"I know," she said. "I'll pray that our dreams come true."

Then she hurried away to the dining room, singing one of her happy Psalms, which Jonathan had recently taught her, "Bless the LORD, O my soul."

Mordecai just stood there, with tears of joy filling his eyes. "Who would have ever imagined that my daughter will get married to the best man in the town. Jonathan will be my son-in-law." He repeated her words, "'I'll pray that our dreams come true.'"

Jonathan felt on top of the world. "I can face anything," he thought, as the vehicle headed for the Centre. "Now I know my sweetheart will be waiting for me, and praying for our dreams to come true. I know God listens to her, and she's my angel who has been sent from Him, to help me, and share my love and joy." He wanted to sing and whistle, as his joy was overflowing.

The driver noticed the happy face next to him. "Jonathan is marvellous," he thought to himself. "He's just going to Lebanon, where heaven only knows what will happen, and here he is, singing away. He must have so much confidence."

Everyone was waiting for him at the Centre. He entered the conference room, where the various heads of different teams were sitting round the table. He apologised for the delay.

"I had a certain important matter to deal with before my departure and the time just flew by. Anyhow, I will not waste any more of your time, so please, fill me in with the details."

Victor produced the facts and the record of events, explaining when and where the incident happened, and gave all the known details of the picture. Jonathan took the pieces and went to his office, to digest the information and draw up a plan of revenge. The other officers withdrew to their various departments, to think up their own ideas to help their leader in fighting back at the enemy.

Jonathan spread out the evidence in front of him, and stared at the information, deep in thought, with his chin resting on his hand. "I can see one thing as clearly as the sun at noon," he thought. "These people are desperate. They recently made an abortive suicide attack on the Christian militia, and now they have shelled a Red Cross vehicle. These are sure signs of desperation and they seem to have gone wild, sacrificing their young sons and daughters to die with their enemies. That indicates they have lost all sense of reasoning, as their hate has blinded them from nature's strongest instinct of self preservation."

He sat there for a long time, thinking and planning, devising a scheme with love as its basis. "I believe this is the best solution. I know it worked in Natanya's case and in my last mission, so I hope the rest will approve of it. Anyhow, I can only do my best."

It was late in the afternoon when Jonathan met with the officers for their discussion. He looked confident and calm as he stood to deliver his proposal. His audience admired his approach to the problem, as his gentleness and quietness was catching, inspiring strength as it spread to the others.

"I have studied the problem with the utmost care," he said, "and this time have approached it from a slightly different angle. I still believe most strongly in disarming without casualties, as the evidence so far shows that it's a very successful method, because our boys are suffering less frequent attacks, with diminishing injuries. I am certain the reason for this is that each time we raid, we disarm, giving us a long period of peace, until they can refill their stores to perform the next attack. This brings me to my new scheme, but, before I mention it, I must tell you what I noticed about today's attack."

The officers concentrated on every single word the young commander uttered, unable to stop marvelling at the way he tackled the problem.

"I observed from this attack, and the suicide car incident, that the people with whom we are dealing are mentally disturbed, so no logic or reason will solve the problem with them, no force will stop their violence. It's like this, imagine yourself meeting with an insane man who is carrying a dangerous weapon. You will not really solve the problem by shooting him down, because human life is sacred. Therefore, you must do two things. One, you need to protect yourself before you meet with him, and second, you must work out a delicate plan to disarm him and then, after that, ensure that he never again lays his hands on weapons. However, before the last step, you must try to help him regain his mind, either by medical treatment or psychiatric help."

Jonathan paused to allow his audience to digest his logic. Then he continued,

"Abu Mansour and his men are desperate, as their sources of money and arms are drying up. So they mentally programmed and trained some young men and women to effectively use what few weapons they still possessed, even though they would act against all sense and die in the process. In other words, we are dealing with dozens of mad men and women who are carrying the most destructive tools in their hands and are willing to use them against others and their own selves."

"Now," continued Jonathan, "the question is this. How are we going to deal with them? The first step is to prepare and cover ourselves well, before we attempt to meet with them. Then we will disarm them. Lastly, we think positively to seek ways to help them return to normal thinking."

The officers glanced at each other, some with smiles on their lips, while others looked puzzled.

"I intend to achieve my objective by what I call 'flushing' tactics," said Jonathan. "We will take Abu Mansour's entire camp, divide it into sections and systematically clean every section from its weapons, but not destroy any homes or property, because we're only interested in removing their dangerous tools. By this method we will be attempting to convey to them that we are not there to harm them, but rather to protect ourselves and them from destruction."

Peres, Jonathan's second-in-command, whispered to Baruch, the head of the air forces,

"Is Jonathan in love?"

"Why do you ask that?" asked Baruch in surprise, staring at Jonathan under his eyebrows.

"Because he is dreaming, living in a fairy world. Flushing?! Helping?! What next?!"

"What's dreaming about that?" said Baruch. "I agree with him. It makes a lot of sense."

The other officers were also whispering and disputing among themselves, some supporting whilst others opposed. Jonathan noticed that his audience was divided, so he understandingly said,

"Please, feel free to sound your objections, because the last thing I want is a divided unit. Let us have the objections and any alternatives and weigh them together. I feel we must start to think of far-reaching solutions, because we're trapped in a deep chasm, as, with every violent retaliatory raid we perform, we slip deeper and farther from the opposite side, bringing us both closer to destruction. So we must try to climb out, by taking positive measures, which will elevate us and make us rise to the proper image of God. Though our climb may cost us a tremendous effort and much time, we will rise higher, until we reach the top of the chasm. Only then will we see the light and leave behind us the bitterness of hate, the scars of wars, and we will be able to live in peace, to raise our families in security. Therefore, we must think carefully now."

Victor, the Centre's senior officer, asked thoughtfully,

"How will you do what you call 'flushing'?"

Jonathan smiled and answered the old man,

"Our team is becoming expert in disarming the enemy, and I have a number of ways to choose, but let us first agree on the principles of the battle, and then I'll give you details of the raid."

Peres stood up to voice his objection,

"I feel we are sacrificing our boys lives by bending over backwards to protect the enemy."

"What do you suggest then, Peres?" asked the wise leader.

"I would do what we usually do. A swift attack, blow up the entire territory. That's fair, it's justice. Why should we have to work hard to protect their lives, while they blow up our people?"

The feelings of the men started to become inflamed, and the majority of the officers took the side of Peres. Jonathan could hear the words of Natanya ringing in his ears, of how she found it difficult to conquer the only real enemy she, and every other human, has; her own hate that dwelt inside her. How she spent nights awake, thinking, until she found the answer in the advice of the wise relative who lived two thousand years ago.

Jonathan spoke calmly,

"What were the results of our previous methods, Peres? What did they achieve? Please give us the results, so I can put them on the other side of the scale."

The audience hushed, as they too tried to find evidence to support Peres.

"We caused a lot of destruction and casualties for our enemy."

"What about our troops? What about our security?" asked Jonathan.

"We lost some of our boys."

"I can think of more than just our boys. Do you remember the nursery school? How many parents are still suffering heartache?" asked Jonathan. "But we disarmed Abu Mansour and had no more rocket attacks on our border towns, plus we've had less casualties ourselves. At the same time, we considered the lives of our enemy, because they are human, the same as us, and created by God. So it's really an act of faith and worship to respect human life, and I can assure you that our God will make sure no harm overtakes us; I know that from a personal experience."

Then Jonathan related his story,

"I am sure you know about the bombs that were planted by Abu Mansour's men around the hostel. Six of them, large enough to blow up half the town, were discovered in a short period of time, and not one scratch resulted. How do you think that calamity could ever have been averted if our God was not protecting us? And how could he ever protect us unless he was pleased with us, and why is he pleased with us? Because we are doing our best to care for human life."

Then he concluded his speech by quoting the famous scripture, "If God does not build the house, it is in vain that the builder works hard, and if the LORD does not guard the city, it is in vain that the guard stays awake."

The officers clapped their hands for a long time, as they felt encouraged and supported by the invisible God. Baruch stood up and said,

"I will personally support your method of dealing with the problem and you can count on my team to give you every assistance possible."

Victor added his support, too.

"I always have confidence in your tactics, because you take time to consider and weigh up the problem, without bias or partiality. So go ahead, and do whatever you feel best. After all, you're the one in command, but thankyou for letting us express our thoughts, without your becoming exasperated."

Jonathan and the officers moved to their planning office, where Jonathan detailed his strategy.

"It should take about two weeks," he said in conclusion. "But if we carry it out as planned, we should achieve a complete victory, with God's help. The main points are these, first, we must take great care in building our protecting walls, which are, as I have already explained, the armoured vehicles and our air cover, which must shelter us continuously. The second point is that our frightening technique must be administered perfectly. Then all that's left is to pray for protection and wisdom."

The team heads agreed to start extra early in the morning, to prepare their teams for the first stage of the two week operation. They were in a relaxed mood, as they could see the wisdom of avoiding violence, and gradually working for a peaceful solution with the enemy.

Jonathan was preparing for bed, when he glanced at his watch and saw it was almost midnight. "What a long day!" he exclaimed. "So much has happened. Imagine it, today my angel agreed to wait for me, and I haven't even had any time to sit and dream of her! But I can have a few minutes now, to dream myself to sleep with my sweet Natanya next to my heart."

Jonathan lay dreaming on his bed, without any worry about the next day. "I've never felt as happy as I was this morning, when I held her so close in my arms, heard her gentle voice, and gazed into those beautiful eyes. It made my whole body tingle with delight." He dreamed for a long time, reliving every moment they had shared together in his room, especially her laughter when she discovered her misunderstanding of the word 'keep'. "I had been worrying myself silly about that ring, but she had kept it safe all that time, to wear for our engagement this morning," he said, smiling to himself. "I've never met such a sweet person in all my life, and I'm a very lucky man to have such a precious present in the form of Natanya." Then he whispered, just before he shut his eyes in sleep, "I love you, my sweet Natanya."

At the hostel, Natanya lay on her bed, thinking and dreaming, praying and singing in her heart. "How lucky I am," she said. "Even in my wildest dreams, I never thought that Jonathan would ever consider me, as I'm only an orphan, with nobody to call my own, or even to turn to when I'm in need, except my invisible friends, but now I have the best man in the whole world, to love me and hold me in his arms, and I will call him my own." She kissed his medallion and the ring. "What a stupid girl," she smiled, "to keep such precious presents for all this time, without realizing the love and care they represented. Anyhow, now I know what they're telling me, that my Jonathan loves me, and I love him with all my heart."

She lifted her hands to her God and prayed, "Please Father, protect him for me, so that our dreams can be fulfilled, and together we will do your will." Then she lay down her head and whispered, "I love you Jonathan, ever so much," and dropped off to sleep.

Early in the morning Jonathan left for Lebanon, to administer the raid personally, as his officers and troops began training to put the strategy into action. After a day all was ready to start the first phase. The entire camp of Abu Mansour was under observation from the air, while the ground troops began their manoeuvres, exercising around the Israeli camp. The eyes soon carried the news to the leaders of Abu Mansour's faction.

"Jonathan is back, and there's no end of army vehicles and troops, hundreds of them, covering the place."

"We must act quickly," said Mansour. "They'll soon raid us, so we must hide our weapons, before he does like last time."

"Better we move them out of the camp," said Abu Mansour to the anxious men, "because last time he blew up the houses where the weapons were found. I think we should fill our cars and any other vehicles with our ammunition and take them away, then, when he does as usual, he'll find nothing."

"How are we going to manage, as we have so much and a lot of it's very heavy?" asked Shakouri.

"I think we can do it, if we organize ourselves quickly. We can move the most valuable equipment first and put it in our hide-out caves, then we can return to move the rest."

Jonathan sat in the camp, waiting beside his radio for the first message from the flying watchmen. Abu Mansour had quickly organized a removal team and the transfer begun.

"Mission Disarming reporting," blared the sound from the loudspeaker. "Trucks and cars are moving from the camp, mainly from section 'A', and heading east. We are following."

Jonathan had his model of the camp and a map in front of him, which enabled him to follow the movement of the fleet.

"Thanks to God," he said, smiling to Peres, "we have made the right move. It's lovely to see the place flushed clean from all that mess."

The troops spent the day going in circles around their own camp, giving the impression of great activity, as they organized and reorganized themselves, whilst going nowhere. Abu Mansour and his men carried out their weapons removal without realizing they were watched and followed.

"It's been a very successful day," said Mansour to his team that evening. "Although we've moved a number of our important items, we need to start very early tomorrow, so we can continue moving our treasures, but we must be very careful, as we don't want anyone to guess our intentions. That means we have to take different routes and use some of our other hiding places, because we mustn't forget about our other enemies, as their eyes will surely follow us, and we don't want them to gather our weapons."

Jonathan did not stop the entire day, not even for a meal, as he was fully occupied in following the movements and marking the weapons stores, besides assigning his troops in preparation to scoop out the contents when the camp had been fully flushed.

The next day proved to be more tasking, as Abu Mansour spread his men out all over the country.

"We have to stop them from scattering so much," said Jonathan to his second-in-command. "We'll send some of the troops and block off a number of the routes, otherwise it will be very hard for us later, to spread out all over Lebanon."

The order was soon made and troops sent to close off some of the roads, forcing Abu Mansour's men to restrict their movements to where Jonathan decided.

A new courier now delivered messages between Israel and Lebanon, daily carrying reports on the progress and success of the mission.

"Any more messages?" asked Solomon, as he gathered all Jonathan's reports and commands.

"Yes please. Take a message to Natanya for me. Tell her not to stop praying, that everything is going well, and that I hope to see her soon." Solomon wrote the message down. "And tell her to think on good things. Also give my love to everyone in the hostel, including Natanya, of course."

Solomon smiled and wished him good luck as he left for Israel.

Natanya was anxiously waiting to hear about the safety of her love, and everybody else, so she never ceased to pray.

Mordecai was also feeling tense, as he hated it whenever the boys went away to Lebanon. "I wish our boys didn't have to make these raids as I never feel relaxed until everybody is safely back home again. Then a person feels like eating and singing, but not now, although Natanya is always happy and seems to be the only one singing, in spite of the fact that she must be feeling concerned about Jonathan. I don't know what makes her so calm and steady."

Solomon drove in, to deliver his messages from Lebanon to the various individuals. Natanya saw him coming towards her, so left her washing-up and ran towards him.

"A message for you, Natanya," he said with a smile. "Jonathan sends his love and asks you not to stop praying. He said that everything is going well and he'll soon be coming home." Then he looked at his paper to see if he had forgotten any other points, "and said, 'think of good things'. That is all."

"Thankyou," she said, with happiness all over her face. "I feel good to hear that. Tell him I pray all the time, and think of good things all the time." Then she laughed softly and with bashful eyes added, "I make a big party, when he come soon, insha-allah."

Solomon wrote down her message and left.

After three days, Abu Mansour's men had moved all their weapons out of the camp and then they ceased their feverish activity. This was the signal for the second stage of the mission to start, so the troops surrounded the camp at dawn, before any of the militia would have chance to leave. At the same time, the air watch concentrated on the camp, as well as the new stores, towards which a fleet of armoured vehicles and trucks were heading.

"We must take the utmost care," warned Jonathan, "as we can't be sure if Abu Mansour has left some of his men to guard the stores. If so, we'll have to chase them out with tear gas and smoke bombs, and then we can empty the stores."

The delicate technique progressed with difficulty as the area was hilly, covered with rocks and full of caves. The army was well prepared with special infra-red glasses and masks as the fighter planes dropped several smoke bombs. A few men ran out of their hides and fled as fast as they could from the smoke, with their eyes burning and stinging, temporarily blinded with tears. Troops quickly moved in to guard the men and their vehicles as they advanced, many of them fitted with loading equipment to speed the operation. The men rushed to the new stores, pushing and dragging their gear to help them in their task of moving the great amount of weaponry from the caves to the trucks, which were gradually filled.

Mansour and his men were trapped inside the camp.

"Well, we are ready for the Israelis to come and search," said Mansour, laughing. "And let us see how many items they will take away!"

Abu Mansour was delighted with himself, as it was his suggestion that the weapons be moved out, so he said, with a big grin filling his face,

"We're well ahead of them this time, with our weapons hidden away and our execution cars in their garages, ready for action. I wonder what Jonathan will say to his government this time?!"

Peres became very excited as the air-watchmen kept sending progress details of the removal procedure.

"I think this is the best disarming game we've ever undertaken," he exclaimed.

Jonathan smiled and said.

"If God is not with us, let Israel say 'Our enemies would have overtaken us', but thanks to God, he has helped us so far. In fact, we are ahead of schedule. I hope my angel is still pleading on my behalf, then I can't see why we shouldn't finish this phase of the mission tomorrow, God willing."

The following day the troops finished their loading and the last convoy started to move back to base, protected by armoured vehicles and the fighters in the air.

"No need to enter the camp," commented Jonathan. "I think we've established what we came for."

"We can't do that, Jonathan," objected Peres, disappointed. "Abu Mansour will be very hurt if we withdraw without paying him a visit."

"Better we withdraw right away," laughed Jonathan, "as that's the best way to tell him we're not interested in hurting anybody or in destroying homes, but only in removing the dangerous and destructive tools from their hands. I hope we'll soon be able to go on to the third stage of our strategy."

Then he issued the command,

"Return to base. Mission accomplished."

The troops began to withdraw and drive slowly away from Abu Mansour's camp.

"What's the matter with them?" asked Mansour, disbelieving his eyes. "They're going away, without paying us a visit. I wonder what's happened to Jonathan? He's becoming very soft these days."

"No Mansour, I have a feeling that something has gone wrong," said the old man, holding his heart.

"But what could go wrong, Father?"

"I can't believe that all these troops encircled us since yesterday for nothing, my dear son."

"Well," said Mansour, joking with his anxious father, "you never know, maybe he's trying to tell us one of two things. Either he is mad, or is trying to provoke us."

The men who fled from the hide-outs on the hills were now able to enter the camp and deliver their bad news, sad and disappointed, with their eyes still swollen from the smoke and tear gas.

"What's happened to you?" asked Mansour.

"The Israelis raided our new stores and carried away every single item. We just managed to escape with our lives."

Abu Mansour shouted with bitterness and Mansour banged his fist on the table in frustration, bellowing,

"If I don't kill you and get rid of you, Jonathan, my name is not Mansour."

It was worse than a funeral in the camp, as they realized they had been tricked and outwitted. They gathered for an urgent meeting to find a way out of their predicament.

"Jonathan must go," said Mansour, angry and full of rage.

"We have done all we can to fight them, but have failed everytime, while they have succeeded," Abu Mansour said thoughtfully. "I just can't understand why, as we are in the right. We are all believers, praying five times a day and never missing one prayer call. We fast the thirty days of Ramadan. So why is Allah not supporting us?"

Shakouri thought for a long time, seeking to find an answer for his leader. At last he said,

"I think Allah is listening to our prayers, as we have not had even one casualty in the last few months. Although we lost a few houses in the last raid, not one brick came to the ground today. I feel life is more valuable than weapons and ammunition. If only we could find a way to deal with our problems, other than fighting, then that would be the day!"

"I will not consider any other way," said Mansour, boiling and screaming. "Even if it costs me my own life, I shall fight back. I'll deal with Jonathan personally as he's the brain behind all these attacks." He paused to think, as he stared with eyes full of bitterness and hate. "I'll drive my suicide van and crash into the Israeli camp, to die with my enemy, as he's sure to be there tonight."

"No Mansour," objected his father. "You can't do that. We need you. You're our right hand, and if you die, who will train the boys and carry out our missions?"

"Plus it will be impossible to get near the Israeli camp," added Shakouri. "You know how they guard themselves and have eyes everywhere. You can see that from what has just happened, how they followed us, waited until we had transferred every single item, and then took the lot, although how they did it, I don't know."

Mansour was not deterred.

"I don't care or worry, as I've nothing to live for. I've been a failure all my life, so what does it matter if I die with my enemies. It will just cut short my agony." He stood up and continued, "I shall go by myself, right now, and watch the Israeli camp, to lay in wait for Jonathan. He's bound to leave for Israel, and then I'll crash into him and die a happy man."

"Mansour," begged his father, grabbing him by the hand. "You can't do it. You haven't even said goodbye to your mother and sisters. Please don't go. Let us think a bit longer and maybe we'll think of a better idea."

"Father!" exclaimed Mansour, rebuking his aged father. "How can you hinder me from the Jihad? Only a few weeks ago you stood there, encouraging the others to die with the enemy, and now, when your own son is going to take the same road, you're putting obstacles in my way. But nothing will make me change my mind and I'm leaving right away with Mubarak and Walid, as they're among the best of our team." Then he rushed out of the room, speeding away to get out before his mother caught him.

There was a huge celebration in the Israeli camp in Lebanon, and another one was held at the same time in the Centre in Israel.

"This is the most fantastic raid we've ever made," said Victor, celebrating with the young pilots who had just arrived, tired and worn out from an exhausting week-long mission. "I cannot express my feelings of joy and happiness that you're all safe, with not one life lost or drop of blood spilt, either among our men or those fighting us. I'm so proud of all of you, and most impressed with our Jonathan. He's a unique leader, very thoughtful, wise and caring. So let's celebrate this great victory and I promise an even grander one when our major-general returns home tomorrow."

Jonathan stood to congratulate his team and the troops.

"I would like to thank all of you, and I must say this; everyone of you is a hero, a victorious hero. You accomplished your parts, perfectly and swiftly. I'm very impressed and full of admiration for you all." Then he looked around him and saw the smiling, happy faces. He continued,

"What a pleasant feeling we all have, to know that not one human has been killed during this difficult and tasking operation. As you can see, it's been well worth it, as we've disarmed these mentally disturbed people, and now, with our God's help, we can work hard to find a cure or medicine for the problem. In fact, Peres and myself are going to the local hospital tomorrow, Im Yirtseh ha-Shem, to find out about the medical aid which we sent to help the Lebanese, and we'll see what else we can offer, to help, not only the Christian militia, but others, too."

The celebrating young fighters clapped and cheered, and felt like singing and dancing, but they knew they had to wait to do that at home.

Jonathan went to his room feeling so good, wanting to skip and glide through the air.

"How wonderful to be in love," he said to himself. "I feel like climbing Mount Everest. It's amazing what love does to the person, it gives the most thrilling and enchanting feelings."

He took Natanya's hair from his pocket and kissed it all over. "Darling, I am nearly there, and, all things being equal, I'll be with you tomorrow."

He could hear her message that Solomon had brought to him. 'I pray all the time, and I think all the time of good things. I make a big party.' He smiled, kissing her hair again. "I shall make the party, my sweet, the biggest party there's ever been, to celebrate our wedding. You just wait and see, my love." His mind started to dream, pondering on the happy thought. "I must buy my love some beautiful dresses, to replace that prison uniform. In fact, I can buy her some clothes from here, so she can celebrate the victory in them. I would hate it if anyone ignored her or gave her the cold shoulder because of that alef band on her sleeve."

He smiled at how events had turned out since Natanya had entered his life. "Actually," he said, "she is the alef friend and the best companion. I've never known a person who has influenced my thinking so drastically, not so much by words, but by her loving actions. I never dreamed that I would actually sit down and plan a raid with the thought in it of love and care for the enemy, and I've never before experienced the joy and thrills that come as fruitage of such a divine love."

He looked at his watch, "It's been a long day, but a happy one. I could sit here the whole night, dreaming of my sweet Natanya, but I must go to sleep, so, God willing, I'll be alert and fresh when I again hold her in my arms. Oh how I do long to be with her and kiss her. Just the thought alone makes me so happy." He put the treasured piece of hair back in his pocket, hung up his shirt and went to bed, well satisfied and happy.

Mansour went to see Mubarak and Walid, to explain about the situation. Both boys were in their early twenties, full of zeal and never fearing death.

"We'll support you wholeheartedly, so let's just slip away, for our mothers are against this method of fighting. They changed their minds when Fahid and Nawal died, but we believe it's most effective."

Mansour explained, with concern in his voice,

"Of course, we will not endanger our lives needlessly. We'll only die with Jonathan alone, as he is their leader, so if we die with him, our people will be liberated from him and his schemes. What I suggest is that we set eyes all around the Israeli camp, while we wait on the main road, so the guards won't shoot at us. Then, when we hear their whistle, we'll crash into him, but only when we're sure by seeing him, because we don't want to die without him. He's bound to leave the camp soon to return to his country, either by road or sea, as that's the way he always goes."

"But sometimes he leaves the camp by helicopter," interrupted Walid.

"True, so we'll watch for that, but I'm sure he will not use the helicopter because he thinks he's won the battle and destroyed us. But even if we can fight him with our bare hands, we'll do that."

Then Mansour organized the spies and sent them to the spots he had assigned to them, while he and his two friends sat in their explosive-filled van, to spend their last night in wait for their enemy.

In the morning, Jonathan and Peres had their breakfast, laughing and joking, as they would soon return home, immediately after the hospital visit.

"We had better change our clothes," said Jonathan, looking at the time. "The ambulance from the hospital will soon be here, to take us for our appointment."

"I feel almost naked without my uniform," laughed Peres.

"I know the feeling," agreed Jonathan. "Somehow, I find it very difficult to talk without a uniform, especially on missions like this, but I think it's the best idea to disguise ourselves as civilians and wear white coats. It reminds me of my university days, when I did my physics and chemistry practicals."

Jonathan went to his room, while Peres sat finishing his breakfast.

He put on his shirt and tie and an ordinary pair of trousers. "I mustn't forget my Natanya, or my prayer," he said, moving his two treasured items from one shirt to the other. After that he put his white coat on and slipped the walkie-talkie into his pocket. He looked in the mirror, and smiled at himself, "I don't think anyone will identify me, especially if I wear my sunglasses." Then he went to show Peres his new look.

Peres had just finished his dressing when Jonathan entered, and they both stood admiring each other, laughing,

"I say Jonathan, you really look handsome. No one would ever imagine you're a soldier!"

"I think just the same applies to you," jokingly replied Jonathan. "We must change our uniform, don't you think?"

The eyes were watching all the time, reporting every little movement.

"No cars or vehicles have left the camp so far," they said.

"Give them time," said Mansour. "They've been celebrating and drinking the whole night, so they're bound to be drunk and sleepy. Give them time to get up."

An ambulance drove into the base.

"An ambulance from the local hospital has just driven in. It had a driver and two doctors in it."

"Someone must have been taken ill," said Mansour. "Don't get distracted, keep watching."

Five minutes later the ambulance came out.

"The ambulance has just come out, still with the driver and two doctors. It's going fast towards the main road and will soon appear."

Mansour saw the vehicle, with the two doctors bending down, busy attending to someone.

"One of the Israelis must have had a heart attack. I wish they all had one," he muttered.

Jonathan and Peres entered the hospital with their 'patient' guard. They were met by the hospital administrator and a number of doctors and ushered in the direction of the conference room. Baha happened to be standing in the corridor when the team of doctors and other staff passed her on their way to the meeting. She stared at the first one and smiled, thinking, "He looks familiar. I am certain I've seen him somewhere, but I can't remember where." Jonathan had never met Baha before, but her smile reminded him of Natanya. "How strange, the same kind of friendly face, but not reaching Natanya's quality." Then the men entered the room and the door was locked, leaving the guard keeping watch outside in the corridor.

Baha stood for some time, trying to recall from her memory file the image of the handsome young doctor. Suddenly her mouth fell open. "Oh no, that's Jonathan, the Israeli!" She was shocked and her hands trembled. "And so what. He used to be my arch-enemy and I hated the sight of him, but how amazing, he's changed! Or perhaps, amazingly it's me that's changed! Now he looks like an ordinary human, quite a likeable one, in fact, although if Mansour discovered him, he'd kill him on the spot," she thought, laughing to herself. "Especially after I told him last time that I love everyone, including Jonathan."

Then she changed her thinking and brought from her memory the one who had caused the change. "Amal, the beautiful person with the big heart, who is able to love everybody, she is the one who helped me to see this wonderful love for all humans, 'Love thy enemy'. I wonder if she met Jonathan? Could it be possible that she did? And Jonathan, I wonder what he's doing here, is he coming to work in the hospital, or what?"

The atmosphere of the meeting was very friendly as Jonathan explained his method of help to the hospital officials.

"We will replace the operating theatre that was blown up, as well as supply you with medicine, and we are even prepared to provide personnel, but on one condition."

The men looked at him, wondering about the conditions.

"I hate the strings that are always attached to such aid," said the hospital administrator in his heart.

"On one condition," said Jonathan. "That the treatment will be available to all, to everyone, not just the Christians, but every needy human, regardless of colour, religion, or political party."

That was a surprising piece of string!

"Of course, sir," said the administrator with emphasis. "We always treat everybody equally."

"I want an assurance that it will by all means be equal," repeated Jonathan.

"The only assurance we can give is our word, and we can take an oath in front of God."

"Yes, I'll accept that, for God is the one who will ensure this agreement will be kept."

The news soon spread that the Israelis had come to the hospital to give aid, and many others besides Baha had identified Jonathan. The ears heard the information and brought it to Mansour.

"You are wasting your time here, as Jonathan and another Israeli, wearing doctor's clothes, are in the hospital, where they've been for almost an hour. They escaped and you didn't even notice them."

"What a deceiving fox!" exclaimed Mansour. "Never mind, that's even better as far as we're concerned, as we can blow them up when they come out of the hospital."

He started his van and drove to the hospital street, busy with traffic speeding past all the time.

"Let's park here, where we have a good view of the hospital. As soon as we spot him, we'll rush towards him before he enters the ambulance." Then he thought for a moment. "If we can kidnap them it will be even better. We'll speed towards them and take them by surprise, and if we manage that, it's far better than killing them, because we can demand a big ransom. But if they see us and make the slightest movement to resist us, we'll crash into them and die together."

The idea was enthusiastically supported by Walid and Mubarak.

"Let's prepare the blankets," said Mansour.

In the van they had two heavy black blankets that would be thrown like fishing nets over their victims, who would then be bundled into the van and driven away at speed. Mansour and his two friends had spent hours at their training classes, throwing 'nets' over their catches, so they could perform the operation quickly and accurately, even in the dark.

Mubarak held one blanket ready and Walid folded his neatly, laying it on his lap, while Mansour focused his concentration on the hospital entrance. "The only problem is that if we crash into them, then Baha is sure to die, as well as many other patients," he thought to himself. "But that's a risk we have to take, for the sake of our people." Then he comforted himself by adding, "Well, at least my love and I will die together."

The conference concluded and everyone stayed for some refreshments. Jonathan felt extremely satisfied to see that every step had gone so smoothly. He glanced at his watch. "I have an hour to spare before I leave, but it's better not to shop here, just in case, as there are so many eyes watching us. I'll buy Natanya's clothes from Israel, because the quicker we get out of here the better." He turned to Peres, who was enjoying a good chat with one of the doctors, and tactfully pointed to his watch. Peres smiled and said to the young doctor,

"We'll have to continue our story another day. It's very fascinating, but I regret we have to leave now."

Abu Mansour went to the hideout where they kept their suicide vehicles. It was a large orange grove that belonged to one of his Palestinian supporters, and had a number of stores which were filled with oranges during the harvest season. Abdu had donated two of the stores to be used for hiding Abu Mansour's vans, as the grove was only about six minutes drive away, so making the garages convenient to reach, yet far enough to be unsuspected by the Israelis and other opposing groups.

Abu Mansour found one of the stores with its doors wide open and no van inside.

"He never listens to me," he sadly said to Shakouri, who was keeping him company. "How does he think he is going to blow up Jonathan, while he is surrounded by the army?"

"Don't feel so bad man, this is life; ups and downs, births and deaths, weddings and divorce. We can't change it, but we have to live it."

"He's the only son I have, and I trained him so well, right from birth, to hate his enemies, to fight them and never fear death, but still, I hate to say it, I don't want him to die. I hoped so much that he would get married and raise a family. Then Amal, the mobashira, came to the camp and ruined Baha, with this business of 'Love thy enemy' and she took her away. Now Jonathan, the cursed man, has come, and he will cause my son's death."

The news reached the hostel that Jonathan would be arriving that day. Mordecai ran to announce the good news to his daughter.

"Natanya," he called, with a big smile on his face, "Jonathan will come later."

She hugged him with joy and excitedly said,

"We will make a big party, Mordecai."

"We can have our big party tomorrow, Im Yirtseh ha-Shem, because he will have a party waiting for him and his team at the Centre. You see," he explained, "our team won again, and no one died, not a single one."

"That is good," she said happily, raising her hands towards heaven. "I prayed a lot, and now I say thankyou a lot, for He listened to me."

"I'm very happy, Natanya," he said, holding her shoulders. "You and Jonathan are my only children, and I pray I will have many more soon."

She blushed and smiled softly,

"I pray our dreams come true."

Then Mordecai skipped and danced his way toward the door, hugging everyone he met on the way.

Natanya floated on air, singing and thinking of different recipes to use in her welcoming party. "When I finish, I'll have a shower and wash my hair, ready for tomorrow, insha-allah." She looked at her prison uniform and felt rather disappointed. "Pity I haven't any of my pretty dresses. If only I could have my Palestinian dress back, I could wear that tomorrow, but they took it from me in the prison." Then she smiled and said, "It doesn't matter what I wear, for Saint Peter wrote that the beautiful inner person is what counts, not the external look. I can put on my new prison uniform. It's smart and I like the pattern on its sleeve, the first letter in the Hebrew language is what Mordecai explained to me." This caused her to stop while she attempted to figure out why her uniform was marked with the letter alef. "Maybe it's because I have been promoted and I'm not in prison anymore." Then she changed her mind, as she had the uniform with the letter on before she was promoted. "I know, silly," she told herself. "It's simple, it's because alef is the first letter of my name, Amal."

Mansour's heart was racing, as he kept his unblinking eyes on the hospital entrance, his hand ready to turn on the ignition the moment they appeared.

"The distance is just right," he told his friends. "I have enough space to accelerate, but let's hope they emerge soon, before they ruin my nerves."

"Mansour," said Mubarak anxiously. "Do you think they left from another exit?"

"They can't," said Mansour, looking round. "This is the main road, and the other exit is very narrow and crowded with parked cars. I doubt if they would take that...." and before he had finished his sentence, a few men appeared from the entrance. He started the engine and his friends adjusted their blankets, ready to swoop. A driver opened the ambulance door as two men appeared, dressed in white coats.

"There they are!" shouted Mansour, and accelerated towards his target.

Jonathan and Peres had just reached the bottom step by the entrance when he saw the van speeding towards them.

"Watch out, Peres!" he shouted. "A suicide van!"

"I'll shoot them," said Peres, holding his back pocket.

"No, stay still, or they will crash and all of us will be killed." Jonathan dropped his document case and walkie-talkie, after pressing the alarm button, as he knew he had no time to move right or left, but must face up to whatever would happen.

"We can catch them!" shouted Mansour, and brought the van to a halt right next to his two victims.

Mubarak and Walid jumped out in less than a flash, threw their blankets over their catches and overcame them, then quickly dragged them into the van and sped away, swerving to miss the traffic, as Mansour kept his hand continually on the horn.

The guard and passers-by stood there with their mouths open. No one was able to do anything, as the whole operation was over in less than a minute. After he recovered from his shock, the Israeli guard picked up the case and two walkie-talkies, and went back into the hospital to seek and wait for help.

Jonathan and Peres were in darkness under the heavy blankets, with their captors almost suffocating them. Jonathan kept perfectly still as he reasoned, "Why resist, it will only make matters worse. Just let's hope that the others will act promptly." He could feel the wires all over the floor of the van and thought, "What a tragedy if they had crashed into the hospital. All those innocent people and us, for sure, would now all be dead." His head timing told him they were now quite a distance away from the city centre. "I have a feeling they're taking us to their camp," he reasoned as he counted the twists and turns of the van as it raced along. Mansour stopped sounding the horn. "Aha, we must be in the countryside, as there's now no need for the hooter," he reasoned in his darkness. "So we are not heading for Abu Mansour's camp, but somewhere else."

Peres was suffocating as Mubarak held him so tightly by his head and covered his nose. "I wish he'd move his hands a bit, as I feel like dying." He tried to breathe through his mouth and calm himself to preserve his oxygen. There was no time to think of any other thing, but they both just hoped for the journey to come to its finish.

Mansour and his friends were in a state of dreaming as they could not believe what they had managed to catch. They did not speak a word, as they were more surprised with themselves than were those who had just been kidnapped. "The road is becoming very bumpy," noticed Jonathan. "It must be a farm or citrus grove. I know there are many around the Palestinian camp, and this will make our escape very difficult, as they will be on one side and the Syrian army is camping not far away on the other, with the open valley in either direction."

The van slowed considerably, and then a different sound started to be blown by the horn.

"He's giving his men the good news," thought Jonathan. "What a great pity that it had to end like this, just when we were on our last step. I sensed that something was going on. I wish we had left early, then we could have avoided these madmen and thwarted their scheme."

Abu Mansour and Shakouri were sitting on the ground, bewailing their lot, when they heard the hooter producing the joyful, victorious sound.

"That's Mansour!" cried the old man, jumping up from the ground and dusting his clothes. "He must have changed his mind from the mission."

"Or maybe he shot them instead," added Shakouri, as they both concentrated their attention on the only narrow track which led to the stores. Mansour was flashing his lights and blowing the horn and they could see his face was filled with excitement and joy. He stopped and his father held one door while Shakouri held the other, looking into the van. Mubarak and Walid had magnificently victorious looks on their faces as they held their catches.

"Father," said Mansour in Arabic, "I bet you will never guess what our nets caught for us today?!"

"I caught the shark," Mubarak said laughing.

"And I caught the fox," added Walid.

"And I piloted the ship!" said Mansour, roaring with laughter.

Abu Mansour and Shakouri were smiling and grinning, but frozen from the news and unable to speak or move.

"Come on man!" yelled Mansour happily. "We must welcome our guests. We can't leave them like that, and anyway, we want to have a good look at them."

Shakouri suggested to take them back to the camp and hide them there.

"Don't be stupid," said Mansour. "Their people will be raiding us in a minute or two. We can hide them here in the storeroom, it's the best place. I'll arrange a good guard system, but first let us empty our nets. Have your guns ready, as I don't trust them, even though they're under the nets."

Peres wished they would hurry up, as he felt sick, and the problem was made worse because of lack of understanding of the Arabic language. Jonathan paid deep attention to their conversation, although he too did not understand their tongue, but was registering their sounds in his head, to identify the voices. "We have three men with us, and there are two outside, that makes it five against two. If only they would lift this blanket."

Abu Mansour felt concern as he looked at the nets, so he suggested,

"Let's get more men in case they overpower us. It will only take a minute or two."

"I doubt if they would be able," said Mansour. "We'll take one net at a time. The shark first and tie him well. Then the five of us will bind the fox."

Walid gripped tighter on Jonathan's neck, while the others dragged Peres out, with three guns sticking in him. He was so relieved that he could breathe at last. Still under the blanket, they pushed him into the store, while holding the rope they had taken from the van, ready for just such an occasion. They removed the blanket and the figure of the shark appeared.

"Not bad, eh?" said Abu Mansour, admiring him. "Young, not more than thirty years, but dangerous, even with his white coat on."

The men laughed, staring at the pale face.

"He looks to me as if he is about to faint," said Shakouri. "Let's tie him quick and throw him in the corner to recover."

They stripped Peres of his weapon and then tied him from his shoulders right down to his feet, so securely that he stood resembling an Egyptian mummy. Then they covered some of the floor of the empty store with the blanket and pushed him onto it.

"I wish I had shot them," thought Peres, resenting the ill treatment. "I wish we had blown them right from the start."

Walid was still holding tightly onto his net. "He hasn't moved a milli," he thought, "I hope I haven't suffocated him, but I dare not uncover him, because foxes are cunning. It would be a great tragedy if he died though, for what's the value of a dead good catch?"

"Now we can concentrate on the real diamond," said Abu Mansour, looking at the worried face of Walid, who said to him,

"He is very quiet since we caught him. Maybe he's died?"

"Don't be stupid," said Mansour. "This type of creature won't die, they are tough and evil and I bet he is scheming a plan to escape from here. I'm looking forward to meet him and I can't wait to remove his blanket."

Then they dragged him out of the van, with guns poking his body from every direction. Jonathan took a deep breath and called on his angel to pray for him, "Pray for me, Natanya. I am in difficulty, help me, O my God." His legs were numb from the cramped position in which he had been kept. Walid still gripped him, while the others prepared the rope to tie him. Mansour twisted Jonathan's arms round his back, and the others handcuffed them temporarily, so he could strip him of his weapons and any other items he had on him. Then he lifted off the blanket, as they all peered at him in anticipation, as though a piece of sculpture was about to be unveiled in front of some art connoisseurs.

"Is that him?" asked Shakouri, looking at the emotionless expression of the calm figure.

"Very handsome, with a beautiful suntan, but no expression or feelings."

The men stared at their arch-enemy face to face for a while.

Jonathan stared with his usual piercing look, studying his captors and weighing them up in his head.

"Jonathan," said Mansour with delight, "I can't tell you how delighted I am to see you!"

Jonathan just stood there, staring with his strange gaze, although Mansour spoke in perfect English.

"I've seen you many times from a distance, but now we can talk face to face. I have so much to discuss with you, but first let me search you, as I don't trust you. Look, you are wearing a doctor's uniform, while your hands are full of human blood."

"What about your hands?" said Peres in his head, as he watched the men surrounding his leader, scorning and mocking him.

Mansour pulled the gun from Jonathan's back pocket and studied it.

"It's a very good make. I've always wanted one of them and now I have two in one day." Then he pulled out the contents of the shirt pockets.

Jonathan's heart almost jumped from his breast but he managed to control himself.

The men stood staring at the strange items that Jonathan kept in his pocket.

"Beautiful hair, soft and black," said Mansour, smelling it.

"You dare," cried Jonathan in his heart. "That's my angel. O my God, please let him return my Natanya to me. It's the most valuable treasure I have, and now he is handling it with his dirty hands."

Peres was also surprised to see the piece of hair, "I thought Jonathan was in love, and so he is, and he never told me a word about her."

Mansour looked at the piece of hair for a long time. It reminded him of his own love. "It's just like Baha's hair, soft and black. Pity Amal came in between us." Then he looked at Jonathan with sentimental eyes.

"I would never have imagined that a heart like yours could fall in love, but, just to show you that I'm not cruel, I'll give you back your love's hair, because I'm also in love, and I know how it hurts when you can't have her beside you."

Mansour stuck the piece of hair and prayer back in Jonathan's pocket, and said, "Just to make you realize the loss you are going to have, for you will never hold your love again, because you're not going to get out of here alive." Then he continued to say to the statue in front of him, "Your girl must taste what it means to be without her man, just like our girls whose hearts have been broken because you killed many of our young men."

Shakouri commented about the piece of hair, saying in Arabic, "It's funny, but that hair looks just like our girls' hair. I didn't think the Israeli girls have hair as black as that."

"They are all similar," said Abu Mansour. "You can find all the range of hair colour in every country, but I can see what you're trying to say because somehow that piece reminds me of one person I know well, but I hate to mention her name."

"Who?" asked Mansour, glancing at his father.

"Amal," said Abu Mansour, with a soft smile on his lips. "She used to come into the camp, and her black plaited hair was just like that, like a trademark, it was part of her identity. Every time she bent down to distribute her food to the children, that black hair would hang down, almost touching it."

Jonathan heard the word Amal and realized they were talking about the hair. His heart fluttered. "They are talking about my Natanya. They must have identified her hair as I know her name is Amal, Dudu told me. O my God, what are they talking about?"

Mansour threw away the white coat and started to bind his enemy, talking at the same time.

"Tell me, Jonathan," he said. "What happened to my cousin whom you took from here, after you killed his brother and parents. He is the only one left in the family. What did you do to him?"

Jonathan did not open his mouth or show any expression in his face, as if he was dumb and deaf.

"I'll tell you one thing, my friend," said Mansour. "You are very arrogant, but I'll make you speak to me before long. I have one more question to ask. What happened to the girl you took from here? She is like an angel. What did you do with her? I'm going to make sure you pay for every one of them."

Jonathan knew who was the girl he referred to. "So he too discovered her angelic qualities. That's an encouraging statement," he thought. "So my angel's care and love did leave an impression on this people. I think that together we might be able to help them, although it's a pity to have this interruption in our helping programme, but I'm sure our dreams will come true, even though the road is impassable at the moment."

Abu Mansour was so proud of his son, and how he had dealt with the arch-enemy. He said to Shakouri,

"I told you how I trained this boy from his birth, and now look at him, very admirable."

After Mansour finished neatly mummifying Jonathan with his ropes, he pushed him into the other corner and then sat on the ground in front of him, looking at the immovable expression on his face.

"Jonathan," he said, while the other men stood admiring their catch, "I don't want to kill you in one go, because that will be a great shame, as I can't tell you how much I'm enjoying myself. So I want you to last as long as possible, which means I mustn't be hasty about my decision. I'll go home and think of a way to kill you so slowly, that every day you'll pay for one of those you killed, because I swear that no amount of ransom can take you out of my hand, but I can do some bargaining for your friend."

Then he stood up and spoke to the other men in Arabic,

"Let's leave them to meditate alone, as they seem too stunned to speak. We'll go and make the road to here secure from intruders, and break the good news to the rest."

Shakouri said laughingly to Abu Mansour,

"I told you that Allah listens to our prayers. Look how he's brought us the best catch we've ever had."

The men left, shutting the door behind them. There were no windows, and no light, except for the few rays that shone through the cracks and holes in the wood of the doors. Jonathan and Peres sat still in the darkness as their eyes gradually became accustomed to the dim light that filtered into the store. They kept silent, listening to the movements outside their door of the men who had been assigned to guard them. The others had left to arrange their next move. Jonathan looked around him in the empty room, smelling the petrol and oil that had dripped from the parked vehicle. "So this is where they hide their suicide vans. Nothing in the room, not one window, and no way we can get out of here, not with this wrapping around our bodies," he thought.

"I wish you had let me shoot them," whispered Peres.

"We would be dead now, Peres," Jonathan whispered back. "The van was packed with explosives. I could feel the wires around the floor with my feet, plus I noticed that even the seat they were sitting on was a wooden box of explosives; I felt the wood with the side of my hand." After a little pause he added one of his Bible parables, "'A live dog is better than a dead lion'. I'm sure our men will soon work something out, and my angel will pray for me, so don't feel desperate."

"By the way," asked Peres. "Who is your girl? You didn't tell me you have a girlfriend."

Jonathan remained quiet as he could see it would not be advisable to reveal her under the circumstances. So Peres repeated his question in a different form.

"Do I know her?"

"I've never had a girlfriend," answered Jonathan, "but I do have a fiancee."

"You are engaged?" asked Peres very surprised, as both of them were close friends.

"We got engaged the same day I left to come here."

Peres felt sad and anxious for his friend.

"I am sorry Jonathan, that things have turned into this mess. I know how you must feel as I've left my wife and two children at home. It does create such tension. Poor Naomi will soon be out of her mind when the news reaches her, and I'm sure it will do the same to your fiancee."

"I know, but I am certain my sweetheart can help us, because God hears her prayers. That's why I call her my angel, as she has great faith in prayer and a unique love for humans in general. She always prays for everyone and I know her prayers have been answered so far, except for this little problem, but in the end I'm confident things will turn out alright. Anyhow, we have time until Mansour decides how to kill me slowly, and you have even more time, so don't let us worry ourselves, just try to relax and 'think of good things', as my angel once advised me. After all, most of our team are still here and, if they act quickly, they can flush this area. They know the technique and my policy. So you have a bit of rest. We could do with some sleep, even though we are wrapped up so tight."

The news of the kidnap reached the Centre in a matter of minutes.

"I will not believe it," said Victor in his conversation with their base in Lebanon.

"Just after everything had gone so well. In fact, they were on the last step at the hospital and the guard couldn't do anything much as the van could have been on a suicide mission. We attempted to chase it, but the streets were crowded. Can we raid the camp and bomb it?"

"No, don't do that, in case we bomb our own boys as they could be hidden somewhere there. Give me time to arrange a meeting and see what we can do, for this is the biggest tragedy we've ever had. Jonathan and Peres disappearing on the same day; what a calamity!"

"We will await your instructions," said the depressed young officer.

CHAPTER 7

"YOU KILLED MY LOVE FOR ME"

The Israeli camp turned into a house of mourning. No one was able to believe what had happened, but for the evidence that two boys were missing.

"When a leader like Jonathan is suddenly taken from the team, it's like having both your hands and legs cut off," said one of the soldiers sadly.

His friend responded,

"They left so happy this morning, looking very smart in their doctor's uniforms. I wonder how they were spotted?"

"We are surrounded by eyes full of hatred. I hate Lebanon and this kind of life, as there seems to be no end of war and fighting, but the shame of it is that they can't see Jonathan's motive; how he didn't drop one bomb on their camp. Why kidnap a person like that?"

Mansour and his father organized their men. Some were sent to watch the movements of the Israelis on the main road between the two countries, while others were scattered around the city to gather information about Israeli activity there, and some were positioned near the orange grove to keep a strict watch on the store. The mood was one of celebration and joy. Sweets were distributed to the children in Abu Mansour's camp and the women arranged a party for their neighbours and families.

Mansour sat outside the store on his chair, guarding his captives and thinking hard of a way to torment Jonathan. "I could strangle him, or I could starve him to death," he said to himself. Then he changed his mind. "No, that is not painful enough. I must torment him, especially as he is so arrogant, just staring. He didn't even blink his eyes once. He feels so sure of himself, so confident, although the other one seemed shocked and worried, but not him. I shouldn't have left his girl's hair with him, I must go and take it away from him."

While he was lost in his reverie, some of the Palestinian leaders arrived to congratulate him, as his fame had quickly spread around.

"Mansour, can we see your catch?" they asked keenly.

"With pleasure, but make sure you keep secret the news that they are here."

"Of course man. We all belong to the same struggle, and today is our victory."

Mansour turned the key, which awakened the two Israelis from their sleep. At first the men could not see properly, as the contrast with the light outside was so great, but soon a big smile filled their eyes.

"Charming," moaned Peres to himself, resenting the attitude of his visitors. "We have become like monkeys in the zoo, that people come and visit us, to find entertainment by watching us."

The men came closer, to obtain a better view.

"Which one is Jonathan?" they asked Mansour.

"You will soon guess the answer," he laughed. "You keep looking."

The men kept looking carefully from one corner to the other, while Jonathan watched them, staring into their eyes, observing their features.

"I think this one with the strange look is Jonathan," said one of them after a time.

"You guessed right. He is arrogant."

Then Mansour went and squatted in front of him, looked at the sleepy eyes and asked,

"How do you feel, Jonathan?"

The men waited with interest, to hear if the strange creature would speak. So they all sat near, looking at him.

"You insist not to answer me, but I don't mind. I'll soon make you speak, for I am thinking very hard to find a way that will even drive the stones to scream. Oh, that reminds me of something," said Mansour, standing and going near to Jonathan to take away the piece of hair. He noticed that he would have to undo a lot of his wrapping and somehow felt he could not trust him, especially with Jonathan's determined look still on his face. "I'll take it away from you tomorrow."

"The man is mad," said Jonathan to himself. "He wants to take Natanya's hair from me. How petty can you get! I hope Victor and the others hurry up, because this man is driving me out of my senses."

231

The men continued to sit on the floor, mocking and laughing at their captives.

"Are you going to feed them, Mansour?" they asked.

"I haven't made up my mind yet. I want to starve them, but at the same time I want to keep them as long as possible. So I'm still thinking."

"Why not just give them water with sugar. That will keep them alive for a long while, but starve them at the same time."

"Yes," said Mansour with a smile, "I'll do that. A glass of water for today, and I hope that by tomorrow I shall have fixed his destiny," and he pointed at Jonathan.

The news had not yet reached the hostel, as the Centre was so busy endeavouring to find a way to save the boys' lives. Natanya waited patiently for the return of her love, but there was no sign of him, so she asked Mordecai,

"Why Jonathan so late?"

"I told you, Natanya, they will be celebrating at the Centre. See, none of the boys have arrived yet, so don't worry, he will come later."

She went to her room, but felt restless and unsettled. "I can't imagine Jonathan celebrating for such a long time, for he has never stayed so long before. My heart is telling me that something has gone wrong."

Every time she heard footsteps in the passage, she got out of bed and pricked up her ears, listening carefully. "That is not Jonathan. I must go and ask Aaron." Then she paused for a while, thinking. "Better I wait until the morning. Anyhow, if something has happened to him, what can I do?" She felt so anxious and unhappy. "Jonathan, where are you?" she asked, holding the medallion. "Pray for me, Natanya," she could his words in her head. "I must pray, that is the best thing I can do for him." So she knelt in front of her bed and poured out her soul to her God.

"Father, please help my Jonathan. He worked so hard to love his enemy, that not even one person was hurt. I beg you to protect him for me and bring him home in peace, so our dreams can come true."

She rose from the floor and sat on the edge of her bed for a time, thinking. "I do miss him so much. I love him, because he is mine. We hope to get married soon, but I feel worried in case he won't come back, and that will be my biggest tragedy, after the loss of my family." Her tears streamed down her cheeks. "Life is hard to understand. I can't figure out why all those that I love have been taken away from me."

She noticed her thoughts. "What are you thinking of?" she rebuked herself. "Why do you think such things. He has most probably been delayed for other reasons. Why do you always imagine the worst, and anyhow, my Lord's advice is not to worry for tomorrow. It's better I leave my anxieties and burdens for him, for he promised he will carry them for me." She kissed her medallion and whispered, "Goodnight my love, sleep well wherever you are, and I hope to see you soon." Then she lifted herself into bed and went to sleep.

Jonathan and Peres were so uncomfortable, as their entire bodies were numb from the ropes and the hard ground. They sat there in complete darkness, listening to a babble of sounds which they could not understand.

"I feel dreadful, Jonathan," said Peres.

"I'm sorry. I feel the same, Peres, but we must make it easy for ourselves. Let's ignore our aching bodies and look forward for tomorrow, because I am sure Victor and the boys are working very hard to get us out of here. So let's be patient and wait, and think of good things, as it helps you to take your mind from the pain."

"I have nothing good to think of."

"Well, I can think of one," said Jonathan. "At least you know you are not going to be killed, but I have to wait to hear the method of my execution, so I must be worse than you."

"I feel very sorry for you, especially after you worked so hard to save their lives. It's just not worth it, Jonathan."

"It is worth it. Life is precious and must be protected, because all humans feel the same. If we can help our species to live as humans, and not as cruel animals, then life will be worth living."

"I suppose so," said Peres, and he started to tell Jonathan about his family, of the happy times he had with his children, and the funny things his little son would get up to. Jonathan heard with pleasure, thinking of the fun he would have with his own children, when he would be married.

"What's the name of your fiancee, Jonathan?"

"I am sorry, Peres. I can't reveal her name, for your own sake and hers, but I shall tell you as soon as we are freed."

Peres started to puzzle why it should be a secret. "I wonder who she is? Her hair is soft and black and she must live near the hostel, because he got engaged to her before he arrived at the Centre. That's why he was late, quite late, so she must live between the hostel and the Centre."

Jonathan guessed that his friend was trying to solve the mystery, so he lay down on the floor, to think of his own good thoughts. "My dearest Natanya, I thought I'd be with you this evening, and share the joy of the victory together, but alas, I am sleeping on a hard ground, with a numbed body and feeling extremely uncomfortable, but at least you are next to my heart. Please pray for me, so we can be together. I am missing you immensely, my sweet; your smile, your gentle person. I love you, Natanya, and I beg from Adoni that He will make our dreams come true."

Soon the two men fell asleep as their pain was drowned out by their good thoughts.

Mansour stayed to personally guard his prisoners, but his father insisted he must go home and rest. So they arranged for the enemies to be guarded by shifts, leaving him free to go to bed, to think and dream of a way to kill Jonathan.

"I know how to do it, I'll cut him to pieces. Each week I will cut off one of his limbs, and that will kill him slowly. But that is not enough punishment for him, as I hate him so much, so I must do more than that.... I know, I've an idea, I'll feed him his own body! Then we can make a party on Friday, and he and his friend can have either a leg or a shoulder."

He felt pleased with himself, yet frustrated at the same time. "He looked very pitiful, red eyes staring all the time, but not one word have either of them spoken. That's their policy, they never speak. I hate them, they're arrogant. Why should I feel pity for him? He killed our people. What about my uncle and aunt, and my cousin? What about Amal? He took her and she is innocent. 'Love thy enemy'!! I wonder if Amal would love a person like him? I'm sure she must have changed her ideas by now, as she's most probably stuck in the Arab prison, beaten and mistreated. I'll let him pay for that. She used to make the children so happy, and Muhammad still asks me if the mobashira will be coming again. Poor boy, his father was killed by this nasty fox, so that's why he'll have to pay; an arm this Friday, another one next Friday, and so on."

Natanya rose early in the morning and went to check if Jonathan was back. She tapped on the door of his room but there was no answer. She opened the door and saw his bed was empty, and no one else there, as nobody shared his room with him since Mark left. She closed the door and went to the kitchen to prepare breakfast, but her mind was not on her work, as it wandered from one horrible thought to another.

"Something has happened to Jonathan. I have a feeling he is still in Lebanon. Abu Mansour and his son hate him so much, as Baha used to tell me that he was their most wanted Israeli, although I'm sure she has changed and started to love her enemy, because she told me that I'm her best friend ever, and that she will do her best to be like me, loving everybody."

As she prepared the breakfast, she kept looking out of the kitchen window, in case Jonathan would appear, but the time ticked by without any sign of him. "I wonder where Mordecai is, as he usually helps me with the breakfast? I'll go and see him, in case he is not well, or perhaps he is still tired out from all his dancing yesterday."

Mordecai had received an early morning phone call from the Centre, giving him the bad news.

"Jonathan and Peres were kidnapped yesterday morning, and the hope of rescuing them is almost nil," said a sad and anxious Victor.

"That's impossible," responded Mordecai, wondering if he was having a nightmare. "How did it happen?"

"They were kidnapped by Abu Mansour's men, using a suicide van, so no one could help them at the time; and it was just after they had successfully finished their mission. Anyhow, I thought I'd let you know, but I must rush, I have so much to do." Then he put down the receiver.

Mordecai sat down and covered his face with both hands, shocked and horrified at the news. "How can I face Natanya? She was so worried about him last night, so what will she do if I tell her that her love won't be coming at all? I think I'll keep away from her, as I hate to see her disappointed. Poor Jonathan and Peres. How can we get them out? I hate Lebanon, I hate the Arabs, except Natanya. I hate life altogether." He felt desperately unhappy. "I must go and help the poor girl. She is bound to hear the news sooner or later, and she has a right to know. After all, he is her man."

He stood up and walked slowly towards the kitchen, arriving just after the last boy had left. Natanya saw him enter the room with his face hanging down, so she ran to him and held his arm, while she looked into his face.

"Mordecai," she enquired tenderly, "you are not well?"

He tried to control himself from weeping, as he could not answer her.

"You sit down. I make you coffee, then you feel good."

She noticed his tears and her heart was squeezed with anxiety. "You crying?" she said. "Is Jonathan alright?"

He sadly shook his head, without saying a word. Her hands trembled and her whole body began to shake.

"He died?" she enquired.

"No," he shook his head, then said with a choking voice, "Kidnapped, and Peres too."

"Kidnapped?" she repeated, with terror in her eyes. "Abu Mansour and Mansour," she said, looking at the sad man. "I know them. They will kill him."

Mordecai nodded his head, surprised and disappointed, for he knew his daughter was a relative of Abu Mansour, as David had told him her story in detail, so he had tried to pretend she was not Baha, just Natanya, but now she instantly mentioned the names of the men and recognized the danger. He silently looked at her trembling hands and shaking body, and the anxious eyes.

"I must go to Lebanon. I get them out," she said.

Mordecai's face suddenly changed and he said,

"No, no, you will never leave this place Natanya. You can't get them out."

"Why, Mordecai?" she said with desperation. "I will pray a lot, and I go, and God help me to get them out."

"No way you go back to Lebanon," he said, standing up and walking away from her.

"I can't understand him. He said Jonathan and I are his only children, yet he will not let me go to help his only son. I can't waste time. Every minute is valuable, every second is crucial. I must go and ask Aaron to help me out, as we have an agreement to assist each other. I'm sure he will help me."

She left everything and ran to search for her friend. He was not at his normal place. "Where is he?" she asked herself, as she rushed from one part of the hostel to another. Then she saw a group of boys talking together, looking rather subdued. She spotted Aaron with them, so speeded her steps toward him. He saw her and stopped talking, watching as she approached. The other boys kept quiet, to see what was the cause of Natanya's hurrying. She reached Aaron and took his arm with both of her hands, and said, her eyes almost full with tears,

"Jonathan kidnapped."

"I know Natanya. I am very sorry."

"I can get the boys out. I must go to Lebanon now."

"Can you get them out?"

"God will be with me. I know I can."

He had no doubt that Natanya would not fail, as he trusted her. He was not partial or biased; he knew his friends by their works. That was how he identified them.

"Did you speak to Mordecai?"

She nodded and answered, looking into his eyes,

"He said no, I can't go, no way. You come and tell him that I must go now."

Immediately Aaron rushed off with Natanya holding his arm, like a little child who cannot let her father out of her sight. The other boys watched them heading for Mordecai's room.

"I wonder if she can get them out?" asked one of the young fighters.

"She's very good and kind, even though she's an Arab," said his comrade. "I've a feeling she will help them, but she's a prisoner, an alef one at that."

Aaron found Mordecai in the corridor, wandering around aimlessly.

"Mordecai," he said in Hebrew, "Natanya says she can get the boys out, so why did you say 'no'?"

"I must say no. Natanya can't leave this place, it's an order. No way can she go out of this hostel."

"Why not?" asked Aaron crossly.

"Because I know what the orders are, that under no circumstances is Natanya to be allowed out of here."

Natanya watched the two men with mounting exasperation, hopping from one foot to the other, as she was aware of the danger the boys were in.

"Why can't we at least phone the Centre, and let them make up their mind? If they say 'no', then I must think of a way to take her to Lebanon, because our leader is in serious danger, and all we're doing is talking."

Mordecai went to his office to phone, closely followed by Aaron and his friend.

"Victor," said Mordecai, with Natanya and Aaron standing in front of him. "Sorry to disturb you, but you know Natanya, the Arab prisoner we have here? Well, she says she is able to get the boys out."

"Is that the girl who raised the alarm when you had the bombs?"

"Yes, she is very good, and works hard. I'm sure she can help the boys."

While Mordecai spoke in Hebrew, Natanya spent the time praying to her heavenly Father, for Him to help her, and help the men to take the right decision.

"We will try anything, Mordecai," said Victor. "Bring her to the Centre at once, and bring her file with you. I'll phone Dudu as well, so we can have her prison records. Hurry up, as time is running out for the boys."

"We'll come directly to the Centre," said Mordecai in English.

As Aaron was responsible for army affairs, and Natanya when Jonathan was away, he drove them as fast as he dared to the Centre in an army jeep, with all its lights blazing, to tell everyone he was on an urgent mission.

Jonathan and Peres had a good sleep, considering their ordeal. After waking, they wriggled into a sitting position and rested their backs against the wall.

"We can do some exercises, Peres," smiled Jonathan, "as we don't want to go out of form. We can swing on our behind and do presses against the wall with our feet, to help our circulation."

They carried on exercising for quite a while, until they became hot and the sweat ran down their faces.

"How are we going to wipe our faces?" asked Peres, attempting to wipe his forehead on his shoulder.

"I feel rather hungry," said Jonathan. "Are you?"

"I don't feel so desperately hungry, but I do fancy a good cup of coffee."

"My angel is the best coffee maker in the world. She makes it just right."

That comment reminded Peres of his situation.

"They're dragging their feet, as they've made no attempt to get us out of here."

"How do you know?" asked Jonathan. "I bet everyone is working hard, but it's not an easy situation. I've been pondering about it myself, wondering what I would do in their position. Come to think of it, what would you do?"

"I'd blow up the whole lot," said Peres.

"But how could blowing up the whole lot get the boys out?"

"You tell me how to get them out then," challenged Peres.

"I told you, it's very difficult, but if it happened whilst I am in charge, I would do my utmost to avoid bloodshed. I think I'd do a tremendous amount of thinking and praying."

Then he continued to explain his thinking about how he would attempt to solve the problem.

"I really enjoyed the idea of 'flushing'. It worked superbly well before and could be used now, especially as we're all well prepared and the teams ready. I hope they go ahead and monitor this area, because they would soon discover us. I just hope they don't decide to destroy the camp, for that would be a tragedy, as imagine how many innocent people would be killed."

"You do surprise me, Jonathan," said Peres, irritated by his companion. "How can you find innocent people in Abu Mansour's camp?"

"It's very possible. There are many children for a start, and sometimes you may find real treasure in such places," he said, thinking of his angel and saying to himself, "I nearly killed her, and would have, if that table hadn't saved her life. What a treasure she is to me, and what a precious heart she has, that is so spacious to embrace all."

Peres kept quiet, as he remembered his last conversation with the young doctor the previous day. 'We have a nurse in this hospital,' said the doctor, 'who used to be a most wanted criminal, as she'd killed both Christians and Jews and those of other factions, but if you saw her now, she's another person. She loves all, and her favourite sentence is "Love thy enemy". She isn't a Christian, but does believe in the power of those words.' Peres smiled softly and said in his heart, "It's better I keep this story to myself, otherwise Jonathan will give me another lecture."

Mansour came to see how his guests were faring. As he turned the key in the lock, Jonathan winked to Peres and they both sat erect, ready to receive their host.

"Aha, good morning," he said, laughing, pushing the door partly closed behind him. "I see you got up nice and early, so now we have a lot of time to talk."

Jonathan stared into Mansour's eyes, without any expression on his face.

"Tell me Jonathan, do you stare like this all the time? Because I want to give you a little bit of advice, as you are my guest. It's better that you take that look from your face, or you're going to lose your eyes."

"I can't help how I look," thought Jonathan, but nevertheless he continued to gaze into his host's eyes.

"I see, you are insisting on your policy. Okay, I will tell you what I was thinking about last night. I have decided to give both of you a little party tomorrow, insha-allah. A special one, just for you two."

Jonathan and Peres felt touched. "So he isn't so bad, after all," they thought.

Mansour continued, with a smile in his eyes.

"You are going to have a special meat, and you can decide if you prefer a leg or a shoulder. I don't mind, because I don't eat unclean food."

Jonathan got the point immediately. "The man is mad, absolutely insane."

Peres' mind wandered to unclean food. "I hope he's not going to give us the meat of a pig or a dog."

Mansour saw no change in their expressions.

"I had better tell you what animal I'm going to cut an arm or leg from, depending on your choice. It's a fox. His name is Jonathan, and I hope he'll taste good. I'm also giving you the choice of how you would like me to cook the joint. You can have it baked, grilled, boiled, or any way you like. So tell me, dear Jonathan, would you like your right arm or leg, for I'm coming tomorrow at nine a.m. to get the meat for the party."

Peres felt ill, and so did Jonathan. "O my God, help me. I'm faced with an unreasonable and mentally disturbed human that's acting worse than a wild animal." Then he called to his angel, "Natanya, why have you stopped praying for me? Do pray, my love."

Mansour waited for their reply, but both of his guests were dumb and deaf.

"Alright, I will decide. I shall bake your right arm for you, and I'll cut it from just here," he said, poking his finger into

Jonathan's shoulder blade. Then he stood up and started to go out, when he turned round and added, "I forgot that you have no watch, so I'll bring you a big clock later, then you can count the time to your party." With that he shut the door and locked it after him.

Jonathan remained silent for some time, and Peres felt desperate and frustrated, seeing his friend in a real mental agony.

"I'm very sorry, Jonathan. We're trapped, and this maniac will carry out his evil scheme, while we just sit and watch."

"So many things can happen between now and tomorrow. I hope Victor speeds up the boys, because I know that on some occasions time is wasted in talking and disputing, while life is in danger."

"The stupid man," said Peres, angrily. "How could he devise a vile thing like this, so repulsive and inhumane?"

"It's too dreadful to think of Peres, so let us change the subject."

Peres was too upset to think of any other subject, so he kept grinding his teeth from the frustration.

Jonathan stared at the wooden door and heard the Arabic broadcasts from Radio Lebanon. He could not understand a word, except for the name Israel which was mentioned from time to time. "It will be the most tragic thing that's ever happened to me if I lose my right arm. Then how can I hold my love, how could I carry my children? I am so desperate." His tears rolled down his cheeks, and he brought his head down to his breast, so he could speak to his angel.

"Natanya, you promised me that you would pray for our dreams to come true, but things are getting worse. Please do something Natanya." He remembered the day when she raised the alarm. "I nearly choked her and twisted her hands so hard. I remember her shaking body and terrified eyes when she said, 'There are bombs outside, go now and find them'. My sweet love, even when I pushed you towards that wall and Aaron stuck that gun in your back, you still patiently stood there for an hour, praying for us, your enemies. You loved us even then." The thoughts of Natanya eased the ache from his heart, and he felt happy inside. "I think that just the realisation of that type of love does impart strength," he thought, and then said the words aloud,

"Love thy enemy."

Peres nearly fainted to hear that sentence from Jonathan's mouth. "I wonder if he heard the young doctor say that?"

"Jonathan," he called. "Did you hear our conversation in the hospital yesterday?"

"No," he answered. "What were you talking about?"

"Nothing much. The doctor was telling me a story, but unfortunately couldn't finish it. Anyhow, I only wondered."

Aaron and his passengers arrived at the Centre, where great activity was taking place. David had already sent Natanya's records with Moshe, and Victor read the main heading and saw one sentence, clearly underlined, "Not to be released or allowed to leave Israel under any circumstances." Mordecai and Aaron entered the conference room, leaving Natanya outside to wait for them.

"Let me see your file," said Victor, without wasting any time. He looked tired, as he and the other officers had spent a sleepless night in trying to find a solution for their problem. He read the same sentence, signed by Jonathan.

"I am sorry," said the old man, dogmatically, "We can't use her at all, as both files have a strict warning against her, and one is signed by Jonathan himself."

Mordecai tried to put in a good defence for Natanya.

"I would personally trust her with my own life. Her own works are enough to declare that she's a friend, and not an enemy. Let's use her. She is confident she can help the boys."

Aaron also gave a good testimony about her.

"She saved our lives in the bomb incident. In fact, she told us where to find the last bomb, when only a few minutes were left, so I can't see why we should distrust her so much, when she has proved beyond any doubt that she is a most loyal friend."

One of the officers asked,

"How did she come to know about the bombs?"

Victor looked at the file and checked on the bomb incident.

"Nothing much has been written here, except that 'one of the resident staff raised the alarm and we are grateful for the service she performed'. That's all, so, for one reason or another, Jonathan chose not to enlarge on how she got to know about them."

Baruch was concerned about the Arab girl, as he knew Jonathan's shrewdness and wisdom in dealing with any problem, so he anxiously said,

"I believe that Jonathan must know something about this girl, to impel him to write down such a strict order in the first place, and then to not change the restriction, even after the bombs were found."

Then he looked to Mordecai and asked, pointing to the underlined sentence,

"Can you remember if anything happened in the hostel on the date of this report?"

Mordecai shook his head and said,

"I remember he was very worried early one morning, and he came to my room, asking why she had been brought to the hostel. I was aware something had happened, but he never told me what it was, although we warned the boys to keep an eye on her. It was only a matter of a few days after that when the bombs were found, and I know she was suspected, because Aaron had to guard her with his weapon. That's all I know about the matter, but I swear Jonathan feels happy about her now and trusts her. In fact, they are good friends."

The men shook their heads furiously.

"No. No way," they said together.

Aaron was becoming upset and frustrated.

"I can't understand Jonathan," he said anxiously. "Why didn't he lift the restriction, because whatever happened before the bombs should be forgotten, as she endangered her life to save us. I should know that, as I nearly shot her, because if Jonathan had been a second later, she would be dead now."

Then he pleaded,

"Give her a chance to help the boys. I'm certain she can get them out. I know she can. I trust in her. Anyway, what harm can she do to us if we take her back to Lebanon?"

"A lot," said the irate old officer. "She knows about every one of you in detail, and don't forget that she is Abu Mansour's relative. She will join with them, and then we'll have a greater problem than ever."

Natanya walked from one end of the hall to the other, waiting for Mordecai and Aaron to appear. "They are wasting good time. Talk, talk, talk, while people's lives are in danger. What's the matter with this people?" she asked in desperation. "If only I had wings, I could fly, but I feel so helpless. They dispute as if they have eternity."

She stood near the door and could hear them arguing in Hebrew, and, from time to time, a few words of English were spoken. "I can't wait any longer," she said to herself. "I must go in and demand they take me to Lebanon. I know this is the way they work because when I mentioned the bombs to Jonathan, he thought I wanted to have a game with him and he didn't believe me, and I had to order him out. So it's the same with them here, I must let them take me."

She shut her eyes and prayed for help, then opened the door of the room.

The raging conference was suddenly silenced, and all the heads of the frantic participants focused on the Arab prisoner, with the star of David around her neck. Moshe was astonished to see the incredible girl just open the door of such a private room.

Natanya looked around the table and saw the old man. "That must be the head," she thought, so walked straight towards him and, looking him directly in the eyes, said in her broken English,

"I must go to Lebanon.... NOW."

The men froze from the shock they had just received.

"O my God, help me," she prayed, looking at her dumb, staring audience. "They are all the same, they don't speak, but just stare," she thought, her heart full of anxiety. She spoke again, to get her message over clearly.

"I must go NOW. You talk a lot, waste good time. The boys will die. I must go to get them out."

Aaron felt pleased to hear her say those words. "I wanted to tell them that, but I'm not as courageous as she is. Good for her, they need someone to move them."

The officers looked at each other, not sure whether to smile, or shout her out of the room. She had such command and authority about her that they were in a dilemma, not knowing what to do. The old man scratched his head, looking at the beautiful soft eyes of a determined young lady.

Natanya tried to explain the seriousness of the situation.

"Abu Mansour will kill them. I know. I must go, very quickly. We wasted so much time." She tapped her empty wrist, in just the same way that her father Mordecai usually did to indicate a lack of time.

The old man asked her,

"How are you going to get them out?"

"I pray hard, then you take me to Lebanon and leave me on the road, the main road of Lebanon, where the mountains start. You leave me there. I find Mansour. I know he is always there. Then I go and get them out."

Victor looked to the worried audience, and said in Hebrew, "That is the exact spot where the shooting happened. She knows the place well, and it makes me shudder to let her go out of our sight."

Natanya looked imploringly to the old man and said, "Please, please, let me go. I know Mansour. He is my friend."

The man looked more horrified than ever.

"I can't understand these people," she thought. She saw Aaron standing at the side of the table and said to herself, "He must know the meaning of a friend, because he is my friend." Then she ran to him, took his right hand and placed it on her right hand, and looked pleadingly into his eyes.

The men turned round and saw the silent demonstration.

Moshe smiled. "I see, they are getting involved with each other. Lucky boy, I'd have loved to hold her hand when she was with us in the prison. She's the best girl I've ever met, even though she gives us the shudders."

Aaron was embarrassed by the demonstration, and felt obliged to explain himself to his audience.

"Natanya is one of our team and Jonathan knows about this," he said, as Natanya was still holding his right hand. "We made an oath in front of the Almighty, that whenever either of us is in trouble, then we will come to each other's aid; and she is reminding me of this agreement."

Mordecai's tears flowed easily, and a situation like this caused his emotions to surface, so a few teardrops trickled down his cheeks.

The men were in a quandary. "Better I do not stand in the way of the Almighty," said Victor to himself. "She's an unnatural girl, there's no doubt about that. She prays. Aaron has an oath. Mordecai is full of emotion. I don't know what to do." Then he stood up and said to her,

"Natanya, I will agree to allow you to go to Lebanon, but we must make a good plan, because the road is dangerous and we don't want anyone to get hurt. You go outside, and later we will tell you what to do."

She smiled with relief and ran to the door, so they could start their planning without any more delay.

Jonathan and Peres had lost their appetite for food and drink. They kept watching the door.

"If only we could get these ropes off," sighed Jonathan. "Then we could easily break those wooden doors and overpower them late at night."

"I know," agreed Peres, "but I doubt it very much, as it took them almost half an hour to tie up each of us, from shoulder to foot, and handcuffs on top of that."

"We need to be Samson to break our ropes, but unfortunately we are not," lamented Jonathan.

Mansour walked in at midday, carrying a battery clock and an Arabic newspaper. He was followed by Walid, bearing a tray with two glasses of water.

"Jonathan," he called joyfully, "I've brought you your clock. I shall hang it there on the wall, so you can both see it without difficulty."

Then he brought in the chair from outside and stood on it to reach above the door, to hang the clock opposite his two captives. Walid stood holding the tray, watching Mansour for a while, and then the two men, feeling very proud of himself.

Jonathan quietly watched the hanging procedure. "At least we can watch the time," he thought, his mind becoming tired from thinking. Mansour descended from the chair and sat on the floor, opposite Jonathan.

"I have today's newspaper, but your people have not mentioned one word about you. Maybe you can tell me the reason for that?" he asked, with a smile on his face.

Jonathan ignored the newspaper and kept looking at the man in front of him. He did not trust Mansour, even for a moment.

Then Mansour spoke to Walid in Arabic,

"He feels so brave now, but let's see what he'll do tomorrow!" Walid laughed, nearly spilling the sugared water.

"Jonathan," said Mansour, "I have brought you something else to keep you company. It will give you great comfort."

Jonathan had become used to Mansour's type of conversation. "I bet I know what is his other comforting item," he thought to himself, and watched with interest, to see if his guess was correct. The delighted man drew from his back pocket a dagger in its leather sheath. "My guess is right," silently said Jonathan.

"It's very sharp, and has come from the Holy Land, from Mecca, so you are privileged, as I have never used it before. Tomorrow is our holy day, and the dagger is holy, so we hope that will make the meal holy."

Walid thought that was the best joke he had heard for years. Mansour continued,

"I will illustrate to you how sharp it is," he enthused, as he slit the newspaper into small shreds. "See its sharpness?! I don't want you to suffer, because we have another party next Friday and I must keep you in good shape." Then he took the dagger and stood it on its bare tip on top of the clock, with the handle resting against the wall.

Peres cursed the man in his heart many times, and was also annoyed with his own people. "They're just dragging their feet. I wish they would blow up the entire area and put us out of our misery. That would be far better than this mental agony we're passing through."

Mansour sat down in his favourite place and asked Walid to give the men their drinks. He brought the glass to Jonathan's lips so he could drink, but he kept his mouth tightly closed.

"He doesn't want to drink," he said to his leader.

"I don't mind," said Mansour. "You can stay without water."

Then he told him to give some to the other man. Peres did the same, as both men were distrustful of the water, especially as it lacked clarity.

"You are worried in case I put poison in it, aren't you?" he said, looking at them. "Well, I will drink it in front of you, to show you that I'm not as bad as you think." He took one glass and drank half of it, and said to Walid, "You also drink from the other glass."

After Walid had done so, he said,

"You see, it's only sugar, to make it nice and sweet for you."

Then he offered them the glasses again. Jonathan drank the remaining water and Peres did likewise, as they knew that would be their only meal for the day. When they had finished, Mansour stood up and told his guests,

"I will not disturb you again, to let you have a good rest, but I will come tomorrow morning at exactly nine o'clock, so I can prepare your little party." He took the chair, shut the door behind him and locked it securely.

Abu Mansour and his men held a meeting in the orange grove, which had now become their focal point because of its two new inhabitants. The men spread mats on the ground and sat under the orange trees to discuss the situation.

"The Israelis are keeping very quiet," said Abu Mansour, "which indicates they're planning trouble for us. There's no movement of troops across the border, nor a whisper coming out of their camp or the Christian militia sector, so I fear they will surprise us by an attack." Then he asked Mansour how his catches were faring.

"I don't like Jonathan. He's confident and never even blinks. He has iron nerves, but I'm sure he'll be a different man tomorrow."

"Mansour," said the wise leader. "Kill him, don't hang onto him, as he most probably has a good plan in his head right now. Let's get rid of him and dump his body near the Christian militia sector of the city. That will teach this evil people a good lesson."

"No father," said Mansour, very irritated with his father. "It's my catch and I'm free to do what I like with him. I am enjoying myself. I've never had such a good time in my whole life, and I must make it last, so dare any of you touch my fox; but you can do what you like with the other one if you want."

Mubarak did not like Mansour's suggestion.

"Why you kill my shark? I want him to last, too, and he's worth a lot of money, as we can ask as much as we like for him. So why kill him? We'll keep him for bargaining, plus I'm treasuring him, as he's my first catch ever. Every time I see him, I feel very proud."

Abu Mansour realised he had a big problem on his hands, with Mansour acting like a well-fed pet cat, who was having great fun sporting with a little bird. So he had to plan his manoeuvres with that point in mind.

"We must organize a roster, to help us guard all our posts extra carefully," he said to his team heads. "The main road to watch is the one to Israel. Then we mustn't shut our eyes and ears from the Israeli camp, as most of their men are still here. We'll send our normal group to the Christian sector, and put our people on the alert, so they can be ready to evacuate their homes after a minute's warning. Then we shall transfer them to the Palestinian camp, as I'm almost certain our houses will be flattened."

Shakouri commented doubtfully,

"I don't think they will flatten our homes, as their policy has changed and they are becoming quite civilised in their raids."

Abu Mansour interrupted him and said,

"We are not interested in their policy, whether civilised or otherwise. We must hurry up and work out our shifts."

He took the lists of his men and started work, filling in names on the separate papers. After a short while he handed the rosters to his various captains.

"I'll watch the road from Israel, as that's the most crucial one. I'll take my normal team and a suicide van, in case we need it."

Then he turned to Mansour and said,

"It's better I leave you here to guard your fox and have your fun. I'll leave Mubarak and Walid with you to guard the way to the grove. But before we take up our posts, we must warn our people to keep on the watch and be ready to move out."

Jonathan and Peres each sat in his own corner, watching the time move slowly. Peres knew the desperation that Jonathan must be feeling, as he saw him biting his lips from time to time.

"Jonathan," he called quietly.

"Yes Peres?"

"Do you think we have any chance of being released from here?"

"I don't know," he answered in a depressed voice. "Sometimes I feel it could be possible, but on the other hand, I see the time ticking by and no sign of any hope. I suppose so much could happen between now and nine tomorrow, as it's only 3 p.m.. I don't think the Centre will do anything this afternoon, so we have lost today, but they have all the night, although if they don't move then, I think we've had it."

After a while Jonathan requested his friend,

"Pray Peres. Nothing is too much for God. He can find us a way out."

"I have prayed, and I always pray, but it never makes any difference. Whatever will be will be."

"What do you ask God for in your prayers, if you don't mind my asking such a personal question?" said Jonathan.

"I've asked many times for my enemies to drop dead, yet they never do. I've asked to be a rich man with a villa by the sea, so Naomi and I can spend our lives in leisure with the children, swimming and diving, eating and celebrating all the time, but I've never had any of my requests answered. But I still pray. It's one of the different measures I take in life. If it works sometimes, all well and good; if it doesn't, I have other alternatives."

Jonathan looked at him with a faint smile on his lips.

"No wonder you never have your prayers answered."

"Why? What's wrong with them?"

"You are asking mainly for what suits you and your family, and nothing for the welfare of others."

"Jonathan!" said Peres in surprise. "Are you becoming a Christian preacher?"

"Why do you ask that?"

"Because you sound just like one of them."

Jonathan felt puzzled, as he thought he had always believed in such principles. What about the story of Jonah? That for sure was not Christian, so he asked Peres,

"Does the prophet Jonah belong to us, or to the Christians?"

Peres had to think for a while, as neither of them was religious.

"I'm sure he belongs to us," he replied.

"Well then, what is Christian about that? He prayed for hours for Elohim to wipe out the enemy, but his prayer was never answered. In fact, he got rebuked, as God's will is always the best for all his creation, and that includes the animals, too."

Jonathan stopped and meditated on Peres remark, 'You sound just like a Christian preacher.' He thought to himself, "True, although I believe the Torah and all the stories of the Bible, I never realized their power and the spirit behind them, until I saw them demonstrated by Natanya. She is actually a real Jewess. Her prayers are usually answered because she prays for the welfare of others. 'I pray that no one will get hurt'."

He felt refreshed and prayed a new prayer for the first time. "I beg you, my Lord, to help these people to see commonsense." This made him forget all about his own problem and he found himself feeling good. He smiled as he remembered Natanya's words, 'Try to love your enemy, then you will feel good'. "How extraordinary is this mysterious type of love. I feel like a hero, though I am bound with ropes. I have conquered my 'Big I', as my angel calls it, the love of oneself. How wonderful and amazing."

The officers at the Centre drew up their plan, while Victor presided, and approved their strategy.

"We're taking a big gamble by letting the Arab prisoner go back to her people, but God knows we've tried our utmost to deliver our boys from their enemies, and this appears to be the only viable alternative we have. At least she seems confident, and has done all she can to convince us.

"So the plan is as follows: a convoy of army vehicles will cross into Lebanon, with the last van carrying her and Aaron, acting as her guard. Something will go wrong with the vehicle and Aaron will push her out of the van first, so if there are any snipers around, they will identify her as one of their own people. She will then gradually slip away while Aaron and the driver attempt to fix the engine as they wait for help. Remember that this section is very narrow and twisting, so the other vehicles will not be able to turn round. That will give the girl enough time to run away before we arrive with 'help'."

The conference felt happy with the plan.

"We'll train the team right away and leave at dawn, so giving us ample time to later carry on with our raid."

Natanya was becoming desperate, as the time was speeding by, while the men inside never seemed to want to stop speaking. What made the waiting endless was her ignorance of the language, although she heard the odd sentence in English from time to time. She was standing outside the door, controlling herself from entering again, when she heard some clear English words spoken by one of the officers,

"In the morning we'll raid Abu Mansour's camp and bomb it to the ground, kill them one and all. We have no time for either him or his men, so we'll have to forget about Jonathan's policy, as it takes too long to be carried out successfully. They deserve death anyhow, so why should we spend our time in considering their lives?"

Natanya held her heart with one hand and her mouth with the other.

"Oh no, they are going to bomb the camp in the morning and kill everyone, Baha, Muhammad and the other children. Why kill? Why bomb?" Then she calmed herself down. "I'll pray very hard that no one will get hurt. I hope by that time Jonathan will be free and he will stop them from bombing the place. I wish they would hurry up, but they never seem to stop. Anyhow, why do I feel so disturbed, as my Lord always works things out for the best when humans run out of ideas and time. Then all the glory will be his alone."

She sat down on the floor of the hall and buried her head between her hands, as she felt worn out from the mental and nervous exhaustion. She wished she could open her eyes and discover that the whole episode had been just a passing nightmare, and nothing more than that. Suddenly the door opened and Mordecai walked out with Moshe, both on their way back to work.

"Natanya," said Mordecai with mixed feelings, as he was proud to see Natanya working with the team, but sad at the same time to see her go on such a dangerous mission. "I must go back to the hostel. You be a good girl, and when you come back, I will have a big party ready."

She gave him a wide smile and hugged him, saying,

"I am sorry you work alone."

"Oh!" he exclaimed, as he had completely forgotten about the time, the cooking, and the washing up.

"The boys will have to eat yogurt today. I have no time," he said, tapping his watch and panicking.

"I made some good food yesterday," she said, giggling. "I thought Jonathan would come. You find it in the cupboard. The boys can have it."

"Oh good," he said, and kissed her on both cheeks, feeling much relieved.

Moshe shook her hand for the first time, and said to her,

"Good luck, Natanya. I will be thinking of you, and hope to see you again."

She smiled and nodded her head, as she remembered him in the prison. "I never thought he could talk, but he does speak good English."

Victor had decided to personally administer the training of the Arab girl, as he felt unsure of her.

"Natanya," he commanded. "You are one of the fighting team, so you must do what I tell you, exactly and speedily. You come with me, and I will teach you what to do."

She eagerly nodded her head and asked,

"We go now to Lebanon?"

"No, we have a lot of work to do first, but if you do your part well, then you can go early in the morning."

252

Her face dropped and she felt disappointed. The old man noticed her expression.

"We will be too late," she said.

"That is what we have decided to do. No more talk, and let us start work."

The team were all ready, waiting on the training field. There were a number of vehicles parked one behind the other, with two soldiers in each. Aaron was standing near the last one, holding his gun and acting his part by looking gruff and fierce.

"Aaron looks unhappy," she thought, looking at him.

"You feeling not well?" she asked.

The soldiers roared with laughter, while Victor looked exasperated, and she wondered what she had done wrong. Aaron lost his fierce expression and a big smile filled his face. He walked to her and explained,

"Natanya, we are going to play a game. I am an Israeli soldier and you are an Arab enemy. I know we are good friends, so we are just acting. I will treat you as an enemy and push you out of the van. You then have to try to run away, but you must do it carefully, if you want Mansour to take you to get the boys out. Now take off your shoes and I will chain your legs."

She understood the game.

"I know," she said, as she removed her shoes. "I know how to do this," she thought. "I've been a prisoner before, with my feet and hands chained and a hood on my head as well. It's a horrible game, but I'll do anything for the sake of getting the boys out, especially my Jonathan."

Victor noticed her medallion and the ring on her finger, so he went near and said,

"You take these off."

"Why?" she asked, feeling hurt.

The rest of the team had never experienced such a member before. They had to carry out orders without question and immediately, but this prisoner was special, full of fun, and innocent as a child.

"Because I said so!" shouted Victor.

"Is for me to keep," she said, looking at him. "Jonathan said I KEEP FOR ME."

The frustrated old man looked to Aaron for help, as he seemed to explain things much better.

"Natanya," said Aaron, holding her hand. "Prisoners never wear anything like that, especially an Arab prisoner. If Abu

Mansour sees it, he will think you are a traitor and not take you to Jonathan."

She took the little box from her pocket and returned the ring to its original place, but she left the star of David on and said,

"I keep it, hide it in, no one see. I must keep."

Aaron looked to Victor for his approval.

"All right, you can keep it on, but you must make sure no one will see it."

Aaron then handcuffed her, attached chains to her ankles and lifted her into the van, telling her what to do when it stopped.

"You try to go backwards towards the bushes, and we will time you, so I will know how long to allow you before I look round."

Victor and a number of young soldiers stood nearby, watching the game. The vehicles started to move into a section that simulated the Lebanese road. One by one they disappeared round the corner, until the last one approached the narrow bend and gradually slowed to a halt. Aaron shouted and carefully pushed Natanya out of the van, jumping down immediately behind her, still shouting and sticking his gun in her back.

"Stand there. Don't move!"

She felt shivery and insecure as the game brought back the ugly past to her. "I wonder if I will be able to see Jonathan again? Maybe they have already killed him?" She noticed how trembly she was, "Why do I feel this way?" she asked herself, then answered, "I don't want to die. Abu Mansour killed my parents and I would not be surprised if he kills me, too." After a pause she spoke firmly to herself, "Natanya, you are thinking too much of yourself; there are others in a much worse situation, and you are frightened while playing a game." She made a resolution, "I must do my best and leave the rest for my God, as long as I make myself available so He can use me."

She stood watching Aaron for a while, then she looked around to see how she could quietly move away from him without him noticing her. Victor was watching her and checking the time with his watch. She started to move very slowly, a few inches at a time, while looking at Aaron. The stones pierced her feet and she became quite excited as she neared the bushes, so she moved faster than the chain allowed her. A loud thump and scream was heard, which made Aaron swing round and Victor jump. The audience howled with laughter.

"Natanya!" cried Aaron as he hurried to raise her from the ground. "If this happens in Lebanon, we will lose the battle."

"I know," she said, feeling disappointed.

"Put more links in her chain so she can move a bit quicker, because it's taking her too long to reach the bushes," said Victor.

A few more links were added, and the exercise repeated a number of times, until Natanya was an expert at the game. Victor came and patted her on the shoulder.

"That is very good. Now you can go with the team and have something to eat. You will camp here with them, so you can get up early in the morning and help the boys, God willing."

She nodded her head and said,

"I only pray. God alone can help the boys."

Aaron stayed by his friend's side, watching and looking after her.

"Eat, Natanya," he ordered, as she had hardly touched her plate.

"I feel not hungry," she said.

"Never mind, you finish that, as we don't know what will happen tomorrow. Maybe we'll go for a long time without food, so you eat it all now. Look, all the boys are eating their food."

Mordecai arrived home to a pile of washing up. He saw the baskets full of unprepared vegetables and meat, and went from one work surface to another, not knowing where to start. He opened the cupboards and saw the large serving plates, covered with foil. He partially uncovered one and said to himself,

"That does look very appetizing. Poor girl, she hoped to have a celebration, and now it has ended in tragedy." He felt depressed and unhappy, lost and grieved. "I must ring Dudu," he advised himself. "Maybe he can send me a cook for just a few days, until Natanya comes home. I can't do any work. I'm feeling lost, as she used to do everything, so quickly and perfectly. I have good food for today, but what will I do tomorrow?" He headed for his office and dialled his friend's number.

"Dudu," he said despondently. "Can you help me, please? Natanya is away with the team and I'm in great difficulty. Can you send me one of your kitchen staff, just for a few days?"

"Mordecai," said David, laughing, "if you think there is another Natanya here, you are mistaken. There is only one Natanya in the world; we will never find someone like her again."

"I know," he replied. "I mean, can you send me one of your cooks? I beg you, otherwise the boys will have to eat bread and cheese tomorrow."

David thought for a while, as he found it hard to disappoint his friend.

"We are not too busy at the moment, as most of the recent raids haven't brought any prisoners. All right, I'll send you one of our kitchen staff, but I must emphasise the point that you can only have him for a few days, because I'm anticipating loads and loads of Arabs after this raid."

At the Centre, the officers and their teams felt refreshed after a shower and a good meal. Hardly any of them had slept the previous night, so were looking forward to an early night.

The defence minister arrived at the Centre, to check on progress and supervise the plan for the next move. He requested a meeting with the officers before they retired to their rooms. He looked depressed and worried as he gave them a summary of the latest news.

"None of the factions in Lebanon has admitted responsibility, but we know for sure that Abu Mansour was the man behind the kidnapping, because some of our most reliable agents identified Mansour as the driver of the van. We are also certain beyond any doubt that the boys are not in Abu Mansour's camp, nor the adjacent Palestinian one, whom I would call his right hand supporters. Only God knows where they've hidden them. I have no hope for Jonathan, as he's been wanted by them for a long time, so they can avenge their relative's blood from him, but we may be able to help Peres."

The minister paused, squeezing his forehead with his fingers, then sadly said,

"I can't tell you how distressed I am for Jonathan. He is one of our best leaders in dealing with these wild animals. He worked so hard, especially on this last raid, which he planned perfectly. He administered it with a hundred percent success, until this mad dog carried out his vicious scheme. What makes the problem worse is that we don't know what to do. We are absolutely helpless, and the more time that passes, the more difficult our task becomes."

He looked to Victor and asked,

"Have you been able to work out something?"

Victor felt uncertain about his plan and decision to take the Arab girl back to her people, so he hesitated for a moment, then said to the anxious minister,

"We spent hours going round and round without finding a way out. As you said yourself, it is a hopeless situation, so we are willing to grasp at any straw that floats into sight. Tomorrow morning we intend to bomb Abu Mansour's territory to the ground, as we are also sure the boys will not be there. I know that will definitely seal Jonathan's fate, but we must let our enemies know that we mean business, and that our fighters are ready to sacrifice their lives for the sake of their country. The other decision I took, really in desperation, is to send Natanya to help the boys. She is an Arab prisoner related to Abu Mansour...."

Then he stopped quickly as the minister suddenly sat erect, unable to believe his ears.

"Please, don't get too worried. I'll explain the situation in more detail."

The minister stared at the tired old man, waiting to hear more hallucinations from Victor's mouth.

"She is a remarkable young woman, very lovable and hard working. She was in the Arab prison, but, according to the report, no matter how she was treated, with pleasure she showed love and consideration to us, her enemy. Anyhow, she was taken to help with the cooking in Jonathan's hostel. It seems from the report that he discovered something undesirable about her, so he wrote a warning."

Victor pushed the page across to the minister, who saw the underlined warning and Jonathan's signature.

"Well," Victor continued with his story, while the minister glanced at the following pages in the file. "Abu Mansour's men planted bombs around the hostel only a matter of a few days after that warning, and the prisoner was the one who raised the alarm, although she almost died herself in the process. Nevertheless, she saved the lives of about fifty persons. It seems from what Aaron and Mordecai have told us that she was suspected of being actively involved in the plot, but she was proved innocent. How and why, I can't tell you, because nobody knows, except Jonathan. He obviously thinks good of her, even though he didn't lift the warning, as he gratefully acknowledged her acts and also gave her two presents in appreciation for her good deeds. One is a golden star of David and the other is an expensive diamond ring.

"Anyhow, to cut the story short, she insisted that she can help to get them out, as she is a good friend of Mansour. We know that, because her real name is Baha, Mansour's girlfriend. Also Mordecai feels he can trust her with his own life, and Aaron actually has an oath of friendship with her. He will be the one to drop her on the road, so she can be picked up by Mansour. We hope and pray the plan will work."

The minister took a few minutes to digest the information he had just received, then he said, with annoyance in his voice,

"I've never heard such nonsense in my whole life! I can see what that girl schemed from the start, she only worked hard to avoid the various punishments. Then she was stupidly taken to the heart of our fighting teams, where she had the time of her life among our boys, listening to them, and studying them, especially Jonathan. Now she wants to go back, so they can celebrate their victory by killing him together."

Victor and the officers felt very uneasy, as they could see the minister was correct in his conclusion.

"I don't know what to do," said Victor. "I suppose we can look at the problem like this; we are gambling anyway, as if we send her, it's a tragedy, and if we keep her it's a tragedy. But at least if we send her, we can say that we tried every method possible, even if it seems madness and absurd."

"I want to see her," said the minister. "And also Aaron. I am concerned that these young boys of ours get attached to the cunning enemy and trapped by their acts, and then do stupid things like making oaths with them."

The messenger went in great haste and told Aaron and the girl to go to the office. Natanya felt uncomfortable. "I hate offices. Why do they want us to go to the office?" she asked herself. "Maybe Jonathan has died and there's no need for us to go." She pulled her medallion from her shirt and held it. "My love, even if it has happened you have died, you shall be in my heart." She could hear his last words, 'I won't say goodbye. See, you are next to my heart all the time.' "Oh Jonathan, I will not be able to live without you. We have so many dreams, and not one of them has yet been fulfilled. Why did you have to go so soon. Why couldn't you have stayed with me for even one hour? We only had a few precious minutes, and then you ran away and left me alone, only hugging your pleasant memory."

Aaron was far away in his thoughts as they walked side by side to the office. "I have a feeling Jonathan has died. I knew he was going to die from the way he looked at me when he left. He knew he was not coming back again." He glanced to Natanya and saw that her eyes were tearful. He remembered his promise, "I'll take her as a member of my family."

"Natanya," he said quietly. "Don't feel so bad. I will look after you. You shall be my sister and I'll take you to my house. I have two sisters, one is married and the other is younger than you. You can also see my mother, who is a very kind woman, and she will love you."

"Thankyou Aaron. I lost my family a long time ago, and I need a family. Thanks to God who gave me one now."

They stood outside the door. Aaron tapped and waited for permission to enter.

"Come in," commanded Victor.

Aaron opened the door and ushered Natanya in first, then followed and looked at the sombre men who were gazing at them. He noticed the minister, who glanced examiningly at him but mainly concentrated on the girl. "I don't think Jonathan is the problem. I have a feeling they are worried about my friendship with Natanya," he thought, feeling like a naughty boy who had been caught misbehaving.

"Oh no," Natanya thought, as she stared back at the new member who was stripping her naked with his piercing look. "I have a feeling they are not going to let me go. I bet they will talk and waste more time. I don't like the look of that man, he is similar to the officer in the prison. I can see he doesn't trust me, because his eyes are hard, and have no affection in them. I must be careful, and keep quiet, otherwise I'll never be able to go and help the boys."

"Come here, girl," gruffly ordered the minister. "I want to ask you a few questions."

Natanya walked calmly and stood near the table. Her soft black hair was woven into one large plait and hung over her shoulder. Her golden star shone around her neck, as she had just pulled it out on her way to the office. Her face was open and friendly, her eyes soft and gentle, and they looked into the minister's eyes, waiting for his assessment and questions.

"Where are you going to find the boys?"

"What a stupid question," she thought to herself. "How can I answer that? He is just looking for an excuse to stop me going." She stood looking at him while she thought of an answer.

"Hurry up!" he shouted. "I haven't the whole night to waste with you."

"I go first," she answered quietly. "Then my God will open my eyes to see."

The minister gave her a surprised look at the unexpected answer, but he continued,

"You said you can get the boys out from Abu Mansour. How are you going to do it?"

Natanya shrugged her shoulders and shook her head, and said firmly,

"I not say I get the boys out."

The minister looked at the others and back to her, puzzled at the contradiction.

"I said," she continued, "I pray. God help me to get the boys out. I can't do it myself, I can't do anything."

The minister thought for a moment, "I shall play the same game," he said to himself, then he gruffly said,

"If you think you can cover everything by prayer, hear this." Then he stood in front of all the men and swore,

"May God see to it, Natanya, that you are cut into pieces if you are deceiving us and endangering the two innocent men."

Then he ordered Aaron to the front of the audience and said,

"I want you to swear, in front of God and us, that you will be the one to search out with all your power, and shoot this girl, if she is proved to be an actor and a traitor."

Natanya was horrified at the oath and watched Aaron, her friend and brother, to see if he, too, doubted her motive.

"I swear in the presence of the God of Israel, to personally search and avenge the blood of Jonathan and Peres from the hand of Natanya, if she proves to be a deceiver."

The beast was kicking inside her heart. "Not one of them wants to believe my love, not even my closest friend, who had just assured me of his loyalty, as he has sworn to be the first one to shoot me. Why should I care? Why do I have to be so humiliated, while I am sacrificing my own life to save them. Let them go and get their own boys. I've been shouted at as a criminal, while I only have good in my heart towards all of them." She felt hot with anger and indignation. Her hands trembled and her forehead was wet with the sweat of repulsion.

She noticed herself, "What am I doing? The ugly beast is awake and controlling me, I must rebuke him." She sought the help of the Pattern of divine love. "What did he do in a situation like this?" she asked, searching her mental library, "He saw all his friends forsake him, even Peter, the one who had assured him only a few hours before that he would stand by him, even die for him, but Peter denied and swore that he never knew him. Did he resent that fact?" She stood watching and focusing on the Pattern. "He prayed, and said to him, 'When you return, strengthen your brothers'. He didn't condemn him, as he knew how humans react under severe pressure. Aaron was pressed hard. I must pray for him, and them, and not resent these people, as my aim is to do what I can to save the lives of the two men, even if that will cost me my own."

The minister saw the sad, hurt face, as she quietly watched Aaron and the rest, without saying a word or opposing the oath. He turned to Victor and spoke in Hebrew,

"We have her photographs, and Aaron knows her face well, so if she thinks she can have a free ride to her people, she is very much mistaken. So we'll chance her going, because we have no alternative, but if she goes and joins forces with them, we will fish her out of the deepest ocean and let her pay for her crime."

Then he asked Victor,

"Did you inform her about where she should tell the boys to find us? That's if she's truthful, which I very much doubt."

"No," answered the old officer. "I didn't trust her myself, that's why I didn't mention any places."

"We don't have to spell out their names. We can just tell her the numbers of the points from where we can pick them."

"Of course, we have the five main posts," replied Victor. "But we can cover and watch the secondary posts as well, so if we tell her to tell them that we'll pick them up from any of the ten posts, that's quite enough. Jonathan will understand what we mean, if she is truthful."

The minister looked at the subdued wax image of the gentle girl and said,

"Tell Jonathan, when you see him, that we will be waiting for him at the ten points," and he opened his two hands with the ten fingers clearly separated. "Can you remember that?"

She nodded and repeated,

"At the ten points," and repeated the demonstration of the fingers.

"You go now," said the minister. Then he turned to Aaron, "I want to have a word with you, young man."

Natanya left the room, feeling dejected and sad, and stood a long way from the door, as she could not bear to hear one more hurtful word, for she had just managed with difficulty to hold onto the reigns of the wild beast that roared inside her.

"Aaron," rebuked the minister. "Why did you go out of your way to attach yourself to our enemies? How could you make an oath of friendship with an enemy like this?"

Aaron felt unconfident and stood silent, watched by the whole team of officers.

"Why?" demanded the minister.

"Because she is not my enemy," he replied. "She has proved by her works that she is my friend, and according to her fruits I swore to be her friend forever, just like the friendship of king David and Jonathan."

The minister was stuck for words as he realised that Aaron had not been deceived by the beautiful eyes, but was convinced and believed in her friendship by the evidence of her works.

"Oh well," said the man after a while, "you made the oath, so you will have to pay for it. You are responsible for that girl, and if she proves unworthy of your friendship, you will have to search for her and shoot her. Our country comes before us and our personal feelings. I hope, for all our sakes, that she will prove to be truthful. Anyhow, it's better you go and have your rest, as all of you will have an early start."

Aaron turned round and walked slowly towards the door, then left, feeling uneasy and unhappy. Natanya saw him and understood the reason for his unhappiness, but she kept quiet. They silently walked side by side back to their camping area, where they would spend the night, in their sleeping bags next to their vehicles, as that was how they were accustomed to spend the night before a raid, to keep them alert and mentally adjusted for the battle.

The other boys were already settled and comfortably wrapped in their gear on the grass. Natanya looked to Aaron for guidance as she had never had such an experience before. He went to the vehicle and collected her rolled-up sleeping bag, then looked around to find her a suitable place to sleep. There was a neat line of sleeping men and he pointed to the side of the last one and said,

"I sleep here, and you can sleep on this side of me."

She slipped inside her sleeping bag and turned toward the empty, open ground, trying to get used to her new style of sleeping. There was a fresh smell from the grass and the wild flowers of spring filled the air with their gentle perfume.

"I feel so frightened, and not sure of anything or anybody," she whispered to herself. It was almost a full moon, and it shone so brightly and beautifully, that she felt reassured. "Why do you feel so afraid, my soul? Trust in your God, for he is always there," and she repeated her Psalm. "Imagine it, Jonathan can most probably see the same moon shining on him as I do, if he is still alive. I am sure he must be, because I have prayed for him. So I have no doubt."

Then her mind wandered to what had happened with the officer and Aaron. "Aaron swore to shoot me and kill me. How easy it is for humans to change their minds so quickly. One moment he is my friend, and the next he will be seeking my soul." She felt hurt and her heart grieved. "I wonder if Jonathan would do the same, one minute saying he loves me and the next.... who knows, maybe he has already forgotten me." She felt tears streaming down her cheeks like a hot stream.

"Natanya," she called herself. "I am really getting fed up with you. Since you saw that man in the office, you are insisting to think and feel sorry for yourself. Don't you know that true love believes in good motives and only sees the positive side in humans? That is what my Redeemer did, he believed in our good side and died so that he could save us from the ugly side that keeps all of us in bondage to fear and hate and death." She felt peace resting in her heart. "Yes, I must think of good things; what about that beautiful Psalm that Jonathan taught me just before he left, "Tov lichasout bashem...." (It is good to wait on the LORD, than to trust in humans, or to trust in nobles). She started to hum it quietly to herself, in Hebrew, to see if she could still remember the words and the tune.

Aaron could not go to sleep, as he lay there facing his friend who was at the beginning of the queue. He was tormented by his thoughts and doubts. "I wonder if she is an enemy or a friend?" he thought. "I have only seen her doing good and caring kindly in every possible way. She has never once lost her temper or held resentment. Could she be acting, as the minister thinks, or just misunderstood all the while, because she has a rare type of love?"

He was aware that she was not asleep, for she kept fidgeting. "What I can't understand is Jonathan, as he wrote such a warning about her, but at the same time asked me to look after her. 'She means so much to me', he said. Well, if she means so much to him, why couldn't he have lifted the restriction? Maybe he's like me, and found her to be an impossible enemy, or an incredible friend, too good to be true, but dangerous at the same time. I shouldn't have vowed so carelessly to be her friend, as now I'm endangering my people and my own self." He felt so depressed and unhappy. "I wish I could see inside her thoughts. Here she is, right beside me, but she lives in a different world, and I don't know whether it is a paradise or hell, a world of truth and pure love, or deception and murder."

He could hear her singing quietly under her cover. "O my God, help me," he murmured and lifted his head. "She is singing, while all of us have tremendous anxiety. She must be an enemy.... Oh, of course, she is going to meet with her boyfriend tomorrow and together they will finish Jonathan and Peres!" He found himself sweating from his anguish and he could no longer stay silent.

"Natanya," he called firmly. "What are you doing?"

She turned over to face him. There was a beautiful smile on her face, as the moonlight caught her features. "Aaron sounded just like Mother Teresa," she thought, "when she caught us talking in the orphanage when we should have been sleeping." Then she answered in a whisper to her strict guard,

"I sing a good song," and she started to sing very quietly in Hebrew, "Tov lichasout...."

The words of the song comforted Aaron and its catching tune calmed his fear. "It is good to wait on Yah, than to trust in man. It is good to wait on Yah, than to trust in nobles. All the nations surround me, but in the name of Yah I shall overcome them. The LORD is with me, what can man do to me?" He started to accompany her, singing very quietly, so they would not disturb the rest of the company. Natanya covered her mouth and laughed softly,

"I make only one mistake."

He encouraged her by saying,

"You sang it well, there was no mistake at all." Then he added,

"Natanya, you are the best friend I've ever had."

She looked at him, remembering her friend Baha. "How marvellous, those are the exact words of Baha, so I mustn't lose my faith in the positive side of humans, as they have been created in God's image." She responded to his statement,

"I am lucky, and very happy. I have so many good friends everywhere."

Jonathan and Peres spent their second day in their abhorrent state. Their bodies ached from the tight ropes, which had only been loosened briefly to allow them to relieve nature, but even then their feet remained chained. Each time they were re-tied roughly and, it seemed, even tighter. They made a great effort to keep themselves occupied with various objects, but the dagger and ticking clock did not help, as it reminded them of their unhappy situation and uncertain fate.

"I can't take anymore of this," said Peres, almost screaming because of his aching body.

"We have no option," replied Jonathan, whose own head was throbbing from anxiety and the following day's threat.

"I think they've forgotten us," moaned Peres.

"I think they must be in more anguish than us, for at least we know we are alive, even though we're dreadfully uncomfortable, but they don't know whether we are alive or dead."

He stopped and thought of his angel,

"I feel sorry for my sweetheart," said Jonathan. "She must be feeling terrible. She looked so happy when I left her, thinking of good things. I had wanted to tell her about my feelings toward her for a long time and never managed it, and when I eventually succeeded, we only had a few minutes together; most probably our only few moments, as I do doubt if I will ever be freed. Perhaps there is a possibility for you, but not for myself, as Mansour detests the sight of me. In fact, I am surprised he's controlled his hate for so long."

Peres kept quiet, listening to the desperate man.

"Maybe they will do something tonight, Jonathan."

"What can they do? Whatever they do, it will be risky. They could floodlight the area, but it's almost impossible to find us, as we are in an orange grove, full of trees and shadows and hidden in this store. I feel that the quicker we accept our fate, the better for us."

Peres sensed that Jonathan was in the depth of the pit, so he said,

"Nothing is too much for Adoni."

"I believe so, Peres. That is my only way out of this misery we are in, and it's funny, the last song we sang on Shabbat with my angel was, "Tov lichasout bashem". She told me that was her favourite Psalm and she sang so well, singing from the heart with a beautiful and sincere voice."

Peres was working hard to discover Jonathan's angel. "She has soft black hair, lives between the hostel and the Centre, makes the best coffee in the world, has a beautiful, sincere voice, and is religious, as she must know so many Psalms if her favourite one is 'Tov lichasout'."

Jonathan noticed Peres sorting out the quiz in his mind, so he smiled and started to hum the song quietly to himself. The tune had a slow start, but soon turned into a rapturous and joyful melody that builds confidence in the mighty hand of the Almighty's deliverance. Peres joined in with Jonathan, and soon they were singing at the top of their voices, forgetting all about their troubles.

Mansour was sitting outside, bored and nervous, it not being an easy job to sever a man's arm, so he tried to build up his hate to the maximum, to justify his actions.

"He killed my uncle and aunt. He took my cousin and others captive to his land to torment and kill them, so he must die." Then he suddenly heard Jonathan singing. "What's he doing?" Mansour felt uneasy and shaky. "I told him of his fate, and here he is singing, and a jolly song at that." He listened to it for a time and then said, "Maybe my father was right when he said I must kill him and get finished from him. He's most probably thought of a way to escape before the morning."

Then Peres joined in with Jonathan.

"They're celebrating and sound very happy. What a strange people!" The thought of strange people brought Amal to Mansour's mind. "She is also very strange. It seems as if all my enemies are peculiar like that. We killed her entire family and she came to our camp to distribute free food and clothes. 'Love project' she called it, as she wanted to tell us by her works how she loved us. But why this fox is singing, I just don't know, as I assured him that I mean business, and tomorrow he will have his right arm cut off, without fail, and here he is, singing!"

He felt like entering to see what was going on. "Oh no, better I don't do that, in case they're trapping me. I'm alone out here and the other two are quite a distance from me. It's wiser to ignore them, even though they are getting on my nerves."

Jonathan and Peres felt really good after the song, as they sensed someone powerful was watching over them.

"I know my angel is praying for me," he thought, noticing the moonlight shining through the various cracks in the wooden door. "Natanya, keep praying my love, and I pray that you don't feel too anxious about me, as I am not alone, for God is with me, and you are beside me, next to my heart. He will work some way for us, so that our dreams will come true."

The two men lay down on the floor on their blankets and went into a deep sleep. Mansour was also sleepy, exhausted from the excitement of the last few days, so he lay down on his mat, with his loaded gun beside him, and slept. The next thing he was aware of were the cocks crowing, announcing Friday's sunrise, and the muezzin broadcasting the call for the dawn prayer. He ceremonially washed his hands, face, head and feet, ready for his prayer. He felt anxious and excited at the same time, "because today is a special day for me, as I will avenge the blood of my holy people from this infidel." Then he thought, "I am glad I didn't worry about their singing last night, as they're still there, awake nice and early. I'm sure Jonathan is dead worried, but he's putting on a brave face. I know I promised to see him at nine, but I'll give him his water after the prayer, because I am kind and I can't let him go without his breakfast, and I want to watch his expression, as it's never changed since he came."

After the prayer, Mubarak came with the two glasses. Mansour opened the door and they both entered. Jonathan was sitting in his corner, staring at his visitors.

"Good morning, Jonathan," said Mansour joyfully. "I see you've had a good night's sleep! I heard you singing and thought you have a good voice, so maybe you can sing for us later in our little party?!"

Peres swore and cursed under his breath.

"I brought you your sweet water early, so you can feel strong for later, as I don't want you to suffer, even though you are my enemy."

Jonathan continued his expressionless look at Mansour.

"So insolent," he said in Arabic to Mubarak. "He's had that style of look since he came here, but I guarantee you, he will be another man after nine o'clock."

Mubarak laughed and responded,

"I can already see a lot of change in his face. His eyes are very tired, and he needs a good shave."

The two prisoners had their sweet water. Then Mansour and his friend left, shutting the door securely after them.

Jonathan stared at the clock, it was a few minutes after six. "So much could happen in three hours," he thought.

"My love, Natanya, what's happening?" he whispered, bending his head to her piece of hair. "Has nobody told you that I am in a great calamity? Are you not aware of my desperation?"

Peres heard the faint mumbling and asked,

"How do you feel, Jonathan?"

"I feel as if I'm sinking in a deep ocean, with sharks surrounding me from all directions, and I am tied like this, unable to move away from them, or even to tread water and stop myself from drowning."

"I know the feeling," said Peres, grinding his teeth. "I wish now we had never gone to the hospital."

"What happened, happened. In fact, going there was the best part of the mission for me, as I felt so happy to see those doctors cheered up, especially when we offered them help, on just one condition!" and he laughed when he remembered their expressions. "I'm sure they thought I was going to tie a string to the offer, but when they heard me say that the condition was treatment for all without discrimination, they almost fainted!"

Peres also laughed as he recalled the vision to mind.

"They're laughing," said Mansour to Mubarak. "Imagine it, laughing, while he has only three hours to go."

"I don't trust them," said Mubarak. "I'd better go and watch the road, in case their people will send someone to get them free."

"No one beside our people will be allowed near here," ordered Mansour. "In fact, no one, except my father and you two, because I have a feeling they are certain of some help, and someone could disguise themselves in one form or another and get in. So take this order, that no one, not even from our own team, is allowed into the grove, except my father and Walid."

Mubarak hurried off to take up his post and pass the message on to Walid.

Natanya woke up before the dawn and watched the glittering stars gradually disappearing, one by one, until the moon was left all alone, except for the company of the bright morning star.

"My Heavenly Father," she said, pleading with her creator, "I beg you to help me today, so that my effort will not be in vain. Help me to find Mansour or his father without any delay, and also help me to find Jonathan and his friend well and without any harm, so they can come back to their people, and no blood will be shed anymore."

She looked around and saw Aaron next to her and the neat line of young fighters, sound asleep beside their vehicles.

"All these are your children, Father, and you desire that all of them shall live and enjoy a life of peace and joy, and pure love. So help and protect them, too. Look at them, they are mere humans, and we are all fragile, made from the dust of the ground, so do feel sorry for the make of your hands."

She sat up, waiting for everyone to rise, so she could carry out her mission. The figures of two men approached the sleeping company and clapped their hands to rouse everyone.

"Boker tov," they shouted, while still clapping. "Coffee and rolls are ready in the canteen. Hurry up. You have half an hour to wash and be on your way."

The boys jumped up, rolled up their sleeping bags, then tied them and lifted them onto the vehicles. Natanya rolled up hers and gave it to Aaron. Then they marched toward the building, to the showers and toilets. There were sections for both sexes, so Natanya had hers all to herself, as she was the only girl on that mission. She had a shower to awake herself, making her feel fresh and exhilarated. After that, she combed her hair, cut short to a fringe at the front, and braided the rest into one thick plait which hung down over her shoulder. She looked into the mirror and remembered the day when one of the nuns cut it in that style. 'Amal,' she told her, 'you have grown up now and need to wear your hair differently, as two plaits only suit young girls. I will cut it for you in a very easy way. As you can't see the back of your head, you don't need to touch that area, so we will only cut the part you can see.' Amal smiled as she looked at her hair. "How strange!" she thought. "All these years I have done exactly as Sister Margarita advised me, yet I still look the same, from that day till now, so I think they will recognize me as I haven't changed, and it would be so lovely to see them all again."

The team had their rolls of bread and cheese and drank their coffee. Some filled more rolls with cheese and olives and wrapped them in napkins, ready to eat on the road. Aaron sat next to Natanya, watching her from time to time.

"Do you feel frightened?" he asked.

"No, I just pray we are not too late," she said.

He nodded and started to repeat the rules for her.

"You do one job at a time, and forget all about other things. Don't rush, or we will all lose the battle."

She smiled and said to him,

"You are a good teacher, just like Jonathan. He is very good."

Victor and the other heads were standing waiting to see the team off on its way. Natanya removed her shoes, and Aaron put on her handcuffs and ankle chains, then lifted her onto the truck. The other drivers were all ready to start as soon as they received the signal. Victor came to Natanya's vehicle and said to her,

"We hope you can help to set the boys free. If you manage that, we will reward you very much, but if you try to deceive us, we will follow you to the end of the world, and punish you." Then he asked, "Can you remember what to tell Jonathan?"

She smiled as she firmly controlled her lower nature, determined that nothing would upset her like the previous day.

"He will find you at the ten points," she replied, lifting her bound arms and showing him her fingers.

"That is good," he said, looking at her soft brown eyes and gentle smile, not knowing how to deal with her. "She almost looks like an angel," he thought. "Just let us hope and pray she will be a real one."

Abu Mansour and his group spent the night at their post, guarding and watching the road from Israel. They said their morning prayer and organized themselves, ready for action, with their sandbags heaped, and telescopes focused on the road.

"Our main interest is in watching at the moment," he said to the men, "as Jonathan robbed us bare of our equipment and weapons, which means we can't afford a confrontation with the Israelis just yet. Anyway, Mansour is going to deal with Jonathan at nine this morning, so let us watch carefully, as so far not one Israeli has shown his face or let us hear his voice."

The men sat behind their sandbags, bored stiff watching an empty road.

"Not even a bird," said one of the young men. "We could catch some game though and have a party too, later."

Abu Mansour ignored the remark of the youth and continued smoking one cigarette after another, his usual behaviour when he was anxious. He looked at his watch,

"It's only half past six, but it seems like midday," he said, fiddling with the stones piled in front of him.

Suddenly the peace of the morning was shattered when a few Israeli fighters flew overhead.

"At last!" he shouted. "They've appeared!"

The men sat in their positions, concentrating on the road as more and more planes screamed overhead.

"They're going to raid us today," said Abu Mansour. "We must go and warn our people...." but before he had finished his sentence, the convoy appeared on the horizon. He glued his eye to the lens while the others prepared themselves to snipe if he signalled them to do so.

"That's a very big convoy," he remarked, viewing the large vehicles turning on the narrow bend between the mountains.

Natanya's heart was thumping as they approached the critical area, as she had never been there before, only knowing about it from Baha. 'Our best spot for sniping the Israelis is where the mountains start and the road turns,' she could hear Baha describing the location. 'The vehicles have to slow down and then we shoot them and blow them up, because they are our enemy.'

Aaron was watching the area carefully, but stole a quick glance at Natanya and saw she was tense,

"Natanya, we are almost near the spot. Are you ready?"

She nodded her head without speaking.

"Are you afraid?"

"No. I am praying," she replied. "I pray that you not be killed. Is very dangerous."

Aaron smiled and said,

"I pray for you, that you will not be killed either."

The vehicle slowed down and gradually came to a halt.

"Their truck has broken down!" excitedly cried Abu Mansour. "It's the last one in the convoy and the others are far ahead."

The snipers hands were on their triggers as they asked, "Shall we blow them?"

Aaron pushed Natanya down from the vehicle, with her hands and feet still shackled. He shot a few times into the air and stood behind her, sandwiched between her and the vehicle.

"That's a prisoner!" shouted Abu Mansour. "Don't shoot at all. I think those vehicles are full of our people that they're bringing to exchange for their two men." He was now feeling excited and happy that things were starting to move at last.

"That's Amal, the mobashira!" he yelled out, jumping with excitement, announcing what was happening as if he was a commentator on a horse racing broadcast. "She's looking around, as she wants to escape, but she's chains on her feet and handcuffs, and the Israeli soldier is pushing her." Then he shouted out loud, "Leave her alone, you dog!"

He turned to the team and said,

"We must help her to escape. Some of you watch for us from here, and the rest follow me down and make a chain of warners, hiding behind the bushes, so you can whistle signals of danger or victory. She's come just in time. The best thing that ever happened to us."

Then he was off down the mountain side, running like a mountain goat, without making a sound as he hid behind the bushes and trees on his way to the road.

Natanya looked around her and saw a gap between the bushes.

Aaron shouted his order,

"Don't move, or I'll shoot you!"

The driver climbed down from the cab and looked under the vehicle. Aaron joined him and bent down, to see what was going on, as oil started to stream down the road. The two men became engrossed in their problem as they talked and prodded their hands about under the bonnet, forgetting about their prisoner.

Natanya began to move gently and slowly toward the gap.

"I mustn't hurry or panic, or we'll lose the battle," she counselled herself.

The team behind the telescopes were jumping and shouting, and banging the sandbags with their fists, as they saw Amal had moved quite a distance from the soldiers, who were still busy fixing their engine.

Amal faintly heard the soft whistle, just like a gentle breath. "That's Abu Mansour's men," she whispered, and felt like running, but controlled herself.

Aaron was strictly controlling himself also as he wanted to see if she had escaped, but he kept gesturing and sticking his hands in the oil and looking at his watch. "She has another two minutes, but they seem like hours," he thought.

Abu Mansour was right behind the bushes, following Amal's progress as he could see her, although he could not be seen from the road. He and the others were whistling and following as Amal managed to inch slowly backwards, whilst keeping her eyes on Aaron. She felt so happy to hear the whistles, "God has answered my prayer and let me find Abu Mansour. I will request him to let the men go free, then no one will be hurt or killed."

Abu Mansour was ready to snatch Amal as soon as she was near enough, although her chains were delaying her. The men on the mountain top were sweating from the excitement of the drama, as they could see the whole picture from their vantage point.

Suddenly Abu Mansour grabbed Amal and dragged her backwards, causing her to nearly shriek, as she had never had such an exciting game in her whole life. But she did as Aaron advised her and forgot everything else, and concentrated on the game. The men carried her like a stretcher, with Abu Mansour holding her hands and Abdu her feet, as they ran to join the rest of the team. She laughed and giggled, like a little child that was thoroughly enjoying her game.

Aaron turned round and discovered that his prisoner had vanished, so he shouted and shot in the air and on the ground a few times and went near to the bushes, where he shot again. When he could not find her, his friend joined him and both shouted and loosed off some more shots. Then they retreated to their vehicle, which they had just managed to repair. At that moment a few fighters flew low overhead to protect the delayed truck, so they gave up the search and restarted their journey.

Abu Mansour let Amal down when they reached safe ground and the whole team joined them, laughing and choking and wiping away their sweat. Amal attempted to hug Abu Mansour and the other men, laughing for a while and crying for a while, as her emotions were running high.

"I can't tell you how happy I am to see you. I prayed so much that you would be here, and it's wonderful to see you all," she exclaimed, loudly and excitedly.

Abu Mansour put his hand over her mouth and said,

"Hush, Amal. You talk too loud, don't you know that every tree and every stone has eyes and ears?"

Amal looked around her and scrutinized the trees and stones with wide open eyes, causing the rest to laugh delightedly. She continued,

"The Israelis are very upset as two of their boys have been kidnapped."

"Shush," warned Abu Mansour.

Then he said to the others,

"I'd better take her to Mansour. She's not safe to keep here and will soon give us away, as she doesn't know the rules of our fighting."

He looked at the puzzled girl and smiled,

"Amal, Mansour and I love to hear every word you say, but we can't talk here. I told you that the trees and stones have eyes and ears, but you didn't believe me. Anyhow, first let me take these chains from your legs and wrists, and then we can talk freely."

He sent one of the men to the van for the bolt cutters and they soon freed their long lost friend. Abu Mansour looked at her and commented,

"You haven't changed a bit, Amal. Your hair is just the same, and you look just as you did on the day you were taken."

She smiled and tried to talk quietly,

"I know. I've just grown a bit older since then, and I've seen and learnt so much."

"We will have a party later, and you can tell us all your story," said Abu Mansour, his face full of happiness.

While the man was freeing her hand, she asked,

"How is Baha? I have missed her so much and been thinking of her all the time."

"Don't mention Baha," warned Abu Mansour. "If you want to make Mansour go mad, just mention the name Baha. None of us are allowed to say that name in the house, so I've warned you from now."

"Why?" she asked, feeling very sad to see division in the family. He did not want to hurt her feelings, so tactfully said,

"And don't ask me why, because that is also a prohibited question."

Amal sat in the same van that was used for the kidnapping, but was quite unaware of that fact. She sat quietly, looking from the window, feeling relaxed and at home, almost forgetting she had been away from her country for many months. Suddenly she remembered her mission. "My Jonathan, he is here somewhere and I hope I can find him. At least I'm with him in the same country. I am so glad to see Abu Mansour and now Mansour, and I'll beg them to let the boys go. They are good people in their own way, but the only problem is the ugly beast of lower nature that's robbing them of their peace of mind and joy. Never mind, I'll do my best to explain to them a better way of solving this problem than by hate and killing."

Abu Mansour interrupted her thoughts and asked her,

"Did you see any of our people in the prison?"

"No," she said. "I've been alone in one little room for a long time. I haven't seen anybody or talked to anyone, except to my God, of course, as he is everywhere."

"What did they do to you, Amal?"

She turned to him and smiled,

"It's not good to think of bad things because it brings the ugly beast back to life and makes the hate to grow, so it's much better to just think of good things."

"Amal," said the man, smiling, "are you still believing in the ugly beast? I thought you must have changed by now, as you told me you've grown up. So what is the beast still doing there?"

She laughed and said,

"The older I get, the better I hope to control that ugly beast, because he lives inside everyone of us."

"Okay Amal, better we don't talk about that subject either."

She looked at him disappointedly and continued with her own thoughts. "What shall I talk about at the party? I can't mention Baha, or the reason why, or the beast. Anyhow, it's better I don't upset them, if I want them to release the boys from their prison."

Abu Mansour approached the grove at ten to nine and blew a joyful tune on his horn to announce their arrival.

"Mansour will not believe his eyes, Amal," he said, laughing. "You just watch his face when we go inside!"

She sat up ready to watch the second excitement of the morning. When Walid and Mubarak saw Abu Mansour, they raised their guns in greeting, but a surprised expression filled their faces when they saw Amal beside him.

"Look at them!" laughed Abu Mansour, with tears flowing from his eyes. Amal too, waved her hands and shouted excitedly,

"Ahla wa sahla," as she recognized the boys.

Jonathan and Peres heard the joyful horn blowing and their hearts sank to their stomachs.

"That's Mansour," said Jonathan. "He's coming to prepare for his party."

"I am sorry, Jonathan," said Peres, pale and desperate.

"I am sorry, too. Now it's too late and I will never see my angel again, because I'm sure I'll be unable to survive this barbaric treatment."

"What I resent is our people," said Peres. "They sit in the Centre, talking and doing nothing, not even making a small attempt to save us." Then he broke down and cried from frustration.

"I need my love beside me," grieved Jonathan, "as she is the only one who can comfort me in such distress, but it's too late now for anything to happen to save us. It's just impossible for our dreams to come true."

When Mansour saw the van slowly approaching down the narrow track, he stood up and went to see what was happening, saying to himself, "Surely my father hasn't also caught another catch, has he?" He half walked and half ran to the moving van where Abu Mansour sat almost paralysed with laughter. As laughter is catching, Amal also found herself laughing at the expression on Mansour's face.

"That's our Amal!" he exclaimed. "What a surprise! I've been thinking of her a lot just lately and here she is, as happy as ever!"

Amal jumped out of the van and ran into Mansour's open arms.

"Amal, I must be dreaming!"

As she hugged him with tears of laughter and joy in her eyes, she said,

"I had been praying to meet Abu Mansour and I met him on the road. It's a most beautiful dream come true."

Mansour looked at his father, who was still trying to control his fit of laughter, and asked,

"How did you pick her up on the road?"

"Amal ran from the Israelis when their truck broke down and we had a lovely time. I wish you had been with us, as I've never had such an enjoyable time in my whole life."

"Shush!" Amal said to the excited man, and pointed to all the orange trees around them. "There are many orange trees here, Abu Mansour, and they all have eyes."

"Tislameely," exclaimed Abu Mansour, hugging her, as she sounded so sweet and adorable.

Jonathan could faintly hear the excited voices and laughter coming from the distance as he kept his attention focused on the time. "Six minutes left, if only something would happen. I think I'd rather be blown up by a bomb than face this situation," thought the very anxious man.

Amal quietly said to Mansour,

"The Israelis are very upset, because two of their boys have been kidnapped."

"I know," he interrupted joyfully. "I kidnapped them!" Then he pointed to the closed wooden doors and said, "You see that store?"

Amal nodded her head, anticipating to hear more metaphorical language about 'doors talking' or something of that nature, not dreaming that store could hold her love.

"Well, inside is a fox and a big shark."

"What do you mean?" asked a very puzzled Amal.

Abu Mansour roared with laughter, as he looked at the innocent girl who was learning so many new expressions.

"I will explain to you," continued Mansour. "The name of the fox is Jonathan, the chief, and I'm going to kill him; not in one go, but a bit at a time."

Amal was shocked and horrified, and cried with pleading eyes,

"Please don't kill them. Try to love your enemy and let them go. You will feel good for it."

"Oh no!" said Mansour in desperation. "Amal, you haven't changed at all. Are you still loving your enemy?"

Abu Mansour was in the mood for laughing, as the whole situation was a great comedy, so he just laughed and coughed all the more.

Because of all the excitement and exertion from the escaping game, the golden medallion had gradually worked its way out of Natanya's shirt, and Mansour suddenly spotted the gold chain around her neck, so pulled it to see what it was. His face turned white and his eyes looked suspiciously at Amal.

"Oh no!" she thought. "What can I do now?" She looked guilty, and her face glowed with embarrassment, while Mansour and his father silently watched her. She covered her mouth with her hand, just like a guilty little girl who had been caught stealing. She put her hand into her pocket and pulled out the little box, opened it and slid the diamond ring onto her finger. Then she giggled and said,

"I only have these two."

Mansour could not hold himself, as he thought the preacher had stolen the two items from the Israelis, so both men collapsed laughing and said together,

"You stole them, Amal!"

"I didn't," she indignantly replied. "I only TOOK them."

"Amal, I've never met a sweeter person than you," said Mansour, laughing and looking at the delightful Amal.

Abu Mansour added,

"I can see we are going to have a great time with Amal this evening." Mansour agreed and looked at his watch,

"I'll have to go soon and deal with the fox, as he only has four minutes to go."

The word 'minute' triggered Amal's memory about the raid which was about to take place, as she had completely forgotten it in the excitement of the morning, so she cried out,

"O my God!" and held her heart.

"What's the matter?" asked Mansour.

"The Israelis are going to blow up all your territory this morning," and then she could not talk fast enough to tell them about the seriousness of the situation. "I heard them yesterday. They said they will kill everybody, and flatten all the houses to the ground. Hurry up, you must get the people out. I will come with you."

The two men were stunned, and just stood there, looking at her anxious face.

"This morning, they said. You have no time left."

"Amal, you've been sent by God to help us, and we'll go immediately, especially as the place is full of people, but better you stay here, as you will be more of a hindrance than a help," said Mansour. He paused, then continued, "You can guard the Israelis for us."

"Me?" she said, holding the golden medallion and looking worried and pale.

"Don't worry, they are tied up securely and can't even move from their place, not even to walk one step. All you have to do is sit on this chair. I will leave you the gun as well."

"No, I don't like guns," she said.

"Okay, you don't have to hold it, but I shall leave it nevertheless, in case something happens and you need to defend yourself. I will leave Mubarak at the gate, so if you see someone coming or you're in trouble, just shout, and he'll come to help you, but I swear, Jonathan shall die today. I'll kill him in one go when I come back."

Amal shook from anxiety and desperation. She was worried for the people who were about to be bombed and she was concerned for her love.

"You look so frightened," said Mansour. "But I promise they'll not harm you, and I'll only be forty minutes. No more than that."

"Forty minutes?" she repeated.

"Yes, and I don't know how to thank you, Amal."

"Please don't thank me, but thank God, as I'm a failure. I think I may already be too late to help. I'm sorry, as I got so excited and happy to see you that I forgot, as I should have told you about the raid earlier."

"Don't worry, we have time," said Abu Mansour. "The people are already on the alert. We'll take the van and be back in only forty minutes."

Amal stood and watched the men leave in haste, disappearing in a cloud of dust up the track. She looked around her. 'The trees have eyes,' she could hear in her head.

"I must get the boys out," she said to herself. "I'll have to chance it, even if I get killed myself."

"I don't want to die," cried her heart.

"There is more happiness and satisfaction in giving, and if that means I have to give my life, so that others can live, then it's worth it. I hope Abu Mansour and his son are in time to save the people before the raid, and I hope, at the same time, that I can help Jonathan and his friend."

She walked bare footed towards the store, carefully looking around her. "There's not a single human around," she thought. "Only the sparrows and the trees, and my God, who is beside me."

She saw the bunch of keys hanging from the lock and noticed that some of them were very small. As she held the key to turn it, she found her hands so shaky. "I mustn't feel so frightened." Then she corrected herself, "I am not frightened, but I can't believe that my Jonathan is in here; yet I'm in great anticipation, and yearning to see him."

Jonathan could hear someone at the door as the keys were rattling. He looked at the clock. It was sharp on nine. He bit his lip in desperation, and called in his heart, "Natanya," as all his expectations had evaporated and the ray of hope replaced by a heavy gloom. Peres could hardly breathe for the thought that he was going to witness a most horrifying experience, to see his friend's arm amputated. Both sat erect and centred their gaze on the door.

"Natanya," called Jonathan, his last word in an undertone, as he waited for the door to open and to face his executioner.

Natanya turned the key and pushed the door gently, then stood there with the door partly open. As her eyes acclimatized to the dark room, she was shocked to discover the state of her man. "How terrible he looks. I can't believe that just a few days could reduce a man to such a state, but I'm delighted to find him still alive."

Jonathan and Peres stared at the calm and softly smiling form as she stood backlit by the sun's rays which poured through the door.

"It's an angel," thought Peres, looking at the still figure.

"It's a vision of the Lord," thought Jonathan, gazing at what he was sure was an angel.

None of the three spoke or moved for a few moments, then Natanya entered and partly closed the door behind her, and ran to Jonathan, who still could not believe the message being sent by his eyes. She knelt beside him and looked at his tired eyes and face, then held his shoulders and hugged him, and kissed him on his cheeks.

"Jonathan," she whispered, her tears flowing as she comprehended his severe situation.

"Natanya," he breathed, still in a state of disbelief. "I just called your name, and you appeared, just like magic. It's a miracle!"

She hugged him again and said,

"I came to set you free, both of you. We have to hurry because Mansour is going to kill you. You must run quick, you only have few minutes." She looked around him, searching for the knot to untie his wrapping, as she said, "I thought I never see you again."

"I thought the same, in fact, I thought you were Mansour coming to finish me. How did you manage to get here?"

"Big story," she said. "I tell you later, now I must let you free."

"Where is Mansour?" he asked.

"Mansour going to get the people out. The Israelis are going to throw bombs."

"How do you know, Natanya?" he asked with concern.

"I heard them talking in the room. I was waiting outside, waited long time. They talk a lot, all the time talk. I waited for a long time. I thought I never come, but thanks to God, he helped me."

While Natanya struggled to undo his ropes Jonathan said to Peres,

"All my hard work is wasted."

"I told Mansour to get the people out," Natanya said. "So no one will get hurt."

"I am glad you did, my love. At least then we'll have no casualties."

She smiled and added,

"Otherwise we will loose the battle."

Peres began to awake from his trance and asked Jonathan,

"Are we dreaming, or is this real life?"

"We are in reality. My angel has just arrived and this is what happens when she's around."

"Angel?" thought Peres, contemplating the bare footed alef prisoner. "The soft black hair is exactly the same as that which Jonathan has in his pocket." He struggled to understand the impossible puzzle. "An Arab, an alef prisoner, yet she is Jonathan's angel, and coming to set us free? How is that possible?"

"I can't do it!" said Natanya, almost panicking. Then she ran across to Peres. "I will try this one," she said, kneeling beside him and tussling with his tight knot. She soon gave up using her fingers and pulled in vain with her teeth as she attempted to loosen the knot. The two men had completely forgotten about the dagger until Jonathan turned from watching his struggling angel to see the time. He hastily called,

"Natanya, look up there, above the door. There's a very sharp dagger which you can use to cut the ropes."

She jumped up and ran to the door, saying,

"You are clever."

"Nowhere near as clever as you are," he protested emphatically.

Natanya jumped to knock the dagger from the clock, but she was too short to even reach the top of the door. Peres was becoming so anxious.

"How frustrating," he said, looking from Jonathan to the angel.

"I know, I know," said Natanya, running out of the room and closing the door behind her.

"Where's she going?" asked Peres anxiously.

"Don't worry, Peres. We're in safe hands and she knows what she's doing. We mustn't panic, as God has sent her to save us at the last minute, so she is bound to succeed, somehow."

Natanya looked around her and there was no sign of anybody, so she took the chair from under the trees and ran back to the store. She put it under the clock, and, standing on her toes, just reached the dagger.

"Thanks to God," she said, breathing a sigh of relief, and tested its sharpness with her finger. "Is very sharp," she observed, looking to Jonathan. "It is good to cut meat with."

Jonathan glanced at Peres and then back to the smiling girl.

"Oh Natanya, please don't say that," he said, feeling sick at the thought.

"Why?" she asked, as she went towards him to cut his ropes.

"It's a long story," he replied, looking at her soft eyes. "I will tell you about it later, but, just for you, I'll take this dagger as a souvenir for our kitchen, even though I hate the sight of it."

She cut the rope and started to undo it, wrapping it round her arm in a neat coil, but she wasted no time in telling them how to escape.

"You go toward your left hand," she instructed, glancing to Jonathan from time to time as she unwrapped him. "Mubarak is at the gate, on your right hand, so don't go that way." Then she pointed to the left of the grove and continued, "There are many farms of orange trees that way, so there are lots of places to hide and nobody around, only the trees," the thought of which made her laugh, so she added, "but they all have eyes, and the stones have ears!"

"This is long," she said to Jonathan, looking at the endless length of rope. He stood up to help her but his body was numb and full of pins and needles.

"What an incredible dream!" said Jonathan in his heart, while he listened to Natanya explaining the way out of their tragic situation. "I thought I'd lost everything, and the one whom I never anticipated to be here is the one who is helping me yet again. I still can't believe it, that she is real, until I hold her in my arms."

Natanya threw the ropes onto the ground, and stared at Jonathan with her mouth open.

"Another chain!" she exclaimed, looking at the handcuffs and ankle chain.

"We've had it," moaned Peres, panicking. "Now Mansour will kill the three of us."

"Pray," she commanded, and then she raised her hands to heaven. "Help me, Lord."

Suddenly she remembered the bunch of keys in the lock. "Perhaps those small keys are for the cuffs," she thought, running out of the store again. She looked from side to side to see if there was any change. "Good, nobody is around," she said, pulled the key from the lock and rushed inside again, almost shutting the door behind her, just in case someone noticed it was open.

"I think I have the keys," she said, sitting on the floor to undo the feet first, while saying, "I do the feet first, so you can run."

She tried one, then another, until she found the right one.

"Thanks to God," she announced, throwing the chains away into the corner, and starting on the handcuffs.

"However can I thank you," said Jonathan. "No words or praise can pay for what you have done, my dearest treasure."

She smiled,

"I didn't do anything. God is very good. He heard my prayers."

At last Jonathan was a free man. He hugged her and tried to lift her up, but his hands had lost their power, from lack of circulation and exercise.

"Please Jonathan," pleaded Peres. "Can't you do that later?"

Natanya giggled and nodded her head,

"Yes, we must hurry now."

Jonathan took the dagger and keys and released Peres, while Natanya stood watching, telling him where to find his people.

"You will find the boys waiting at the ten points," she said, stretching her fingers.

Jonathan noticed his ring and the golden star of David. "What a brave girl," he thought. "How did she manage to come here with that round her neck?" So he asked her,

"Did Mansour see your medallion and ring?"

"Yes," she said, covering her mouth and laughing. "Is a long story. I tell it later."

Both men laughed, as there were so many long stories to be related.

"You keep to your left hand," she continued, "the camp is on the right. If you run quick, you be far before Abu Mansour come back."

"Why are you speaking like that, Natanya?" asked Jonathan with concern. "Aren't you coming with us, to show us the way?"

"No," she said quietly, looking at him thoughtfully.

He stopped unwrapping Peres and stared at her, shocked and anxious.

"Why, my love? You promised me...." but before he had finished his sentence she interrupted,

"I will wait for you, Jonathan, but I must stay here for a few days."

"That's the least we can do for her," thought Peres, "to let her stay with her people for a few days. In fact, we should set her free altogether."

Jonathan could not find words to express his disappointment, so she explained her decision,

"If I go now, they will never trust me again. They need help. I must stay and help them to love their enemies, and also I can help you, too."

Jonathan paused as he looked at her gentle person with admiration and respect. "What a unique love! She has no thought for herself, but what is best for others, even though they're not her own family." Then he spoke, while undoing Peres' ropes,

"Mansour will kill you, my love, if he discovers that you let us out, so how do you think I can leave you here to die?"

"We make a plot," she said, using all the words Aaron had taught her. "You tie me on the chair, hit me, not hard, so Mansour will see that you run away, and I not able to shout, because you hit me."

Jonathan and Peres smiled, then Jonathan said,

"It's very difficult for me to leave you behind, but I feel it's better that we carry out your plot, to help our enemies. Later I will come and take you and prepare a big party for us, so we can celebrate and tell all those wonderful stories."

She smiled and said,

"I pray that our dreams will come true, and we will all be good friends. Mansour and his father, and all of us."

Peres was freed at last and he jumped up and down to help his circulation. Jonathan looked at the time and said,

"We must hurry. Let's take the ropes and blankets with us, as it's quite a distance to any of the ten points, and they may come in useful." He cut off a length of his rope to tie his love and then rolled his blanket and tied it into a neat bundle, ready to sling on his back.

Natanya stood watching him and noticed that his white shirt was striped with dirty lines from the ropes. "Poor Jonathan," she thought. "He looks sad and disappointed, tired and weary. Never mind, he will find clean clothes and the boys waiting for him."

Then she said aloud,

"The old man will be waiting for you. He was very sad, but when he see you, he will be happy."

"I would be very happy if you would come home with me," he commented wishfully, hugging her to his side.

Peres looked at the clock on the wall and asked,

"Do you think I can take the clock as a souvenir for my Naomi to put in our kitchen?"

"Of course," replied Jonathan, still holding his love by his side. "You can take it with pleasure."

Peres jumped on the chair and lifted it down, still ticking and indicating they had twenty minutes left before Mansour returned. He wrapped it in his 'net', tied it with rope and slung it over his back. Then the three walked out of the store, with Jonathan holding Natanya by one hand and the chair with the other.

The grove was quiet, except for the sound of the birds and a light breeze through the leaves. Natanya pointed again to the direction they should take.

"You see there," she pointed, "is very good, many trees. You go down the mountain, many big stones, you can hide."

"Thankyou my love," replied Jonathan. "We'll follow your directions, but I don't want to leave you. Can't you change your mind, then maybe we can think of another way to help Mansour and his people?"

"No," she said, "we must not change our mind." Then she sat on the chair under the orange trees and looked around her. "You tie me quick," she ordered, feeling worried in case she changed her mind, as she loved her fiance and hated to see him leave her.

Jonathan put the bunch of keys and the dagger in his pockets and started to tie his love to the chair.

"I will do it loose, so it will not hurt you," he said, looking at her kind eyes. His face brushed by her soft cheeks as he worked, so he kissed them and whispered, "I love you, Natanya. I am so proud of you, and you are the best one in the team."

Peres was looking around and hopping from foot to foot in exasperation.

"For heavens' sake," he hurried Jonathan. "Is it time for romance now, when our time has almost run out?"

Jonathan smiled at his love and pretended he had not heard Peres.

"Do you know where to find us, Natanya?" he asked.

"Yes, I know, Aaron told me. He will wait for me, too," she said.

He stood up and found the gun resting by the tree, not moved since Mansour left it there for Amal. He picked it up and held it over Natanya's head. Peres stood by his side, anxiously looking around him as the wind was building up, creating rushing sounds among the leaves. Natanya looked at the gun in Jonathan's hands, and squeezed her eyes partially shut, anticipating the hit. He saw her expression and his hand refused to move. "How can I hit her?" he thought. "Even to act it is impossible for me." So he lowered his hands and said to her,

"I'm sorry, I can't hit you, my love."

Peres snatched the gun from his hands and said, while looking around him,

"I'll do it. We're running out of time."

His hands were unsteady and heavy from the lack of circulation and he was still looking over his shoulder in panic as he lifted his arms high above his head. A powerful thump was heard as the gun struck Natanya hard on her head. Peres was so quick, that Jonathan stood paralysed, watching the drama, and unable to stop the tragedy. The echo of the thud lingered in Jonathan's ears. Both men stood in front of the girl who looked surprised and shocked for a moment, then the blood vessels burst in her head and her blood spattered on the men's shirts as they stood motionless watching her. The colour disappeared from her face and a pale sheet covered her cheeks as her eyes closed and her head dropped forward onto her chest. They stood frozen for a few moments, shocked and bewildered.

"You killed her, Peres," whispered Jonathan, staring at Natanya. "You killed my love for me," he gasped, almost choking with emotion.

"I'm sorry. It was an accident. I didn't mean to hit her so hard, but I just couldn't feel my hands."

Jonathan knelt beside his angel, calling her softly,

"Natanya, my love. Please speak to me."

But she was deadly silent. He opened her eyes, to see if there was any sign of life, but the tears misted his vision.

"My love, I am sorry. I will never believe that you have gone so quickly, but you are living in my heart. I am only passing through a nightmare and will awake in the morning, with you beside me again." Then he kissed her cheeks and forehead.

"Jonathan," said a trembling Peres. "I can't tell you how sorry I am for what's just happened, but if we don't move, her life will have been sacrificed in vain."

Jonathan knew he could do nothing for his angel, so he stood up and said, looking at the pale body,

"I will not say goodbye, my love, because you are with me all the time. See, your hair is always next to my heart."

Then he turned to the left hand and both men ran away, carrying the blankets on their backs, with Peres still holding the gun.

Jonathan felt in a daze. "Where am I?" he asked himself. "I'm sure this isn't real, as angels don't die. No, Natanya's love will be like a refreshing spring of water that flows forever, refreshing hearts, taking away the bitterness of hate and healing the wounds of war."

The two men came to a wall. 'You keep to your left hand. There are many farms of orange trees,' he could hear her voice in his head. Jonathan looked over the wall.

"It's another orange grove. We'll carry on in this direction," he said, jumping over the wall, with Peres following him. They surveyed the area around them.

"Lucky it's not a busy time," said Peres, trying to distract Jonathan's mind from the great calamity he had just inflicted on him.

Jonathan did not comment as he was concentrating on following the correct direction, mentally marking the north and avoiding the south. 'The camp is on the right hand.' He could hear her voice clearly. "Why should that happen to such a person?" he asked himself. "She came all that way, bare footed, to set us free, then we killed her by our own hands."

"Please forgive me, Jonathan," begged Peres, holding him by the arm. "It was an accident."

Jonathan looked at his friend and stopped for a moment to rest, then stared at the anxious man. "He must be feeling dreadful," he thought. "but it could have happened to anyone. After all, I nearly killed her twice, and both times were deliberate, so I mustn't torment Peres, as his conscience must be in agony." He took his companion's arm and a sad smile appeared on his lips.

"It was an accident, Peres. I know, as I watched it happen. I hold nothing against you, and I can assure you that my angel would do the same, because she is a most understanding person. So, don't let what happened rob you of your peace, but rather let it be a lesson for all of us, to hate and detest weapons and violence, and to follow the way of that divine love, which is so far reaching, even to the depths of Hades, that nothing stands in its way, not even death itself."

CHAPTER 8

"LOVE THY ENEMY"

While they drove to their territory, Abu Mansour told his son part of the story of how they found Amal.

"Amal is like an angel of deliverance," Mansour said to his father. "Her warning was a vital piece of news, as if she had not come when she did, I feel today would have been the saddest and most tragic day for all of us."

"I'm glad we warned our people to be ready for evacuation at a moment's notice, especially as the men are scattered all over Lebanon at the moment," said Abu Mansour, tensely tapping his hand on the window-sill, as was his custom to release the pressure.

Mansour dropped his father in one street, Walid in another, whilst he took another one, whistling the evacuation warning.

The women and children started to pour out into the streets and rush to the nearby Palestinian camp, as both camps had an agreement to open their homes and share their food in case of raids on each other. The important possessions were packed in baskets and boxes and carried on the head, with even the young children carrying their share. Everyone sought to save as much as possible, from what seemed to be an approaching big raid, as the whistles were loud, sharp and continuous.

The minister had not slept the night before, he still being unsure of the Arab girl. "We had a clear warning not to let her out of Israel, and now we have gone and sent her!" he said to himself, tossing and turning and worrying the whole night.

Early in the morning he left for the Centre, intending to administer the raid with Victor, as he was worried and anxious about the situation. While the two men were awaiting news of the convoy's progress, he explained his misgivings to Victor,

"I've never faced such a dilemma before. If that girl goes and joins with her people, we're in dead trouble, because we have no excuse, as we broke a definite order."

"I know," replied Victor, rubbing his forehead. "But I look at it like this: we were faced with an impossible situation, with two of our leaders facing definite death and our hands tied. We couldn't do a single thing to save them and then this Arab prisoner appears and makes an offer, and then insists to help. So, suppose she is genuine and succeeds, that's absolutely marvellous, but imagine if we had refused...! What a dilemma! On the other hand, if she goes and joins her people, all we have lost is a prisoner and important information about our boys living in the hostel, but we can easily change their duties around and not return them to Lebanon. However, either way, as far as Jonathan and Peres are concerned, we know their situation is hopeless."

A radio message arrived from the convoy,

"Natanya disappeared on schedule. Aaron is safely back and we feel the plan is successful, so far."

"I think her people have spotted her," said Victor, "otherwise they would have shot at the broken truck."

The minister followed the progress on the map.

"We must carry out the raid on Abu Mansour's camp," he said to Victor.

"Give her an hour or so," replied the wise old man. "Just in case they are in the camp. At least when they see her, they might suspect we are coming."

"Does she know about the raid?" asked the minister.

"No, of course not. She was outside the room and we conducted our meeting in Hebrew; so no way she could know about it."

"It's a pity in a way that we didn't tell her," said the anxious minister. "Then at least we could be sure that the territory would be evacuated."

"But we are sure our boys aren't there," replied Victor in frustration. "I think I'm going mad, so just let's follow the situation as it is, and forget about what we did or didn't do."

Peres' wife phoned the Centre to enquire if there was any news about her husband. Victor had the responsibility to deliver information on the current situation and said to her,

"We have no news yet, Naomi, but I will ring you immediately I hear anything."

"It's been so long," she objected, "and every time I ring, the answer is the same. Can't you feel sorry for me? I haven't slept for three nights now, and the children are driving me mad. Can't you give me one little ray of hope?"

"My dear, none of us have slept for the last few nights and we're doing all we can, as well as the impossible. If only you knew the lengths we are going to, to save the boys; so please, pray for us, for only God can help them," he said with a faint smile, remembering Natanya's sentence.

As he replaced the receiver, Jonathan's mother phoned. She and her husband had left England without delay when they heard the news of the kidnapping. They were staying at their flat in Jerusalem, their second home, which they kept for holidays and festivals, as well as for Jonathan's use, although he hardly ever used it.

"Can you kindly inform me of the progress," asked the anxious mother, in English.

"There is no change in the situation," replied Victor. "We are working flat out to release them."

"Is any effort being made to have an exchange or pay a ransom?"

"No, my dear, in no way will we do a deal with these terrorists. If we can get them out by a different means, all well and good, but there's no way to do an exchange or ransom."

"It's alright for you, sir," said Sara, feeling exasperated and in absolute despair. "He is not your son, so it doesn't matter much, but this boy is my son, and I've worked hard to bring him up and educate him, and now what a criminal waste of a young life! Can't you feel for us?" With that she burst out crying.

Victor covered the receiver with his hand and said to the minister,

"Everyone is blaming us for the boys' tragedy and feel we are not doing much. Sara, Jonathan's mother, is asking for either an exchange of prisoners or that a ransom be paid for her son."

The minister shook his head and bit hard on his pen.

"Tell her that we hold no hope for Jonathan, and that he is most probably dead by now."

Victor could not bring himself to shatter Sara's heart, so he consolingly said,

"Please, don't feel so upset. Aren't our people suffering and dying all the time, like we have from the beginning of history. I assure you that we are doing everything possible, and even more, but as Jonathan is the head of the mission, he is facing extra hardship, and it will be a miracle if he comes alive out of Lebanon."

"I see," she said, trying to adapt to the ugly reality. "You feel that most probably he's already been killed?"

"I don't know where he is, or his position, but I personally feel that his position is hopeless. As I said to Naomi, all we can do is pray."

Sara replaced the phone and broke down, weeping. Her husband put his arm round her to comfort her and asked, "Has he died?"

"No," she sobbed, "but he is as good as dead."

Jonathan and Peres ran with all their strength to put as much distance as possible between themselves and Abu Mansour's territory, just stopping from time to time to catch their breath. They felt shaky and exhausted from their ordeal, especially from the last stage of the drama. Jonathan had almost convinced himself that what had happened was a nightmare and not reality, until he looked at his shirt. "Natanya," his heart ached, "this is your blood covering my shirt. You died so you could set us free."

Peres noticed Jonathan looking at the blood on his shirt, so he glanced at his. "I wish I had never snatched that gun. What a situation to be in, as now I feel so guilty, and I don't know how I'm going to live with myself," he groaned, with torment showing in his eyes.

Neither of the men talked, as they sought to preserve their energy. Jonathan walked down the slope of the mountain side, hiding behind bushes as he went, trying to find his bearings.

"I think we had better hide here until nightfall, because we're approaching open ground and someone is bound to spot us soon. As it's a full moon tonight, we can cross then, hiding from one shadow to the next."

He had hardly finished speaking, when he heard men approaching who sounded excited and angry.

"Quick Peres," he warned. "Let's get inside this bush."

Peres used his gun to lift the thorny branches, heavy with inedible berries, and the two men hid, watching the others approach. They heard the word "Israelis" mentioned many times.

"They're after us," thought Peres.

"The raid must have started," thought Jonathan.

"Amal gave Abu Mansour the warning just a few minutes before it happened," said one of the men, as they continued gesturing and talking in Arabic.

"And just when the last person got out, the Israeli planes blew the whole area to the ground," said his companion, angrily kicking the ground with his feet.

"At least we have Jonathan, and Mansour is going to kill him," responded another one, stopping so near to the bush that concealed the two fugitives.

"They are talking about my Amal," thought Jonathan. "Maybe they've found her, as they seem very angry, or perhaps they're looking for us, as they are talking about me. Please Adoni," he prayed, as they stood beside the bush, "cover their eyes, so they don't see us, as we're only a few feet from them now."

"We've had it," thought Peres, as he heard Jonathan's name mentioned. "They will kill us if they find us. I wonder if it's better to shoot them now, from here?" Then he quickly changed his mind. "No, I mustn't use violence. I'm already feeling bad enough over Natanya and I can't kill anymore. As Jonathan rightly said, we must learn from her loving example."

The men stood for what seemed like an eternity, talking and shouting and looking in the direction of the bush. At last they continued on their way down the mountain, allowing the two men to leave their hideout.

"That was a narrow escape," commented Jonathan, unhooking the thorns from his shirt and wiping spider's webs from his hair and face.

"A very narrow one," responded Peres, clearing the mess from his body.

"I feel it's wise not to move from this spot until nightfall," said Jonathan. "We are high enough to see what goes on around us, plus we have these dense bushes as a good screen for us. We can sit and rest on these stones in the shade of the bush and think." He paused for a moment, looking around him, "Our only real problem is water. It would help if we could find some wild berries or fruits."

Peres surveyed the area.

"It's early spring," he said, "so nothing much around, except the grass and weeds."

"We can chew some grass," said Jonathan. "It's good enough for the animals, so it will do for us."

They pulled some young grass stalks and sat on the stones, sucking and slowly chewing them, while keeping a careful lookout.

Mansour and his father stood some distance from their previous homes, watching the smoke and dust rising.

"Imagine it," said Mansour, "if Amal had arrived just a few minutes later, all our people would be dead now."

"Allah has been very good to us lately," said Abu Mansour. "He must be working with us, as he saved you from death, and let you catch the best prize ever. And now he has sent Amal, all the way from Israel, to inform us of the raid and save all these lives."

"She is a hero," responded Mansour. "We will make her our hero, as all of us owe her our lives. She has proved herself to be our best friend, even though we annihilated her family."

"Do you have to remind me of the past, Mansour?" said the old man, with distress in his voice.

"No, I am not mentioning the past. I'm only marvelling at the quality of her love, as she really does believe in that sentence, 'Love thy enemy'. I admire her for that, because I know it's an impossible love to put into action, yet she has managed to live it." Then he took his father's hand and said, "Let's go and deal with that fox. I'll cut him into pieces, as he well deserves it."

Abu Mansour laughed and said,

"Just make sure Amal isn't looking, otherwise we will upset her, especially as we're going to kill one of her beloved enemies."

Every five minutes the lookouts at the ten posts kept sending in their reports to the Centre.

"No sign of the boys yet."

"Oh well, we are not really anticipating to see them any more," said a despondent Victor, as he received the latest dispatches.

Then the reports from the raid started to pour in,

"The area has been flattened to the ground. Not a single building remains standing."

"Ah, good," said the minister. "That's one job accomplished, even though we lost two of our best men. At least their blood is well avenged."

Peres and Jonathan sat watching their planes returning from the raid.

"What a great shame," remarked Jonathan. "I explained my policy in detail, but as soon as I'm off the scene, they revert to their old habits."

"They had to do something," said Peres, watching the busy sky.

"That raid will not solve any problem, nor our predicament. Natanya came without a single weapon or any armour, yet she was able to set us free, just by her pure love. Somehow, I'm sure that we could also disarm and conquer by the same powerful method." Then, after watching the aircraft flying low for a while, he added,

"Pity we can't communicate with them, as they're so close to us, but at the same time, so far."

"Shall I shoot at them to attract their attention then?" asked Peres, in desperation.

"Don't be silly, Peres," answered Jonathan, while he watched the planes. "You'll attract the wrong people to us, and also the pilots will think we're Abu Mansour's men shooting at them, and then they will attack us as well."

"If only I had a mirror," thought Jonathan, "then I could signal to them, as the sun is very bright." Suddenly he remembered the dagger. "Just the thing, that will reflect the light perfectly." He immediately pulled it from his pocket and withdrew it from the sheath.

Peres saw what Jonathan had in mind and became quite excited.

"Brilliant idea, Jonathan!" he shouted.

"Shush, Peres. Remember what my angel said, 'The trees have eyes and the stones have ears'."

Then he lay flat on the ground, with the bush behind him, and Peres watching and guarding. He adjusted the position of the dagger and started to reflect his message to the planes which kept roving around in the sky, as they had only just concluded their raid.

"He missed us," lamented Peres as another plane passed over them and flew away.

Jonathan continued systematically flashing his dagger without stopping.

"If they miss us, we'll just have to wait until tonight," he said, concentrating on his dagger. Another fighter approached them.

"Please help us, God," said Jonathan, focusing his attention on the plane and flashing the sunlight directly at the cockpit.

"I'm sure I saw a flashing light down there," said Baruch. "I'll turn back and you look towards the slope of the hill."
Then he banked sharply.

"They've spotted us!" shouted both men excitedly. Jonathan kept flashing and watching the fighter as it approached for the second time, much closer than before.

"Blessed be Ha-shem," said the co-pilot. "I'm certain that's Jonathan, as he's flashing our signal; very clearly."
Baruch circled the area above the boys and transmitted his message to the Centre.
"The boys are out!" he cried with great excitement. "We've spotted them on the slope of the mountain, north of Abu Mansour's territory!"

Victor nearly fainted, as the message sounded unreal.
"Are you sure?"
"Definitely. He's in front of me right now and sending us our signal."
"Stay where you are. I'll send you two helicopters and more fighters so you can guard them while they are lifted out."
"The boys are out!" announced Victor to the minister.
"What! Out?! They can't be!! She must be an angel!" he exclaimed.
Victor immediately directed other fighters to the area, together with the two helicopters, and soon a skilful operation of air acrobatics began, the result of ingenious thinking, as the boys were located on the slope of a hillside and surrounded by enemies.

The Syrian soldiers were watching the busy Israeli fighters.
"What are they up to?" asked one of the officers.
"They're blowing up Abu Mansour's area, as he's holding some of their men," replied his friend.
"I feel they're up to mischief," said the first officer, as he watched the fighters weaving themselves into impressive patterns. "They're showing off and telling us that Lebanon belongs to them."

He then reported the display to his headquarters,

"At least ten fighters are circulating like vultures waiting for a dead body."

"They have just flattened Abu Mansour's area," they responded.

"I know, but they are circulating around the north slope of the mountain and provoking us by performing impressive air acrobatics."

"I think they're very upset because of their men and are just trying to frighten Abu Mansour. Anyhow, we'll send you a few tanks to show we are aware of them, but it's better we stay out of any confrontation, especially when they are raging mad, as at the moment."

The helicopters were soon on their way from the direction of the Mediterranean, escorted by more fighters, and anxiously awaited by Jonathan and Peres.

"I hope they speed up," said a very concerned Jonathan, looking around him, "as soon everybody will be alerted to us. I wish these fighters would go away, instead of hovering above us, at least until the helicopters arrive."

"Oh, I don't know, Jonathan, as to see them around gives us tremendous moral support, and just when we need it."

Baruch spotted the tanks moving towards the area.

"Help," he radioed the Centre, "the Syrians are sending their tanks towards the boys. We're in dead trouble."

Victor was almost in a panic as he repeated the message to the minister.

"Oh, hell!" he shouted. "They're really in trouble now!"

"Baruch," ordered Victor. "All withdraw immediately and join the helicopter escort. I will send more fighters to another location to distract their attention."

In a moment, all the planes disappeared towards the sea.

"Wonderful," breathed Jonathan with relief.

"How long do you think we'll be trapped here?" asked Peres anxiously.

"I don't think it will be long now, so it's better we get ready because I have a feeling they will swoop suddenly. Let's squat in readiness to jump, as I can see our helicopters on the horizon."

The Syrian officer saw the fighters disappear out to sea.

"They were right in our office," he said to his friend. "Now the tanks are coming in vain."

"No, I think we frightened the Israelis," said his companion, watching the fading fighters with a proud smile.

Jonathan and Peres squatted right close to the bush, to screen themselves, whilst they scanned the horizon. Their rolled-up blankets were tied to their backs and Peres could hear his clock ticking. Jonathan had the dagger ready in his hand, to direct the planes when they returned. Suddenly they saw a group of fighters appear some distance away from them and proceed to give a brilliant aerial display.

"That's what I call real strategy," said Jonathan, with satisfaction in his voice. "I'm always proud of our boys," he continued, "as they're quick thinkers and do their utmost to save their friends." That statement brought Natanya to his memory, so he looked down to his shirt and added, "But no love will equal that of my angel, for she displayed heroism and love towards her enemies. In fact, she died while helping others."

"I do admit," said Peres thoughtfully, "that I've never met such a person like that in my whole life. I just could not believe my eyes when I saw an alef Arab prisoner coming to release her captors. It's such a pity and a great tragedy that my hands are the ones that snuffed out her pleasant light." Then Peres could hold his emotion no longer and wept.

Jonathan held him by the arm and said,

"As far as I'm concerned, Natanya hasn't died. Her love will remain alive forever, as she is personally living in my heart. So, as long as my heart lives, she is situated right in its centre."

Victor and the controllers at the Centre were sitting on their nerves, as they received reports and sent orders.

"We're distracting the Syrians, as they're now moving towards our new position."

"Good. Keep them busy, but stay high and fast so they can't aim at you."

The attention of those on the ground moved away from the trapped men, allowing the helicopters and their escort to approach unobserved.

Jonathan flashed his dagger to indicate his position and their readiness.

"We're going to swoop!" blared the message from the radio at the Centre.

The minister could not sit down, so he stood leaning over his chair, and concentrating on the map, as if he could see the lifting procedure happening in front of him.

"It will be a great pity if we fail, especially after the Arab prisoner got them out in a matter of only three and a half hours, and here we are, the experienced fighters, panicking!"

"Pray!" shouted Victor, as he was convinced that prayer was the secret of Natanya's power and he could hear her voice, 'I pray'. So he repeated the advice to all.

"Pray minister," he commanded again.

One of the helicopters approached the mountain slope, with the lifting line dangling underneath it. A group of fighters acted as an umbrella while others swarmed around it.

"Are you ready, Peres?" shouted Jonathan, trying to make himself heard above the tremendous noise from the planes. The two men centred their gaze on the helicopter hovering above their head.

"Jump Peres," ordered Jonathan.

Peres bounded like a wild cat from beside the bush and grabbed the line, which immediately started to be winched up and he soon disappeared inside the aircraft.

"One is lifted," came the message.

"Thanks to God!" shouted everyone in the office.

The Syrian officer turned round and saw the helicopter.

"Look! What are they doing now?" he shouted excitedly. "I told you they're up to mischief!"

He contacted his headquarters immediately.

"The Israelis are dropping some soldiers on the slope of the mountain. We need help urgently."

"We're sending you some fighters immediately," came the reply.

The line was dropped to pick up Jonathan. As it came down, he took a last look round and saw someone firing at him.

"O my God, help. They've seen me."

"The Syrians are shooting at Jonathan," announced Baruch. "Shall we bomb them?"

"No," shouted Victor. "We don't want a confrontation. Don't lose time, just pick him up quickly."

Jonathan crouched on the ground, watching the line slowly coming towards him, taking what seemed like an eternity. "I think I can just catch it if I jump high enough," he said to himself, as he took a deep breath and leapt upwards, hanging on with all his might.

"He's got it!" shouted Baruch, as he watched the drama from his elevated position.

Jonathan was lifted high above the ground, still dangling below the helicopter as it started to move away, with the Syrian officer firing at him from a distance. The fighters continued to surround the helicopter to protect it as they all headed away towards the sea.

"Jonathan and Peres are safe on board," declared the delighted pilot.

At the Centre the men hugged each other with joy, and Victor was so overwhelmed that tears flowed down his cheeks and he hugged the minister, saying,

"Thanks to God, who sent his angel and rescued the two men from a definite death."

Another message came from the helicopter pilot as a warning to the Centre,

"The boys are looking dreadful, so I thought I'd better prepare you, as I hardly recognized them, especially Jonathan. I have a feeling they've been fighting because their shirts are spattered with blood." Then he added, "I thought I had better warn you, so you don't get a shock."

"I'm not surprised," replied Victor. "We are looking shocked enough without a battle, so I can imagine their state. Thanks anyhow."

He lifted the phone to inform the relatives of his happy news.

"I love to deliver good news," he said to the smiling minister while he dialled Naomi's number. Then a big grin crossed his face as he continued, "I may just be in time to save her before the children drive her completely mad!"

Naomi heard the phone and ran to answer it.

"My poor man," her heart fluttered. "I know what this message is," she told herself, "as good news never travels that fast."

Her knees were knocking as she lifted the receiver. The children ran to her and tightly gripped her skirt as she asked,

"Who is it?"

"Victor. I have just received some news for you."

"Don't tell me, Victor. Please don't tell me as I know what it is."

"I assure you that you know nothing about my news," he said, laughing.

She was encouraged by his laugh, so hastily answered,

"Alright, go ahead and tell me."

"Peres is on his way home. Our boys picked up both of them just a few minutes ago, so if you hurry up and come to the Centre, you will meet him. Bring the children with you, as we are having a welcoming party for them."

"Are you joking with me, Victor?" asked the bewildered wife.

"I don't know how to joke. I only know how to deliver good news."

"Do you know that I have been praying since you told me to do so, and thanks to God, he has answered my prayer."

"That's wonderful, Naomi. I must go now though, as I've other people waiting for the good news. Oh, just one little warning," he added. "I'm sure you appreciate that the boys have been through a very hard time, so you'll have to ignore their appearance."

She laughed and said,

"I don't care what they look like, as long as they're alive and well!"

He dialled the second number, and while he waited for the reply, he said to one of the officers,

"Go to the canteen and tell them to quickly prepare a celebration for us, as our mourning has turned into joy."

Then he commented to the minister,

"Jonathan's parents don't want to pick up the receiver, and I know the reason why."

They were sitting by the phone, anticipating only bad news. When it rang, they both jumped to their feet, but neither was brave enough to lift the receiver.

"My Jonathan is dead," said Sara, looking at the ringing phone.

"Would you like to answer it?" asked her husband, with trembling hands.

"No, it's better you take the message. I might have a heart attack."

Dan lifted the phone, and a loud, joyful voice almost deafened him.

"Is that Sara?"

"No, I am Dan," answered the man, shaking from top to toe.

"Can you both come to the Centre directly, as the boys have been found."

"Found?" queried Dan.

"What's found?" asked Sara. Then she screamed hysterically, "Have they found the bodies?"

Victor heard her and said,

"They are sound and well and on their way home. Come quickly, or you'll miss the celebration."

"Jonathan is alive!" shouted Dan.

"That's impossible! Give me the phone! I want to talk to that wonderful man," cried Sara, snatching the receiver from her husband.

"Hello, my dear," she said to Victor, feeling as if she was in a dream. "How did you manage to save my son?"

"Me? I didn't Sara, but I am waiting like you, to see who rescued them and how. But whoever did it is an angel of God, and we must give all the thanks to Him."

Victor's next call was to pass the good news to Jonathan's hostel, to a low and depressed Mordecai who was missing Natanya and worried to death about Jonathan.

"Mordecai," came the familiar voice. "Jonathan is out, alive and well, and Peres, too. They have just been lifted by our helicopter, both of them."

"Ole!" shouted a joyful Mordecai. "This is Natanya's work. She's wonderful, as she got them out in no time. You know, she's like that, she never wastes time and does things like magic. She is the best girl in the whole world. She's my Natanya. I told you that I trust her with my own life. Now I will prepare a party, a very big one...."

Victor had to interrupt the excited man.

"I'm sorry to interrupt Mordecai, but I have to phone so many people to tell them the good news, plus I have other work as well. But, if I were you, have your party tomorrow, as we're having a mighty big one here, and you are welcome to come."

"No thankyou, Victor. I must do my own; that will keep me busy."

Then the phone was cut off and Mordecai walked out of his office, floating on air, dancing and singing and hugging everyone he met in his way.

"The boys are out, safe and well," was the news he passed to all, so turning the hostel into a home of celebration.

The staff at the Centre, headed by the minister and Victor, stood by the runway, waiting for the aircraft to arrive. Many fighters had already returned, while the others accompanied the helicopter.

"Do you know what I feel like?" said the minister as he watched the sky. "I feel as if I'm in a dream that started with a nightmare and ended with the most fantastic miracle. I can't believe that Jonathan is on his way here, I just can't believe it."

"I know the feeling," laughed Victor. "But what I can't believe is that girl. Is she a human, or what? I've never met a person like her before. How amazing that an alef Arab prisoner begged to go and help the boys, but we just couldn't trust her. Imagine if we had listened to her yesterday, then we could have had one less horrific night."

The helicopter approached the field and all who were watching its arrival started to clap or wave their handkerchiefs, with some dancing or jumping in the air. Jonathan and Peres looked at the crowd below and smiled.

"They must have suffered more than we did," remarked Jonathan, than added, "Pity my sweetheart isn't with us, as then it would have been the most joyful occasion." Then he touched his top pocket and said with a smile, "Of course she is with me. She is in my heart."

No sooner was the door opened than the minister and Victor rushed with wide open arms to welcome the two men.

A sad smile appeared on their lips and they looked tired and bewildered.

"I see what he meant by the warning," said Victor quietly, looking first at Jonathan's face, then at his filthy shirt which was a mixture of black stripes, dust and blood. They hugged each other without exchanging a word, after which Jonathan and Peres hugged everyone else and they all walked quietly towards the building. The assembled crowd stood looking with astonishment at their faces.

"Poor boys," one whispered. "They must have been through a horrifying experience. I think they would have died if Natanya hadn't arrived when she did."

Jonathan walked silently between the minister and Victor for a few yards, then he said,

"Thankyou all very much for the effort you made to get us out of our calamity."

"My dear Jonathan," said Victor, holding his arm. "We did nothing. We felt absolutely helpless as we didn't know where you were or what to do, until Mordecai phoned us on Thursday morning and told us that Natanya said she would get the boys out, and then we were stuck in the biggest dilemma we have ever faced."

Jonathan sighed deeply. The two men noticed his sigh, so they stopped and looked at him, enquiring with their eyes.

"I take it that she got you out?" asked the minister.

Jonathan nodded and kept silent, as he felt like weeping.

Peres and the other officers joined the three men, and all centred their gaze on Jonathan.

"What happened to the girl?" queried Victor, feeling uneasy.

"She died," answered Jonathan, almost inaudibly, as he did not want to hurt Peres, nor speak about her death.

"Died?" said the two men together.

"They killed her?" asked Victor, looking at the shirts of the two men.

"We killed her," said Jonathan, holding back his emotions.

"Oh my God!" said the minister to himself. "So Jonathan was right about his statement."

"You killed her?" enquired the pale faced Victor, shocked and unable to puzzle out the drama. "The least thing they could have done was to set her free, not kill her," he thought, as he waited for the answer.

Peres quietly confessed in a grief stricken voice,

"I killed her. It was an accident, a complete accident. She had just set us free...." and then he broke down, unable to continue his statement, while tears streamed down his face.

"Come on boys, let's go inside," said Victor to the distressed men. "We can sit down and have a cup of coffee, and then you can tell us your story from the start." He saw Jonathan move his head away, so he added, "I feel that the best thing is to get the whole subject off your chest, and then you will feel relieved of your burden, as the proverb rightly says, 'a problem shared is a problem halved'."

Jonathan nodded, as he saw the wisdom of the saying. He lifted the rolled-up blanket from his back and placed it on the table. Then he pulled the dagger from his trouser pocket, removed it from its sheath and placed it next to the 'net', watching the expressions of his audience and smiling softly.

Peres laid his blanket down and started to unroll it until he reached his ticking clock, which he gently placed upright. The time was a quarter past eleven when he uncovered it. Then he put the gun next to it and sat down, watching the men looking at the objects on the table, their eyes full of questions.

'It is a long story. I tell you later.' Jonathan could hear Natanya's sentence in his head, remembering his puzzlement when she arrived at the store just a few hours before.

"So much has happened this morning," he began, "that I hardly know exactly where I am. At nine this morning, by the time on this clock in front of you, my right arm was to have been amputated with this dagger which Mansour brought from Mecca. He was to use it for the first time on me, as a privileged guest, and then roast the arm for our first meal since our breakfast on Wednesday."

The audience shuddered at the thought, and the style of the story. Jonathan stood up, lifted Peres' rope from the table, and continued to relate his nightmare.

"You see this rope, yards and yards of it. We have been wrapped from our necks to our feet with it since Wednesday until six minutes past nine this morning, when Natanya cut it with the dreadful dagger that Mansour had placed on top of the clock, to torment us. I must confess that I have never experienced such mental anguish in my life, and I know for a certainty that I would have died if he had carried out his scheme, but my angel came sharp on time at nine o'clock. When the keys were rattling in the lock, we thought beyond doubt that it was Mansour, and it took us a few moments to awake from our trance and believe that the gentle, loving angel had come to set us free, after we had lost all hope."

The men looked at each other in amazement, not knowing whether they were listening to a fairy story or reality.

"It must be reality," thought the minister. "I can see Jonathan with the rope in his hand, and the other items on the table, as well as the dirty marks of the ropes on their shirts."

A soldier entered with a tray full of cups of coffee. He looked to the standing figure and smiled with respect.

"Give Jonathan his coffee first," said the minister to the waiting soldier, who promptly handed him a cup and asked,

"Milk?"

"No thankyou. Black will suit me fine."

Then he gave Peres his cup and asked the same question.

"Black please," he said, then looked to the audience. "This is our first cup of coffee since Wednesday morning."

Jonathan continued,

"We have been living on one glass of sugar water a day, after Mansour and his friend drank a portion of it, as we just couldn't trust them. Our exasperation was beyond description, especially as our bodies ached from the lack of circulation and we were shut in a storeroom in one of the orange groves near Abu Mansour's area. Anyhow, to cut a long story short, we hoped and prayed that you would flush the area adjacent to our raid, but, with every hour which passed by, our hope diminished."

Victor rubbed his forehead and commented, with shame in his voice,

"We felt sure that you would most probably be killed, although we had a bit of hope for Peres, so we didn't waste time to flatten the area to avenge your blood, because we felt panicky and frustrated, especially as we didn't know where you had been hidden, until Natanya came here. Then we were faced with an even worse dilemma than before."

Victor paused for a few moments to wet his throat.

"Knowing that the girl was an alef Arab prisoner, with an underlined warning, 'Not to be set free or leave Israel under any circumstances', put us in real difficulties, made worse because one of the warnings was signed by you. So we were stuck. She begged and pleaded," said Victor with a smile, as he remembered her demonstration. "She opened that door and walked in, without permission, and without fear, came straight to me and ordered, 'I must go to Lebanon now'."

Jonathan smiled, as he remembered his own experience when the bombs were planted. Victor continued,

"She ran to Aaron in desperation and put her right hand in his right hand, to illustrate to us that they had an oath of friendship between them."

Jonathan felt so grieved that he bit his lips, thinking to himself, "I caused you all that trouble, my love, all that anxiety."

Victor interrupted his thoughts by asking him,

"What had she done to merit that severe warning against her?"

"Nothing, nothing at all, except unfounded suspicions. One of the boys at the hostel was reading a spy novel at the time when I asked him about her. I was about to write the report and he convinced me that she was acting. I accepted his reasoning, believing it, because she is too good to be true, so loving and caring in a unique way. Then what made the suspicion worse was the bombs."

"That's what we concluded," said Victor. Then he quickly asked, "Why didn't you remove the restriction after the bombs were found?"

Jonathan hesitated and looked about him. The eyes of all those around the table were fixed on him. After a moments' pause he quietly answered,

"I am a very selfish man."

The men looked at him in surprise, enquiring with their expressions.

Then he continued his confession,

"When I discovered her unique personality, I fell in love with her. I didn't want her to be moved or released, until I found a way to take her as my wife."

"I see," said Victor sadly. "That was why she refused to take off her ring and medallion, as they represented a great deal to her. I managed to remove the ring, but no way could I budge her star of David."

"She was wearing both items when she opened the door for us," said Jonathan.

"How did she manage that with Mansour around?!" asked the amazed old man.

"It was a long story," said Jonathan, with a faint smile on his lips. "I'm afraid we'll never know that story now. She promised to tell us later, as she was hurrying to set us free."

The relatives arrived at the Centre and waited for a long time for their men to appear from the conference room.

"How amazing," said Sara to Naomi as they sat in the comfortable waiting room, "that men never stop talking, while we are waiting here all this time, and they are enjoying themselves inside."

"I don't mind this type of waiting," said Naomi, laughing, "because I know my husband is well and back home. Let's enjoy ourselves now, and later we'll catch up with all the stories."

Jonathan continued relating the drama, of how Natanya suggested that she be tied and hit, so as not to lose the trust of Abu Mansour and the rest, because of her hope of helping them to find another way to solve the problem.

"She believed in the statement, 'Love thy enemy'," he said. "That by such love you can conquer and win your enemy."

"I've heard that proverb before," said the minister. "I think it's one of Jesus of Nazareth's sayings."

Jonathan nodded his head and carried on.

"She told us which road to take, and what to avoid. In other words, she saved our lives, whilst dying in the process."

"No Jonathan," emphasised the minister, standing up. "Natanya never died. She will live in our memories and hearts, and her loving deeds will blossom for ever. In her honour, we will cancel our celebration, as a great hero died today."

Then he stretched out his hands to hold Jonathan's, and said,

"Please accept my heartfelt condolences for the tragic loss of your fiancee. We shall arrange a memorial service for her in the hostel on Sunday, after Shabbat is over."

Jonathan was comforted by the minister's offer, feeling even better when Victor rose and offered his condolences, saying,

"We will plant two trees in her memory, one here at the Centre and the other at the hostel, so she shall be a living example for all of us to eternity."

Jonathan felt proud that he had had the honour to know the "unnatural girl", and was comforted by the way all the officers and friends accepted her as a hero.

The minister then said to the two men,

"You need a long break from everything, so you can have a month off from tomorrow. I'll be happy to pay for both of you, and your families, to have a holiday. You can choose anywhere in the world, so let me know later of your choice, but now we must meet those poor ladies who have been in torment these last few days."

Abu Mansour and his son sped towards the grove, as they were over the time they had given to Amal.

"I dread all the work we have to do now, as those pigs have ruined our homes," said Abu Mansour, fuming with rage.

"At least our house is still standing, as it's on the edge of the Palestinian camp, but I'm confident in the strong will of our people, that soon they will raise the ruins from the ground. This is our life and we are accustomed to it; they break down and we build, we snipe and they drop dead," replied Mansour. Then he added, "It will give me the greatest pleasure to kill Jonathan in a minute, as he is the brain behind all these raids."

Abu Mansour responded quickly to that remark,

"To be fair, Mansour, he can't be behind this raid, because he's with us. In fact, they've returned to their old habits this time, and just when we thought they had improved a bit."

Mansour approached the grove and blew the horn to announce their arrival. Mubarak stood up, as he was bored stiff from sitting behind his pile of bricks, guarding the area. Mansour stopped and had a few words with him, enquiring if everything was alright.

"Not a sound or a single person, whether friend or foe," he said, and then he enquired about their mission.

"The Israelis ruined our homes," said Abu Mansour. "If Amal hadn't come when she did, not one would have been left alive."

Mubarak's mouth opened in horror.

"Honestly?" he asked.

"I swear," said Mansour. "The first bomb was dropped just when the last person was safely out."

"Better we kill both men," said Mubarak in anger.

"I have the intention to do just that," answered Mansour, moving the van slowly down the bumpy track.

"We must teach Amal our various whistles," he said to his father, "so we can announce our movements to her, and then she can also communicate with us."

He played a joyful tune with his horn, and looked ahead of him, anticipating that Amal would come out to meet him.

"I wonder why Amal hasn't come to meet us?" asked Mansour.

"I can see her on the chair," replied the father, looking hard. "I think she is tied to it."

Mansour felt his hands lose their grip.

"Don't tell me they have escaped," he exclaimed anxiously, driving as fast as he could. Then he stopped the van, opened the door and ran the last few yards towards the girl, as that was quicker.

His father followed him and they both stood paralysed at the sight before their eyes.

"They've killed her!" mumbled Mansour, as the shock of seeing the bleeding girl with her head resting on her chest tied his tongue.

Neither of them moved, they just looked toward the partly open door of the store and then back at Amal, both as white as a sheet and trying hard to digest the situation. Then they moved slowly to the chair and knelt by her side.

"They took the gun," said Mansour, looking to where he had left his gun. "I think they opened her head with it. I wish I had taken it with me, as she said she didn't like guns and now I've caused her death."

"Amal," called Abu Mansour softly. "Please Amal, forgive us." Then he looked with anger at his son.

"You should have killed him when I told you to. Now he's escaped, and killed the one who saved our lives."

Mansour kept quiet, as he felt wounded to the heart. Then he answered, almost crying,

"I know I'm to blame, but we all make mistakes sometimes. She was so frightened to stay, but I assured her that they would never move one step, and look what happened? That's why they were singing so joyfully last night, and even this morning I heard them laughing. The pigs, the sons of dogs, the vipers...."

"Please stop all those words and give me a hand to untie her. We have to prepare for her burial and that will take a few hours. I just can't believe it, she saved all those people and she alone had to die, the loving angel. I do hate life!" lamented Abu Mansour, as he wiped the blood from her forehead with his hand, while Mansour knelt by her side, looking at her pale, sweet face.

"They must have hit her hard," remarked Mansour. "Look how deep the cut is, and the lump, it's almost as big as a tennis ball."

As his father wiped away the congealed blood, he noticed fresh blood start to flow.

"She isn't dead!" exclaimed the old man, getting to his feet. "The cut is bleeding. That means her heart is still pumping. Hurry up, give me a hand!"

Mansour whistled sharply for Mubarak to come and assist them. Both men looked up at the sky when they heard the roaring of the fighters to their left and saw some of their display, but they did not bother much, as their main task was the rescue of Amal. Mansour undid the knot so easily that he said to his father,

"They don't know how to tie a knot; and look how loose this rope is."

"They must have done it in a great hurry," said the father, resting Amal's head between his hands.

"I think they had someone to open up for them, and loosen their ropes and chains," said Mansour, looking at the door. "The keys have gone; that's another mistake I made. We were in such a hurry, that I left the keys in the lock."

Mubarak came running up, and then stood stock still, aghast at the sad sight. He noticed the open door and exclaimed,

"They killed her and escaped?"

"She is unconscious," replied Mansour. "Get me the stretcher from the van. Quick."

Mubarak ran to the van and returned with the two poles and the sheet of canvas. He slipped each rod through its loops and laid it on the ground. Then Mansour and his father gently carried Amal and lowered her onto the stretcher.

"We'll take her home and bind her wounds," said Mansour. "We can't go near the hospital, as everyone will be waiting for us, so I will nurse her myself. She shall be my patient, as I've nursed many of our injured people before. I just hope she'll recover, because she seems to be in a deep coma."

Mubarak and Mansour emptied the boxes of explosives from the back of the van and carried them into the empty store, while Abu Mansour stood beside Amal.

"The thieves!" shouted Mansour. "They've taken our nets, ropes, the clock, and my precious dagger!"

He banged the boxes with his fist, screaming with bitterness,

"I swear to follow you to the end of the earth, Jonathan, to hunt you and kill you, even with the last drop of my blood!"

"I wished we had listened to Abu Mansour, but both of us insisted to hold on to them like treasures, and now look at the result!"

"Don't worry, Mubarak. I will think and plan, and we'll win, but let's save Amal's life first. She's our hero; and we'll declare her a man hero. We will honour her, protect her, and never forget what she has done for all of us."

Then he ran to his waiting father.

"We can lift her into the van now, and I'll drive, to make sure of a smooth journey."

Abu Mansour jumped into the van, whilst Mansour and Mubarak carefully carried the stretcher to him. Mansour gave his father the front end and then Mubarak gently lowered the rear of the stretcher onto the floor of the van, and hopped in. Mansour shut the doors and started the drive home.

"Poor girl," said Mubarak, looking at the saturated shirt and trousers. "She bled a lot."

"They must have hit a large blood vessel," commented Abu Mansour, looking at the peaceful body laid in front of him. Then, gazing at her black hair, he said, "Funny, her hair colour and the thickness of her plait is identical to that piece of hair in Jonathan's pocket."

"Please don't be ridiculous, Father," shouted Mansour. "There's no connection, but I have an idea of how those men escaped."

"How?" asked Mubarak.

"I think that piece of hair was bugged. I bet you he had a micro-transmitter hidden in it and that gave his position, so his people came and hit Amal before she had a chance to scream. Then they tied her quick and ran, after they stole everything."

"We should have taken that piece of hair," said Abu Mansour.

"I'm such a failure," sighed Mansour, regretting everything. "That will teach me a lesson for the future, not to torment my enemy, but kill him as quickly as possible. At least he can't run away when he's in the grave."

As they passed through the flattened area, Mubarak whistled in astonishment.

"They've ruined us! There's nothing left standing."

"I told you that, and you didn't believe me, but I'm going to avenge from those wolves for every brick and every drop of Amal's blood," vowed Mansour, as he quietly blew the horn to announce their subdued arrival.

"That's your father," said Om Mansour to Nahid, her youngest daughter. "Why is he blowing the hooter so sadly? I wonder who has died?"

They ran to the door and opened it, just as Mansour jumped out and opened the rear doors of the van. Mubarak hopped down, took the stretcher handles, and slowly walked away from the vehicle.

"It's a body!" exclaimed the mother, trying to have a good look.

Abu Mansour handed the stretcher handles to his son, and went towards the house.

"Sad news," said Mansour to his mother. "We have lost everything."

She looked at the body, and screamed with horror.

"That's Amal! Who killed her?"

Mansour replied quickly, to calm his mother.

"She's not dead, just in a coma. She will soon recover, insha-allah."

Shaking with shock, she opened the door wide, while Nahid ran ahead and opened another door, to one of their bedrooms.

"The Israelis escaped, after hitting Amal and tying her on the chair," explained Abu Mansour, sounding very disappointed.

"How?" she asked. "I thought you said they were well wrapped with ropes, and had a good guard."

"They signalled to their people, by a bugged piece of hair that Jonathan had in his pocket. They most probably dropped their men from the air by parachute, from the orange grove direction," he explained. "Mubarak didn't hear or see anyone, as they came from the opposite direction. They stole everything, and, as far as they are concerned, killed Amal, and ran away. We saw a group of planes displaying in the sky in that direction, so I'm certain they've gone back to Israel."

Then he bitterly added,

"They are able to do that because the Americans help them, giving them all the latest equipment, so of course they prove superior to us. We are only struggling by begging weapons and money from the Arab countries, who are not really supporting our cause."

"Don't feel so bad, Abu Mansour," said his wife understandingly. "At least no one has been killed, and we will soon help Amal to recover. I know she seems badly injured, so we have to try hard to help her, and pray."

Mansour and Mubarak lifted the limp body gently onto the bed, then he said to his mother,

"Can you take her clothes off and wash her, Mother. Then call me when you've finished and I'll attend to her wound."

Nahid rushed to collect a basin and water as the men left the room to sit outside, waiting for Om Mansour to change Amal. Nahid soon returned with a basin and soap, entered, and closed the door behind her.

"Mama, I can give her one of my nightdresses. She can have my new white one."

"Yes, that's a good idea. I think it will fit her, and she deserves the best. After all, she always helped us with her free clothes and cakes, and now she has saved our lives. It's such a great shame she has to suffer like this."

She unbuttoned the shirt and started to take it off gently, while Nahid helped support Amal. Suddenly. she noticed the medallion.

"Oh, the prophet Muhammad!" she exclaimed. "Look Nahid, Amal is wearing the star of David!" She gently lowered her to the pillow and ran outside to the men.

"What's happened?" asked Mansour anxiously, seeing his mother looking concerned.

"Amal is wearing the star of David round her neck!"

Mubarak jumped up, exclaiming,

"She's been planted by the Israelis!"

"Oh no she hasn't," said Abu Mansour and his son together.

"I know all about the medallion, and the ring. Amal stole them from the Israelis," said Mansour with a smile, "but she insisted to say that she 'only took them'!"

The mother smiled at first, then she broke into laughter and remarked,

"She is the first mobashira I've ever known to take such valuables from the Israelis, but at least she was able to keep her catch!"

Everyone laughed at the situation, and then Om Mansour went in to finish her job. She washed the blood from Amal's body, put on the clean white garment and stood to admire the peaceful, sleeping girl.

"She looks just like an angel, don't you think so, Nahid?"

"Yes Mama. I do hope she can stay with us for good, then she can share my bedroom and be a sister to me."

"I hope she recovers, and I can't see any reason to prohibit her from staying with us, especially as she's an orphan. In fact, I can be a mother to her."

She covered her with a sheet and went to call Mansour.

"I haven't touched her head," she said. "I will get you some more warm water and disinfectant, so you can deal with her cut."

The three men entered the room, where they saw Nahid standing at her side, holding her hand. She looked at them and smiled, announcing,

"She is my sister."

The men smiled, and gazed at the angelic sleeping person.

"White suits her much better than that prison uniform," said Mansour, and he sat on her right, the side of the wound, and carefully lifted her hair, which was sticky and dyed by the blood.

"Get me the first aid kit," he asked Mubarak, who immediately ran to the van, and came back carrying a white box, marked with a red crescent on its four sides.

Mansour gently and skilfully cleaned the cut, then filled it with an antibiotic powder.

"I'll have to shave off just a little bit of her hair so I can stick the wound together with the special plaster, but it's much better than stitches, and won't show."

His father handed him the razor. He shaved around the cut and joined the wound together, then placed the plaster over it. As he finished, Om Mansour arrived with coffee for the men. She looked at the black hair in Mubarak's hand and then at Amal.

"Oh, good," she smiled. "I would have hated it if you'd spoilt her hair, but it doesn't show at all. She has such lovely hair, black and soft, and plenty of it."

Mansour put his coffee on the floor and held Amal's hand, then he gently called her name,

"Amal, please speak to me."

There was no answer or response.

"Amal, look, we are all around you. All your friends are here, so please open your eyes."

He looked about him and saw everyone watching sadly.

"Maybe she will wake up tomorrow, after a good rest today," he said, picking up his coffee and taking a sip.

The three men left the room to start work. They had so much on their hands, having to organize themselves right from the beginning. As Mansour left the house, he said to his mother,

"If Amal awakes, or her situation worsens, you know where to find me. Send Nahid, and I'll come straight away."

"Don't worry, my love," said his mother. "I'll look after her for you."

The eyes behind the trees and the ears of the stones soon heard the news of the Israelis' escape and Amal's injury, and before much time had passed, Abu Mansour's house started to fill with visitors.

"Can we see Amal?" they requested.

"Yes, of course," replied Om Mansour, feeling proud to have the honour of looking after the hero. "But you must keep very quiet. She is unconscious."

The women, children and some men softly walked in and stood for a few moments, staring at the sleeping angel. Some drew near and kissed her forehead and cheeks, then left her in peace.

As soon as they had departed, more tapped on the door.

"We've hardly done any work today," said Om Mansour to her daughter. "Anyhow, everyone has the right and an obligation to Amal, so we can do our work tomorrow," she said, while on her way to open the door.

"Ahla, Muhammad." She greeted her young visitor with a smile.

"Can I see Amal, please?" asked the young boy.

"Yes, you can, but she is asleep at the moment."

"I know," he replied. "Mama told me the Israelis hit her and escaped. Pity I was not with her, as I know what to do with them," said the boy with indignation.

"Speak quietly, Muhammad. I told you she is asleep," said the woman in a whisper.

Then she took the boy by the hand and they entered the room. He walked across and stood by the bed, looking at Amal. After a moment he stretched out his hand and touched her forehead with the back of his hand, and said,

"She is alright, she doesn't have a fever."

The kind lady smiled and whispered,

"Yes, that's true, but she has a headache instead."

"Give her one tablet of aspirin. That will soon take her headache away," said Muhammad, acting like a competent doctor, who would diagnose the illness and then prescribe the right medicine.

Om Mansour nodded her head and said,

"I'll tell Mansour, as he is the one looking after Amal."

The boy smiled and said,

"I'll come and see her again tomorrow."

Then he turned round and left the room, ran to the street door and disappeared into the street.

Abu Mansour and his son had one of their busiest days. All the heads of the movement gathered in the local mosque, and after the prayers, they discussed the situation, informing each other about the missing pieces of the jigsaw puzzle.

"The Syrians saw the helicopter dropping some men on the slope of the mountain, on the left side of your grove."

"I know," commented Mansour, looking to his father and Mubarak. "We figured that out for ourselves. They timed it very well, as they knew we would be evacuating our people, so they almost killed Amal."

"How is her condition now?" asked Shakouri.

"Very serious," answered Mansour. "She's in a deep coma, but at least she is alive, thanks to God."

"We must hit back," said Walid, angrily.

"Better we control ourselves," said Abu Mansour. "If we hit them now, they will flatten the Palestinian camp as well, and we don't want that to happen, especially with Amal fighting for her life. So let us first concentrate on rebuilding our homes, and after that we will take revenge."

Then he added,

"We're lucky that our bank balance has just been refilled by the subscription from Kuwait, so we'll soon organize ourselves, and then we'll fight with all our power."

Mansour listened to the men for a while, subdued and feeling unhappy, as his conscience was upsetting him. His mind wandered back to Amal, "I am the one to blame. I was so confident of myself, that I left her there, assuring her that she would be safe, and look at her now." He glanced at his watch. "I must go home and look after her; that's the least I can do after what I've caused her." He stood up, and the men looked at him with surprise.

"We haven't finished yet, Mansour," said his father.

"I must go to Amal. I can't leave her unattended for so long," he replied, with worry showing on his face.

"Your mother is looking after her, and we've had no message, so she must be as we left her."

Mansour walked away, not wanting to waste any more time.

317

"You tell me later about the result of the meeting," he called over his shoulder as he went out of sight, leaving the assembled men silently watching his departure.

Abu Mansour felt obliged to explain his son's behaviour.

"He's feeling responsible for Amal's injury, especially as she asked to come with us, but he assured her she would be safe."

"Why didn't you take her with you?" asked Abdu.

"She doesn't know any of our whistles, plus she had no shoes on, as she had just escaped from the Israelis, so we thought she would be an obstacle rather than a help. We never anticipated that such a complicated manoeuvre would take place."

The minister came out of the conference room and made an announcement to the waiting crowd at the Centre, all anxious to meet with their two escaped men.

"I am sorry to have kept you waiting for so long, but we have been listening to a long story about a brave and amazing self-sacrificing person, who set the boys free, after we had lost all hope of getting them out."

The relatives and soldiers clapped warmly, smiling and cheering.

Then the minister continued,

"Unfortunately, the story ended with a tragic accident for our hero."

The crowd opened their mouths and gasped.

"Yes, I regret to say it, but she died, just on the last step of the mission. It was a complete accident, so please don't ask how it happened. It was one of those situations, when so many little and unexpected things happened that completely changed the desired course of events. So, in her honour, I announce the cancellation of our celebration. Our hero is Natanya, an Arab who resided in the army hostel, and it is not the first, but the second time that she has saved the lives of others. The first time she saved fifty persons, including Jonathan, and now she has saved hundreds, including our two boys."

The people stood up and bowed their heads in respect for a few minutes silence. They all looked shocked and saddened by the news, so the minister continued,

"On Sunday we shall have a service in her memory at her hostel. After that we will plant two trees to commemorate her loving deeds."

At that moment, Jonathan and Peres entered the room and stood at the side.

He concluded,

"Natanya is alive in our hearts and minds. She is a perfect model for us to follow, and her method, 'conquering hate with love', shall be a new goal for us to try to achieve, somehow. So, don't let sadness cover the achievements of this angel, but let us celebrate her deeds, and concentrate on her pleasant memories."

The audience clapped to show their full agreement with the minister, and then they turned towards the entrance, to see Jonathan and Peres smiling softly. Peres' two children ran with excitement to greet their father. His wife looked at him and realised the hard time he must have passed through.

"How grateful I am for this stranger who died to save my husband for me," she thought, smiling. Tears filled her eyes while she waited for the two children to get down from hugging their father, who had one on each arm.

Sara and Dan rushed to embrace their son, pushing the chairs out of the way in their hurry.

"I hardly recognized Jonathan," she said to her husband, "but I am ever so grateful to Natanya. Pity I didn't meet her before."

Jonathan hugged his mother and kissed her many times, then he kissed his father. They were unable to speak because of emotion for quite a time. Eventually Sara spoke, eyeing his filthy shirt, which was spattered with blood,

"We'll go home directly, and you'll feel a different man after a good bath and a nice meal."

Jonathan looked at his mother with understanding, and softly said to her,

"I must first pass by the hostel, Mum, as I need to talk to Mordecai."

"Can't you talk to him on the phone?"

"No. Natanya is his adopted daughter, and he personally helped her to come and set us free. Plus, I want to pay a little visit to her room, to thank her."

Then he sadly gazed into his mother's eyes and said,

"The hostel is full of Natanya's memories, so I can only stay with you for Shabbat, and then I must return, especially as there are a lot of preparations to be made for the service on Sunday."

"Whatever pleases you, my dear," she replied. "If there is anything we can do, please let us know."

"Thankyou. I think we'll need a great deal of help, as we're anticipating many visitors. The minister is coming, as well as many from his office, most of the officers, and many others besides. So I must be back on Saturday evening."

"We'll come with you," said Dan. "We can prepare some sandwiches and help the poor man, as I don't think he will be in a mood for any work."

Dan drove his son to the hostel, with Sara sitting on the back seat. She sat behind Jonathan and held him by his shoulders.

"We have been through misery, my love. We haven't slept for the last few nights and have almost gone out of our minds. In fact, just this morning my frustration burst out on Victor, as I never anticipated to see you again, alive or otherwise."

Jonathan turned round to speak to her.

"I'm sorry for all the anxiety I've caused you," he responded. "I also thought I would never return to Israel, either, as my hour for execution was nine this morning, and, at that precise moment, my sweet angel opened the door. We thought we were seeing a vision, but it was a miracle. Anyhow, that beautiful dream passed by so quickly, but, as far as I am concerned, Natanya is living in my heart."

Sara kept quiet, as both parents had ignored Jonathan's remarks about her when she was alive and now they felt lost for something to say. Jonathan noticed their situation and understood their feelings, so he tried to console them by saying,

"I consider myself very privileged to have met such a unique person, so the memory of these last few months will sustain me until I die."

His father kept glancing at him while he was driving, and said in admiration,

"It's wonderful to know that there are people around like her. It makes me regret our attitude toward her in the past, when you kept writing about her, describing her care and love. We just thought you were infatuated with her and felt quite concerned. Your mother was in desperation at the thought of your being involved with an Arab prisoner, so when your uncle came to see us, after your promotion, we asked them about Natanya. They were so impressed by her behaviour, to such an extent that we couldn't change the subject, as your aunt kept telling us over and over again about the gentle smiling alef prisoner, with beautiful kind brown eyes, who made the best coffee in the world."

Jonathan smiled as he remembered the time when they visited him, how Mark had screamed at her, yet she had so kindly served them.

Sara carried on with the story,

"She told us that there was a very boisterous and ill-mannered officer with you, who shouted out her name at the top of his voice. They anticipated black looks and resentment, yet were amazed to see a soft smile and polished etiquette, which excelled that of a high class lady."

She laughed as she retold the story, then remembered the last part.

"They said they were so surprised, that they forgot to say thankyou, so Natanya said it for them!"

Jonathan put his hand in his pocket and brought out the treasured piece of hair. He tenderly kissed it and said to his parents,

"This is a piece of her hair."

They looked at him with surprise.

"Did you cut it off?" his mother asked.

"No, she cut it with her own hand, taking my penknife from my belt. Then she told me, 'It is for memory'. So that every time I saw this piece of hair, it would remind me that she would be praying for no one to be hurt, and that I would come back home in peace."

He kissed the hair again, and said,

"She gave me this treasure long before my last raid into Lebanon, and I'm sure that her prayer was answered. In fact, this pleasant memory that I held in my possession kept me going during this impossible period of imprisonment."

"You must have been very good friends," remarked Dan.

"At the time I was mistreating her, but she was loving all the time, no matter what one did to her, because she loved her enemies. As far as she was concerned, none of us are enemies, but real friends."

"Well, that's just incredible, Jonathan," said Sara. "That is just out of this world. She must be an angel!"

Jonathan smiled, as he loved to talk about his angel. He said to his mother,

"I asked her to marry me, on the very day that I left on this last tragic mission, and she promised to wait for me, and pray for our dreams to come true."

Then he burst into weeping and his tears wet the soft black hair.

"Well, all my dreams are shattered now," he said, sobbing like a little child. "All that I'm left with are memories, but most pleasant memories."

Dan stopped the car by the roadside, as he too, found himself weeping.

"Time will bring healing, my dear," said his mother. "I never realised that you are so much in love with her. Anyhow, I'm in love with her now, even though I've never seen her. So I can imagine what my feelings would be if I'd had the pleasure of meeting her in person."

As Dan drove into the hostel, he was spotted by Mordecai, who immediately ran to greet Jonathan, with a joyful face and wide open arms.

"Shalom, and a hundred times shalom, my dear Jonathan," he exclaimed, hugging and embracing him. "I can see you've been in a fight, but I don't care what happened, as the main thing is that you're out and well."

Then he waved to the parents, who stayed sitting in the car.

"Now, my first question is this," said Mordecai, holding the tired, red-eyed figure by his arms. "When is Natanya coming back, as we have a big party to prepare together?"

"I knew he would ask me this question," thought Jonathan, looking at the happy man, and hating to disappoint him.

"She will not be coming, Mordecai."

"Why? Now tell me the reason why you are not bringing her back home?"

Jonathan stood and stared sadly at Mordecai, without any words daring to escape from his lips.

"Jonathan, you must tell me."

"I came here personally to tell you, my dear Mordecai. I am sorry to disappoint you like this, but Natanya is dead."

Mordecai froze like a snowman, looking unbelievingly at Jonathan. Then a few mumbled words came from his lips.

"Impossible. Natanya is dead! They killed her, those Arabs killed her?"

"No, Mordecai. It was a dreadful accident that happened in less than a minute, so quick, so fast, that we couldn't do anything to avoid it."

Then Jonathan took the old man's arm, and they walked slowly towards her room.

"I want to say a small prayer for her, in her room," said Jonathan quietly. "That is life; we have to accept it, with its bitterness, and its short, sweet moments."

Mordecai kept quiet, as the shock had robbed him of his thoughts. Jonathan opened the little cupboard room, and both men slowly entered.

"She made this bed two nights ago," he said, kneeling beside it and touching it with his hand. "My dear love, I am sorry I dragged you out of your little home, to your death."

Mordecai spoke in a whisper,

"She wanted to go. No one dragged her; in fact, I refused her, so she ran to Aaron, and both of them forced me to phone the Centre. Even there, she was the one who insisted to go - she was happy to help both of you, regardless of the cost."

Jonathan said his short prayer, requesting the Almighty to receive her spirit, and place it with the righteous. Then he raised himself from the ground and said to Mordecai,

"Please leave this room as it is, don't let anyone use it, change the sheets, or anything. It shall be a resting place for Natanya for ever."

Mordecai nodded his head, and Jonathan continued,

"The minister announced that a memorial service will be conducted in her honour here on Sunday, and he, as well as a great many other people will attend. He will also plant two trees in her memory, one here, and the other at the Centre."

"That is very good," said Mordecai, feeling comforted by the kind gesture.

"I will return tomorrow evening, Im Yirtseh ha-Shem, and my parents are going to give us a hand in preparing some sandwiches and coffee for our visitors."

"Good. We will need a lot of help, especially if the minister himself is coming," said Mordecai.

Then Jonathan asked,

"Has Aaron arrived back from Lebanon?"

"No, not yet, but he should be here late this afternoon."

"Would you ask him to ring me, please, because I want to tell him the news personally. You have the number of my parents' home in Jerusalem."

Mordecai nodded, looking at the blood on Jonathan's shirt. Then he asked,

"Is that her blood?"

He nodded sadly and said,

"Yes, I watched her when she died. It was the worst nightmare I have ever passed through, and much worse than the kidnapping. But please let us centre our focus on the good memories, and the wonderful times we shared with her, because her works and loving deeds shall live forever."

Mordecai smiled and looked around him, saying,

"Every inch of the hostel is full of Natanya's loving deeds. I will cherish every one of them."

"Yes," agreed Jonathan, smiling sadly. "I'll be looking forward to come back to her memories on Saturday evening."

Then he went to his room to collect a change of clothes. As soon as he opened the door, he was met by one of his sweetest memories. "This is where we stood holding each other so tightly, the most thrilling feeling I've ever experienced." He stood for a while on the spot, deep in the sweet dream. Then he woke up as he heard cars driving into the hostel. "My parents are waiting patiently for me, so I must leave my sweet dreams for tomorrow."

Mansour was met by his mother as soon as he stepped into the house.

"Oh Mansour," she said, looking tired and worn out. "We haven't stopped since you left, as so many visitors have called to see Amal. I haven't even had a chance to cook any dinner for us, so I'm afraid we'll have to eat bread and cheese today."

"Don't worry yourself. I personally don't feel like eating anything," he said, as he hurried to Amal's room. He entered and found his sister sitting on a chair by her bed, holding Amal's hand. When she saw him, she stood up and gave him her chair.

"I've tried to speak to her," she said, "but she doesn't want to awake. I know she is alive because I've found her pulse; very faint, but it's there."

"I'll take over, Nahid," he said, taking Amal's hand to find her pulse. Then he said,

"Mama needs help in the kitchen, if you can give her a hand, please."

She nodded, and left the room immediately, quietly closing the door behind her.

Mansour found the weak pulse, and looked at the pale, gentle face. "Just as if she is in a deep sleep," he thought.

"Amal, come on Amal, you've slept long enough. Come on, let me see your eyes."

He stretched out his hand and stroked her cheek. Then he drew closer to see what had happened to the big lump on her head. "No change. If it's swollen like this on the outside, I can just imagine what it's like under her skull, and I think that's where the problem lies."

He was examining the lump, moving the hair gently with his hands, and thinking hard of a way to deal with it, when his mother walked in with a cup of coffee for him.

"How is she?" she enquired in a whisper.

"It's this big swelling," he said, still concentrating on it. "It must be causing pressure in her brain and I must get it down somehow."

Om Mansour put the tray down and went closer to have a look.

"I wonder if we could squeeze it very gently?" she suggested.

"No Mama, we mustn't use any force. I think we'll use an ice compress. That should help."

"I'll go and get you some ice," she said, and hurried back to the kitchen.

Mansour sat back on his chair, drinking his coffee and looking at Amal.

"She is so pleasant," he murmured, "that I could sit here watching her for the whole day."

Om Mansour soon returned with the ice in a bowl, and a towel, and placed them on a little table next to her son. Then she stood with her hands folded, ready to watch the treatment. He put a few ice cubes on the towel and folded it, sandwiching the ice between its folds, and then he carefully placed it on the swelling.

"Can I support her for you?"

"I will look after her, Mama, as you have enough on your hands and have been looking after her most of the morning. Now it's my turn, that's why I came home early to attend to her."

He left the towel in position for a few minutes, then took it off and checked it.

"It's taking the heat away!" he exclaimed, putting on more ice, and all the while talking to her as he supported her head on his arm, just like a nursing mother attending to her sick child.

"I hope that pressure will soon come down, and then you can tell me your story.... You have been away for a long time, and I've often thought of you.... I do admire your courage and love, even though I can't abide by it, but nevertheless, I respect you for it."

Abu Mansour arrived with some of his top men, and all walked directly to Amal's room, where they saw Mansour busy with his treatment.

"Any change?" he enquired, lifting her hand and kissing it.

"Speak quietly, please," said Mansour, looking at the men surrounding his patient. Then he answered his father,

"I'm attempting to get this big lump down."

Shakouri drew near and started to examine it.

"She might already have brain damage," he observed.

"Can't you say something a bit better than that?" answered Mansour with irritation. "I'd rather have her die in peace, than spend all her life stuck in this bed." Then he replaced the towel on her head yet again.

Abdu sat down on the edge of the bed, looking at the angelic face. After a moment's thought he softly said,

"I've never seen her from such a close distance before. She is very pleasant, like an innocent child. It would be a tragedy if her brain is damaged."

"I'll tell you what I'll do to Jonathan," declared an angry Walid. "I'll blow his brain out!"

"Shush," ordered Mansour. "Please, speak quietly. The girl is fighting for her life, and she doesn't like bombs or guns, so don't speak about blowing or killing whilst you are in her presence."

The men became quiet and stood watching him. His father was still holding her little hand, and he whispered to them,

"You see this beautiful ring? She stole it from the Israelis." Then he gently held the medallion in the other hand. "And this star of David. Just these two, she said. She took, not stole!"

Smiles broke out on the faces of all, and, when they had digested the sentence, they laughed, and then roared with laughter.

"That's the best thing she's done!" laughed Shakouri.

The phone never stopped ringing in Mordecai's office. First Victor phoned from the Centre.

"Mordecai, I am sorry to bring you sad news, but I thought I must warn you before Jonathan arrives that...."

"He's arrived," interrupted Mordecai. "He told me what happened, but we must accept life as it is."

"Yes, my dear, that's the best policy, but I am very sorry, especially as I distrusted her so much. And all those threats; absolutely unnecessary. I could have kicked myself many times for my attitude."

"I told you that I trusted her with my life, but none of you listened to me, until it was too late."

"I'm sorry, but I learned a valuable lesson. Anyhow, I'm sending you a few of our canteen staff to give you a hand, because you are going to have a great crowd on Sunday."

"Thanks, Victor. I do appreciate that, because so far I don't know whether I am coming or going."

"Don't worry, man. I'll send them directly. They're excellent workers."

Mordecai put the receiver down, mumbling to himself.

"There is only one excellent worker, and that's my Natanya. No one else can reach to her level."

Before Mordecai left his office, another call was on its way to him.

"David here."

"Hello Dudu," answered Mordecai in a subdued voice.

"I've just heard the news, and isn't it tragic! A great loss, and I can't tell you how sorry I am. As I've told you before, if I lived for hundreds of years, I'd never understand that girl. Imagine it, she died to save her enemies, that's just incredible!"

"She doesn't have enemies," replied Mordecai.

"I know that, she's been here with us, and viewed us all as the best of friends, although I showed her the stars in the day time from the ill-treatment we gave her. Now I have a dreadful conscience."

"I assure you, she doesn't hold any ill-feelings against you, because she only has good and loving thoughts toward all."

Then he added,

"Good people like her always die young. My Esther was so good and kind - she died in an accident, and now my Natanya has also died in an accident. That's my luck in life, that I should live alone, sad and unhappy."

"Come on, Mordecai, don't feel so down. At least she's going to have an honourable service on Sunday, and two trees planted for her memory. I would be satisfied if one tree were to be planted in my memory. Anyhow, I'm sending a few more of my staff to give you a hand; you're going to need it."

Mordecai began imagining all those hands in the kitchen, and thought to himself, "I'd better get out of the way, otherwise we'll be stepping all over each other."

Aaron arrived at the hostel full of joy, unaware of the last events of the mission. He whistled and skipped as he danced his way to find Mordecai.

"Oh Mordecai," he called, dancing his way towards him. "We won the battle, without any casualties."

Then he noticed the sombre man just staring at him.

"Well, where's your smile? Is Jonathan back yet?"

"Yes, he wants you to ring him. You will find his number on my desk. I've left it there for you."

Aaron was puzzled by Mordecai's attitude, but he thought to himself, "I know Mordecai well. I expect he's just flustered because the work must be accumulating while Natanya is away. Never mind, he'll be on top of the world when she returns, I know I will be for sure."

He entered the office and saw the number on the desk. "I wonder why Jonathan wants me to ring?" He dialled the number and waited a few moments before Sara picked up the phone.

"Is Jonathan there, please?"

"Yes. Who is speaking?"

"Aaron, from the hostel."

Jonathan was already on his way to the phone when his mother announced, "Aaron." He was feeling much better, having had a bath and a change of clothes, as well as a light meal of soup and salad, quite enough as he had no appetite. He took the receiver from his mother.

"Aaron, I am glad to hear your voice again."

"And to hear yours, Jonathan. I nearly thought I was never going to see you again, but I knew Natanya would get you out. In fact, I nearly felt like arranging my own way to take her to Lebanon, as everyone made such a fuss. Anyhow, the plan worked perfectly."

"I don't know how to express my thanks and appreciation to you, Aaron," said Jonathan warmly, "as you have been a great friend to Natanya, and gave her tremendous support, which she really needed."

"That was my duty and pleasure, but what I would like to ask is when will she be coming back? I told her where to find us, and waited as long as I could, but I can appreciate that she will find it difficult to come just yet. Did she mention anything to you about when she will be coming?"

Jonathan kept quiet for a few moments so he could arrange the tragic news without hurting Aaron too much.

"Natanya bravely came and released us from a desperate situation, but unfortunately the last step of her mission turned into a nightmare."

"What do you mean?" asked Aaron anxiously, with Mordecai's depressed image on his mind. "I wonder if she has been hurt?" he thought, but could not ask such a question, rather waiting to hear Jonathan's reply, which seemed to take an eternity to reach him.

"I regret to say it, Aaron, but Natanya is dead."

Aaron felt like fainting. He could not believe his ears, and sank down onto the chair.

"Dead? They killed her?"

"No. It was an accident, a horrifying one."

"What do you mean by an accident?" queried Aaron.

"It was a plan Natanya herself suggested, so that she could help us, as well as Mansour and his father. The problem was that both Peres and myself were numb and partially paralysed from our tight binding, so we failed in doing our part successfully, and it ended in her death."

"Did she suffer?"

"I don't think so. It happened in a fraction of a second, and we felt helpless, watching her in front of our eyes. We couldn't do a single thing, except to run away and leave her, as it happened in the place where we'd been held."

He sighed with grief and continued,

"The minister announced a memorial service for her on Sunday, and also said that two trees will be planted in her memory, one at the Centre and the other at the hostel. At least her memory shall live through them, and in our hearts."

Then he added thoughtfully,

"I personally will not accept that she died. Perhaps I'm still in this terrible nightmare, and tomorrow will wake up and discover that it's just a passing black cloud."

Aaron, still suffering from the shock of the news, felt numb and detached from any feelings. Then he said,

"I thought you would be the one who would not come back, so I phoned my parents and told them about Natanya, to prepare them, as I promised you that I would take her as a member of my own family. I was amazed how my parents loved the idea and wanted to come to the hostel to meet her, but we had to leave in a hurry, so now I don't know how to break the news to them."

"I am sorry I have put you to so much trouble, Aaron."

"No Jonathan, I do consider it an honour, although I'm sad and disappointed to have lost the best friend I ever had. Anyhow, I think I'll also refuse to believe that she's died. As you say, perhaps it's just a passing nightmare."

Mansour did not leave Amal's side, so his father gave him the result of the morning meeting which took place while he was attending to her. He spoke with bitterness to his father,

"I've made up my mind. I will not rest until I avenge Amal's blood from those pigs, so as soon as she's out of her emergency, I shall go and hunt them, and find a way to kill the fox. If he thinks that we're defeated, he'll have to think again."

"Now who is talking of killing in Amal's presence?" asked Abu Mansour, with a grin all over his face.

Mansour kept checking the lump. Sometimes he thought it had improved, but the next time he measured it, it seemed to have worsened.

"I honestly feel we should go to sleep," said his mother, seeing him exhausted and irritable. "I'm sure she will get better, especially if Abu Mansour prays for her, as he is a righteous man."

Mansour sighed and kept quiet, as he thought to himself, "We spent a whole day praying and fasting to blow the dogs, and we failed. Then we prayed hard again, and, in the moment when we thought God was on our side, we failed again. It's better we leave Amal alone, without any of our prayers, otherwise we'll fail again." He stood up, feeling tired and depressed, and adjusted the pillows at what he thought was the right height. Then he kissed her forehead and said softly,

"Goodnight Amal. I hope you have a good sleep, and awake bright and well in the morning."

His mother stood watching him and smiled as she remembered the past. "You would never think Mansour would do all this for Amal, as it was just less than a year ago that he was seeking her blood, but now I could swear he would die for her."

Jonathan went to bed and tried to sleep, but he could not wipe the image of Natanya's last moments from his eyes. He got out of bed and took her soft hair from his shirt pocket, then returned, holding it in his hand, and looking at it. Immediately his mind brought her pleasant memories to his eyes; he could see her smiling, hear her laughter and giggles, her songs and words. He talked softly to her, "Of course, my love, you are with me. I never said goodbye to you, for there was no need, as you are next to me. I can hold you tight next to my heart; I can kiss your hair and pretend you are sleeping beside me, and that might help me to have sweet dreams." He hugged the piece of hair next to his heart and soon drifted into a deep sleep.

Dan and Sara talked together on their bed about the problem of their son.

"I think we must take him with us to England. The change will do him good and take his mind from Natanya," said Sara.

"That's a good idea, but I think he wants to stay where her memories are," said Dan. "It's understandable. After all, she was his fiancee."

Sara felt sure he must cut himself off from the past as soon as possible.

"She has died and gone, so I can't see why he should tie the rest of his life to memories."

"Sara, my dear," said Dan reprovingly, "we never thought we would see him alive altogether. She died to set him free; she achieved what the entire army failed to do, so we must honour her with all our heart. She only died this morning, so we must allow him at least a month of mourning, and share the sorrow with him. She's my daughter and I'm proud of her, and I only regret that she had to die. Anyhow, we must go to sleep, as we need our strength to cheer him up tomorrow."

Mansour awoke early, while it was still dark, and the first thought in his mind was Amal. He went straight to her room, even before he ceremonially washed for the dawn prayer. He turned on the light to see his patient. "She looks exactly the same as I left her last night," he thought with disappointment. He examined the area of the wound.

"Nothing has changed. Cursed be you, Jonathan," he muttered in an undertone.

Om Mansour was also up early, and, seeing the light on, she entered the room.

"Good morning, my love," she said, fixing her attention on Amal.

"I wish it was a good morning," he answered sadly.

"Why Mansour?" she asked anxiously. "Is she still alive?"

"Yes, but only just; nothing has changed since last night."

"Well, that is good news. We can repeat yesterday's treatment, and I feel she will improve."

"I'll come after the prayer and see to the wound and change its dressing. Then we can repeat the treatment," he said, as he gently laid Amal's head back on the pillow.

Abu Mansour and his family had their morning coffee beside Amal's bed, where they discussed her problem. The wise old man watched her silently for some time, thinking. Then he commented, with concern in his voice,

"Our problem is how to feed her. If she doesn't get up soon, she will die from dehydration."

Mansour had thought of that problem himself, and he knew of an easy solution, but his pride would not allow him to take that course. "Baha would help us, as she's a good nurse, and Amal's friend. But I'm not going to see her, especially after the way she treated me last time. Just to upset me, she told me to my face that she was quite happy to love Jonathan. Huh! Now he's damaged our Amal - I'll never go and see her again," he thought, while he tried to think of an alternative solution for the problem. Then he said to his father,

"I think she can stay without water for today, as many people have survived for a few days without food or water, but if she continues like this for longer, I'll have to force-feed her by inserting the tubes through her nose, although I hate to do that treatment because it's quite painful."

He changed the dressing on the wound and was pleased to find it clean, with no sign of infection.

"Actually, the swelling has slightly improved," he remarked.

"That's good progress," responded his mother, with hope in her eyes. "We will take over from you now, Mansour," she said, as she could see her husband was waiting for him, so they could start their day's busy schedule. "You set your mind at rest. Nahid and myself will stay by her side until you return."

Jonathan attended the Sabbath service with his parents in one of Jerusalem's main synagogues. Many people were aware of his release and of the miraculous escape which had been achieved by the Arab heroine. They gathered around him after the service, to express their joy for his safety and to show their keen interest in the story of the girl, which story he found it a pleasure to relate.

"Her name is Natanya, although I call her my angel, for that's what she is. Tomorrow we're holding a service in her memory at the hostel."

"We would love to attend," was the wish of many, "as she's a unique person. We've heard of people who died to save their friends or relatives, but not their enemies."

"You're welcome. The hostel is her home, or, to be precise, she turned it into a beautiful home, for all of us."

The heads of different units spread the news to their various departments and hostels, eventually reaching Mark in Beer Sheva's army hostel.

"I can't believe it!" he said with alarm. "She's too wonderful a person, young and gentle, and extremely cute, to die like that!" He went to his room so depressed and secretly cried,

"Forgive me, Natanya," he begged. "I wanted to come and apologize for my stupidity, but I felt so ashamed of myself, and now it's too late. You remained the same, that loving, caring and self-sacrificing person, right up till the last moment. Pity I lost the pleasure of your company."

He made up his mind to attend the service the following day. "I hope Jonathan won't be offended by my presence, but I feel I must go and pay my respects."

The stream of visitors increased at Mansour's house, as everyone was interested to follow Amal's progress. Om Mansour received much advice and numerous remedies, which she carefully registered in her head, giving the same reply to all,

"I will tell Mansour when he comes. He's the doctor, we are only the nurses."

Muhammad arrived to visit his friend the preacher.

"Is Amal awake yet?" he enquired.

"Not yet, Muhammad, but you can come and see her for yourself."

He followed the kind lady to the room, where he noticed Nahid placing the towel of ice cubes on the sleeping girl's head. He watched for a while, then held Amal's hand and called out,

"Amal, goomi." (Get up).

Nahid smiled and said quietly,

"I've been telling her to get up all the time, but it's no use."

He looked at Om Mansour, and gave some advice as usual,

"You must wash her face with cold water. That will make her wake up."

The lady smiled and nodded her head, so he said with conviction,

"My mama always gets me up in the morning by throwing freezing cold water on my face, and it always makes me jump from the bed."

Then he repeated,

"It must be ice cold, otherwise it will not work."

"I'll tell Mansour about it, Muhammad. Thankyou for coming to see Amal."

"I will come again tomorrow, because I want to ask Amal about something, so she must be awake by then."

"We will pray, Muhammad," said the lady, sadly.

He nodded his head and said,

"I will pray, too."

Then he turned round and left.

Abu Mansour organized his men to rebuild the ruins. They worked without stopping, some laying new foundations, while others gathered any usable materials from the wreckage. Mansour could not concentrate on any work, his mind being preoccupied. "I don't seem able to do anything," he thought. "Amal keeps haunting me. How I wish she would get up. I do want to talk to her; I was so looking forward to hear her stories. She even made my father feel so thrilled, and I've never heard him laughing so much as he did when she arrived yesterday. He told me that was the best time he's had for as long as he can remember - what a great shame."

He looked at his watch. "I must go home, as Mother has to do some cooking. I know my father won't like it, but I must stay beside her."

He tried to creep away, but his father spotted him.

"Mansour, you're not going yet?!"

"I'm only going for a few minutes. I must go and see Amal, and you have so many men."

"I can't understand you, Mansour. You are the leader here, yet you keep leaving everyone working and then disappear."

"I'm working too, Father. Amal is our hero. She needs someone to look after her, and that's my duty. I can't neglect it again; once bitten...."

"Your mother promised to do that," he interrupted his son. "So no need for you there."

"See you later, Father," Mansour said, rushing away and moaning to himself, "If I want to look after Amal, I shall, and no one will stop me."

Peres related the whole story to his wife in all its finest details, including his desperation and feelings of hopelessness.

"The first night was bad enough, but the second one was just unbearable, my body ached and throbbed and I wished to die, or even be blown up by our own men. But Jonathan was marvellous, calm, and having faith in prayer. He sang his angel's favourite song, 'It is better to trust in the Lord, than to trust in man'. It was amazing how that song cheered us up, and we felt comforted and able to sleep well for that night."

Naomi heard the story without interruption, until her husband related to her how he hit Natanya on the head.

"No, Peres!" she said in horror, holding her head as if she was the one who received the blow.

"It's my nightmare," he said, swallowing his saliva. "My hands were paralysed and I could hardly feel them. The wind was blowing through the trees, making it sound like people were coming in our direction. It was such a panic. Adding to that, Jonathan was hesitating to do it himself, so I had no alternative but to carry it out myself, and I killed her in a moment."

"How dreadful!" she exclaimed, still holding her head with both hands. "How can we face Jonathan again?"

Peres answered, in a voice full of grief,

"He forgave me, and he's sure Natanya would do the same, as it was a complete accident."

"We owe so much to this angel," said Naomi, "and I feel for poor Jonathan, so I think we must take a real part in the service tomorrow. We'll let the children offer our flowers, and give Jonathan a letter explaining our sincere heart feelings, and our regret for her loss, as well as telling him that our house is open to him at all times, so that, if he ever needs a friend, or some company, we are his."

Peres agreed, and added,

"We'll tell him that we will plant a little garden in her memory, and if God gives us another daughter, we shall name her Natanya."

Jonathan arrived with his parents to begin preparations at the hostel, and they found the place buzzing with activity. The boys and girls were cleaning and tidying up. The common room had been rearranged to accommodate the guests for the service. There were so many hands in the kitchen that there was no room for Mordecai or any more assistants. Aaron's parents and sister were busy sweeping the yard, as they felt that Natanya was one of their own family.

Jonathan was so comforted and touched. He had a few words with each person, thanking them and expressing his gratitude. Then he went to Natanya's room and opened the door wide, saying to his parents, as well as Aaron and Mordecai,

"This room will be the centre of our service tomorrow. We will place our flowers and any offerings of respect on this bed, as it represents Natanya's resting place."

Sara felt concern, and said,

"We can't use the room like this; we'll have to empty the shelves from the linen and do something to cover them up, because it's a disgrace to let the minister see a cupboard like this."

Jonathan looked at his mother and replied adamantly,

"Mother, I am not ashamed of this room, for this cupboard tells about the great person who humbly dwelt here, while none of us were worthy of her. How many great people who affected world history dwelt in such places? Palaces and imposing buildings are no guarantee of producing great people, but persons like my Natanya are the driving power to generate the light of love and pleasantness in the world, so I do not want any change made to this room. This bed will stay as it is, just as she left it, and I will honour her memory here, as long as I live."

Mordecai and Aaron nodded their heads in full agreement. Sara was outnumbered, but she still felt uncomfortable, being very class conscious, and appearances meant so much to her.

A second night ended, and Amal was still fast asleep in her unconscious state. Mansour spent the time trying to think of a way to rouse her, as otherwise he would have to start the second step of his treatment, of pushing the feeding pipes through her nose.

"I'd better go and say my prayer first," he advised himself, "otherwise my father will give me another lecture. Then I can spend some time beside her before we go to work."

Abu Mansour was surprised to see Mansour already ceremonially washed and on his prayer mat before him.

"You're early," he remarked. "Have you seen Amal?"

"Not yet. Prayer first, then Amal."

"That's a good boy," said his father, commending him, as he was anxious that Amal seemed to be taking over his mind.

Mansour said his prayer so fast, looking just like an athlete training in a gymnasium, that he finished long before his father. Then he jumped up and rushed off in the direction of Amal's room.

"What a man!" exclaimed his disappointed father, watching him disappear into the room.

"Amal," he called softly, gazing at her face as he walked slowly towards her. He sat down beside the bed.

"She definitely looks much better today, and there's colour in her cheeks." He touched her forehead. "Quite warm, that's a good sign." Then he examined the lump on her head. "Good!" he exclaimed, "It's almost disappeared!" He called her name over and over again.

"Come on, Amal, you've slept for such a long time. Wake up, we have so much work to do, and I need you, my Amal." (My hope).

Om Mansour and Nahid soon joined Mansour, while his father was still saying his prayer.

"Good morning, my love," said his mother, yawning, feeling so tired from the busy time she had experienced over the last few days.

"Don't you think Amal is looking better this morning?" he responded with delight in his voice.

"Yes, she is," both women said together.

"She just looks as if she is asleep and about to wake up," said the mother.

Then they all called together, while Mansour gently shook her shoulders,

"Amal, goomi."

Amal was dreaming for the first time, as the pressure eased from her brain. She could hear the sound of a crowd in the far distance, but her eyes were so heavy and her head swimming, that she dreamt she was on a ship in a stormy sea. One moment she was on top of a wave and the next she was crashing down to the bottom of the depths.

Om Mansour remembered Muhammad's advice, and with a smile, said to her son,

"Yesterday, Muhammad came to visit Amal, and he suggested that if you wash her face with cold water, she will get up. He said his mother always wakes him by throwing cold water on his face."

Mansour smiled and said,

"We'll try anything, and cold water won't harm her. Let's try it."

Nahid ran to the kitchen, put cold water into a big bowl, emptied the ice cubes into it and ran back to the room. Mansour stirred the water with his hand, to mix the ice and cool the water.

Amal was still in the midst of her stormy sea. "We are going to drown in a few minutes. Look at the hailstones and the rain," she thought in her dream, as her ears registered the sounds around her in the room, and her headache contributed to the rest of the nightmare.

Nahid held the bowl near Amal's face, while Mansour supported her head on his arm. Then he filled the hollows of his hands with the iced water and threw it on her face.

The shock of the cold water on her face created a mighty reflex that caused her to jump up from her sleep, just at the moment that her ship was wrecked and she fell into the cold sea.

Mansour and his mother and sister screamed with delight, shouting and laughing.

"Amal, him-dilla alla salama!" (Thank God for your safety).

She stared at them, gazing as if in a trance at the jubilant people.

"Amal, how great to see you!" They shouted and screamed, still hardly able to believe their eyes.

Abu Mansour heard the tremendous excitement, so stood up in the middle of his sentence to God, and said,

"Please forgive me. I'll say a double prayer at noon." Then he ran to the room.

Mansour hugged his patient, and his mother threw herself onto the bed, hugging her from the other side, while Nahid cried with joy.

"Amal!" exclaimed Abu Mansour, his eyes almost popping out of their sockets. "What a miracle! To see you awake and sitting up in bed!"

Amal was trying to find herself. "We are not at sea, although my face is dripping with water, icy water, too. And these people who are crying and laughing, who are they?" She stared at them, as she did not recognize Om Mansour or Nahid. She turned and saw Mansour holding her to his chest.

"Amal, can't you recognize any of us?" asked Mansour, looking at her eyes. "Look, I am Mansour, and that is my father. Remember, he helped you to escape from the Israelis?"

"Ah, I remember," she thought to herself. "Of course, Jonathan and his friend, I helped them to escape." Then she touched her ring and medallion, and smiled softly. Her excited audience burst into laughter and Mansour said to her,

"I'm glad they didn't steal your catch from you. Mind you, they stole my dagger and gun, but I'm going to kill both of them as soon as I recatch them."

Amal shut her eyes and frowned, but her tongue was too numb to utter any words.

"Don't Mansour," begged the mother, as she saw Amal shut her eyes. "We've waited long enough for her to awake, and now you're sending her back to sleep."

"Amal," hastily begged Mansour. "Please open your eyes. I'm sorry. I will not mention the fox in your presence again."

She opened her eyes and looked at her friends. "They must have been looking after me," she thought, wanting to ask many questions, but only her eyes spoke.

Mansour understood her questions, and gave her the information.

"You have been asleep from Friday morning till now, which is exactly six o'clock Sunday morning. We almost went crazy at first, when we thought Jonathan had killed you, but my father noticed that you were unconscious, and since then we've tried every method to get you better. Thanks to God, your little friend, Muhammad, had a good suggestion that worked perfectly," he said, laughing.

She smiled and nodded her head, and attempted to say thankyou in Arabic, "shokra", but the word did not come out clearly.

"Never mind, my love," said Om Mansour. "You'll soon recover, and then you can tell us what happened."

Amal shook her head, as she did not want to talk about the experience, so Abu Mansour said to his wife,

"We don't want to know about what happened, as we already know, nor do we want to upset Amal. That's now a closed page of the past and we shall not bring it back to mind."

Amal smiled and nodded.

While Mansour still proudly held his patient, he said,

"You know what I'm going to do, Amal? I'm going to make the biggest party ever to celebrate your recovery, and all our friends and yours will be invited, as they have been coming to ask after you every day since you've been unconscious."

The family agreed immediately, although Om Mansour suggested they wait until Amal regained her speech.

"We can have another one when she is completely recovered," said Mansour, "but tomorrow, insha-allah, we can have one to celebrate her raising."

The family sat with overjoyed faces, eating their breakfast around Amal. Mansour suggested a cup of warm milk with a spoonful of honey as a suitable first meal for Amal. She sat resting on a pile of pillows, holding her drink and sipping it from time to time, watching her happy friends, and thinking all the while. "It is good to see everyone so happy and to know that no one got hurt in the raid. I am personally happy that my love was able to escape, and now all I have to do is pray that all of us here will become good friends, just like Baha, Jonathan and Aaron; then that will be the most wonderful dream ever to come true." She looked at Mansour with her soft, gentle and hopeful eyes, and smiled. He noticed her and smiled back.

"What a wonderful smile," he thought. "So pleasant that it refreshes the heart. Now I can see what Baha meant when she said that 'Amal is an unnatural girl'. She told us that after she went to gather information about her, and since then, she's been hooked on her."

"Come on, Mansour," said his father. "We can't sit here all day looking at Amal, however much we would like to do so, but we'll hurry up and soon come back, and hopefully by then, Amal will be able to talk to us."

Mansour stood up, looking at her happy face. Once again she attempted to say "shokra", but did not quite succeed. He smiled and encouragingly said,

"You've already improved, Amal. I look forward to seeing you later." Then the two men left, dragging their feet away from the room, although their hearts were full of joy.

"How strange," said Abu Mansour. "Amal has something about her that you can't resist, a sort of magnetic pull. I can't identify it, but whatever it is, it does produce peace in the heart."

Mansour smiled and nodded. "I'm glad I'm not alone in feeling that way," he thought to himself.

The hostel started to fill up with visitors. Half an hour before the service the car park was full, so one of the soldiers had to direct the traffic to park outside. The minister and other members of the cabinet arrived. David, the prison governor, together with Moshe and other prison officers also arrived, as well as many guests. The common room and corridors soon filled up, so many had to stand in the yard.

Jonathan, Mordecai and Aaron took their places at the front, to take a leading part in the service, as Natanya was their close relative. Peres and his entire family arrived, including his and Naomi's parents. Their children carried flowers to offer in memory of the angel. The 'beautiful girl' and her parents also came to offer their condolences.

"Look at all these people," said Sara to her husband. "I've never seen so many people coming to a memorial service before."

"No," whispered Dan, looking around him. "That's because people like our Natanya are few and far between."

"I don't know about you," she said, "but I feel very proud of her, and impressed. I never realized she was so famous."

When Jonathan looked around and saw how the people kept pouring in, he felt so good that Natanya was being honoured so much. He turned to Mordecai and whispered,

"It's good to see many people coming to share our loss."

"Yes, Jonathan. I am very proud of my daughter, and I wish she could see them."

Jonathan held his shirt pocket and smiled softly.

"I think she can," he said.

The rabbi began the service, reading some prayers, and then a few Psalms were sung by the hundreds of mourners. After that the minister stood and gave a brief talk about Natanya's qualities.

"A unique person that bore in her heart a most wonderful love, a love impossible to achieve unless one is a hero and able to conquer the impossible, and that's what she attained to, in the land of her enemies."

Then Victor, the Centre's commander, gave his contribution about Natanya.

"Jonathan calls her his angel, and I didn't realise he was referring to this strange girl, until I saw her with my own eyes, and then I came to the same conclusion. When we thought the hope of saving our boys was nil, the angel came and intervened, prayed a lot, and, in no time, the boys were out, safe and sound. We don't feel she has died, no, never may that be. Natanya shall live forever, through what she has done and performed, and, just to illustrate this point, look around you. All these people attending this service testify that good deeds never die, no matter who produces them, and good deeds are the product of the pure love, the divine love, that is able to spring up new from year to year, from generation to generation."

Jonathan headed the congregation, followed by Mordecai and Aaron, each carrying a wreath of spring flowers. He walked between rows of people to the little room. He entered and knelt beside her bed, laying the wreath on it and whispering in grief,

"I will not say goodbye, my love, for you are living in my heart."

Then Mordecai entered and laid his wreath, unable to speak at all, with tears streaming down his cheeks. He was followed by Aaron, who laid his and saluted. Then they moved away from the room and stood outside to receive the condolences of the guests. As they left, the two children entered, walking side by side, and laid their flowers on the bed. The queue followed them, and soon the bed was covered with flowers, until there was no place left for any more, so a second layer was started.

The minister headed the mourners to the yard, where a beautiful myrtle tree was waiting to be planted. Jonathan had chosen the myrtle, it being evergreen, with pleasant, fragrant flowers and medicinally useful leaves. The minister planted the tree, while Victor supported the trunk.

After the service was over, the young fighters offered drinks and sandwiches to their guests. Jonathan never had a moment without someone chatting to him about his privilege of knowing the amazing girl. Mark appeared and warmly shook his hand, saying apologetically,

"I hope I haven't offended you by my coming?"

"Of course you haven't!" replied Jonathan. "It's good to see you again."

"You are always so gracious, Jonathan," he said. "I can't tell you how grieved I am about Natanya. I wanted to come a long time ago and apologize for my stupidity, but I lacked the courage. Anyhow, if it's any consolation, Natanya caused me to start a new page. I used to be a selfish beast, just thinking of my stomach and what I desired, until that dreadful night, when she taught me the lesson that love is not what you receive, but what you give. She was a young girl, but very strong, who kicked and pushed me and was quite happy to die by my pistol rather than lose her purity. I saw the abhorrence in her eyes at my behaviour, and that's what changed the course of my life. Since that night, I've detested my lower selfish nature, and have tried ever since to lift myself up, to her level." Then he paused and asked, "I hope I'm not upsetting you?"

"No, Mark. I love to hear anything about Natanya, because whatever I hear is only good and never shameful. I am privileged to have had the pleasure of knowing her." He smiled and asked softly, "Did you know we were engaged?"

"No," he answered, surprised. "When did you get engaged?"

"A few minutes before I left for Lebanon."

"How dreadful for you that events turned out like this. I am sorry." Then he added sheepishly, "I thought you had a soft place in your heart for her, so I told her a lie about your cousin, and what amazed me at the time was that she felt very pleased and said to me, 'I will pray they will be happy together'."

Jonathan smiled and said,

"I know, she told me. In fact, she nearly refused me because of that and I really had to work hard to convince her that I had nobody else besides her. Anyhow, that was a pleasant dream that soon passed by."

Abu Mansour's house started to receive its endless visitors, enquiring as usual about Amal.

"Come in," said Om Mansour, welcoming them with a big smile filling her face. "Come and see what's happened to Amal!"

They followed in anticipation, as the beaming face announced the unveiling of good things.

"Amal!" was the joyful scream which everyone uttered when they entered the room and saw the gentle smiling person sitting on the bed; meeting people whom she had never seen before, as she only used to see their children, never the adults. The women folk went near and hugged and kissed her, while Om Mansour retold the story from the beginning of how they woke her up. After that, she would invite each one to the party, and they in turn, would offer to come and give a hand in the food preparation.

"Tislameely," she would say, "I would be so grateful for your help, as you can see that Amal still needs attention, as she can't speak yet, although she has improved since the morning."

Abu Mansour was in a good mood, joking and laughing with everyone. Even one of the Druze militia had a handshake from him, which was remarkable, as he usually cleared his throat loudly and spat on the ground to show his contempt for his enemies.

Mansour kept watching the time. "I really feel we must finish early today, as Amal has got up after a long period of unconsciousness and been left alone, without any companionship. So I must go and keep her company for a bit," he told himself. "I'm sure my father won't mind, after all, I have to carry on with the treatment as she could hardly speak this morning, so I'll go and see what I can do." He got up and told Shakouri,

"I must go home right now, Shakouri, because I have to attend to Amal. Don't forget to tell my father." Then he disappeared before he was spotted.

Muhammad arrived to see his friend. Om Mansour hugged him and kissed his cheeks and said to him,

"Come and see what happened to Amal after we followed your suggestion."

The boy ran to the room, and, when Amal saw him, she opened her arms and shouted,

344

"Muhammad, ahla."

He threw himself into her arms and they hugged and kissed each other.

"That's wonderful," thought Om Mansour. "Amal spoke quite normally." Then she said to Amal,

"Muhammad came yesterday and said he wanted to tell you something, so I had better leave you alone."

Amal also had many questions to ask her right hand.

"How are you?" she asked slowly and softly. "And how is school?"

"I'm okay, but I've hardly been to school this year, because I've been very busy."

"Why?" she asked with concern.

"You see," said the young boy, explaining his situation like an adult who had just met up with a long lost friend, "I am the only man in the house, and have to look after the family, especially since the Israelis took you away and I couldn't buy any clothes or medicine or free food, so I had to earn some money."

Amal was shocked and hurt, and asked him,

"What job do you have?"

"I go to the market and carry shopping for the women. Sometimes I earn some money, and sometimes no one wants me to carry their shopping."

"So what happens when nobody hires you?" she asked.

The boy shrugged his shoulders and said,

"We just have to go without food until the next day."

Amal felt speechless, and detested war and hate more than ever. "If only people would stop killing each other, and spend their money and time on love projects, then this lad would never have to suffer like this," she thought, looking at him. Then she asked him,

"What did you want to tell me?"

He smiled bashfully and answered,

"I wanted to ask when you are going to sell free things again?"

"I don't know," she said thoughtfully, as she was thinking of going back to her waiting love as soon as possible, but now she found herself in a dilemma. "They need help. I must ask Jonathan. I'm sure he is willing to help them, but I need time. I can hardly move, as my head is feeling giddy, and I don't think I can return for at least a week." She spoke to the waiting boy,

"Give me time to think, Muhammad. I will pray, and will discuss the situation with Mansour when he returns, and see what he has to say."

He nodded and said,

"I know. He must know, because he is the doctor."

She smiled as she tried to see the connection. Then she said, holding his hands,

"You pray as well that God will help us."

"I will. I have been praying that He get you up from your sleep, and He did."

"Thankyou." Then she remembered the party, "Oh Muhammad, ask your mama and brother and sister, and of course, yourself, to come and share in our celebration. Mansour is making a big party tomorrow."

"Tislameely," he said gladly, hugging her. "I'll tell them."

He jumped up and excitedly ran off to carry the news of the party to his mother.

Mansour successfully arrived home, without having been spotted by his father. He headed for Amal's room, entering just as she was praying, so she was delighted to see him.

"Ahla, Mansour," she called, smiling.

"Amal," he rushed to her, "my Amal, your speech is almost back to normal!"

"I have been praying for you to come home," she said, looking at him.

"I must have heard your thoughts, as that's why I left early, to be with you. So tell me, what do you want me for?"

"I've heard a sad story, and I want to share it with you."

Mansour felt privileged, that he meant so much to her, that she prayed to share with him her story, so he said,

"Where did you hear this sad story?"

"In this room." She looked at him with her soft, kind eyes, then told him the story, without giving any names.

"Did Muhammad come to see you?" he asked.

"He did," she replied, then asked, "Is it a true story?"

He nodded.

"We must do something to help him, and others like him," she said with concern.

"We are going to help them, but now we have a struggle on our hands. When that's out of the way, we'll be able to concentrate on the other problems."

"Mansour, that will be too late for Muhammad and his family. Plus, what you call a struggle, will produce more cases like Muhammad and more tragedies. Why can't we stop? Why can't we start to conquer the hate with love?"

Mansour stared at the girl without speaking. "She has just risen from the dead, as it were, after a horrific experience, and the first thing she starts to speak about is love! What on earth can a person do with someone like her?"

Amal waited for Mansour's opinion, which was slow in coming, so she asked again,

"Why is it difficult for us humans to see the simple truth which baffles men, yet even the common sense of children enables them to see the solution?"

"Amal, I can't understand your logic," he said, trying not to lose his calmness. "Our struggle is more important than our life, for what good is it if you have life but no security with it? Take yourself as an example, those dogs almost killed you, and they are the ones who killed Muhammad's father, and destroyed our homes in their last raid, and, if you hadn't warned us, Muhammad would not be here to tell you his story. So how can you tell me to conquer the hate of those pigs with love?! I tell you right now, I hate them, and I'm going to fight them with the last drop of my blood, and you ought to support us in our struggle. Not only that, Amal, but I took an oath to avenge for every drop of your blood which they spilt on the ground."

She looked at him with understanding, but was determined to explain her superior way of conquering the evil by love, so she said,

"I forgive the Israelis for what they did to me, and I am forever grateful for the care that you showed me, and the vow which you took on my behalf, but I release you from it, as I will be hurt and personally injured if you fulfil your vow, because you will be killing my friends, as I have no enemies. I only have friends."

He stood to leave the room, so she held his hand.

"Please do not go, Mansour. I need you. Together we can help our people, our friends."

He sat beside her, as he could see she only wanted to help, and was desiring the best for all. She kept holding his hand in case he would leave without first reaching a positive conclusion.

"Mansour, I forgave your father and family first, as they killed my entire family. I came personally to illustrate to myself and to all of you, that it is possible to conquer hate with love.... It's the best way to solve the problem. Now I am doing the same to the Israelis. I have forgiven them for their injury to me. Then the next step is to help Muhammad, and those suffering like him. I promised him I would talk to you, so that we can together think of a 'love project' to pull us out of this vicious circle which is dragging all of us to destruction."

Mansour could see her point. "I know we killed her family, yet she came and endangered her life to help us, by working hard, and now she's saved the entire camp from extinction, while she almost died in the process. So I must try to understand her way of thinking, even though it's impossible to comprehend, and I mustn't upset her, because she must still be feeling quite ill." He looked at her eyes and tenderly asked,

"How are you feeling, Amal?" Then he stood to examine her wound. "It's looking much better."

"I feel good when others are feeling good, but in the meantime I don't feel so happy."

He sat beside her and comfortingly said to her,

"I promise to help you in your love project, and think about what you told me, and try to understand your thinking, but I don't guarantee to agree."

"That's very good, Mansour. I will pray for you, so you can see the simple way to solve this huge problem. I suddenly saw the light after spending many nights thinking by myself, and I know you will see it, too."

"Mansour," called his mother. "We need you." He stood up, smiled at his friend, and said,

"We can talk later about our project."

She smiled happily, and added,

"I'll be thinking hard, if my brain lets me."

"I think nothing is wrong with your brain, Amal. It works perfectly." Then he left to find out about his mother's requirements.

"We need so much shopping for tomorrow," she said, as she sat washing up a pile of china, ready for the party.

"I'll go to the market early in the morning, because most of the good shops are shut for today, but don't worry, I've already prepared the list. The main thing is, do you have someone to help you?"

348

"Yes, most of my friends are coming to give me a hand, so our kitchen will be flowing with women tomorrow."

He smiled, but was surprised at the same time, so remarked,

"I never realised how much Amal meant to all these people. Even the boys are keen to come and give their assistance. In fact, Shakouri offered us a complete sheep from his farm for the party. He said his wife and daughter will prepare it ready, so we only have to roast it, and Walid and Mubarak are coming to build the open fire."

"That's excellent," said his mother. After a pause she added, "I'm feeling very excited. There's a wonderful atmosphere of love and cooperation here now, as somehow Amal just inspires such feelings."

Mansour sat thinking, quietly watching his mother piling up the endless plates that the neighbours had lent for the celebration. "It is an exciting feeling, but why?" he asked himself. "Why does Amal inspire such an atmosphere?" He stared at the pile of china. "My father feels the same way about her, and now my mother. Nahid is already telling everybody that Amal is her sister, the team consider her as one of their members, and I just want to be beside her, regardless of her philosophy. If I can find the answer, then I've found the secret of her magnetic pull."

Abu Mansour walked into the kitchen and was astonished to find Mansour sitting on the chair watching his mother washing, rather than sitting beside Amal.

"What are you doing here?" he asked, with a grin on his face, feeling guilty for misjudging his son's motive.

Mansour answered with dreamy eyes,

"We are preparing for the party."

"To be precise, your mother is; but you are dreaming as usual, leaving the work for everyone else to do."

Om Mansour laughed and said, rebuking her husband,

"Mansour has been working very hard. Don't forget he's the doctor, and without his treatment we would not have a party to prepare."

Abu Mansour laughed, and gave his son a friendly slap on the shoulder, saying,

"True, we mustn't forget the valuable work he's done for our hero." Then he said to his wife, "I think we're going to have almost everyone coming to this party, so now the problem is where to accommodate them? But at least we won't be short of something to eat, as all our men and other supporters have offered food and sweets."

Mansour answered him as he stood up,

"We shall have our party on top of the ruins, the whole area that the Israelis flattened for us. We might as well use the ground for our celebrations, marking a new era of love and cooperation."

Abu Mansour looked at his son with his mouth open, as he heard the word 'love'. His wife noticed him, and said,

"Don't look like that, Father. Mansour is only quoting my sentence."

"This is the second time I've misjudged Mansour," he said to himself. "I mustn't be so suspicious of his motives. Anyhow, my only concern is that Amal doesn't change him like she did Baha, as then I will really be in a mess; but I'll worry about that when she regains her speech."

Mansour's idea of using the flattened area was an excellent one, and soon his team and the children of the camp had cleared a huge square and erected shelters all around it. As they were working he said,

"Tomorrow we'll spread carpets and mats around the outside, so we can sit down, and use the centre for dancing."

The children were charged with excitement, and ran to the centre of the square, where they jumped and danced, illustrating to him his own suggestion. The men stood laughing, happily admiring the results of their efforts.

"I wonder what the Israelis would say if they saw what we're doing?" said Walid.

"I think they'd feel we had gone crazy," replied Mubarak.

Then Mansour passed a piece of advice to his men,

"Don't mention the words Israeli, enemies or killing in front of Amal; she is allergic to all of them."

The men laughed and carried on to finish their joyful work.

Amal was left alone to rest, while the rest of Abu Mansour's family were busy preparing for the celebration. She laid her aching head on the pillows, alternately thinking and praying. "I wish my headache would ease a bit, as I feel like screaming," she thought, shutting her eyes to concentrate on Muhammad's problem. "He must go back to school, otherwise his future will be ruined, especially as he is a bright child, considerate and kind. Pity nobody gives him a hand.... I know, I must start my project again, but this time I'll make my cakes and give him the tray to sell after he returns from school, and he can keep the money for his family." She smiled softly as the idea pleased her. "I'll tell Mansour when he comes. He promised to help me."

Mansour crept in quietly and stood by the bed, watching the smiling face. "Amazing how she resembles an angel; the white clothes, the soft black hair and the beautiful smile, even in her sleep."

Amal's thoughts travelled to her love. "I wonder what he is doing now? I must let him know about my state as soon as possible, otherwise he'll worry about me; and also poor Mordecai, I hope he's found someone to help him in the kitchen." She opened her eyes, and saw Mansour standing watching her.

"Did you have a nice dream?" he asked curiously.

"I've had a good idea for Muhammad," she replied.

"So that's what makes her happy," he thought, drawing his chair near. Then he asked,

"What's the idea?"

"I must start baking my cakes again, but this time I'll give them to him, after he's finished his school day, and he can sell them and have a secure income for his family. I will take back some of the money from the sale so I can make him more cakes, as I want to train him to work and earn his living. Otherwise, he will take things for granted."

Mansour looked at his friend and said,

"I will supply you with the ingredients, but you mustn't start work yet. Leave it for a week or so."

"No Mansour, that's too far ahead, and I don't know what will happen to me by next week, so I shall start on Tuesday, insha-allah. I will speak to him at the party tomorrow, and that will make him happy."

"What do you mean, you don't know what will happen to you by next week?"

"Well, we don't know what will happen to us in the next hour, do we?" she said. "So why postpone a good scheme while it's in our power to achieve it sooner?"

"Amal, I admire you a lot, and we'll make a good team together. I'm very busy today, so haven't much chance to think, but I hope I can think of a way to help you in your project."

After the service was over, Sara asked Jonathan to go back to England with them for a few weeks, so his mind could be eased from the pressure he had passed through.

"I'm happy here, Mum," he said kindly to his mother. "I love this hostel. That's why I stayed here after my promotion, as Natanya transformed it into a welcoming home, even making Shabbat become the best day of the week. It was so wonderful; everyone sang Psalms and danced to them, and she made us special food for the Sabbath celebrations. So how could I leave all these pleasant memories and go to England?" He paused and dwelt on his pleasant memories for a time, and then said to his mother, "I would like to stay here for a few weeks at least, to think over my future. Then I shall contact you, and inform you of my decision."

"What do you mean, Jonathan?" asked Dan. "Are you intending to leave the army?"

"I don't know what I want to do in the meantime, as my life has been turned upsidedown. So I need time to think, to reflect on the last few months and the change I have experienced since I met Natanya. She changed many of my fundamental views about life, but unfortunately, I hardly had any time alone with her, as the place is always full of people. But I do have her example, so I desire to sit alone for a time, to consider her model, and then I'll tell you my decision."

"Don't be hasty," advised Sara. "You have reached a high position in the army, so don't go and throw all that achievement down the drain."

Jonathan smiled and responded to her remark,

"Most of my achievements were the result of Natanya's advice. Anyhow, I promise to take my time. First I need to be alone with her, and my room is the best place for that."

Dan and Sara left their son, with a pile of letters and cards to read and answer, and returned to their home in England, to await news of his decision.

Amal lay on her bed, suffering with a tremendous headache, trying to sleep, after having had a busy day of visitors and thinking. She held her medallion in her hand and talked to her fiance. "Jonathan, I do miss you so, and it seems as if months have passed since I saw you last. I have been told that I've been sleeping for a long time, but I'll find the boys as soon as I can, I hope." She stopped to think of a way to let them know about her. "I am surrounded by friends, who are looking after me so well, but at the same time, they hate you a great deal. I'll do my best to help them see the way to the true love, then we will all be able to enjoy the fulfilment of a most amazing dream. My only love, I'm waiting for you, that our dreams may also come true. It will be lovely to spend all our days together, sharing each other's love, joy and happiness. I shall pray with all my heart that the Lord will grant us our dreams."

Jonathan lay on the bed that Natanya had made, holding her hair, and cherishing her memories. "What a strange feeling," he observed, while he looked at the hank of hair. "I can almost hear my love talking to me." He kissed her hair and spoke back to the soft brown eyes. "I am missing you ever so, my love, although only a few days have passed since I saw you last. What am I going to do after a month has passed by? Why did you have to leave me so soon, when not one of our dreams has come true?" He could see her in his mind's eye, holding the medallion close to her heart, and smiling, telling him she would pray for their dreams to come true. "How can that ever be so, Natanya? I'm sure we left you dead." Then his mind started to wonder about what happened to her body. "I would like to know where they buried her. I'm sure Mansour and his father would give her a good burial, as she saved their people from a definite disaster." He sat up on his bed, feeling anxious, and almost asked aloud, "Where are you resting, my love? I'd like to know." Then he lay down again, advising himself, "I mustn't dwell on such thoughts. I must think of the good memories only, after all, she is here beside me, and that's all that matters."

Monday brought great activity to the territory of Abu Mansour, especially to the women folk. They gathered to the house, singing and dancing, and preparing the banquet. Amal felt frustrated, sitting on her bed.

"I must come and give you a hand," she entreated Om Mansour.

"No, my sweet. Mansour left strict orders that you do not move from that bed."

"Okay, I will stay here, but bring me something to do. I can peel the potatoes, or something."

"No, you try to sleep."

"I've been sleeping for days," she objected. But Om Mansour won, and Amal sat thinking, hearing the noise of the chattering. She heard her name mentioned many times, as well as her title, 'Mobashira'. She smiled to herself, and marvelled at the accuracy of Jesus' words, 'Let your light shine, then people will observe your good deeds, and glorify your heavenly Father'. She said to herself, "I thought all that hard work was wasted, but in reality, those little seeds of love I sowed have been growing, and now they are beautiful trees, bearing sweet fruits. I do feel so happy and grateful that my Father helped me to see his love, and experience the sweetness of this divine love, the love of the enemy. I think it's the best advice ever written, 'Love thy enemy', as it suddenly opens an endless horizon of new friends and treasures in human relationships."

Nahid gave Amal a selection of dresses to choose from, for the celebration.

"I don't want to take your clothes, thankyou Nahid. I can keep this pretty nightdress on, as I'm staying in bed."

"No, Amal. I will be very upset if you don't choose one. Mansour said you are allowed to sit in a comfortable chair at the party, so you can't go in your nightdress."

Amal felt embarrassed to select a dress from her friend, so she said,

"You choose one for me, please, and I will make sure not to spoil it for you."

"Don't be silly, Amal. All my dresses are yours, and I'm glad we are the same size." Then she brought the pretty Palestinian hand embroidered and decorated garments to Amal so she could select one to suit her colour. "This deep blue will suit you, Amal. You will look like a princess, I'm sure."

Amal smiled and said bashfully,

"I like the colour. Can I try it on?"

"Of course, but let me lock the door first, as we don't want any of the men to walk in, as they all seem to have forgotten that you are a woman. Since they made you our hero, they have forgotten you're still a girl!"

Amal laughed and said,

"If only they know how useless I am. I've done nothing to deserve all this hero treatment, and what I did was only my duty, and even in that, I seem to lack confidence. Anyhow, I hope we can do better next time." Then she stood up, and nearly fell back onto the bed, had not Nahid held her.

"Are you alright?" she asked anxiously.

"Yes, just feeling giddy. Horrible feelings, as if I'm in the midst of a stormy sea." She sat back on the bed, until she felt steady, then she rose gently and put on her new dress.

"That suits you perfectly!" Nahid exclaimed, admiring the smiling girl.

Amal said quietly,

"I haven't worn dresses for such a long time, that I've almost forgotten what it feels like to wear one, as they took my clothes when I arrived. Since then, I've always worn my prison clothes, with that big letter on it. I was told it is the letter alef."

"What does that stand for?" asked Nahid, with interest.

"I think it stands for my name, Amal, as it's the first letter of my name."

Nahid smiled and said,

"I'll ask Mansour, as he knows all about these things. Anyhow, Mama washed the blood from your prison clothes and I've ironed them for you." Then she stopped and rushed to the drawer and brought out the ring box. "We found your little box in the pocket, wrapped in this tissue paper."

Amal smiled and took the box.

"It's the box for this ring."

Nahid laughed and said to her with pride,

"You shouldn't feel ashamed of it. That's compensation for what they did to you."

Amal paused as the box brought the pleasant memories of their engagement to mind. "Poor Jonathan, he gave me the ring such a long time ago, to tell me he loves me, and I, like a stupid girl, kept it wrapped all that time! If only I had known what the word meant, we could have been married by now," she thought, looking at the box, while Nahid stood watching her.

"So," Nahid re-started the conversation, "you are going to wear this dress. Now we can look for some shoes to match."

"I am sorry to take all your things like this," said Amal apologetically, "but as soon as I start my work, I shall replace them for you."

"You are upsetting me, Amal. I told you, we are sisters, I'll wear your things, and you wear mine."

"Oh no!" thought Amal, staring at the girl. "I can't take off my ring, or my golden star, for that represents the love of my

355

man, so what else will that leave for Nahid to wear?" Then she said with concern,

"You can't wear my prison clothes?"

Nahid laughed and hugged her.

"Of course not! I'm only trying to illustrate to you that what is mine is yours."

Amal hugged her and kissed her cheeks.

"Tislameely. I thank my God who gave me a lovely sister like you."

The sun was setting as Abu Mansour and his men erected stands all around the square for the lights and decorated them with coloured lamps.

"You would think we're having a wedding!" he said, laughing to his son.

Mansour looked around and began to dream, "My beautiful Baha, I wish she was here, to share our joy." Then he turned back to his work, still thinking, "How strange the way events have turned out, as we threw her out of our house because of Amal, and now we have Amal here as our hero!"

Abu Mansour noticed how his son went quiet after his remark, so asked him,

"What's on your mind, Mansour?"

"Events that I can't understand," he answered quietly. "But I must keep on thinking, until I see the light."

"What are you talking about? Since this morning you've been speaking in riddles. What's happened to you?"

Mansour looked at his watch and said,

"We must hurry up and get ready before our guests arrive. Now I just want to go and have a bath, as I'm feeling all hot and sweaty, and after that all I desire to do is sit beside Amal, so we can think together." Then he walked toward the house.

"I think my worries are well founded," the father muttered to himself, watching his son disappear into the house. "I must keep a close watch on Amal, as Mansour is hooked on her already. 'Sit beside her thinking', huh! 'To see the light'! What light? I think I'll send her back to the orphanage as soon as she is better, otherwise I'm going to lose my son, just as I lost Baha."

He looked around him and saw the other young men joyfully working, spreading the carpets and mats on the ground. "I can't help it, I feel hooked on her, too, and so is everyone here. It's a strange atmosphere, one of love and cooperation." He smiled to himself, "Now who am I quoting, Mansour or his mother? Or is it my own observation?"

The guests started to pour into the square from all directions. The children ran ahead, skipping and shouting, wearing their best rags, some with sandals on, whilst others were bare footed. Some families were able to buy the best clothes, but the majority lived from day to day, as their homes and daily lives were constantly interrupted by wars and raids, and their men snuffed by death at the hands of their many enemies.

Nahid helped Amal to put on her deep blue velvet garments. Then Amal carefully combed her hair, as she could hardly bear to touch her head because of the ache and throbbing. The golden star of David and its chain shone around her neck.

"You look beautiful, Amal," said Om Mansour. "And that is how our hero should look, because all these people are coming to see you. It's your party."

Amal hesitated and felt uncomfortable.

"But why? I'm only an ordinary human, why do you give me so much honour? Our God is the one who did all the work, so why should I be the centre of attention? I feel like putting on my prison garment, then nobody will consider me something special, because I'm not."

Mansour entered the room while Amal was objecting to the first class treatment. He stood and stared at her in admiration, without uttering a word. After a moment his mother said to him,

"Amal would like to put her prison clothes on, as she is objecting to being the centre of attention."

"You're our hero, Amal, whether you wear your prison clothes or any other garment. Nevertheless, you look like a princess, and I am proud of you. I want everybody to see what an angel looks like." Then he said to her, "Can you walk? Because the square is only a few metres away."

She slowly took a few steps, but felt very faint. He immediately came and supported her.

"I don't think I can walk," she said, tightly holding onto his arm.

"Don't worry, you sit here. I'll call the boys to give me a hand, and we'll carry you to the party."

Before she could open her mouth, he had rushed from the room. Om Mansour and Nahid laughed at the modest girl and her expressions. A few moments later Mansour returned with two of his team, carrying an armchair.

"Give me your hand, Amal," he commanded, and gently helped her into the chair.

Walid and Mubarak stood watching her with a big smile on their faces and admiration in their eyes. She sat in the chair, holding onto its arms.

"Why do you have to go to such trouble?" she asked, looking at her stubborn audience, as the strong young men grasped the chair and lifted it up high. She shut her eyes, as her head began to swim. "I feel dreadful. I wish they had left me where I was," she thought.

"Amal," shouted Mansour, as he noticed her eyes shut. "Lay back in the chair, as we're nearly there, and then you can rest. We can't have the party without you, as it's made in your honour."

The guests clapped and cheered and whistled when Amal appeared, although she kept her eyes shut, feeling sick from the giddiness, and the sound of the people seemed to be miles away. "I'm going to drown again," she thought, covering her face with both hands. Mansour gently lowered the chair to the ground, then took her ice-cold hands and held them between his to warm them.

"You look very pale, Amal. I'm sorry to drag you out so soon."

She opened her eyes and smiled softly.

"I think I will be alright, Mansour. I'm looking forward to meet my friends, especially Muhammad," she said, quietly forcing herself to forget her discomfort, for the sake of others.

The square was soon overflowing with celebrating throngs, with the women seated on one side and the men opposite them, while the children freely crossed from one side to the other. The young men of Mansour's team offered soft drinks and sweets to the men, while Nahid and the other young girls took charge of the ladies. The open fire was in one corner of the square's centre, sending sparks from the dripping fat of the roasting sheep, preparing the guests for their dinner. The sound of laughter, and the shouting of the excited children, filled the air.

The first thing every woman did was to give Amal hugs and kisses, and bless her for the way she saved their lives.

"I assure you, I did nothing of the sort," she protested. "I only did my duty, and I'm sure you would have done exactly the same."

Muhammad appeared, carrying his baby sister, and bringing his mother to introduce her to Amal.

"Oh, Muhammad!" Amal's face shone with delight as she welcomed his mother and took the baby from his arms. The child was too small for her age, due to lack of proper diet and medical attention. "Even with my weak arms and swimming head, I can lift this girl," she thought. Then she looked at the mother who was concerned in case the baby would spoil her pretty dress.

"Nahid will not mind," soothed Amal, smiling. "She kindly lent me her dress, but I'm hoping to start my dressmaking soon, and then I can replace it for her." Then she said to the shabbily dressed young woman, prematurely aged by her hard experiences in life, "I want to ask you a favour, and I hope you will agree."

Siham opened her mouth with surprise, "What? Me? What can I offer that she should ask me for a favour?" she thought.

Amal noticed the woman's surprise, so she continued, while Muhammad was trying to take the medallion from his sister's mouth, saying,

"Don't, my sugar, this is the Mobashira's catch. We don't eat treasures."

Amal spoke to the mother,

"I wonder if you would allow Muhammad to help me with my selling? As I just mentioned to you, I hope to start my work again soon, but I don't feel well enough to do it all by myself. So, if you agree, Muhammad can be my manager and sell my cakes for me, and I will pay him."

The woman hugged Amal and the tears rushed to her eyes.

"Of course, Amal. You don't have to ask me, or call it a favour. It's the other way round, you have shown me a big favour."

Amal held her emotions, as she also felt like crying. Then she added,

"But I will employ Muhammad as my manager on one condition."

"Are you listening, Muhammad?" said his mother to the delighted boy.

"Yes, Mama, I am."

Amal stated the condition for the job.

"Muhammad must do the selling after school, because I want the man who does my business to be able to read and write and do my accounts properly, as we don't want to lose any of our profit."

"Yes, of course, Amal," answered the boy. "I will work hard, and bring you my exam results, when I pass."

Amal looked at the smiling mother, then to the manager, and said,

"If it is God's will, we shall start tomorrow, after you come from school. Then I will tell you where to sell, and the price of the cakes. Of course, we shall have some to sell for free as well, but we can deal with that separately."

The boy felt so good and important, and charged off with all his might, to tell the good news to his friends. As he was running across the square, Amal said to his mother,

"I do trust Muhammad, as he is a reliable man. In fact, he told me he is the only man in the house, and that's why I'm employing him in my company."

Siham laughed and hugged Amal, and exclaimed,

"May God bless you, my only Amal, and prosper your company. You have made me so happy." Then she took her baby and moved away, to allow others to have their turn with the preacher.

Mansour kept looking at Amal from time to time, to see when he would have a chance to sit by her side and do some thinking. "Everyone is hugging and kissing her, and looking so happy," he thought. "I've never seen so much laughter and joy like this. What's the secret; why does Amal inspire such an atmosphere? Who could imagine that the person sitting down there, with that lovely happy face, was our enemy one day, and I planned to shoot her. The times I nearly pulled the trigger while she tried to show us love, the mysterious love, 'Love thy enemy'."

Muhammad told his friends about his new job. He explained with great excitement,

"Amal has made me the manager of her company, and I'm going to start tomorrow, after school!"

The boys looked at him with envy and delight, but at the same time, they were stunned by the news, so he explained the qualifications of his new job.

"You must be the only man in the house, and know how to read and write and do the accounts, because we do not want to lose any of our profits."

"I am the only man in my house," said Salah, challengingly. "I need a job, too."

Soon there were four boys fitting the qualifications to the dot.

"Can Amal let us work in her company, too?" They looked at the manager.

"I'll go and ask her. You stay here and don't come with me, as she's ill. I will explain everything to her." Then he ran back across the square, leaving the boys watching from a distance, hoping for a job in Amal's company.

"Amal," said the breathless boy. "Can you take more managers in your company?"

Amal looked with surprise at the lad, and asked,

"What do you mean, Muhammad?"

"I've found four more boys, who are the only men in the house, and they need a job urgently, otherwise their families will die without food."

"Four?!" she said in amazement. "How am I going to employ all these boys?" she thought, looking at the waiting boy.

"Muhammad, give me time to think. I will speak to Mansour and let you know, but I must have time."

Muhammad nodded, having become accustomed to wait until Mansour had been informed. He pointed to the other side of the square.

"You see those boys, they are my friends, and we will be waiting there." Then he ran across to rejoin them.

"Help me, Lord," she prayed, while looking around to find Mansour. "All this human tragedy, whilst time is wasted in killing and fighting. Aha, there is Mansour." She smiled as she spotted him looking in her direction, so she waved her hand and beckoned him over.

"Amal wants me. I wonder what she wants to share with me?" He jumped up and rushed to the women's side.

"Yes Amal, I am all yours," he said, with a big smile on his face. He knelt by her side, as she was the only one on a chair, all the rest sitting on the carpeted ground, reclining on pillows and cushions.

"I spoke to Siham about Muhammad's new job, as I have made him manager of my new company," she said, with laughter in her eyes. "But now the problem is that he's found me another four employees, and I just can't supply that many with cakes. It will flood the market."

Mansour laughed, although he saw the point at the same time. "I will think of a way to help all of them, Amal."

"Yes Mansour, but we must think now, as they are waiting for an answer. Look over there." She pointed across to the boys, who saw her pointing at them, so they all waved their hands. "How can I disappoint them?" she asked, looking at him.

"What an angel, only thinking of others," he thought, staring at the soft, kind eyes.

"I heard Shakouri has a big farm," she said, thinking aloud. "Could he help us with our love project? I mean, if he could donate some eggs or any other product, then we can employ more boys, so they can help their families."

Mansour stood up, scanning the other side.

"I'll go and find him," he enthused. "Then we can discuss the plot together." And he dashed off to the men's side.

Abu Mansour spent a lot of time watching Amal, and everytime he looked in her direction, there was someone hugging her or they were joyfully laughing.

"It's lovely to see everyone so happy. There's something about her that attracts and pulls the heart to her, especially the children. I think it must be because they remember her free cakes." Then he turned round and noticed Mansour talking to Shakouri, and holding him by his arm. "At least Mansour has kept his distance from her so far. I have a feeling he's forgotten all about the business of thinking by her side."

"Mansour," he called out to him, "don't you think this sheep is done by now?"

"Not yet, give it a few more turns, Father. I just have an urgent discussion."

"Not during the party, boy, leave discussions for another time. We set tonight aside to enjoy ourselves, not to talk."

Mansour led Shakouri by the hand, and both crossed to the women's side and sat down at Amal's side, ready for business.

"Shakouri is willing to support our love project," announced Mansour.

"It's a lovely idea, Amal," said Shakouri. "I'll be happy to daily supply you with eggs and vegetables, and, later in the summer,

I can donate fruits to the project. I also have vineyards and orange groves."

"Tislamly," responded a joyful Amal. "If you can donate the eggs just to start the project, then we'll pay you the going rate after that."

"No, Amal. I'm feeling bad that we did nothing before to help our own people, and spent so much of our time and money on weapons, so it's my duty to share fully in your love project."

The mention of weapons triggered Amal's mind about one of the obstacles, so she said,

"There is one point I must mention before we start."

"What's that?" both men asked together.

"I would like to use part of our profits to help others who are in even worse conditions."

"Of course, Amal," said Mansour.

"What I mean is that we must distribute without any partiality or distinction to those who are suffering, because the aim of the project is to help suffering humanity, regardless of their religion, colour or nationality."

"No objection," said the men.

"Then I am grateful for your help. We are hoping to start tomorrow, if God wills it."

"I'm ready to support you, Amal, so we can discuss the details right now." He turned to Mansour. "I feel very excited, as if I'm about to start a new company myself."

Amal lifted her hand up high and signalled to Muhammad to come. He ran to his friend with all his might on his bare feet, kicking off his slippers as they were coming apart.

"Tell your friends they can start the job after school tomorrow, insha-allah. They can come with you and I will explain to them what to do."

Muhammad hugged Amal and said,

"Tislameely, the boys are going to be very happy." Then he ran off to deliver the good news.

Mansour and Shakouri watched the happy boy running across to his friends, then they both turned to their hero, and saw the happy face and kind eyes shining with tears of joy. "That's what I call happiness," thought the men in their hearts, as their hearts also experienced a leap of delight. They sat down beside her again, feeling somehow soothed and refreshed. Then Shakouri started to detail his offers and gave Amal a list of the items he would donate, enabling her to organize the jobs for the boys.

The four managers ran to their mothers and delivered the joyful news.

"I'm working in Amal's new company, Mama. Starting work after school tomorrow!" said each to his mother.

"Company! What company?"

"It's true, Mama. Look, Mansour and Shakouri are also in the company."

The women looked around and started enquiring about the new company. Siham heard their questions, and laughed joyfully.

"It's true. She has employed Muhammad and he is starting tomorrow. She is an angel sent from heaven to help us."

Then the boy mentioned the qualifications for the job,

"You must be the only man in the house, and...."

"Well, that's not fair," said one mother, who had lost her husband and only had girls, and none of them were at school. "They need a job badly," she said, looking at Muhammad and the other excited boys. Another mother supported her.

"And my daughters, too. They can't find work, even as servants, and we are in real hardship."

Muhammad knew what they meant, as he experienced that almost every other day. He said to her,

"I will go and speak to Amal, and see if she can give them a job, too."

Amal was discussing the business with Shakouri when Muhammad arrived and stood in front of them.

"Yes, Muhammad?" she enquired, wondering if he had found more men needing a job.

"Can you employ girls in your company?"

"Girls?" she queried, glancing quickly to Mansour, then focusing her eyes on Muhammad.

"Yes, all girls, and the problem is they have no man in the house at all," he said, frowning like an old man who is faced with a most tasking problem. "And, adding to that, none of them can read or write."

"None of them?" repeated Amal, holding her aching head.

"None," said Muhammad, shaking his head sadly. Then he added, "It's urgent. They need a job badly, otherwise they will all die very soon without food."

Mansour and Shakouri smiled at the boy's description, but they noticed how Amal took him seriously. Before she had time to open her mouth again to answer him, he said,

"You need time to think." Amal's lips broke into a gentle smile. "I will wait for you just there," and he pointed to a spot a few metres away.

Amal nodded and turned to her two helpers.

"Muhammad is a good manager," she told them. "He has a kind heart. Since the day I first met him, he always thinks of the needs of others, and that's why I trust him." Then she continued, still holding her head, "It's a big problem."

The two men nodded in agreement, looking to her for inspiration, forgetting all about the roasting sheep, the noisy laughter and chatter.

"I can help the girls in sewing. I can train them to make dresses, and they will pick it up very soon, as it's quite easy." She smiled victoriously and added, "I can cut the material, and they can help me to machine them. Then we can give the products to the boys to sell with the other items."

"That's a wonderful idea, Amal," exclaimed Mansour.

"I only have one problem," she said, looking at him. "I need sewing machines. We used to sew hundreds of dresses in the orphanage, but then we had so many machines. Although I can cut three dresses at a time, you need three machines to sew them, but I know for a certainty there's always a demand for good cut dresses, whether for children or adults, and I used to earn good money from it."

Shakouri concentrated on her words, while his mind searched for sewing machines.

"We have a machine at home that my wife hardly uses. I can lend it to you for a few months," he offered.

"That's very good. At least we have a start."

Then Mansour added,

"We also have a machine, so you can have that; and I know the mothers of some of the boys in our team have machines. We can arrange something for you, Amal, at least for now, and then I will talk to my father, to see about funding us to buy others. At least we'll be helping our people to escape from poverty and starvation."

Amal nodded, and felt comforted by the way the love project was starting.

At the same time, Abu Mansour was becoming anxious, as he saw Mansour next to Amal, thinking, but when he saw Shakouri on the other side, deep in thought, he stopped his worrying. "Shakouri is one of our main leaders, so he'll keep Mansour in line, but I wish they would hurry up with whatever it is they're doing, because we have to start soon. I'm feeling starving, with this lovely smell filling the air."

Mansour looked around to spot the members of the team among the guests.

"I'm never going to have time to find them now," he said with exasperation, because he knew he had to carve the meat and start the dinner party. "I know," he said, and he stood up, stuck two fingers in his mouth and blew a piercing whistle. "That will soon bring all of them!" he said, as he sat down smiling at Amal's side again. "That's how you whistle to gather the team for a secret meeting, for planning a plot against the enemy."

Amal smiled with intrigue in her eyes, and said gently,

"I haven't heard it before."

"Never mind, Amal, I shall teach you all of our whistles. I wish I had taught you before, as then you could have whistled to Mubarak when the Israelis escaped. Then we could have killed them by now."

She shook her head and turned it away from Mansour.

"I'm sorry. I forgot about my promise. Will you forgive me, Amal?"

She looked at him, and said,

"Of course I forgive you. I'm not upset with you, I am only sad for you, as I want you to be happy, and the only way to be happy is by loving and helping everyone, but especially if you manage to love your enemies, because only then will you be a mighty hero, able to achieve the impossible."

The team members started to appear from different parts of the square and headed towards Mansour.

Om Mansour was surprised to hear the whistle, and said to herself, "What's Mansour up to now? Is it the time for a secret meeting to fight the enemy? Can't we forget about them for one night?"

Abu Mansour found one of his friends to attend to the roasting of the sheep, as he wanted to see what the meeting was all about. "The funny thing is that Mansour is with Amal. I wonder if she's told him about the Israelis? That would be wonderful, the best thing that ever happened to us."

Mansour briefly explained the plot to the men, before his father managed to arrive. Different ones promised to support the project with tremendous zeal.

"There's another problem," said Mansour. "We need a big room."

"I think the room where I am at present is big enough," said Amal. "With a bit of rearrangement we can change it into a little factory."

"It's very exciting," said Walid. "We'll have our own industry right in the camp."

"How many girls can you employ, Amal?" asked Mansour.

"Until I am fit enough, at least ten. Some of them can also help in the baking."

Abu Mansour sat in front of Amal, trying to catch the thread of the conversation, as Mansour continued his leadership.

"The vans will be ready for transporting the machines in the morning, and you can bring them straight into our factory, so Amal can start immediately."

"What machinery?" asked Abu Mansour, thinking of manufacturing weapons or explosives with which to fight the enemy.

Mansour guessed what was in his father's mind, so just for fun he said,

"We are turning Amal's room into a little factory."

"Amal's?!" he said, with surprise written all over his face. "Does she agree to have a factory in her room?"

"She suggested it, and is taking the main part in organizing it."

"Amal, you're wonderful!" cried Abu Mansour, jumping to his feet. He hugged her and kissed her cheeks, while the women stopped their chattering to see what was going on, and Muhammad patiently stood nearby, waiting for the result of the meeting.

Amal blushed and modestly said,

"This is the least I can offer to all of you, to thank you for your care, and also your help in fighting our worst enemy."

"I must be dreaming," thought the old man. "Amal has changed her policy completely."

Mansour stood up, smiled to Amal, then advised his father,

"Please, don't ask Amal about the worst enemy."

"Why not, Mansour? You feel that Amal belongs to you alone, but you're mistaken. I have the right on her. After all, I'm the one who helped her to escape from the enemy."

The men sitting around the hero all laughed, as they could see that Abu Mansour had grasped the wrong end of the stick. Mansour shrugged his shoulders, and stood to see the conclusion of the meeting before he started the dinner. Abu Mansour asked Amal,

"Who is the worst enemy?"

Amal put her hand over her mouth to hide her laugh, especially as she noticed Mansour's big smile.

"My worst enemy is the big ugly beast that dwells inside us and robs us from the joy of true love and happiness."

Mansour burst out laughing and ran off to deal with the meat carving, leaving his father gasping like a fish out of water.

"C..can anyone inform me about what is going on here?" he demanded, looking at the laughing faces around him.

Shakouri stood up and held his hand to lift him from the ground, explaining,

"We have been discussing a most exciting plot. It's a love project...." but before he could add another word, Abu Mansour hushed him,

"Don't talk to me about love! I want to enjoy my party in peace, without the nightmare of the ugly beast and love projects."

Amal spoke to her manager and told him she would employ the girls in her new company. Then she set the time for work,

"I will see them in the morning, as they don't attend school; and tell them that I will do my best to teach them to read and write as well."

Muhammad did not have to cross over to the men's side, as the waiting mothers were only sitting down on the far side of the women's section.

The uncontainable joy and laughter vibrated the atmosphere, charging it with divine love. The news of the company spread through the guests, like fire in dry hay, and resulted in more generous hands donating various items to the enterprise. Mansour carved the tasty roasted sheep, while a queue of young men and women filled their large serving plates, ready to serve the guests. There was so much food, in such variety, that if a stranger stepped into the square, he would think he was attending a royal banquet.

"I can't get over this happy feeling I'm experiencing," thought Mansour as he watched the queue of serving volunteers, while he sliced the tender meat. "I can never remember a time when I really smiled because my heart impelled me to, because, even if I try to hold back my laughter, I'm unable." Then he looked across to Amal, and saw her with a wide smile and a face shining with happiness. "Look at her! She's like me, she can't hold her happiness in. Now I'm just beginning to understand Baha's words when she said that Amal showed her the meaning of happiness, and why she would not come back here under any circumstances, unless the atmosphere of hate changed." He looked up to the laughing eyes of his team, and continued his thoughts, "Well, if only she was here tonight, I wonder what she would call this atmosphere?"

After the happy crowd had their plates filled with the delicacies, Mansour filled his own and crossed over to sit and enjoy his meal next to his hero, to watch the dancers and local musicians play their drums and flutes, while the rest of the company clapped in time with the rhythm.

"How are you feeling, Amal?"

"I am very happy, Mansour. I don't know how to thank you for all the help you have given me."

"Amal, you must be joking in thanking me; do you know what you have done to me tonight?"

"No," she answered, intrigued.

"You have opened my eyes to see the pleasant light of happiness for the first time in my life. So I'm the one to thank you, and I'm certain all these happy people would like to tell you that, too."

She looked at him, and smiled with satisfaction, saying,

"Actually Mansour, you helped your own self, because the real happiness is generated inside, right in the centre of your soul, and when it reaches saturation point, it floods out and overflows to the outside."

Abu Mansour saw his son sitting by Amal's side, talking and laughing. "Oh well, I suppose he needs a bit of cheering up after he lost his catch, but I fear that if he continues sitting at Amal's side, thinking or talking, he will never recatch his enemies. He'll lose them forever."

The boys and girls who had joined the new company were beside themselves with joy and anticipation for the next day. Rays of hope shone brightly in their mothers' eyes, which made them jump up and join the dancers, dancing an old Lebanese folk dance called 'Dabka'. One of them commented,

"Do you know, this is the first time I've danced since I got married, and even then I never really enjoyed it as I was tense and worried about the unknown, but tonight I feel completely different. There's something about the atmosphere; difficult to explain."

Her companion nodded,

"Yes, I know the feeling, as I'm going through it, too."

The hours of the night ticked away. Amal held her head, which was bursting from all the thinking and arranging for the new company. That, as well as the excitement of the evening, made her yearn for her bed. "I must attract Mansour's attention, for I need my sleep, to be ready for the first day of the love project." She looked around, but could not see him, as there were so many people dancing and jumping up and down. She smiled to herself, "I could try the new whistle, but I don't think Abu Mansour would appreciate it!" Her mind travelled to Israel, so she held the ring and gazed into it. "Jonathan, I wish you were here beside me, as we are having a most wonderful night. So much has happened and a great deal has been achieved, and I do hope that soon I'll be able to go and meet the boys. But I must tell you this, my love for you is growing into a huge tree, full of pleasant blossoms that are filling the air with their fragrance, representing my feelings toward you. Oh for the day when we can share our dreams together underneath its refreshing shade." She was so far away in her dream, that she did not realise Mansour was sitting by her side, gazing at her dreaming eyes while she was admiring the diamonds in the ring. She lifted her eyes and saw him smiling at her.

"I'm going to buy you another ring, so you can wear one on the right hand as well."

She looked at him with bashful eyes.

"Please don't do that, Mansour," she replied, as she only wanted Jonathan's expressions of love to array her body, and nothing else. "But I would really love it if you donated the price of the ring to our love project, as we are desperately in need."

"Of course, Amal. I will do both. The project is one thing, and you are another."

She did not want to be deviated from her only love, so she changed the subject immediately.

"I wonder if you could take me home, as I have to start early. The girls will be arriving for their first day's work, and I'm feeling tired, and my head is aching."

"I'll call the boys, but what about another fruit drink? Then we can talk while you are drinking." Before she could answer, he had called his sister to bring a glass of juice for Amal.

She thought it advisable to warn him from getting too involved with her, so she tactfully said,

"I'm trying to organize the project in such a way that it can continue without me. I want to train the team to be like bees in a hive, so that when one worker is missing, it will not affect the honey production."

"Why are you talking like this, Amal? You are the queen of the hive, and without you all work will cease. Anyhow, you are in your own home and among your family, so why are you thinking of leaving?"

She found herself trapped. "How can I tell him that Jonathan is my fiance, and that we are hoping to get married soon?" So she continued,

"I hope to go back to the orphanage, because my parents are there who brought me up. I hope to leave as soon as I'm able to, but as you are all my friends, I'll make sure to visit you regularly, to help you with all my power, as you've been so good to me."

"Amal, you're breaking my heart," said Mansour, feeling very hurt. "My parents are yours, and Nahid and I are your sister and brother. So here is your home, and you're not going to leave this house, no matter what happens. I just will not let you leave, and I want you to promise me right now that you'll stay with us for good, and make our home yours."

She looked anxiously at Mansour while she tried to think of a way out. "I can't promise him. I wish I had never started the subject." Then she prayed for help, "Help me, Lord. I don't want to hurt Mansour by refusing his kind offer, but at the same time, I know it will be a mistake to reveal the situation to him and tell him about my real home. So give me wisdom, please."

She held her head with one hand, and her drink in the other, staring at it.

"Please promise me, Amal, because you mean so much to all of us, especially me, as I've just started to see the light. I need you beside me, so we can think together, talk together, and work together."

"I must have time to think," she replied, then, with a smile on her lips, she quoted Aaron's advice, "'We will do one job at a time, otherwise we'll lose the battle'."

Mansour smiled and said,

"That's a good idea. We'll concentrate on the love project in the meantime, and I'm sure that's going to take us years. Then we'll worry about the next step later, because we don't want to lose any more battles."

Shortly Amal was back in her bed, trying to sleep, while the noisy party continued outside on top of the ruins. She talked to her God, and thanked Him for all the blessings she had received, and prayed for Jonathan not to be anxious about her. Then she stopped and tried to think of a way to contact him. "I wish I could fly, Jonathan, then I could fly to you tonight and tell you all about my lovely story, and be back here again in the morning, ready for the new company. Please forgive me for not contacting the boys, but I fear it's going to be a long wait. All that I hope and pray is that you never doubt my love for you, because you are my only one, and I will wait for you." She soon dropped off to sleep, holding her love's medallion close to her heart, and whispering his name.

Jonathan spent the day reading his way through the piles of letters and answering them. With each expressed thought he read, his love for Natanya grew stronger. "My love, all these people are expressing my own thoughts toward you. How I do regret your loss, but the strange thing is that I feel as if you're talking to me. I suppose it's because your love is alive all around me, as your deeds and memories are everywhere. I'm looking forward to see your beautiful myrtle tree grow and be covered with blossoms, as then I can sit beneath its shade and dream of the pleasant time we shared together, even though it was too short."

The dawn broke, sending new hope through the camp with the birth of the love project. The family gathered in Amal's room whilst Mansour changed her dressing. After carefully inspecting it, he informed her he would soon remove the plaster completely, as the wound was healing perfectly.

"I'll go to the market and buy some material as soon as we've had breakfast," he said. "Shakouri will send his products with Walid, and Mubarak will collect the rest of the items." Then he stopped and looked at his parents. "We have so much to do, with the building project outside and the love project inside. I have a feeling most of the camp are already employed."

"It's wonderful," exclaimed the mother. "I'm feeling so excited that our house is becoming the centre of such great activity." Then she looked at Amal, "And your room is a workshop with so many employees."

"I will need Nahid," Amal responded, as she could see how big the scheme had become. "She can be my secretary."

The family laughed and looked to the delighted Nahid.

"And what about me?" asked Om Mansour.

"I need you badly," replied Amal. "You can supervise both departments, the workshop and the bakery."

Abu Mansour looked at Amal and jokingly said,

"I'm already employed, Amal. Sorry I can't accept any further work."

Walid arrived early and off loaded the farm products. Om Mansour supervised the operation and showed him where to leave the trays of fresh vegetables and tomatoes. Another van arrived with Mubarak announcing his arrival by joyfully blowing on the horn.

"That's Mubarak!" Nahid proclaimed with delight in her eyes and excitement in her voice.

"We're ready," responded Amal, trying to stand and walk toward the door of the room, but she felt the same odd feeling. "I wish this giddiness would leave me alone, as I've so much work to do. I hate to see everyone busy while I'm sitting in bed." But she had to sit back on her bed, as she realized her body was refusing to cooperate with her spirit.

Mubarak greeted her warmly, and said with pride,

"I've been able to collect seven machines, and there are more to come, later, when their owners have finished their sewing."

"I think that's more than enough for our immediate needs," replied Amal gratefully. "May God bless you."

"And you too, Amal." Then he said, "I'm interested to see the end product. How long does it take to make one dress? A few days?"

"I hope not," she laughed. "It all depends on my staff, but I'll pray the Lord will bless our efforts, and that by the afternoon we'll have a few dresses to sell."

Mansour returned from his shopping with rolls of colourful material and an abundance of thread.

"What do you think, Amal?" he asked, showing her his choice of cloth.

"Wonderful!" she exclaimed. "Lovely colours. I hope we can soon turn it into pretty dresses."

"I'll try to come later to see the progress," he said, wishing he could take the day off to watch everything personally.

The girls arrived with their happy faces and respectfully greeted their employer, eager to receive her instructions. Amal remembered her days in the orphanage, of how Mother Teresa used to allocate the children their daily assignments and remind them of the golden rules. She asked them for their names and ages and registered them on her list. Then she divided them, saying,

"We're going to work in shifts. Some will work in the kitchen, to help bake the cakes, and the rest will work at the machines. Tomorrow, insha-allah, we shall reverse the order, so all of us will become expert in cooking and sewing."

Then she remembered how Jonathan's teams had great fun by having friendly competition, as a goal to work toward.

"We'll be working as two teams. The winning team is the one who produces the best product, without any mess or damage."

Om Mansour and Nahid stood by, smiling and excited, like young children eager to start a game.

Amal then showed the older girls how to use the machines, and soon discovered that some of them had already had some practise.

"That's good, then we can start straight away," she said, unrolling the yards and yards of soft cotton material. She demonstrated how to cut a simple pattern using newspaper, and then use that to cut the cloth.

After each of the team in the workshop had her assignment, she asked Om Mansour and Nahid to help her walk to the kitchen, while she supported herself on their arms. There she sat down and started the cookery course, explaining,

"We are dealing with life sustaining food, so we have a great responsibility on our hands, as we don't want to poison people, or make them unwell. That means we'll pay careful attention to our hygiene and ensure everything is spotlessly clean before we attempt to start, and we keep it that way. Other essential rules involve taste, appearance and nutritional values."

Then she illustrated how to achieve the objectives in front of the audience of young girls. The students watched their teacher working, while her face shone with happiness and she hummed one of her happy songs of praise. Shortly, she turned to them and said,

"What makes the food taste good is the motive behind why you are making it. Love is the best motive to make any recipe taste unique, so we're sure our cakes will be the best, because we're working in the love project."

Muhammad and the four other managers could not wait for school to finish, but at the same time, they knew they must work hard for a good mark to impress their employer. They sat down at playtime to discuss their new business.

"I only hope I manage to sell all my shop," said Muhammad. "I'd hate to go back with some unsold cakes, as that will lose us our profit."

"I don't know what I'm going to sell," responded Salah, wondering. "I hope Amal will give me something easy to sell, then I can shout loud to call people." At that, he jumped to his feet and called out at the top of his voice,

"Farm products, fresh farm products. Come and buy farm products. Very cheap farm products."

The other boys in the playground heard the proclamation and rushed to the standing boy. He surveyed the outcome, while the rest of his colleagues felt impressed with the result.

"I told you!" he said with a big smile. "Look how many people are coming to buy!"

"What are you selling?" asked the boys, looking at the fascinated salesman, delighted with his initial success.

"My shop will be open later, after school, and we're going to sell everything. Farm products, cakes, dresses, and everything else," he said, boastfully.

"Where's your shop?"

He looked to Muhammad for the answer, as he was the main manager.

"I don't know yet," Muhammad replied thoughtfully. "But if you want to know, you can follow us after school. Then you'll find out."

Mansour kept watching the time, as his heart and mind was at home with Amal and her project. "The queen of the hive," he thought. "In no time she's organized the whole camp, although she's unwell. I wonder how she is managing, as it's a big project and so many people are involved. Not only that, they are anticipating great results, but Amal is not fit at all and can hardly stand. I must go home and give her a hand and tell her to take it easy, as I've already explained that the project will take years, and I don't want her to get despondent if we have a slow start."

Abu Mansour noticed his son was getting ready to leave.

"Mansour, may I ask where you are going?"

"Yes Father, you may ask with pleasure."

The old man stared disapprovingly at his son.

"Did I say something wrong?" he queried.

"Your intention is wrong, Mansour."

"Okay, what is my intention?" he asked his father.

"You're skiving again, leaving us here doing all the hard work, while you go and sit beside Amal, talking."

A disgusted look appeared on Mansour's face and he challengingly said to his father,

"Well, tell me if you can answer this question. Do you know of a worker bee that sits down doing nothing in the hive, especially next to the queen?"

Then he turned round and left for home, as his father sought to find an answer. "This boy is becoming a philosopher. What do bees and hives have to do with Amal?"

Mansour entered the house, then stopped for a few moments to listen, as he could hear unfamiliar sounds. "They're singing!" His heart flickered with happiness at hearing the joyful song. "I have a feeling Amal is doing well," he thought, trying to decide which room to go to, the bakery department - the kitchen, or the workshop, as each pull was stronger than the other. "The smell is terrific, and welcoming; and the song is joyful and sweet."

He followed the sound of joy and stood at the door, watching the happy, busy girls, sewing and singing an Arabic song with a Jewish tune, one of Natanya's latest songs which Jonathan had taught her. Amal sat on the middle of her bed, designing and cutting new patterns, while some of the girls sewed and others finished the garments. She lifted her head and saw him at the door. She laughed and enthusiastically called him,

"Come in, Mansour. Look at what our team has done!" she exclaimed, lifting up a pretty child's dress. "It's been wonderful," she continued. "The cakes are ready, we have weighed and priced all the vegetables, and I hope we'll have a few dresses ready for our salesmen when they come this afternoon."

Mansour could not hide the surprise that covered his face and oozed out of his eyes.

"That's magic!" he exclaimed.

The girls burst out laughing, feeling proud of the commendation expressed by their leader. Amal readjusted the statement, and said,

"That's love, the fruit of pure love."

Muhammad and his management arrived at Abu Mansour's home, followed by a crowd of schoolmates, curious to see where the shop was located, so they could tell their parents where to buy the best farm products. They did not have long to wait, for Amal had everything ready and priced. She handed each boy his items and gave them her advice,

"Be careful not to charge more, or less, as the prices are fair, and don't lose any money. Try to do one job at a time." Then she added, "I'll pray that you'll sell every item, so we can continue in our good work."

Lastly, she gave them instructions as to the best locations for their selling.

Abu Mansour's fighting team, headed by Shakouri, gathered at the location of the new project, to find out about its progress and discuss their normal subjects.

"Muhammad should be back in about an hour's time," said Mansour, looking at his watch. "I was so impressed with Amal. She organized the whole scheme so well that by the afternoon, she had managed to establish with her team what would take us months."

"Pity she can't join our struggle," said Shakouri. "We would win the battle with the Israelis in no time."

Abu Mansour was swaying from side to side, thinking, and fearing the unknown.

"Amal is an amazing girl," he said, after a long pause. "But she has one fault which is really spoiling her, and disqualifying her from being a perfect angel."

The gathered men gazed at him, keenly waiting for his observation. Then Abdu asked,

"What is her fault? I personally can't see any, except her religion, and she can't help that, as she was born a Christian. Yet she doesn't view us as enemies and takes us all as her friends, so we must shut our eyes to her religion and accept her as a misguided child, that might one day turn to Islam."

The men nodded their heads in agreement with Abdu's comment. Mansour kept silent, thinking and weighing their comments in his mind.

"Her one fault," said Abu Mansour, "is that she loves her enemies."

The men puzzled over that declaration for a while, then erupted into laughter, as the statement sounded incongruous to their ears. Mansour quietly commented,

"Aren't we glad that she loved us, and forgave us for killing all her family?"

"Why do you always love to drag up the past?" said Abu Mansour angrily. "I'm sure you do it just to upset me. I want to forget about the past. True, I killed her family, but I also saved her from the Israelis."

"I am not desiring to upset you," said Mansour in his calm voice, "but I'm just mentioning an ironic fact about this type of love, because I am personally trying to comprehend it, as this fault of hers is the foundation of her strength and joy. She's a great hero, because no barrier could block her from loving her enemies. She conquered the impossible, and...."

"Don't go on, Mansour," shouted his father. "I don't want to hear any more lectures on this subject, so let us carry on with our discussion about our struggle, and forget about Amal for the time being."

Before Abu Mansour had turned round to discuss the struggle and fight against the enemies, Muhammad rushed in with the other four boys in his trail, shouting with tremendous excitement.

"We've sold all our shops, nothing left! We earned a lot of money!" Then he entered the women's quarters on his way to Amal's room, carrying the empty one and a half metre long tray on his head.

Amal took one look at the boys, and she knew the result. "That's exactly how I felt when I sold all my products when I started a couple of years ago."

The men rose to their feet and followed the boys, completely forgetting about the separation rule for men and women, and all entered Amal's room with beaming smiles on their faces. Before she touched the money, Amal lifted her hands and thanked God, and then she looked to Nahid.

"You're the secretary," she said, smiling. "Please keep the money for the different items separate, so we can balance the accounts."

The men sat around Amal's bed, watching Nahid counting the pile of money on the bed and Om Mansour recording the amounts, while the workers stood around Amal, trying to control their joy. Amal took a portion of the money and put it in a separate purse, remarking,

"This is back to God. He gave us all this wealth, so we will give him some back." Then she put another pile in a different purse. "And this is to buy our goods for tomorrow, insha-allah," she said, looking at Shakouri.

"No, Amal. I promised to donate for the project."

"I know, Shakouri. You did donate and started us, but now we can pay you for the next delivery, otherwise we will not be fair in our trading. Anyhow, what does the parable say? 'If your brother is honey, don't eat all of him'."

Shakouri felt delighted that Amal likened him to honey, but he still argued and bargained with her, until he managed to settle on an agreement to sell his items to the new company at half price for the meantime.

"Now we can pay the wages," she said to the excited boys and girls. "We'll start with the smallest and work up to the oldest."

Nahid paid the salaries according to the list that Amal had already prepared, looking under the column, 'all sold', although there were another two columns on the sheet, one for if half was sold, and the other for three quarters.

The employees started to go out, when Amal interrupted,

"Don't leave yet, we're not finished."

So they returned, still counting their liras, as they had never experienced such generous wages before. Amal looked to the supervisor and said,

"Please, can you sell the teams their free parcels, as their mothers will be waiting for them."

"Yes, my love," said Om Mansour, rushing off to collect her tray that was full of items wrapped with newspaper. She returned and 'sold' the contents to each child.

"Thankyou all," said the smiling Amal. "I hope to see you all tomorrow, as I have more items in mind for our love project."

"Tislameely," said each child, hugging her and kissing her cheek, and then they ran to their homes.

The men showed no intention of leaving Amal's side, but stayed with Om Mansour and Nahid, watching the happy hero, whose eyes shone with stars of joy and hope for the next day.

"We've had a very successful start," she said, looking to Mansour. "Muhammad and his team sold out in half the time I had anticipated. I don't know how he did it, but anyhow, the money is right to half a lira. Now I hope to start sandwiches as well. Only 'falafil' (small balls of fried vegetables), but that means we'll need more salesmen and cooks."

"That's an easy task," said Walid. "I can soon get more boys and girls for you. The camp is full of them, all living from day to day."

The time swiftly ticked by as a new list of names was written and a new plot drawn up, aided by each person's constructive contribution.

"We'll have to discuss our items tomorrow," said Abu Mansour, "as we haven't had a chance to deal with any of them tonight."

"We're not in a hurry," said Shakouri. Then he quoted the new expression they had all learned, "We deal with one job at a time. At least we're winning on the love project."

Mansour spent hours thinking, both while he was working on the building project and when he was sitting at home. Even as he tried to sleep at night, his thoughts never released him. "Amal, why are you possessing me?" he asked himself on his bed. "You've been on my mind the whole time since you came here, and now you're taking me over during the nights as well."

He noticed his feelings towards her, and felt anxious and concerned. "What am I doing? I have my own love waiting for me, so why is Amal allowed into the centre of my heart?" He demanded an answer from his heart and head.

"Baha is my only one, with whom I desire to share my dreams and love, but Amal is something else," explained his heart and mind. "It's hard to define my love for her in words, as it's a different type of feeling." He turned to the wall to try and sort out his emotions. "If I liken my love for Baha to the moon, which inspires dreams and romance, starry eyes and yearning for a touch from her hand, then I can easily explain what kind of love Amal inspires. Her love is like the sun, too elevated to reach, never romantic, but at the same time generating heat, life, and the light of hope, so essential that the moon would cease to function without its light."

Mansour smiled with satisfaction as his thoughts explained his strong feelings of love toward Amal. "I need her, as well as Baha needs her, just as we all need the warmth of the sun. It's a pure, far reaching love that revives the soul and supports life. It's a divine love, a superior love, that enables men and women, young and old, to gain from its light, so I don't need to feel guilty of getting close to my Amal, as she's the common agent for all of us."

A week passed by, and the love project had grown into a huge tree, with its shade almost covering the entire camp. Mansour's friendship with Amal became stronger the more he sat by her side, so that he came to resemble her in many ways; his expressions, his smile, even his gentle way of speaking. His phraseology became identical with hers, which in turn affected the entire team of fighters, causing their conversations to be centred on buildings, love projects, celebrations, and new hopes for tomorrow.

Abu Mansour noticed the change in his men, and was almost panicking. "I must revive our fighting spirit, as no one has mentioned our fight against our enemies, not once. Everytime something has to interrupt our discussions, and it's always around Amal's project. I know it's important, and is giving employment and happiness, but what's the use of that without security? We need to liberate the holy lands as well, and how on earth are we going to achieve that, while everyone is turning sentimental and singing about love?!"

He decided to inflame the spirit of war at the mosque on Friday, so he set about preparing one of his most enthusiastic talks for the meeting. "Well, there's enough fuel in this talk to inflame the stones," he said to himself, as he believed his men needed recharging, especially Mansour. "He's become hopeless; no training now. I bet he can't even aim one shot right and has forgotten all his skill, sitting next to Amal and talking about love!"

Amal sat alone in her room to rest, as it was a holy day and the workshop was closed. "It's good to sit alone for a change, and have time to be with myself, though I do miss Jonathan so much. I wish I could contact him somehow." She sat staring at the closed door of her room, thinking. "I feel fine in myself now, so I could walk to the Christian sector of the city and leave a message for him." Then she stopped and thought. "I don't know how to write English, so I'll have to write it in French, or perhaps Arabic, but he's bound to find someone to translate it." She picked up her pen to start writing, all the while looking anxiously toward the door, her heart beating loudly. "I do feel afraid, because if Mansour or anyone else enters the room while I'm writing, I'll be in dead trouble. Then I'll lose the battle altogether."

She put the pen away. "Jonathan, I love you, I miss you and I need you," her heart screamed inside her. "Although I'm free among my friends, yet I'm not allowed to be alone for long because they want to be so close to me - Mansour, Nahid, and almost everyone else. So I'm not free after all."

After the prayers were over, Abu Mansour sat at the head of his group, delivering his fiery message and working hard to revive the spark of hate in their hearts.

"We are born to struggle," he said to the attentive men. "Now we're progressing in rebuilding what our enemies destroyed, although they try to keep us down all through our lives, to prevent us from regaining our land that they took from us. But we mustn't let them win. We must fight to the last drop in our veins."

Mansour felt his feelings becoming agitated, as the ugly beast of hate started to be roused from its drowsiness.

"Jonathan, our arch-enemy, escaped from our hands, after he almost killed our hero. We vowed vengeance on him, so why are we sleeping? Why is no one doing any training? Where has our zeal gone?"

'I forgive him. I release you from your vow.' Amal's words sounded loud and clear in Mansour's head. 'I love him too, just as I loved you first.' He held his head, and looked around, wishing his father would finish his speech.

"Mansour, we are relying on you," his father continued. "You are the one with the ability and the brains. You are the one who promised revenge, so why aren't you training your team?"

"We agreed to do one job at a time," he answered. "So we're rebuilding our ruined homes, and supporting Amal to help renew our people's morale. I can't do everything."

"I understand that, but Amal doesn't need any support now, as she is well and capable of dealing with her own business, and we are ahead in our rebuilding, so you must start to train tomorrow, and we must plan a new plot to fight our enemies."

Shakouri asked tactfully,

"Which one of them?"

Abu Mansour gave him a surprised look.

"All our enemies, Shakouri. Our policy hasn't changed and our enemies are exactly the same as before, so I don't understand your question."

"I feel we have to drop the Christians from the list, because we don't want to hurt Amal's feelings, especially after what she has done for us."

The rest of the group nodded their heads furiously in support of Shakouri.

"I think you're all becoming useless men," replied Abu Mansour despondently. "The Christians are supporting the Israelis, so how can we take them off the list? As regards Amal, everyone on the list is her love and friend, so we'll be hurting her if we fight any of them, so I feel we must carry on with our existing policy, regardless of anyone's feelings."

"I disagree," said Mansour. "I don't want to hurt Amal's feelings, as she's my friend. So let's just concentrate on fighting the Israelis and the Druze for the meantime. Later we can consider the others."

The meeting finished and the men returned to their homes, depressed and unhappy. Their wives and families noticed the difference in their men and enquired,

"What happened? You went to the prayers happy, and now you've come back home as if you met the devil himself."

Mansour also arrived home, despondent and unhappy. He sat alone on the veranda, outside Amal's room, thinking of his father's talk. Amal heard him sighing. "Oh dear," she exclaimed. "What's happened to Mansour to make him sigh so deeply?" She stood up and opened her room door, and looked at him, while he was deep in thought and looking very gloomy. "He must be bored stiff," she thought. "It's just like the boys in the hostel during Shabbat. I must go and help him to find joy on the day that's set aside for worship."

She walked softly and sat beside him on the settee.

"Mansour," she said gently. "Did you have a good time?"

"No," he replied gruffly.

"I see," she thought, still looking at him, as he tried to hide his depression. "These are the signs of wrong thoughts, not boredom, so we need to exchange them for good thoughts, and then we'll have a happy Mansour again."

He glanced at her eyes and noticed a soft smile on her lips.

"I'm sorry, Amal," he said, apologizing for his testy answer. "I just feel unhappy."

"I know," she said. "You must be thinking disturbing thoughts that have awakened the beast." She laughed as she saw the surprised look on his face. "How does she know what I'm thinking?" he wondered, looking at her kind eyes.

"I know, because I used to react the same way whenever I fed the beast with the wrong thoughts, but as soon as I controlled my hate and love of self, and started to think of others and put them first in my heart, I felt happy again. So I can see that when I look at you. I can immediately tell what thoughts you are cherishing, whether they are good, or unpleasant."

Mansour kept quiet and just looked at her. "She's right. I know the feeling when we're planning and discussing the love project; all of us are very happy. Then as soon as we discuss fighting and vengeance, the same agitating and distressing feelings return, but how can I conquer this hate? It's impossible. I can find it easy to love Amal, but how could I ever love Jonathan, or his people? Even the thought of it makes me sick!"

"You're getting upset again," said Amal, as she watched him.

"Amal, please stop looking inside me. I feel uncomfortable when people can read my thoughts."

"I want to help you, Mansour, because you're my friend. In fact, more than a friend, a dear brother; as you yourself told me, I'm one of the family. So how can I see you tormenting yourself with hate and anxiety, and I sit beside you doing nothing? I want you to be a hero, a great conqueror who is able to fight the monster and overcome it."

"I can't Amal. I love you, and will do all I can to make you happy, but I can't be like you - we're all different. You find it easy to love people like Jonathan, and those pigs with him, but I hate the sight of him!"

The mention of Jonathan made Amal's heart flutter, and she was just able to control her feelings, to prevent them from surfacing.

"It's up to you as to whether you win the battle or not. I admit that the first step is the most difficult move, but you've already made that; so the rest is easy!" She smiled as she remembered her childhood and the history of her battle, so she told him her experience.

"I remember how, when my family was blown up, I was so unhappy, and I prayed every night that God would blow up all of you up with a big bomb and kill you."

Mansour sat at the side of the settee to could watch Amal's face as she told her interesting history.

"One day the Father heard me praying like that, and he directed my attention to the light. He told me that God would never hear a prayer like mine."

"Did he really, Amal?" asked Mansour, extremely surprised, as he thought that all the Christians, especially their leaders, spent all their time in fighting and converting the Muslims.

"Honestly," replied Amal. "He said to me that God is our father, and as a father, he loves every single child of his, regardless of what they believe and do, and his will is to save all his children from the agony of hate and death. He also said that God only answers prayers that harmonize with his will, because he loved humans to the point that he sent his son to show this unique love. So I had to change my prayer, because God would not answer mine unless I loved all his children, even though some of them were my enemies."

Mansour listened intently to the story, his chin resting on his hand, looking at her soft brown eyes.

"I found this fact impossible to put into action, so I spent my time thinking, as the Father suggested to me. I couldn't pray much at the time, as my hate was so intense and blinding me from my own God. Then one day I read the advice of Jesus where he said, 'love thy enemy'. That really made me think. How could I love my enemy? He said you should go as far as to hate your own self in order to make room for your enemy, and only then did I discover the real enemy, that it was me, myself, my own feelings, which turned my fellow humans into enemies. So that was where the battle started, not outside, on the battlefield, or in Israel, or in Palestinian territory, but in my own heart. But then I needed a weapon, a powerful weapon, to fight this impossible enemy of mine that dwelt in the centre of my heart. Well, the weapon is so easy to use, and so delightful, that a person would never normally think of it, as it sounds quite ridiculous." She laughed as she related the solution.

"The powerful weapon is love, the pure love like God has, which has no partiality and all understanding. When I applied this weapon to fight the beast, I experienced a happiness and satisfaction which I had never known before, and suddenly I was at peace, as I was in the midst of friends, wherever I went or turned, whether in Muslim territory or an Israeli prison; it made no difference. So now I'm at home with any human, as long as I keep the ugly hate under control."

Mansour smiled and said,

"It's alright if your enemy loves you, but what if you love and he comes and kills you and destroys your home for you; that's not fair. You can't just sit down with your hands folded, as he'll destroy you."

"I do trust in the love of my God," replied Amal, "for He makes sure that you never lose, even if sometimes the road seems impassable. He makes sure you are blessed, and I can say that from experience, for every time you pass through one hardship, you receive many blessings as a reward. He also answers your prayers, so you are never alone, but have the Almighty as a friend with you."

Mansour responded to his friend, as he felt refreshed by the long conversation,

"I love you, Amal, but I don't think I will ever love my enemy."

Amal felt a failure, so she sighed and said,

"You'll have to think about the problem for yourself, as I did before you, but may I suggest one thing to make the battle easier for you?"

"Please do," he requested.

"As you said, you love me and would do anything for me, so, if next time you are facing an enemy, whether an Israeli or someone else, and you want to snipe at them or blow them up, just imagine that I am in front of you, and then perhaps you'll see them differently and love them too, for I was once your enemy but am now your friend."

He laughed and said,

"I promise to do that, just for you." Then he rested his two hands on her shoulders, and said, "Amal, you're the best friend I've ever had, even though I can't follow all your reasonings."

She looked at him with appreciation, and said,

"I can't tell you how much that sentence means to me." She paused for a while, thinking, "Baha said that to me, and Aaron, and now Mansour. I'm so lucky."

Then she said,

"I feel just like a student, who is incompetent, but works hard, and has just received his certificate. When he opens it to discover his result, he finds he's succeeded with full marks. I have just received my certificate, with full marks!"

Mansour laughed and said,

"I hope I'll also be a hero one day."

"You will be. I shall pray for you, and I'm certain God will answer me, as it's in harmony with His will."

Om Mansour looked out of the kitchen window and saw Mansour's hands resting on Amal's shoulders. "They're in love," she remarked to herself. "That would be so lovely if they get married, as they suit each other just right. Although I know Abu Mansour would explode if he saw them like this, I'm sure he'll like the idea after a time."

The second week was now almost over, with Amal still busy, training and teaching her team by day, and dreaming and calling her love Jonathan by night, feeling desperate to contact him but hindered by the many eyes that never departed from her side the whole time. Mansour thought a great deal, and his views were gradually changing. "There must be another way to solve this problem. I can't see why Amal's method won't succeed, but if only I could be sure of the other side first, or if we could meet together and discuss our difficulties round the table. Then we could save all the human and material resources that are wasted in fighting, but that's an impossible dream. Now my biggest problem is Father, as he wants me start a new schedule for fighting the Israelis, but I'm not in the mood, at least, not just yet with the love project progressing so well. I'd rather spend my time with Amal, planning its expansion, rather than losing my inner peace planning destruction."

Abu Mansour's teams were also thinking of the love project.

"Amal's room is too small. We must move her to a bigger place."

"What about our stores? We have plenty of room there and then she can have a proper workshop."

The venture had now become huge and organized, with so many employed, that the atmosphere in the camp had completely changed. The women felt a measure of security, as they could see a new hope for their children. In turn, the young boys and girls had a purpose in living, which caused them to sing and dance as they shared in building such a happy hope, and, for a change, forgetting about hate and enemies.

The week came to an end, with Amal looking forward for some rest and time to be alone. "It's amazing how the week has flown by," she said to herself on Thursday night. "I wonder how Jonathan is now, and Mordecai? I hope they haven't forgotten me, for it seems such a long time since I last saw them. I promised Aaron that I'd leave a message for him as soon as possible, but now two weeks have passed and I've done nothing." She sat up on her bed, feeling very anxious. "Jonathan, I am waiting for you. I haven't forgotten my promise, but I'm trapped, as I want to come to you, but, at the same time, we're progressing here and love is growing; and even Mansour has become my best friend, and everyone else."

She paused for a while, thinking of a way to contact Aaron. "I'm coming Aaron, but I do wish one of you would come here, near the area, as I have never yet walked outside the house. Please do come." Then she realized the danger that would pose for whoever ventured into the camp. "No, I must go out tomorrow. I'll tell Om Mansour that I'm going to visit the Father and Mother Teresa, as they are my parents. Then on my way there, I'll slip into one of the places which Aaron showed me, and contact the boys." She knelt on the ground and prayed for her plan to succeed. "Please Lord, help me to find them tomorrow, while Mansour is in the mosque. I'll go quickly, as I want to keep my word and I desire to be with the one I love, so together we can plan to praise You."

Mansour lay on his bed, trying to sleep, but his thoughts kept him awake. "Amal is changing me so much," he thought. "But I do feel happy for the change and I'm able to laugh and plan for a better future. Now wouldn't it be wonderful if Baha came back and then the three of us would make a perfect team. We could plan a huge love project to cover the whole of Lebanon, because if in just two weeks the camp has become a haven of joy and songs, imagine what the country will be like after a year!"

The happy thought made him excited and he continued in his dream. "I'll tell Amal about the idea tomorrow, after the prayer." Then he remembered the routine. "Oh no, my father will ask me about the training, and I've done nothing about it this week, so that means an argument for sure. I think the best thing is to leave immediately after the prayer and take Amal out to a restaurant, then we can talk alone, without any disturbance, as I'm sure my father is trying to separate me from Amal. I noticed him this week; every time I went near her, he found one reason or another to keep me away." He smiled as he remembered the past. "We used this trick before, to keep Baha away from her! Poor Amal, and when she came to ask about her friend, the Israelis took her. Well, I'll never let her out of my sight again; we'll live together and die together, but most of all, we'll plan and work together."

Jonathan was also thinking, about his future, and he found himself unsettled and disturbed. He had Natanya's hair in his hand, as he gained comfort from it, like a baby who finds reassurance from his dummy. "The hostel has never been the same without Natanya. In fact, nowhere is good for me now. I just feel lost and shattered, and all I want to do is sit with this beautiful piece of memory in front of my eyes, and stare into those gentle eyes, which I can see so clearly; and listen to her voice." He paused as he gazed into the past. "What I can't understand is that I feel she's calling me. I must be going out of my mind, as how could she be calling me when she's been resting in her grave for these last two weeks?" Then his thoughts started to disturb him. "I can't rest until I see her resting place. Maybe that's why I can't settle."

He rose from the bed and went to his office, to check the Palestinian camp and their cemetery on the large scale map. "Here's the cemetery, so close to Abu Mansour's territory, but I think I can work out a way to slip in and find her grave." He stopped and thought of the great difficulties in the way of his finding the grave. "It will be a freshly dug one and I'm sure will be marked, as she must have been treated like a hero; but I don't know Arabic, so how am I going to read the inscription? That means taking someone who knows the language, but I suppose I can do that. I can also disguise myself and wear...." He quickly changed his mind. "No way I can safely hide myself. I tried it once before and ended up in deep water. If I took such a reckless move, I could endanger myself and others, too, and there is no Natanya around this time to get me out of trouble."

He stood up, switched off the light, and turned towards his room. As he passed Natanya's room, his feet stopped. He quietly opened the door and turned on the light, then partially closed the door behind him.

Menachem was on guard, and when he saw the light on in Natanya's room, he walked down the passage and quietly stood peeping to see who was there. "It's Jonathan. He does break my heart, as he's never been the same since Natanya's death. In fact, Aaron and Mordecai have changed too, and this hostel has become a miserable place." He stopped in his thoughts, as he could hear Jonathan talking softly.

"My love, where are you resting? I can't settle until I know what's happened to your body. I know you are in my heart, but nevertheless, I want to know."

Menachem heard Jonathan standing up, so he quickly moved away and disappeared down the passage. The sad man gently closed his love's door and walked slowly to his room.

Amal rose early, rehearsing in her mind what she was going to say to Om Mansour, and praying that she might find someone in the places which she had in mind. She heard Abu Mansour and his wife talking.

"We'll be quite late today, as we have a tremendous amount to discuss and plan, so Mansour and myself will be late for dinner."

"That's very good," said Amal to herself. "My prayer has been answered, as I hope to be back long before them."

Mansour took much longer than usual to get himself ready, as he put on his smart clothes. "I must take extra money with me, to take Amal to the restaurant where I used to take Baha. It's expensive, but a most enchanting place."

Amal cleaned her room and made her bed. Her stomach was fluttering. "It's my chance today, otherwise I'll have to wait for another week and that will be too long. My Jonathan will think I don't love him anymore." She had her bath and put on her dress, which Nahid had given her on permanent loan.

Om Mansour and Nahid were sitting on the veranda, talking and laughing about the happy experiences they had enjoyed during the week, when Amal walked towards them with her soft smile. They stopped their talk and looked at her with admiration.

"The sweetest girl in the town," said Om Mansour proudly, thinking of her as a beautiful bride for Mansour. "Come honey, sit here with us and talk. We have all the morning for ourselves, as the men won't be back till quite late."

Amal sat down between her relatives and softly said,

"I am hoping to visit the orphanage this morning, as I'm missing the Father and Mother Teresa. They brought me up and I'd love to see them again."

"Have you asked Mansour?" asked the mother.

"No, but I'm sure he won't mind, as I'll only be away for an hour or so."

Om Mansour hesitated and said,

"I think you had better ask him first, my sugar. He is the doctor, and if anything should happen to you, we'll never live it down."

"I assure you that I'm very well and I promise to be back before they return."

"Okay, you can go, but Nahid must go with you."

Amal's face dropped, "Oh help me, my God. I need to go alone." Then she said to the kind lady,

"Why disturb Nahid, it's her day off and she must rest. The other thing is that there's a small church there, and I want to pray for a little while and don't want Nahid to feel uncomfortable, as she's a Muslim."

"True, Amal," said the woman, thinking. Nahid stood up and said,

"I don't mind, I can stand outside while you pray, but I'd love to go with you, to see what the orphanage looks like inside."

"No, my love," said her mother. "Your father would go mad if he knew you had gone inside a Christian place like that. No, let Amal go alone." Amal felt relieved and stood up to go, when Om Mansour remembered something else. "Amal, I really feel you mustn't go."

"Why?" asked the girl, looking pale.

"Because the Israelis will spot you. You know that mark you had written on your prison uniform?"

Amal nodded.

"Well, Mansour said that means you're a dangerous prisoner, most wanted. So imagine if one of them sees you, they will take you back to the prison."

"I'm not frightened of the Israelis," said Amal with determination. "But I must go, please, otherwise I will not have another chance for a whole week."

Om Mansour anxiously agreed, then she said,

"You stay and have a cup of coffee first, and then you can go," hoping someone would appear and take the responsibility from her hands.

Mansour sat at the end of a row in the mosque, far from his father, so he could slip away as soon as the prayers were over. Abu Mansour sensed his son was up to a trick, so he watched him all the time, and even during the kneeling his head was turned towards him, which caused him to bump his head hard on the ground a few times. "He took ages in the bath this morning. I know him well. Amal is taking him over, body and soul."

The moment the prayers were over, Mansour jumped up from the floor, and so did his father, who tried to avoid stepping on the feet of the praying men.

"Mansour, where are you going?"

"I'm going home. I want to take Amal out for lunch."

"You can't, Mansour. You know it's our meeting day and I have a plan for you, so leave Amal for later."

"No, I can't take her out at night, otherwise people will talk, and she's been shut in the house like a prisoner, so I must take her out today. You have the meeting and tell me about the plan later." Then he rushed out of the mosque.

"I have a useless son," complained Abu Mansour to Shakouri and Abdu, who were still sitting on the floor, where they had been watching the two men.

Shakouri smiled and said,

"What's wrong with taking Amal out for lunch, the poor girl needs a bit of recreation. Anyhow, he's lucky, many of our young boys would love to do that, but they daren't ask, with Mansour around!"

Amal had just finished her coffee and was about to open the door to leave when Mansour appeared in front of her with a surprised look on his face.

"Amal! How did you know that I'm going to take you out today?"

She froze with shock and her tongue stuck in her mouth.

Om Mansour was delighted to see her son just in time.

"Oh Mansour, you're early, but I'm so glad you've come. Amal would like to go to the orphanage to visit her people, so now you can decide for yourself about the matter."

"Of course you can visit your parents," he said, looking at her pale face. "I'll take you. Then I'm taking you for lunch afterwards, to celebrate your recovery."

"Oh what a great pity," sighed her heart. "I prayed the whole night, and now everything has gone wrong."

"You're not looking happy, Amal," remarked Mansour. "What are you thinking of now?"

She smiled, as she noticed he was using her analogy.

Then he continued,

"Come on, we don't want to waste any time, because I've a new plot for our love project and I want to discuss it with you, after we've visited your people, of course."

Amal kissed her mother and sister and walked out with Mansour. He opened the door of his car and she sat in the front. Om Mansour and her daughter stood watching them.

"Isn't she a lovely girl, Nahid?"

"Yes Mama, I think she's the best girl I ever saw."

"I think Mansour is in love with her."

"Do you think so?"

"Yes, I am definite. I hope they'll marry each other; and what a happy house we would have!"

"But what about Baha?" asked Nahid.

"Well, Baha has left, and Mansour must settle down."

"But she is a Christian, and we are Muslims."

"It doesn't matter much what religion you are, Nahid, as long as you practise goodness, and I feel Amal is the best Muslim I've ever met. She does good work, and shows her goodness, not by words, but by her deeds. She prays a lot and loves everybody. That's why I love her; she's our angel!"

"I love her, too, but I think Baba will really get upset if he finds out."

"We'll keep quiet, and let Mansour fight his own battle."

Aaron was looking more depressed than usual, as he sat by the myrtle tree, gazing into space. Menachem saw him and went and sat by his side, as they were close friends.

"Come on, Aaron, cheer up for a change."

"I can't, I feel so restless."

"Why?"

"I want to find Natanya's grave, and then I might be able to rest, as I feel she's calling me to go and visit her."

"How amazing!" thought Menachem. "That's what Jonathan was asking last night in Natanya's resting room." Then he said to Aaron,

"I'm going to Lebanon later for my three months duty. I could always nip along and find her grave."

Aaron sat up erect, as he liked the idea, but was terrified at the same time.

"That'll be very dangerous, and risky," said Aaron. "That cemetery is near Abu Mansour's area and they'll shoot you, if they spot you."

"I'll plan it carefully. It's not far from the main road, so it should be okay if I go early tomorrow morning and find out where she's been buried."

"No, Menachem, don't go. I'd rather do that myself, so if I get killed, it's my own responsibility. I can't let you venture into that area, just because I'm feeling depressed."

"I want to, Aaron. Natanya is my best friend, too, and that's the least I should do. Then you can rest, and I'll rest my mind as well."

"I think we should talk to Jonathan about it."

"No, don't let Jonathan know, because he'll say 'no', and then we'll be disobeying orders. Keep Jonathan out of it."

Aaron sat anxiously looking at the beautiful tree, then he said, "I wish I'd kept my mouth shut."

"But I want to go and find out, because I know that when I find her grave, all of us will rest, especially Jonathan."

"Why do you say that?"

"Because I heard him last night asking her where she is resting."

"Did you?"

"Yes. I'm sure he's feeling like you, and me. So I promise to take it very carefully. After all, the Arabs view cemeteries as sacred, so they won't shoot me, I hope. Anyhow, I'll go early in the morning, when there's no one about."

Aaron smiled faintly as he repeated Natanya's sentence, "'I'll pray that you do not get hurt.'"

Mansour felt proud to have Amal sit by his side, but he noticed she was despondent, and sighing from time to time.

"What's up, Amal? Are you anxious about something?"

"Not really. I just hope you don't mind waiting for me when I visit the Father."

"No Amal, I'm not going to wait outside, I'm coming in with you."

She looked at him with her mouth open.

"Will they allow me in?" he asked.

"I am sure they will," she said hesitantly, although inwardly thinking, "The Father will have a heart attack if he sees Mansour! I remember when I mentioned him in the past, he nearly fainted, and now he will see him in person! What am I going to do?" She thought and then prayed with all her power, "My Father, I know you have a plan in mind, that is why things have turned out like this, so please help me by letting the Father welcome Mansour."

He parked the car outside the gate, and they walked towards the high walled building. Mansour noticed how Amal's hands were shaking. "She must be nervous because of me, and I can quite understand her feelings, as I personally killed a number of the parents of these children. But I was blind before, and now I'm just starting to see the light of love."

Amal tapped gently on the door, while she looked at Mansour and smiled softly.

The Father was strolling around when he heard the gentle tap. "That sounds just like Amal," he said, smiling to himself. "She's been on my mind lately, poor girl. I wonder how she's faring in Israel?" As those thoughts passed through his mind, he unbolted the gate and opened it.

The next moment his face turned white as a sheet, as if he had seen a ghost, as he gazed at the smiling princess, and the young man by her side. Amal threw herself into his arms and her tears flowed copiously. "She's real. It's not a ghost," the man muttered to himself.

"Amal," he said at last. "Is it really you, my daughter?"

"Oh Father, it's so wonderful to see you again. I thought I would never return to Lebanon."

"My dear, I have been praying for you every day. Come in, both of you. Mother Teresa will have the best surprise she could ever wish for, as she was only talking about you just a few hours ago."

The Father took Amal by the hand and led them to his office. Then he sent for Mother Teresa.

"Amal, you haven't changed a bit. You look just the same as the day you left, except for the dress - now you look like a princess."

Mother Teresa opened the door, and stopped, her eyes wide open and her face white. The Father laughed and said,

"She's not a ghost, but real! She's Amal in person. I touched her, and wiped her tears with my hand."

Mansour felt so touched by the welcome which Amal received from her people, that he had to wipe away his own tears of emotion. Amal saw him, and remembered she had not introduced him to her parents.

"Oh, I am sorry, I haven't introduced you to my friend," she said, while still hugging her mother. "This is Mansour. He is my best friend."

The Father had another shock, and supported himself on his desk, while Mother Teresa supported herself on Amal. "Mansour himself!" thought the Father. "Help us, Lord. This man killed your people, and now he is here to...." then he stopped as his words sounded just like the disciple Ananias when he was sent to meet Paul. "I am sorry, Lord. This must be your hand." So he stood up and went towards Mansour, who opened his arms and both men hugged each other.

Mother Teresa took off her glasses and wiped them with her handkerchief, as she thought she was seeing a vision. She put them on again. "It's not a dream," she thought, as Mansour came and hugged her too.

"Please sit down, Mansour," said the Father. "I've heard a lot about you, but, as far as I'm concerned, all Amal's friends are mine because the parable says, 'birds of a feather flock together', and I know that's right, because I've met one of Amal's best friends. Her name is Baha and she's a most wonderful person. She works hard in the hospital as a nurse, where she loves everybody and helps everyone, just like Amal. So I do trust anyone who associates with our Amal."

That was the first news Amal had heard about her friend.

"How wonderful!" she exclaimed, looking at her father.

Then she turned to Mansour,

"So Baha is a great nurse! I'd love to see her!"

"You haven't seen her yet?" asked the Father.

"I haven't had a chance, but I'm sure Mansour will take me to visit her."

The happy company sat talking for more than an hour, during which Mansour told them about Amal's new love project. Then he asked her parents,

"Are you full?"

"We are always overflowing with children which war and hate have robbed of their homes and families."

"I'd love to help you," said Mansour with deep sincerity. "Our project was started on one condition, that we shall help all, without any discrimination because of religion, politics, or colour. So we've set money aside for God, as Amal said, 'From God, and back to God'."

Mother Teresa glanced to the Father, and then back again to Mansour. "What a transformation!" she thought. "It's almost like listening to a fairy story, as in just a few weeks the divine love has changed this young man from a ferocious beast into an agent of mercy."

The Father asked Mansour to stay for lunch.

"I'll take the offer another time," said Mansour, standing up, for the time had passed by swiftly, "as our lunch is already booked for today, but thankyou so much for the pleasant conversation. We shall work closely together from today onwards, as I'm intending to cover the entire country with our love project, and I'm sure it will succeed."

The Father and Mother Teresa accompanied the happy pair to the gate, and there they stood, waving back to them until they drove out of sight.

"I can't get over this," said the old man. "I remember this girl, when she knelt in the chapel and asked Jesus to blow up the Muslims, and now they are joining hands together in a wonderful project of love and care."

"I wonder what Amal did in Israel?" said the shrewd mother. "I have a feeling she wanted to tell us about her experience there, but was somehow unable. I noticed her sighing at the mention of Israel."

"Perhaps she had a bad experience, and was trying to forget it and wipe it out of her mind."

The mother nodded her head in her usual way, to indicate that there was another reason.

The restaurant was in a pleasant part of Lebanon, with mountain scenery and flowing streams of cool water. Many tourists used to enjoy their meals there, but since war had ripped the country, the wealthy local inhabitants used it, and, of course, spies from all parties found it a profitable place for gathering information.

Mansour was proud to have the princess accompany him. "This will make the town talk!" he said to himself, as he held the door for Amal. She walked gently, with a pleasant smile on her lips. Her innocent eyes glanced around her, then she quietly said,

"There are so many people, Mansour."

"I know, but we'll sit down there, near the stream, far away from everyone."

The eyes followed the young couple; voices hushed and heads turned round.

"Beautiful girl, uh!"

"Palestinian, rich Palestinian. You can tell from her dress."

"That's Mansour, Muslim militia. I wonder what happened to his number one girl?"

The waiter arrived to take the order, while his eyes were on Amal.

"Try kibba, Amal," said Mansour. "It's beautifully cooked here." Amal smiled and answered,

"I'll have whatever you suggest, as you're the doctor, and this is my first meal ever outside. I got used to eating at the orphanage, and prisons, and...." she stopped as she could not continue, "and, of course, at home."

The waiter collected the order, and the information, which he would pass on to whoever wanted to know, after bargaining the price.

Mansour and his best friend sat talking about their project, and how they could advance it.

"We need a lot of support," he said.

"I know, but that's easy. We already have the Father and Mother Teresa promising us assistance, as they will receive our help, and that reminds me, Mansour," said Amal, with concern. "Why didn't you mention Baha to me? You know she's my friend."

He looked ashamed and said quietly,

"We had a big argument and separated."

"That's very sad," remarked Amal. "She's a wonderful girl. You heard with your own ears what the Father said, and she's also a good nurse, so will really be a great asset for our work, but most importantly, she loves you. I remember the times she used to talk about you and say that her only dream was to marry you."

Mansour sighed, as he loved Baha so much.

"I was thinking of her last night," he said dreamily. "In fact, the three of us will make a perfect team, and now she can come back home." He smiled and continued, "She promised to wait for me, if I changed my policy towards my enemies."

"Have you changed your policy?" asked Amal excitedly, while at the same time the eyes and ears were trying to gather information.

"Amal, be careful," said Mansour, bringing his head closer to hers and whispering, "don't you know that every chair has eyes and every table has ears?"

Amal smiled with intrigue, like a little child, and looked about her with her happy face and smiling eyes, to the people who sat not far away. "I wonder if some of these eyes and ears will carry a message to my love for me?" she thought, while looking and searching, in case she found one of the boys.

"Amal, please don't stare at people like that," said Mansour, laughing, as he was tickled by Amal's behaviour.

"I want to see where are the eyes on the chairs."

"You are so sweet and innocent. I like you. Would you like to be Baha's bridesmaid?"

"I'd love to, that will be one of my happiest dreams." Then she looked at him in delight. "I take it that you have changed your policy towards your enemies?"

Mansour smiled with joy and responded,

"I'm on my way. It takes time, but I'm thinking hard."

"That is another of my best dreams which is starting to come true," she said joyfully. "So now we'll soon have Baha in our team, but we need support," she paused as she thought aloud. "I wonder if the Israelis would join our team, too? Say someone like Jonathan. Wouldn't that be wonderful?"

"Amal, please don't dream so much. Let's take a step at a time, and not mention the Israelis at all, especially Jonathan."

She looked at him, disappointed.

"I am trying to love my enemies, but one at a time."

"Yes Mansour, you're right, otherwise we'll lose the battle. But you are winning, as the first step is the most difficult one, because the ugly beast is the worst enemy. After that, the outside world is easy to conquer."

While they were talking, some of the Christian informers were bargaining with the waiter for some information about the princess.

"How much do you want then?" they asked in exasperation.

"Well, you don't have to pay. You go and find out about her for yourselves." The price was agreed and the information started to pour out. "Her name is Amal, she was brought up in the orphanage, has been in prison, this is her first meal out and she's sharing the same home with Mansour."

Mansour and his friend spent hours talking and planning, joking and laughing, forgetting about the world of hate and mistrust.

"Amal, do you know what time it is?"

"No, I haven't a watch. I lost mine in the prison."

"I'll buy you one, but now we must fly home, or otherwise my father will shoot both of us!"

Amal stood up immediately.

"We can't have any casualties," she laughingly replied, quoting Jonathan's golden rule.

Abu Mansour was fuming at Mansour's late arrival and angrily remarked as he walked through the door,

"I thought you said you're worried about people's talk? So what do you think they'll be saying now?"

Mansour was in a good mood, after the wonderful time he had just enjoyed with Amal, so did not reply to the angry man.

"Well, I'm telling you right now, that's the last time you take Amal outside alone. We're Muslims, so what will people say when they see you with a Christian girl?"

"She's my friend. Anyhow, I'm not worried about what people say, as I'm proud to be seen with Amal. She's a hero, and a princess." He paused, as he remembered the Father's comment, but knew his father would not understand, so added, "That was how one of the people commented about her."

Then he disappeared to his room.

Amal lay down on her bed, tired but satisfied and happy with the progress. She sent her thoughts to her love. "I tried ever so hard to contact the boys, but I failed. I will try again, but at any rate, Mansour is starting to love his enemies, so just let us be patient." Then her mind brought back the day's discussion. "Mansour will soon be getting married, and he would like me to be Baha's bridesmaid. I wonder who will be mine as I don't have any girl friends in Israel? Perhaps Aaron's sister, although I have never met her yet. I nearly did, as he had arranged for the whole family to come and meet me in the hostel, and then Jonathan was kidnapped. At least he is out and safe now, and the time will soon pass by and then we'll have our dreams fulfilled."

Jonathan tried to understand the feelings that were controlling him, as he was yearning more than ever for Natanya. "Maybe my mother was right when she advised me to go back with them to England and have a complete change, but I'm pulled towards my love. I feel I'm bound to her. If only I could comprehend the reason why."

He sat up in bed, thinking, as if he had a difficult puzzle to solve. "I must be reasonable. I do love Natanya, but she's dead now." He heard his own voice in his head, 'See, I will not say goodbye, for you are with me all the time'. "That's true," he reasoned with himself.

Then another sentence flashed through his head as he remembered the minister saying, 'Natanya is not dead, as her work will live forever.'

"Ah, I think I'm beginning to understand, she must be telling me to continue her good work, what she called her 'love project'." He felt excited and a smile broke on his lips. "Of course, my love, I shall continue where you stopped. You loved your enemies, so I must continue on that strange yet most pleasant road, but how?"

Jonathan spent most of the night thinking about how he could achieve that hard goal. "Education," his mind suggested. "We need to educate the younger generation to love and trust, to talk and reason as humans, not to kill and tear each other apart like wild animals. Yes, to teach our young people a new view, a superior way of resolving our problems."

Jonathan made up his mind about his future, so, feeling happy, he went to sleep with a new purpose in life, and hope of helping to resolve the tangled mess by following the pattern drawn and illustrated by Natanya, and left for him to continue and finish.

Menachem arrived in Lebanon and planned his trip to the cemetery for dawn on Saturday. "As I'm on my tour of duty, I'm exempt from breaking the Sabbath. I have my camera with me, so all I have to do is take some photos of the latest graves, especially the prominent ones, and later we can translate the inscriptions. The whole process will only take a few minutes, and no one will know where I've been, particularly as the road is not too far from our camp."

Abu Mansour woke his son at dawn.

"If we start right now in training our team, as we decided at our meeting which you missed yesterday, then we'll not interfere with our building programme."

Mansour was ready in no time, as he wanted to restore their friendship. "I enjoy training the team," he thought, "as it's a game of fun, and no one gets hurt. We just have a good time."

The training ground of Abu Mansour's men was the partly filled cemetery as it occupied a huge area, with one section accommodating the graves while the rest was empty space, except for many stones and boulders which were used as targets. It was also suitable because hardly anyone went near the entire place, either because of respect for the dead or fear of the ghosts who toured the derelict ground.

Abu Mansour and the young men began erecting their hideout on the far side of the unoccupied area while Mansour set up the gun and telescope, ready for the training. As they worked, the sound of a vehicle drawing near was heard. The men stopped and peered in the early morning light to see what it might be.

"A transporter," said Abu Mansour, turning back to his construction work.

Menachem drove slowly along the main road, looking carefully around him and through the mirror. "Not a single person around. It's so quiet, so fearful." He climbed down, leaving his truck at the side of the road, and started to walk through the cemetery, examining the graves, not aware that there were eyes in the stones, watching him closely.

"An Israeli!" whispered Abu Mansour, looking towards Mansour, as he was the only one with the gun and telescope ready at the time, and none of the rest had their weapons with them, because they were building their little barricades for practise firing.

Mansour looked through the viewfinder and saw the young soldier on the far side, looking at the graves. "What's he doing here?" he asked himself. "Maybe he's lost his way, perhaps a newcomer who's missed his road, as their camp is not too far from here."

"Shoot Mansour! It's a bird for you," whispered his father excitedly.

Mansour looked closely at the viewfinder and saw the young face and dark eyes. "Amal!" he called in his heart, as he could hear her voice in his head. 'Next time you see an Israeli, or any one of your enemies, try to imagine that is me.' "Amal, how can I shoot you, while I love you?"

"Mansour, shoot! What are you waiting for?" said his father with mounting frustration.

Mansour felt his heart thumping and his hands trembling as a fierce battle raged in his head and heart. 'You said you love me, so imagine your enemy is me, then perhaps you might love them, too.' 'I promise I will do that, just for you.' 'I will pray for you, and you will win.' "Oh help me, my God, I can't shoot at my best friend!" he cried inside himself, as Amal's words kept going round and round his head. He gazed at the Israeli, and could only see Amal, with her soft, gentle eyes and trembling hands as she stood by the convent gate. "You are the best friend I ever had," he whispered.

Abu Mansour could wait no longer, so he crawled on all fours, hiding behind the stones, until he reached his son. He looked at him and saw the sweat pouring from his pale face, his hands shaking and his eyes full of tears.

"Shoot boy! He's almost out of view." Then he pressed the trigger in anger, looking at his son. A shot sounded, shattering the peace of the dawn, and a painful cry heard from Menachem, as he fell to the ground.

"You killed her!" said Mansour, trembling, with sweat pouring down his forehead. "You killed Amal, my best friend."

"Have you gone mad, Mansour?" said the old man, looking anxiously at his son, as he had never seen him in that state before. He held him by his shoulders and could feel his entire body shaking fiercely. "You are ill, boy."

Walid and Shakouri came near and saw Mansour's state.

"He must have an attack of malaria, as he's hallucinating."

"Let's take him home," said his father, lifting him up, as Mansour shook and sobbed like a child, repeating the words,

"Why do you have to kill?"

Menachem was shot in the abdomen and was able to raise the alarm through his walkie-talkie.

"I've been shot," he muttered his message. "I'm in the Palestinian cemetery."

Abu Mansour and his men hurried to their vehicle, anxious about Mansour and worried about retaliation from the Israelis. They disappeared out of the cemetery in no time, back to the house.

Israeli armoured vehicles soon covered the area around the cemetery, and Menachem was quickly found, lying on the ground.

"Menachem," said the officer, "how are you, lad?"

"I've been shot in the abdomen," said the young man slowly, as he tried to control his pain.

"What are you doing here?" asked the man as he administered some first aid.

"I wanted to find the grave of Natanya. She's my friend."

The officer looked at him in surprise, so Menachem added, fearing for Aaron's future in case something should happen to him,

"Please don't blame Aaron. I wanted to find out as she's our hero and has done so much for us, so I wanted to pay her my respects."

Menachem was lifted by air to Tel Aviv hospital, for an urgent operation to remove the bullet from his intestines.

Abu Mansour drove speedily, as he was concerned for his son, but angry with himself at the same time. "Mansour's big problem is Amal. She was with him most of yesterday, and now he can't even shoot at an easy target. But the most disturbing matter is his question, 'Why do you have to kill?' That's what Baha said when Amal brainwashed her. It's my fault. I should throw that girl out of my house as soon as I get home."

Amal was weighing, wrapping and pricing the fresh farm products with Nahid when the men came rushing into the house, with Mansour being supported between Shakouri and Abu Mansour. The girls jumped to their feet, looking anxious and worried for the shocked young man.

"He must have been shot by the Israelis!" exclaimed Nahid.

"Oh help us, Lord," cried Amal in her heart. "Just after Mansour had started to change and really support and love his enemies, this had to happen to him!"

Om Mansour rushed after the men with Amal and Nahid following, all of them in a state of shock. Abu Mansour saw Amal in front of him, trying to hold Mansour's hand, and he burst out in anger at her.

"Don't touch Mansour, Amal! You're the cause of all his trouble. Go out and leave him alone. Go back to your people. I don't want you in this house. Go out!"

Amal was surprised, and so were the others in the room.

"Why do you talk like that to Amal?" asked Shakouri. "Why blame her for Mansour's illness, while she's innocently working in our love project?"

"She's the one who's dividing my house with this love of hers. She separated Baha from us, and now she's making Mansour go mad!" he screamed, repeating his order,

"Go out!"

Amal, almost in tears, looked at her dear friend, and their eyes met. Mansour conveyed to her his friendship, and regret for what had happened. She noticed the glimpse of a victorious light shining from his tearful eyes, so she smiled softly at him and withdrew from the room.

Everyone stood looking at the angry man, and forgot about Mansour.

"Why are you all standing there like images? Are you also blind to this girl's motives? She's going to be the cause of our losing the battle, as the Israelis will come and take us over, while we're sitting with our arms folded, talking about love!"

"No one is sitting doing nothing," objected Abdu. "We're all working very hard. In fact, since Amal came, we've established so much. Look at our women and children, they're all happy and have a purpose in living, so it hurts all of us, when our hero who helped us with love, is thrown out by us like a dirty dog." Om Mansour and Nahid nodded their heads in agreement, feeling very hurt for Amal.

Amal went to her room and sat on her bed, too shocked to think. Resentful and agitating feelings began to rise and boil up inside her. "How awful and shameful of Abu Mansour to treat me like that, throwing me out of the room; in fact, out of his house." The ugly beast of lower nature was waking up from his long period of dormancy. "I will go, and leave his house. I'll go back to 'my people', as he put it, and then let him see how he'll get on with the new company." She covered her eyes and started to cry, feeling hurt and sorry for her injured feelings. "How dare he throw me out in front of all those people! I felt so small and belittled. I'll leave, and I hope the Israelis come and blow him up!" Suddenly she stopped as she heard her words 'blow him up'. "Oh no!" she covered her mouth. "The beast is up." She jumped to her feet. "I mustn't let him control me. Help me, my God, as it's very difficult to do what's right when others are unfair." Then she remembered her own advice to Mansour, that the battlefield is inside the person, and that it is up to the individual to fight his own hate and prejudice. "I'll forgive Abu Mansour, and pray for him, but I must stay for the sake of Mansour. He looked so unwell. I wonder what happened to him, as I didn't see any blood on his clothes, so I don't think he's been shot."

Suddenly her thoughts terrified her and she called out,

"Oh help! Maybe they shot an Israeli? Perhaps Jonathan came to find me, and they killed him!" She went outside her room and wanted to go back and enquire about what had happened, but she knew Abu Mansour would be very angry. "After all, it's his home, so I must respect his order," she thought, as she went back to her vegetables, to carry on with her love project while unloading her anxiety onto her Lord.

The team and Mansour's family decided to leave him alone for the morning, to allow him to recover from his shock. The team left to continue their rebuilding work, feeling uneasy and concerned.

"I wonder how long it will take the Israelis to retaliate for their man?" asked Shakouri.

"Give them a day or two," replied Walid. "The pity is that they'll ruin what we've just rebuilt. I wish we hadn't killed the boy."

"Don't you start!" shouted Abu Mansour, feeling nervous and unhappy. "This is our life. We are born to struggle and suffer, but we're bound to win at the end of the road."

Om Mansour and Nahid returned to their sad and weeping hero.

"I am sorry, my love," said the mother, hugging her. "Don't you feel hurt by Abu Mansour. He doesn't mean what he said, but he's always like that when he's worried, and this morning he had two things that made him anxious. First, Mansour refused to kill his enemy, and second, he's worried about another raid as they just killed an Israeli."

The vegetable dropped from Amal's hand and her muscles turned to jelly. "That's what my heart feared, they've killed my love for me," she thought, looking anxiously and tearfully at the mother.

"Don't you worry, Amal," said the elderly lady. "We won't throw you out, and the men will soon think of an idea to move us out of the area, in case the Israelis raid us again."

"Why can't we learn to love our enemy?" asked Amal as she wiped away her tears.

"My sugar, don't mention those words to Abu Mansour, as he hates them. I know it would be a lovely dream if we could all love each other, but it will never happen."

"It will if we want it to, and if we start work on ourselves."
Then she asked, "Can I see Mansour?"

"Better not, Amal. None of us are allowed to be with him.
He had a nasty shock, as the Israeli they shot was a young man
who had lost his way and was wandering in the cemetery. Walid
suggested that perhaps Mansour mistook him for a ghost, or
something, as he said that it was you, his best friend."

Amal felt pleased for Mansour that he had put her advice
into practise. "But what was an Israeli doing in the cemetery?"
she asked herself. "I have a feeling they think I'm dead, and
perhaps that was Aaron, searching for my grave." She covered
her eyes and wept.

"Come on, Amal," said Nahid, consoling her sister.

"They killed my best friend," she sobbed.

The two women looked at her in surprise, as she said the
same sentence as Mansour about the shot young man. "They
can't both know him," thought Om Mansour, looking at Amal.

"I have no enemy," continued Amal, explaining her words.
"Everyone is my best friend, and brother and sister."

Mansour sat down, weighing up the situation in his head and
feeling upset that Amal had been badly treated by his father.
"She is so loving and kind, working hard in loving us, and now
we throw her out and treat her like this." Then his mind took
him to Baha. "We did the same to my angel of mercy, and my
father declared her blood as of no value, while she was working
hard to help others." He tried to sort out his mixed and confused
feelings. "I'm surprised at myself," he thought. "When I saw that
young man, I felt no hate toward him. In fact, I pitied him, as
he looked insecure and lost. He almost looked the same as
Amal, a normal human." Then he thought deeper. "Of course he
is a human, isn't he?"

He sat for a while to puzzle over the question in his mind.
"I think I can see the issue. What makes him an enemy or friend
is my own view of him, how I look at him, for when I viewed
him as Amal, I looked at him as the best friend, but my father
viewed him as an enemy, so he shot him with severity, as a dirty
pig."

He smiled as he began to understand the meaning of the
sentence, 'Love thy enemy.' "How true is that advice, as Amal
and Baha found out for themselves, that the minute the
individual, I, start to change my view toward those I personally

hate, I make them friends and they are no longer my foes. The moment I, only I, love them, then they become my friends."

He felt as if a heavy burden of hate had been moved from his shoulders, to be replaced by feelings of warmth and tender compassion. "I do regret that the boy died, but I'll do my best to sort out our struggle by another method, the most powerful method; by love, the divine love, Amal's type of love. I know my father won't understand it, but I must copy Amal's example and show it, by my works and not just words."

Mansour left his room and walked to where the three women sat, as they were preparing for their day's work.

"Amal," he said, sitting down on the floor beside her.

"Thankyou for everything."

The three looked at him in surprise.

"I do feel happy inside, even though the road is lined with blazing coals, but love will conquer at the end of the journey."

Amal put both her hands on his shoulders and said,

"You are the best friend I ever had."

Then he stood up and said, as he made to leave the house,

"We have a lot of work to do, and a great amount of thinking." He paused for a moment, then added, "Thinking of the right things."

The women burst into laughter, as that had become the motto of the love project teams.

Jonathan sat at his desk, arranging his thoughts before he could put his decision into action. "I'm sure I'm taking the right step. I must continue in the way that Natanya started, so I'll concentrate my ability and talents on solving the problem using peaceful methods; by training our young people to learn how to overcome the barriers by love, and reasoning with their opponents; by controlling their hate and considering the other side's views. Then, for sure, the whole Middle East will be the centre of peace, the throne of the Messianic kingdom, where no weapons will be found, but rather the high and elevated principles of the Almighty, who loves all his creation equally."

He began to write his letter of resignation, and explained that he would like to change his career to one of teaching, as a lecturer at the university in Jerusalem, where he could teach and direct the young generation in the art of achieving a peaceful settlement for Israel, in trying to find ways of living in peace with their many enemies. He was only half way through his long explanatory letter, when the phone rang.

"Is that you, Jonathan?" blared the clear voice of Victor.

"Yes. Good morning, Victor. I'm just writing a letter with a copy to you."

"Oh!" he said, guessing what the letter was about. "I know, he must have had enough of the army and Lebanon, and I bet he wants to leave," he thought, so he quickly answered,

"Can we talk about the letter later, Jonathan, as I have a mixture of news for you. I'm sorry to interrupt your holiday, but as the news concerns you, I didn't hesitate to ring."

Victor continued before giving Jonathan a chance to comment.

"I have two items of news for you; both have a good and a bad side, and both need you to deal with them."

"Oh no," thought Jonathan, tapping his pen on the desk. "I can guess what the news is, and I don't want to go to Lebanon. I've had enough of raids and fighting."

"Are you listening?" asked Victor, as the line had gone silent.

"I'm listening, but I must explain before you...."

"Don't explain just yet, please," interrupted the old officer. "Let me tell you my two items, then you can explain about your letter."

Jonathan kept quiet, waiting to hear the news.

"One of your team was shot early this morning in Lebanon."

"I guessed that right," he thought to himself, feeling distressed. Then he asked,

"Which one of the team?"

"Menachem."

"Oh no! Has he been killed?"

"No, thankfully, and that brings me to the good side of this first item. He was shot in the abdomen, and his operation in Tel Aviv hospital is over, with, happily, the possibility of a complete recovery."

"That's good, as we don't want to lose Menachem; he's an excellent member. Anyway, how did it happen?"

"Well," said the man with hesitation. "It happened in the Palestinian cemetery, early at dawn this morning."

"What was he doing there?" asked Jonathan in a surprised voice.

"He said he was looking for Natanya's grave, because he wanted to pay his respects to her."

Jonathan's heart sank as he felt responsible for Menachem's injury. "He must feel like me, as I also wanted to find out," he thought. Then he said,

"I am very sorry, but I can see what happened. Both he and Aaron are good friends. I bet they put their heads together and prepared such a reckless plan, without speaking to me. In fact, I saw both of them talking yesterday, sitting under Natanya's tree."

"Ah," said Victor. "Actually Menachem cleared Aaron from any part in the plan. He said it was his own idea. Anyhow, I have the other item to tell you."

"I wonder what that could be?" thought Jonathan in his mind, trying to guess.

"I'll give you the good news first, then the other side, because both will give you a shock," said Victor, laughing.

Jonathan held his breath and gripped his pen hard, as he could not imagine what the news item was, either its good or bad side.

"I'm ready," he said quietly.

"Our Natanya is alive and well."

Jonathan almost jumped out of his skin.

"It can't be! Impossible! I must be hearing things," he said, transferring the receiver to the other ear as he tried to comprehend the news.

"It's true, Jonathan. The news has come from very reliable sources," said Victor to the shocked and quiet man.

"Of course," thought Jonathan. "The informers saw Baha, and our men thought that was our Natanya, not knowing her real identity." Then he conveyed his fear with a disappointed voice.

"How can we be sure that it's our Natanya, and not someone similar to her?"

"You do amaze me, Jonathan," said Victor in a fascinated voice. "You must be psychic, as it's quite true that a person can mix personalities, and that's what happened to us all the time. Apparently our Natanya is not Baha, as we believed, but she is Amal, as she told us all along. She is a Christian orphan, brought up in the orphanage, as her family was blown up by Abu Mansour. We mistook her for Baha, as she had become her good friend and was found in her house."

Then he paused.

"Actually there's so much information about Baha, that it's difficult to relate it all on the phone."

Jonathan felt as if he was in a pleasant dream. "That's my love. So she was talking to me all the time."

"Jonathan, are you with me?" asked Victor, as there was no response to his message.

"That's the best good news I've ever heard. I'm not sure if I'm dreaming or it's reality."

"Well," replied Victor, laughing, "now I'll give you the bad side of it, and that will soon prove to you that you're not dreaming. Natanya was seen with Mansour, in one of his usual spots, and here is the bad news; she's living with them, so how are we going to get her out of that place?"

"I'll come immediately to the Centre," replied Jonathan, feeling excited and confident that his dreams were on their way to be fulfilled. "Then we can plan a way together, to bring her back home; and also deal with the case of Menachem."

"Thankyou, my dear. Now you can tell me about your letter."

Jonathan laughed and quickly answered,

"We'll forget about the letter for the meantime, as my first priority is to get my girl out."

He jumped up from his chair, feeling like dancing, folded his half finished letter and put it away.

"I'm coming, my love," he said, touching her hair. "No matter what it costs me, or how great the price, even if it's my own life, as you're everything to me and life is empty without you. I must tell poor Mordecai and Aaron the good news first, then I'll pray for God to inspire me with a way to get you out."

Mordecai had become withdrawn since Natanya's death. He visited the myrtle tree many times a day, to water and look after it. "My sweet myrtle, I want you to blossom and fill your branches with beautiful flowers, so you can resemble the tree of the righteous one which is planted by the water; whose leaves never wither and who bears fruits every year."

Shalom and Dan were walking to their room to pick up some papers, and passed by Mordecai who was talking to the tree.

"Mordecai does worry me," said Dan. "His health seems to have deteriorated a lot since Natanya's death, and now he's talking to the tree. I wish someone could do something about his problem."

"It's sad," answered Shalom, "but I'm sure time will heal the wounds. I feel that when Jonathan starts work again and cheers up a bit, Mordecai will improve."

Jonathan went to find his father-in-law, and knew exactly where to start his search. "Near the myrtle tree," he thought, and was right in his assumption. He stood by Mordecai's side, and noticed the tears in his eyes.

"No need for the tears, Mordecai, but it's time to prepare for the wedding!"

"What wedding?" he enquired, looking shocked at the transformed man.

"Natanya is alive, and I'm on my way to bring her back home."

The man stood there, not knowing what to believe, while holding the hose in his hand, squirting water everywhere except in the right place.

"I'm telling you the truth. Look, I'm just going to pack my bag and then I'm off. So, no more tears or crying."

Mordecai threw the hose on the ground, hugging and kissing Jonathan, while his tears flowed down his cheeks.

"I'm not crying," he said, wiping off his tears, as Jonathan ran to find his brother-in-law, to deliver the good news to him.

Dan and Shalom had collected their papers and were approaching the myrtle tree when they saw Mordecai hugging the tree and dancing around it. They stopped and looked at him in horror.

"D'you think Mordecai has already gone out of his head?" said Dan.

"I fear so. It's too late now for any help as he's completely gone. Just look at him."

They walked slowly towards him, feeling depressed and sad. As soon as he saw them, he left the tree and pushed himself between them, held them by their waists, and started dancing.

"What a happy dream! What a lovely day!" he sang.

"Mordecai, please!" they said, trying to calm him down.

"Come on, let's dance. We have a happy time in front of us. My Natanya is alive and will soon be home."

"Natanya!" they both exclaimed, while Mordecai whisked them round and round with him as he danced.

"I'm telling you the truth. Jonathan just told me the good news."

Jonathan found Natanya's friend, looking depressed as he was worrying about Menachem, not knowing about the news of his accident.

"Just the man I want to see!" said Jonathan, trying to contain his joy. "I want you to come with me to Lebanon."

"Lebanon? Why?"

"Don't look so worried, Aaron. I'm going to get my love out, and I need your help."

"Who's love?" asked the puzzled boy.

"Mine, and your best friend. Natanya is alive!"

"Natanya is alive?" he said unbelievingly.

"As sure as that sun is there. So come quickly, there's no time to waste."

"So no need for Menachem to search for her grave, as she's not there."

"Ah," he said, smiling, "so you know about Menachem's plan?"

"Yes, we were talking about it yesterday, about her resting place, and he suggested to go and find out where she was buried, as he said you would be pleased to know."

"Did he?" he asked.

"Yes, he heard you talking to her."

Jonathan felt touched and said to Aaron,

"I'm sorry to inform you that Menachem has been shot, but not seriously. He's recovering in Tel Aviv hospital."

"He's been shot?!" The smile disappeared from Aaron's face and an anxious look covered it instead.

"Don't worry, he'll be alright," said Jonathan, to reassure him, "but his effort has not been in vain, as we discovered about Natanya through his accident. He was shot while he was in the Palestinian cemetery, but I'm so relieved that his injury wasn't too serious, otherwise it would have marred our joy, but now we can celebrate."

The two young men held each other by the waist and skipped and danced their way to their rooms to get ready.

Mordecai was still trying to convince the two boys of his sanity when he saw Jonathan and Aaron dancing their way to their rooms.

"Look," he said, laughing. "They're doing the same as me, so why do you think I'm mad and talking out of my head?"

Dan and Shalom jumped for joy when they saw the evidence, and also began to dance. Soon the entire hostel was turned into a house of joy and laughter.

Mansour went to the building project, although keeping his distance from his father. Abu Mansour saw him and thought to himself, "He's recovered quickly. Anyhow, it's no use talking to him, as everyone seems to support him and Amal, but I must talk to his mother, as she's with her most of the time. I must know what she's doing in my own house, otherwise she'll brainwash the entire family." He left his building work and returned home to talk to his wife about Mansour's problem.

When he walked in, the first person he met was Amal, who automatically smiled, as she had already forgotten about his harsh treatment. "Talk about the devil," he mumbled, trying to avoid the soft, gentle eyes. "I can't understand her, it's as if nothing had happened! In fact, my men are the ones who are really upset, but she doesn't seem to mind."

"Ahla, Abu Mansour," said his wife in greeting, wondering what else had happened to bring him back home in the morning.

"I want to talk to you, alone," he said, glancing at Amal.

"Of course. Let's go inside," she answered, walking to her bedroom.

"We're in great difficulty," he said to his wife. "Mansour is changing, and I know the reason. It's Amal; she must go. I can't have her here, living in the same house with us."

"Why not, Abu Mansour?" asked his wife, entreating him. "Amal is our hope. She has filled our house and hearts with joy and laughter. How can you throw her away? She works so hard the whole day, thinking of nothing except how to help others and make them happy. Look how many girls are working outside with her. Why do we have to hurt our best friend?"

"I don't mind her, but I don't like her policy. She is affecting Mansour. Today he couldn't shoot his enemy, but was calling her name."

"I can explain everything to you," she said, holding his arm to calm him down. "Mansour is in love with her. I'm sure they both love each other, and like all young people, they dream of each other, so you don't have to worry about Mansour's behaviour, or Amal's. She's a lovely girl, and easy to love, so Mansour has fallen in love with her."

Abu Mansour looked at his wife with his mouth wide open.

"What do you mean, they are in love?" he asked with disgust.

"You know," she said, looking at him bashfully. "I saw them holding each other. So please don't upset them, as it will be lovely if they get married."

"I think you're also brainwashed by her. How can you talk about them getting married while she is a Christian and Mansour a good Muslim? Did you forget that fact? Imagine what the people will say about me, a devout Muslim, allowing my son to marry a mobashira?"

"What's wrong with that, my dear? Don't we all worship the same God? She can practise her religion, and we practise ours. Anyhow, everyone loves her; they all think she is the best girl around, and Mansour deserves a good wife like her."

Abu Mansour felt like screaming, as his wife could not see any of the important issues, nor could his men.

"Have you thought of their children, my grand children? With a mother like her, she will soon convert all of us to Christianity. No, no way will Mansour have her for a wife. I'd rather have Baha back, at least she is a Muslim, and also my niece, and Mansour's fiancee. How could he forget his promise to her as soon as another girl appears on the scene?"

"But you prohibited her from entering the house, or even the area, so how can you expect him to marry her? He had to find another girl, as he can't stay single all his life."

"I'll speak to him later, and tell him that I don't mind Baha coming home, and their getting married as soon as possible."

"Okay, speak to him, but please don't upset Amal. Don't forget what she's done for all of us. Let's live and let live," pleaded the kind lady with her husband.

"Well, I'll feel better when Baha comes back, especially as I need him now more than ever, with the anticipation of retaliation ahead of us. Then she can control Mansour before this girl ruins him completely." He turned and left the room, hearing the happy company of workers singing while they worked. He had to smile, as it was so refreshing and reassuring to hear the sound of joy in the midst of a furious storm.

Jonathan was back in his room, busy packing his bag, whistling for a while and thinking for a while. "How amazing life is," he thought. "Less than half an hour ago, I felt like dying, as everything seemed so black, except for the bright memories of my love; but now I've completely forgotten all my sorrows and

I can't contain my heart's joy. My sweet Natanya is alive and well!! It's just like receiving a dead one back to life. I'm aware that my mission will be difficult and dangerous, but nothing can keep me from my bride, no obstacle, nor death itself, as I'm sure our dreams will be fulfilled. She's my angel, and her prayers are always acceptable to Adoni."

Victor and the other officers were waiting for their leader at the Centre, in an atmosphere of joy and celebration. Peres was especially delighted, as his conscience had been heavy with guilt, made all the worse as Jonathan and the rest of Natanya's friends had been grieving beyond comforting.

"There, our happy bridegroom!" said Victor, hugging the overjoyed young man. "We shall get straight down to business, so we'll not delay you from meeting your Natanya," he said, taking his seat. "I'll give you all the details of the case, so we don't lose any time in getting Natanya back home, then leave the entire decision for you, as I'm sure none of us will come up with a better idea.

"As soon as Menachem was shot, our men gathered the following information from very reliable sources," said Victor, as Jonathan listened intently to him.

"Mansour was seen with Natanya in his usual restaurant, and both looked extremely happy."

"My love is always happy," thought Jonathan. "So I can imagine that anyone in her company would feel the same."

"This was the first time she had been out with him for a meal," continued Victor, looking at his notes.

"So my darling had most probably been confined to bed during all that period," concluded Jonathan.

"Mansour was talking to her for hours, much of the time with their heads close together as he whispered words into her ears."

"I wonder what he was telling her, and why were their heads so close together?" thought Jonathan, feeling uneasy. "I don't want to lose my girl to Mansour, or anyone else. I know how easy it is for people to get hooked on her, as she has that unique pull that even pulls unfeeling stones towards her."

"She was seen looking around many times, staring at the other diners, as if she was searching for someone," said Victor, surveying his silent audience.

"She must have been searching for our boys," commented Jonathan. "I guess she hadn't been able to meet with us before because Mansour had been guarding her all the time."

"It could be," said the old man, sensing the tinge of jealousy in Jonathan's tone as he tried to convince himself about the reason for the closeness and long conversation. "The other point," continued Victor, "is that Mansour left his girlfriend, Baha. In fact, the family disowned her."

"Oh no," Jonathan's heart ached. "That is worrying, and he'll deceive my innocent Natanya in no time, especially as he's good looking as well. But she promised she would wait for me, and pray for our dreams to come true."

"Do you know what was the reason for the separation?" asked the worried man.

"Apparently our Natanya was a Christian preacher who used to go to the camp and distribute food and clothes, to show her enemies, who had killed her family by a bomb, that she was able to conquer hate with works of love. That was when she converted Baha to her way of thinking."

"Did she convert Baha, the informer and number one killer?" asked Jonathan in surprise.

"Yes," said Victor laughing, and proud at the same time. "Baha was thrown out, and became a devout nurse in Beirut hospital, where she treats all without any discrimination or partiality, and her favourite motto is, 'Love thy enemy'."

"Oh, so that's what that young doctor was telling me about!" said Peres, with his mouth wide open in surprise. He looked to Jonathan, "You remember, when we were in the store, I told you that I'd had a strange conversation with the doctor."

"Yes, but you didn't tell me what it was about, nor about Baha."

"No, because he was about to complete his story when you suggested that we should leave."

"Anyhow," interrupted Victor, "Baha is no longer our enemy, and we can thank Natanya for that. But now our problem is how to get her out, as she's living with Abu Mansour, who is still insisting to fight us, and we know that without any doubt because the evidence shows that his men shot Menachem, but, at the same time, they are giving her a first class treatment. We gathered that from the clothes she was wearing, as she looked like a princess, according to the informer's mind. Fortunately, from the way they shot him, it seems they saw him too late, otherwise he would certainly be dead now.

"I know he shouldn't have been there all alone, but I can understand the feeling of wanting to know, as I've also spent hours thinking about what happened to her body. However, I'm glad our tragedy has turned into a happy dream, and now it's up to you to convert the dream into reality."

"I can only try," said Jonathan. "I'll pray and try to put the pieces together, and see what picture will appear, and then we can hopefully carry it out by tomorrow. It's still only early afternoon, so that gives me ample time to construct a plan."

"I have no doubt about your ability, my dear, so we'll wait for you," said Victor, pushing towards him the various papers relating to the case. "By the way, you also have photographs of where the incident took place, and a detailed map of the area. I'll pray for you, as I do believe in prayer, and actually started to do that since Natanya showed me how," he said, smiling.

Jonathan gathered together his files, put them under his arm and departed for his private office, while the rest of the officers left for their various departments, until their leader would decide on a plan. On arriving, he spread out the details on the table and sat down, staring at the information in front of him. His heart was anxious and his mind pictured Mansour so close to Natanya.

"Please, my love, don't consider another man. Don't you know I've suffered so much because of you?" He placed the treasured piece of hair in front of him, and could see her gentle kind eyes and soft smile, 'I'll pray that our dream will come true.' He saw her nodding her head, 'I'll wait for you.' He could hear her voice grooved deeply in his memory.

"I mustn't doubt your love, Natanya," he said softly, then he remembered Mark's words after the service, 'She is very strong, and she kicked me hard. When I saw the detestation in her eyes, I hated myself for my behaviour.' "You are my angel, so pure, so faithful. I have no doubt about that. Please forgive me, my love; I'm just anxious as I don't want to lose you again. I thought you had died, but heaven showed me great favour by keeping you safe for my sake."

He was still holding the hank of hair which seemed to bring only pleasant thoughts from his memory. He could see her standing at the door of the store, then running towards him, saying, 'I come to get you out.' "My dearest, you ventured into the dangerous unknown, to set me free; your love reached so far that it's madness to even let the thought of doubt cross my mind. Anyhow, you told me you would stay to help them, too, but I fear from what's happened that the road is too difficult for you, because I know the depth of hate in Mansour's heart, especially for me. It will be impossible to convert him, or his father, as they have just proved their insistence in killing us by shooting Menachem on sacred ground."

Jonathan returned the soft black hair to his top shirt pocket and gazed at the large scale map, studying it for a long time.

"They're using the empty space here as a training ground. That would explain why they didn't spot Menachem earlier, as they would have been concentrating on the other side of the cemetery. They must have taken this road to escape back to their territory, without being seen by our men." As he marked the map with his pencil, he thought to himself, "We could use the same route to enter their camp as it's almost empty land, and if we started before dawn, that would be even better."

He sat back in his chair to weigh his steps carefully, before he took any decision. "My aim is to get Natanya out, without injuring her, or anyone else. I don't want any casualties and I don't want to announce our raid in case they take her into hiding with them, and then I would lose knowledge of her whereabouts for weeks, and, to be honest, I can't bear that, especially with Mansour so close to her, and away from his girl at the same time."

The young officer started to direct his steps toward the goal. "I must concentrate on only one house, Abu Mansour's, as he's the leader, and the entire camp will be lost without his direction, and especially his son's, as I know from personal experience that Mansour is the power behind his father. He's the main one, young and full of zeal for the movement, and burned up with the fever of hate. I'd like to lay my hands on him. He needs help as he's surely out of his mind to suggest severing my arm and then cooking it for a party." He shook his head with terror, as he remembered his experience with the arch-enemy.

"Fortunately his house is standing right at the edge of the Palestinian camp. It was missed in our last raid, so we can use the flattened area here as a base for our troops, and I can face the house direct, while we surround the entire camp, so no one will be able to escape. I'll use one of our hydraulic platforms as a mobile watchtower, and we can encase the cradle with bullet proof material; that will do the trick perfectly. I can have Aaron and Peres on the tower, as Aaron will not mistake Natanya, nor will Peres miss Mansour. They can act as guides for us for the immediate distance, while our high flying aircraft can scan the camp for any firing or movement by the rest of Abu Mansour's team."

Jonathan sat resting his chin on his hands, while he peered at the map, calculating his steps to the limit. "We made the last attack less than a month ago, so I doubt if there are many weapons, plus they've been busy rebuilding, which means their resources have been spent on reconstruction for the meantime. Now my problem is how to flush the house of its inhabitants. I don't want any violence, so none of our boys will be shot at by Abu Mansour's men, nor do I want anyone in the house to be shot at. We've already hurt my angel enough, and it will be my end if anything should happen to her again, as I've already proved to myself that I can't live without her. So I'll have to take my time to think out the matter precisely."

He thought of one way, then changed his mind and re-directed his steps towards another course, until he had satisfied himself from all possible angles. Finally he said to himself,

"I feel this plan should work, God willing. We'll enter their territory through the cemetery road, under cover of darkness, as it will be completely deserted at that time and they would never anticipate a raid at that hour. I can set the mobile watchtower here, where it will be protected from the side by the mountain, and by our armoured vehicles from the front." He marked the position of the tower on the map, then continued his strategy. "The troops will dig in in the flattened area. We have loads of stones, and many walls have just started to rise from the ground, so we can hide behind them. Then, when we're all in, we'll signal our army to close up and encompass the entire area, so no one will be able to move out of his house and cause us any risk. Peres and Aaron will closely watch Abu Mansour's house for us, and this road that will lead me to him. He's bound to come out of his house when he realises we're surrounding the area, either to fight or carry out some plan or other, and when he's at that point, we'll announce to him over the megaphone for him to surrender or we'll shoot. By this method we can arrest the men and then search the house, and we're bound to find Natanya, who 'escaped' from the convoy, recapture her, and take her back with us."

A happy smile broke out on his lips. "I must control my feelings when I meet her, for I've a strong feeling my emotions will betray me in front of Abu Mansour's family, and that will just not do."

After he had arranged the details of his strategy, and the number of men and vehicles needed, he stood up and went to the conference room, to announce that his plan was ready for discussion.

As soon as everyone had assembled, he explained his plan and then waited for their response.

"We promised we would not waste any time in discussions," said Victor, as the rest of the officers nodded their heads in agreement. "I think your plot is very simple and easy to follow. As you said, we're mainly interested in one house, and I feel your plan is an excellent one for flushing the house without violence. We can start our practising immediately, and hopefully our men will be at their posts before dawn, to give your friends a good surprise. The main thing, as you emphasised, is to guard ourselves from all directions, so no one is sniped at, and, who knows, maybe by tomorrow we'll meet your two men and listen to their story!"

The officers laughed and then hurried off to train their men in preparation for the mission.

Abu Mansour had a meeting with his men in his house, to prepare for the anticipated retaliation from Israel. Mansour sat quiet, listening, and thinking hard to find a solution for the endless struggle.

"I'm sure the Israelis are brewing trouble for us, perhaps tomorrow. It usually takes them two days or so, and I'm certain that this time it will be a serious raid, as Jonathan is back and holding a big account against us for his kidnapping and imprisonment," said the anxious Abu Mansour, looking to his worried men.

Then he said to Mansour, with regret in his voice,

"If only you'd killed him, instead of tormenting him like a cat with a mouse, and then now we wouldn't have any of these worries."

Mansour sighed and kept quiet, looking at the ground.

"Mansour, can you tell me what's in your head?" asked the father, feeling exasperated with his son's attitude.

"I am thinking, Father. I am trying hard to find a solution for our problem."

Abu Mansour sat back on his cushion, relieved at the answer. "That's my son," he thought. "Just as his mother said, he's in love with Amal, but he does hate his enemies."

So he asked him,

"Please, tell me if you've thought of any solution yet."

"I think I've found a simple solution, but there's a big wall and obstacle between us and the solution, and only a very fierce battle will remove it from the way."

The men nodded, as did Abu Mansour, who said,

"I know, my son, but we hardly have any weapons left with which to fight even a small battle, so can we think of another solution for tomorrow, and then we'll stack up our ammunition for the battle after that."

Shakouri held his head from desperation and moaned, mumbling his words,

"Pity we shot their man, just when our buildings have started to rise from the ground. Now they'll come tomorrow and bring them back to the earth."

"That doesn't concern me much," said Walid, "but what does torment me is that they'll blow up the adjacent camp, and that's absolutely full with people. Where can we move them to? And look how many children there are. Take your home as an example, Mansour. It will have at least twenty girls working on the love project, and what a tragedy it would be for us if they dropped one bomb there."

"We must move the factory," said Mansour. "We'll transfer it to your farm, Shakouri. At least then we'll have our love project still functioning. Amal is a very caring girl, so I'm sure she'll take care of the children, but that doesn't solve the problem of the rest in the camp."

"We can empty it temporarily," said Abu Mansour, "and scatter the residents around the orange groves, just for the next few days at least, until we see what Jonathan has in mind."

"No, Father," said Mansour. "Not the orange groves. They'll be the first places he'll bomb and he knows them inside out. Plus that's the way their policy goes, they bring to the ground any place where they suffer, so we must think of another place to evacuate to."

"I think it's better to erect tents on the flattened area, and move everyone there, then they can go home at night, until we can find another alternative," said Mansour.

"Yes, that's a good idea," responded his father.

"Better we get a move on right now," said Mansour anxiously. "We can move Amal and the machinery right away, and make shelters for the rest."

"No need for that, Mansour," objected his father. "Not at this hour of night, but early at dawn we'll evacuate everybody. However, we can tell them now about our decision, so they can prepare themselves. You know the Israelis, they never raid us at night, because they're arrogant and want to show us how strong and brave they are in killing and destroying us in full daylight."

The men agreed to carry out the mission at dawn, with each having a section of the camp to which they would deliver the warning and help in the evacuation at sunrise.

Jonathan and his teams finished their training and prepared to have a few hours sleep before they were transported to Lebanon just after midnight.

As was his custom, Jonathan went to the office to telephone his parents. "I think they'll be convinced I've gone out of my mind when I tell them about Natanya and my going to Lebanon," he thought, as he dialled England.

While he waited for someone to pick up the receiver, he looked at his watch. "Good, it's only nine p.m., so they should be at home," he said.

"Hello," answered Sara, wondering who was on the other end.

"Mum, it's nice to hear your voice again."

"Oh, my Jonathan, my dear boy, how are you? I've been thinking of you the whole day and anticipating a call from you, as the period of time you gave to me is over and I'm looking forward to hearing your decision."

Dan heard his excited wife talking so fast, as was her way whenever she received a call from her son, so he left his book and stood by her side, trying to hear, and guess what the conversation was about.

"It's Jonathan, dear. He sounds happy," she said to her husband, as Jonathan began to tell her his news.

"I've just made my decision, and am ready to carry it through, but I need your prayers, lots of them, and more than ever before."

"What kind of decision have you in mind?" asked his mother, puzzled, and worried at the same time, as she thought to herself that prayer is only needed when someone is in trouble.

"I'm going to Lebanon, later this evening, for two reasons. One...." but before he could mention any of his reasons, she interrupted, almost screaming,

"You must be mad! You're on holiday, so why are you going to Lebanon? Why you? I must contact Victor; he's taking advantage of your sincere heart and devotion to duty. He doesn't care about how we feel or that you've just escaped from death, and now he's sending you back again!"

Dan was becoming anxious, as he could see his wife starting to get hysterical, so he was hopping from one foot to the other, and sticking his ears as close as he could to the receiver.

"Mum, please, don't get so upset. I have good news to tell you, but first of all, I want to go to Lebanon. Victor has nothing to do with this decision. It's mine, and I'm going with pleasure."

"What good news?" asked his mother, doubtfully.

"My Natanya has been found, alive and well, so I hope to go and bring her back home."

"Natanya!!" exclaimed Sara, looking at her husband. "Natanya has been found alive and well in Lebanon," she repeated.

"Wonderful!" shouted Dan with excitement, trying to snatch the phone from his wife, but she pushed him away while she clenched the receiver.

"That's one of the reasons," continued Jonathan, "but the difficulty is that one of my team has been shot by Abu Mansour's men, and unfortunately Natanya is living with them."

"She's living with Abu Mansour?! Why does she stay with people like that? Anyhow, can't one of the other men get her out?"

"She's my bride, Mother, and it will be my pleasure to free her. She didn't hesitate to come and rescue me and gain me my freedom, so do you imagine I could possibly allow another to carry out my duty? Anyhow, can I have a word with Dad, please, because I must go and have some sleep."

She handed the phone to her husband and sat down, hating the word Lebanon, as it immediately gave her nightmares.

"Jonathan, what good news to hear that our Natanya hasn't died! How did you find out about that?"

"It's a long story, Dad, but as I tried to explain to Mum, one of our boys was shot, and during the enquiries into his case, we discovered about her recovery. So now I hope to leave tonight, and we'll be ready in our positions by dawn, God willing. So please pray for us."

"I will, Jonathan, but does this mean we can get ready for the wedding?" he asked with delight.

"I'd love to say yes, but one can never tell in a matter like this, as I know from past experience. But I'll let you know as soon as I get my girl out, and then, yes please, I would appreciate your help, as Natanya is an orphan, and has no relatives or anybody, except us."

"Have no fear, my dear. Your mother will soon adjust to the situation, as usual, but that's how she reacts every time you go to Lebanon. I have to suffer for weeks. Anyhow, tomorrow is not too far, and I'll look forward to hearing from you soon."

"Thankyou Dad. But if I may say one thing before I go, and that is that, if it happens I lose my life, I will die very happy and satisfied, just to realise that my love is alive, and we didn't kill her."

Abu Mansour and his men went around the Palestinian camp warning their people, and then they returned home.

"Amal, I want you to pack all the machines, because tomorrow we are going to move you from here," announced Abu Mansour sternly.

She looked at him in surprise, "Why does he want to move me from here?" she wondered. Then she turned to Mansour, who understood her thought.

"Mama and Nahid will go with you, Amal," added Mansour. "We are evacuating the whole camp because we're anticipating a raid from the Israelis, and we don't want anyone to get hurt or killed. Our house will be the target of the hostility, so we must move everything, to ensure our love project will not be interrupted."

Amal stood looking silently, as she knew in her heart that no one would be killed, as Jonathan would not approve of casualties. "I am sure my love is coming to take me home, so I don't want to go away from here, as then he will never find me," she thought. Then she spoke with hesitation about what was in her mind,

"We shouldn't worry about the Israelis. I will pray, and no one will get hurt. I know God will answer our prayer, as we are busy doing His will by our love project, so He will not allow any of us to be killed."

"Amal, no argument," warned Abu Mansour. "We have decided to evacuate the place, and you must cooperate. I want you to be ready at dawn. Shakouri will come to collect you, so make sure all your things are ready."

Om Mansour and Nahid gave her a hand to pack the materials and other items.

"My sugar," said the kind lady, trying to encourage the disheartened girl. "Don't feel so sad. You will get used to this kind of life in time, just as we have. I've spent most of my married life moving from one place to the other, running from our enemies. I've lost furniture and valuables, and had uncounted sleepless nights, but now I'm used to all of this. As long as we have life, then we can do something with it. All I hope is that the Israelis don't blow down the camp or the new buildings, because that would break my heart."

Amal sighed, and said quietly,

"I trust in the hand of my God. I'm sure nothing will be blown down."

"You can't tell, Amal," said Nahid. "We thought they had improved in their raids, but as you know, only a few weeks ago they blew down our houses, and if you hadn't warned us, all of us would be dead now, so it's the best thing to move out. I know it's very inconvenient to sleep on a mat on the floor in a crowded room, but at least we can continue our work from there, as we'll be on the farm, picking the fresh produce ourselves."

Amal went to bed late, as she had been busy preparing for the move. She felt depressed and unsettled. "I wish I could tell them about Jonathan, or even just Mansour, but his father is changing towards me, and has prohibited me from getting near him. At any rate, I'm not sure it would be a good idea to speak, because they will misunderstand my intentions, and then I'll lose all I've been able to achieve so far." She held her ring and felt like crying from desperation. "Jonathan, please don't blow the camp, it's full of my friends. They are poor people, with many children, and also Mansour is my best friend, so please, don't kill. I know you have the same view as me, but I am worried about the other officers who meet in that office, as they don't have any time for their enemies."

Then she comforted herself because she knew her man would be in charge. "I really long to see you tomorrow, as I know you're coming for me, but now, alas, I'll have to wait for heaven knows how long, and I feel so lost. I'm unable to talk about my heart's desire to anyone, for fear of harming them, and myself."

Mansour also had an uneasy night, as he considered his new method of dealing with the problem. "If only we could sit down and talk with our enemies, with understanding and truthfulness. Then we could stop all these nightmares. I must talk to Amal, as she mentioned the Israelis. I wonder if she would be able to shed some light on the way, so we can get out of these endless entanglements and frustrations, a vicious circle that leads to nowhere, except destruction. Pity my father can't see the good Amal is doing, even though he's enjoying the fruits of her love, which are joy and peace, but somehow, he can't see the connection between the good blessing and its source; that peculiar love, love of the enemy." Then he repeated her words, "'The minute you, only you, love the enemy, then he is no longer your enemy, but a dear friend. So it's up to you.' Well, I must talk to her on the farm tomorrow, away from my father, as it's impossible to even have a few words here without him coming and interrupting us."

Baha was trying to sleep in her shared room at the hospital, but she felt unhappy, as she was yearning for her only love, and at the same time feeling sorrow and pity for him, because he was losing so much joy, the joy which comes as the result of helping humans without any discrimination. "If you only knew how much I love you, and dream of the happiness which we can share together, Mansour, then you would never treat me like this. I'm here alone, with no relative or companion to confide in, and you are there with uncle, planning hate and destruction, and causing our people to suffer and die as a result. Why can't we sit together and plan for good, in things like Amal's love project. Then we'll soon spread such peaceful ideas to the entire country, and even beyond. After all, Jonathan is not as bad as I thought, because Doctor Gamil told me how he's supplying us with free medicines and medical equipment, and even surgeons, to help our people, without showing any discrimination, yet you went and kidnapped the poor boy, but I'm glad to hear he escaped. If only you would come to see me, I could tell you all this information about him, and then I'm sure you would not feel so determined to fight him."

Just before midnight, the alarm awoke Jonathan, and his heart began to flutter in simultaneous anticipation and anxiety, as he wondered if his mission would be crowned with success, or whether he or his team would fail in carrying out their role in the plan. "My love is dwelling with my arch-enemy," he thought, as he put on his gear. "The problem is how to meet both of them at the same time, without hurting anyone, or injuring her loving feelings. I've never felt like this before, excited, but dead anxious at the same time, as death and happiness will be on the same doorstep for me. I wonder if she's still waiting for me?"

Then he pushed the doubt out of his mind. "Of course she is waiting for me, that's why she's been talking to me through her thoughts all during the last few weeks, giving me those strange feelings of her presence which I couldn't define. I somehow knew she was alive from the strong messages she was sending to me and the boys, and that's why Menachem was injured. Anyhow, the quicker I go to the area, the better I'll feel, as I hate suspense."

The teams had a quick snack and black coffee to alert their nerves, then Victor gave his good wishes and a few words of encouragement to the young men.

"I'm the one who'll be hanging on his nerves, as usual, so do take the utmost care. Don't rush, and take it easy, a step at a time. Keep us informed constantly, remembering that we have our fighters ready if things take a wrong turning, plus you have ample support from the tanks, and I'll be praying non-stop!

"Look after our hero, as there's a reward waiting for her, which I promised her from her last mission, which she performed while all of us sat here as useless men! So I must pay my debts, otherwise I'll never be able to sleep again," he said, winking to Jonathan.

As the men were airlifted to Lebanon, Jonathan experienced hundreds of butterflies fluttering around in his stomach. "I can't wait to meet you, my love, my princess. I can imagine you with your royal garment, which I've never seen, but even in your prison uniform you resemble an angel. Only a few hours to go, and then hopefully you'll be in my arms. After that, I'll never let you go out of my reach again; we will live together, and die together."

It was two a.m., and pitch dark, as the sky was lit only by a hair-thin crescent. The cemetery was fearfully silent. One truck switched off all its lights, except for one dim front light, filtered from the main road, and drove quietly along the side of the cemetery, heading for the dark side of the mountain, where it stopped at exactly the point marked by Jonathan. Peres and Aaron jumped out and entered the heavily armed and shielded cab which was then gradually lifted to a suitable height. The two men adjusted their telescopes to the outline of the distant black buildings.

"This is about the right height," said Peres. "When dawn breaks, we can adjust our view precisely."

A number of other heavily armoured trucks took up their positions beside the tower, acting as a shield along the side of the mountain. The troops crept along, stooping down almost double, and headed for the open area, with Jonathan in the lead.

"Let's follow the deep shadows," whispered the leader. "Fortunately, we have so many short walls to hide us."

The troops dug themselves in behind the stones and brick walls, setting the aim of their weapons in the direction of the dark, high building that rose in the distance, just in front of the sleeping camp.

"First step is achieved," announced the young officer, whispering his message for the army into his walkie-talkie.

A convoy of army vehicles promptly started to move off, to encircle the camp and shut all exits to the main roads. The camp was in a deep sleep, with no one being aware of the activity going on outside. Each vehicle found its assigned position and parked. All lights were switched off and the troops were ready to block the exit or entry of any man or vehicle.

"I'll hide here," said Jonathan, pointing to the only open route from Abu Mansour's house, which led to the cemetery at the rear of the Palestinian camp. "Then I can welcome Mansour and his father. Just let's hope they decide to leave their home, as it's much better we meet them here on the open ground, than inside the house, as then I'm sure they'd use force, and I don't want anyone to be killed, especially Natanya."

Amal was sure she could hear some movement outside. "I can hear a few cars passing by on the road to the new buildings, but perhaps I only heard them tonight because I'm awake," she said to herself, sitting up in bed, listening and praying. "I wish the morning would hurry up. I hate darkness, as I always imagine all sorts of horrible things, which sometimes prove to be reality, but other times they are only mere imagination."

She continued listening for a while longer, but heard nothing. "Well, for sure there hasn't been a single movement outside for the last half an hour," she said, trying to make herself sleep. "I must get some sleep. Why am I sitting here worrying about tomorrow, as I can't do anything to change it either way. I only know one thing, and that is that love, the true love, will win in the end, even if in the meantime it seems impossible to see the way out. We are so tiny and fragile, but it's amazing the power it does impart to people like me, lonely and weak, and in the hands of events. Oh, if only my Jonathan was here, then we could hold each other's hands and walk this impossible road together, side by side, toward victory; and triumph over hate and wars. What a dream, a most beautiful dream."

Natanya finally dropped off to sleep, but her thoughts continued into an amazing dream, that refreshed her for a few hours, before she woke up in the morning. "What a dream!" she said, smiling to herself. "I could have happily stayed dreaming that for the whole night. It's a pity I couldn't sleep properly, as I'm worried to oversleep because Shakouri is coming early, and anyhow, I may as well get ready now, as it's almost dawn and the sky is beginning to brighten."

She switched on the light and went to have her shower.

Mansour saw her up early and said to himself, "Poor Amal, she is so conscientious. I bet she hardly slept at all. Anyway, I'll have a talk to her for a while when she comes out of the bath, just to reassure her of my friendship, and tell her about my thoughts."

"There's a light on," said Jonathan, rubbing his hands, as he was tormented by boredom and concern. "They get up very early, so I'm glad we dug in during the night, as we're now ready to welcome them."

Peres and Aaron adjusted their telescopes sharply onto the house, focusing on the light that had appeared. The rest of the army was alerted by Jonathan,

"They are up. Be on your guard."

Victor received the news of progress as he sat with a full flask of coffee, waiting for Abu Mansour and his son to rise.

"At last," he said, wiping his tired eyes, and speaking to the officers who were directing the mission from the Centre.

"Time for action, and stomach ulcers."

Amal put on her dark blue dress which she wore outside the house.

"Good morning, Amal," came Mansour's warm greeting as she walked out of the bathroom.

"Good morning, Mansour," she replied with a happy smile. "I am sorry to disturb you so early, but I just can't sleep well when I know I have an appointment."

"You shouldn't worry to that extent. It's only Shakouri, and there's no need to hurry, either, as we're only anticipating a raid that could take place today, or may never happen."

"I hope it will never happen, Mansour, and then we can think of another way to solve this tragedy."

"Funny you should say that, as I wanted to talk to you about that subject. Perhaps we can have a few minutes now, before my father wakes up, as he gets upset very easily these days."

"I know, but that's natural. Mama told me that he always behaves like this when he's worried, or anticipating a raid. So we must be understanding."

"You're a most amazing person, Amal. You allow so much room to others, who in turn do not allow you even a milli. We can sit on the veranda over there," he said, holding her hand, just like a friendly child in a school playground.

Abu Mansour rose from his bed, and the first thing he saw was Amal and Mansour, holding hands and walking towards the settee.

"Oh no! Stupid boy! You assured, and promised me, that she means nothing to you, and that Baha is the one you love, so what do you call this?!" He quickly dressed himself and rushed towards the couple, just as they sat to discuss their important thoughts.

"Mansour, what did you promise me yesterday?"

"Oh Father, why can't you leave me alone for a little bit? Amal is like a boy friend to me, and she knows that. We're just good friends, nothing more, and I want to talk to her."

"No Mansour, there's no time for talking today. We have hundreds of tasks to do, erecting all those shelters and booths. So leave Amal alone."

Om Mansour and Nahid joined the rest of the family.

"You are ready nice and early, my love," said the mother.

"I thought I'd better be ready, so I won't delay Shakouri, because he'll be here as soon as dawn breaks."

"A van is approaching along one of the main roads to the camp," announced the pilot of one of the spotter planes.

Then, a few minutes later,

"The same van is trying other routes. He's on the southern road."

Shakouri saw the Israeli tanks on the main road, so tried a side road. "Oh no! They've blocked everyone in! How can I pass a warning to Abu Mansour? I know, I'll leave the van here, and whistle from the south edge of the camp." He left his watched van and crept between the bushes, but the Israelis were everywhere. "They've really caught us, and all our fighters are trapped inside," he groaned. He whistled as he tried to find a way to enter unseen.

Badrawi was living in the southern part of the camp, and had woken early to begin the evacuation. While he was dressing, he heard the faint whistle of a lonely grasshopper.

"The Israelis are here!" he exclaimed in surprise. He ran to his door and opened it.

"Go in, or we'll shoot!"

"Oh my God! We're not prepared, nor do we have a plan ready to fight this great army. If I shoot any of them, they'll flatten the house with their tanks. I'd better go in, and pass on the warning."

Then he whistled, and soon the entire camp turned into a grasshopper chorus, as each person discovered what had happened.

Abu Mansour heard the warning whistle, and his face turned into a white sheet. Mansour and Amal looked at each other in horror.

"They're here!" he said to his friend.

Nahid and her mother started to panic.

"Oh my God, help us! The Israelis are here! They'll blow us up!"

Abu Mansour ran to his room and picked up his and Mansour's automatic weapons. Mansour went to the window and looked towards the flattened area.

"I can't see anybody there," he remarked, then turned back and sat beside Amal, trying to devise a peaceful plan which could help defuse the tense situation.

Shakouri went all the way round the camp and eventually saw the only open route. "I'll take this road to Abu Mansour, before the Israelis come and block it off as well. At least I can take Amal before they can find her, but I wish we'd listened to Mansour last night when he suggested to move everyone out then."

Peres announced the approach of the van along the only open route,

"He's coming toward you, Jonathan. The van seems to be empty, with just the driver in it."

"Let him pass. We'll stop him before he reaches the house, as we don't want to confront any more people than we have to."

The van was being driven fast towards the house when an Israeli soldier suddenly jumped out from the roadside and ordered the vehicle to stop.

"Oh prophet Muhammad!" he gasped, almost jumping out of his skin. "From where did this demon appear?!"

The young soldier ordered Shakouri out of his vehicle.

"Hands up!" he commanded. He searched him for weapons, while another soldier kept him covered. Then he carefully searched the van, and found only a few trays of vegetables.

"I'm only selling these vegetables," objected Shakouri.

"Perhaps, but the road is blocked for the meantime. You stand at the side of your van with your hands up. Keep facing the van, and dare you move."

"Lucky I left my gun at home, as I didn't anticipate this, and these robbers would have taken it. I bet they're searching for weapons," thought Shakouri, trying to glance at Abu Mansour's house from time to time. "How can I warn them that the place is full of ambushes? They're hiding all over the place."

Victor received the news of the van, and details of various men and women who had been temporarily detained. But his main concern was to know that Mansour and his father had been arrested.

"We'll wait for another half an hour, before we raid the house," said Jonathan, looking at his watch. "They're bound to appear very soon, as the sun's just above the horizon."

Abu Mansour had his gun on his back, and held Mansour's in his trembling hands.

"Come on, Mansour, here's your gun. We must get out before they surround us, too. They've already hemmed the camp in, so let's get out and hide, and try to organize a plan, or seek some help."

"I am sorry, Father," said Mansour calmly. "I am not going to carry a gun again. I am not going to kill another human, because it's a waste of time and life, but I'll try to solve our struggle by another method, a peaceful one."

"Are you insane, boy? Or crazy? How can you speak like that, with our enemies surrounding us and our people needing defending? Anyhow, I'm not going to argue with you, as time is pressing, so I order you to take this gun and come with me, as you're one of the leaders of our fight."

"I am unable to join you in using this method, Father," said the gentle young man, "as I believe we can conquer our enemies by love, because didn't our Lord Eesa advise, 'Love thy enemy'? So I'm certain we can win the battle by love, as I've seen it working with my own eyes, and I choose to believe the facts, the simple facts."

Amal and the other two women stood shivering in anticipation of a great explosion from the angry man, as he stood there holding his gun and trembling with rage.

"Please Lord, help," prayed Amal, watching the gun. "Don't let him kill his son, as he does look extremely upset. If he attempts to shoot, I'll jump quickly, because I can't see my friend

435

killed in front of me, while I stand doing nothing." She did not move her eyes from Abu Mansour's hand and gun, ready to push him if the situation got out of hand.

The whistles had changed to warn that the Israelis were now around Abu Mansour's house, too.

"You know who you are, don't you?" said the wild man, foaming at the mouth. "You're a useless woman, a coward, a worthless dog, a good-for-nothing woman who's afraid to face his enemy, and disguised it under the cover of love! - You're just a stupid woman!"

Mansour jumped to his feet, as he had never been hurt so much in all his life, to be called a useless woman by his father, in front of his sister, mother and best friend. It was unbearable.

"I AM NOT A WOMAN!" he shouted back. "And just to show you that I don't fear death or enemies, I'll walk straight out to the Israelis who are surrounding the place, because I trust I'll win the battle with LOVE." Then he turned round and headed for the street door, to leave the house.

"Mansour, please don't go," cried his mother, running after him. "The Israelis will shoot you. You know they're after you. Please don't go, my son, my only one." She tried to grasp his hand, but he was too quick.

Abu Mansour regretted he had upset his son to that extent, but it was too late, he had opened the door and gone, shutting it behind him.

"A young man has walked out of the house," shouted Peres in excitement.

Jonathan's heart leaped.

"Watch carefully, see if you can identify him."

"It's Mansour! He's walking towards you, with his hands in his pockets. He's looking straight ahead of him, with no sign of fear, or haste in his steps."

"That's very strange," thought Jonathan. "He surely knows we're around, as we've just moved our tanks quite close to his house. Oh no!" he nearly jumped out of his hiding place as the thought struck him.

"Try to see if there are any bulges in his pockets, as it sounds to me like a suicide mission."

Peres and Aaron enlarged Mansour in their viewers, to the point that they could count the hairs on his arms.

He walked gently, with his heart sensing that there were Israelis all around him. He saw Shakouri's van in the distance, with a few soldiers nearby. His father's insult was ringing in his ears, 'Useless woman!' "How dare he call me a woman! I don't fear anything. I'm a man. I'm a conqueror of the impossible beast. So who is there who can frighten me? I must go to Baha and try to talk to her, if I can manage to pass by. Otherwise, let me die by the hands of those I'm trying not to fight."

Victor and the officers with him stood in their anxiety, as they followed the mission in their mind's vision.

"That will be a tragedy if he goes and blows up our Jonathan this time," said the anxious man.

"I sincerely hope not," said another. "I hope he shoots him before he gets too near."

They then had to hush as Peres continued his report.

"No sign of any bulges or weapons, but he does look upset and his face is pale. He's almost thirty metres from you."

"Thanks. I'll surprise him right now." Jonathan jumped out of his hiding place, together with an officer holding a megaphone.

"Hands up, or we'll shoot."

Shakouri saw Mansour coming out of the house and he grew numb. "Mansour, why did you have to come out? Now you've had it, man; there's no way you can flee." He glanced again and saw Jonathan jump out with another man. "That's the fox himself, the cunning devil! I am sorry, Mansour, now you'll die in that horrible prison in Israel, where they will knock you into the grave. What a great tragedy for us, our blackest day ever."

Peres continued his commentary,

"They are walking towards each other. Mansour's hands are up in the air. Jonathan is a few feet from him."

The other troops who were in hiding behind the rocks and walls were all ready with their guns in their hands, watching the development of the hair raising meeting between the two arch-enemies. They had a clear warning not to shoot unless commanded to do so, and even then, only to incapacitate, not kill.

Jonathan walked steadily, staring directly into the eyes of the young man. But he noticed a change in them. They were not the eyes of the Mansour he remembered.

"Hello, Mansour," he said, while still staring at his eyes.

Mansour looked straight at his enemy. 'Every time you see one of your enemies, pretend you are looking at me.' "Those haunting words of Amal are back again," thought Mansour, not knowing what to say or think as Jonathan searched him, while two of his officers stood at his side.

Jonathan was surprised that he did not find a single weapon, not even a penknife. "What's happened to him," he wondered.

"Where is your gun, Mansour?" he asked.

A victorious look shone in Mansour's eyes, and he answered in a quiet and confident voice,

"I do not carry guns anymore."

Jonathan almost lost his balance. "That's incredible!" he thought, trying to adjust to the strange drama that was unfolding in front of his eyes.

"Why are you not carrying guns anymore?" he asked, wondering if Mansour had lost all his weapons, or perhaps because of some other cause.

The young hero felt excited to answer Jonathan's question, and fascinated at the same time to watch his expressions, as he felt like a superman, even though he had no weapons.

"I do not need any guns."

"WHY?" Jonathan's heart almost jumped out of his breast.

"Because I have no enemies, not a single one." Then he added, as a soft smile appeared on his lips, "Have you heard of the advice, 'Love thy enemy'?"

"I have," answered Jonathan, with great amazement on his face, as he looked intensely into Mansour's gentle eyes. Then he quickly added, "I believe in it."

"You do?" said Mansour with surprise.

Then he continued, as if he was in an impossible dream,

"I practise it."

"Has he arrested him yet, Peres?" shouted Victor into the radio.

"No. They're having a conversation, a relaxed one."

"Maybe he's enquiring about Natanya," said Victor to his men, while he almost chewed his pen in half out of anxiety.

Jonathan hesitantly stretched out his hand to shake Mansour's hand. He instantly responded by firmly grasping Jonathan's.

"This is wonderful!" they both said together, with smiles on their lips. Then their left hands gripped each other's arms.

"How marvellous!" they said with one voice, as the handshake developed into a hug.

Peres' commentary continued,

"They are shaking hands. They're smiling. They're firmly gripping each other's arms. They're hugging."

"What do you mean, 'hugging'?" enquired Victor, thinking he was hearing things, or perhaps completely out of his mind.

"You know, embracing."

"What do you mean by 'embracing'?"

"You know, like when you meet a long lost friend," answered Peres.

"I know the meaning of the word, man. What I'm asking is what are they doing?"

"They are still hugging."

Shakouri kept glancing underneath his lifted arms and saw the handshake, then the arm grip, and finally the hug.

"Blessed be Allah! What are they doing?! I must be seeing things! It can't be true, not Jonathan and Mansour hugging - that's impossible!"

Jonathan continued gripping his new friend's hand, as he knew Natanya had been very busy spreading the most effective way of conquering hate. He said,

"I do respect anyone who believes and practises those words, because beyond any doubt, those who manage to do so are heros who have conquered the impossible. So I do greatly admire and respect you, Mansour."

"I can't express my delight to find that you feel that way, too, Jonathan. I've been thinking hard to find a way to solve our common problems, and am so glad to meet you face to face."

"I just feel as if I'm dreaming, because I've also spent days thinking the same thing," answered Jonathan. "We must meet again, and now I can arrange for a meeting. Then we can sit down and talk like good friends, caring and loving ones, and I'm certain our talks will be crowned with success."

"I'm ready for discussions at any time, and in fact, I have some good friends who are working for the same aim. Do you know where to contact me?"

"Perhaps through the hospital, as I know of another hero there by the name of Baha," suggested Jonathan, with a twinkle in his eye.

Mansour laughed and gave Jonathan another hug.

"You're very shrewd. I like you, and I admire your wisdom. Yes, that will be the best place, and actually, I was on my way to her when I left the house just now."

"I will not detain you any longer," said Jonathan with a warm smile, and he announced an order through his walkie-talkie to the troops,

"A safe passage for our friend Mansour."

The men's ears tingled at hearing the strange command.

"Please repeat the order. It is not clear," they asked.

"A free and safe passage for our friend Mansour," repeated Jonathan, with a wide smile on his face.

As Mansour walked past the tanks and armoured vehicles spread all around the place, he felt like skipping and dancing. "What a wonderful feeling, to actually love the enemy. I've never experienced the like of it before, and it's far superior to any other love; it is indeed a divine love. Baha won't believe me when I tell her that I've just embraced Jonathan, but I know for sure that she will no longer refuse me, as she told me she would wait for me until the day that I love my enemy, and I did, today. But how did Jonathan get to believe in that statement, 'Love thy enemy'? I wonder who taught him? I'll have to ask him about it when we have our meeting. He really is a delightful man, and a very good friend. How amazing!!"

When Abu Mansour saw his son leave, he knew he would never see him again. He was shocked and angry, and his feelings were made worse when he saw his wife almost collapse as she watched her son walk straight into the arms of the enemy. Then his eyes fell on Nahid, weeping and crying for her brother, while Amal stood praying with all her strength for Mansour's safety. When he saw Amal standing beside his wife, with the star of David shining on the dark blue velvet dress, then his ugly beast kicked inside him.

"Amal, you're the cause of all my trouble. You're the one who's lost me my son!" and he rushed to her, grabbed her shoulders and gave her a severe shaking. "We were alright until you appeared, and then you divided our family. First we lost Baha, our own flesh and blood, and now you've lost me my only son!"

Amal stood staring at the angry man, knowing that if she opened her mouth, he would strangle her, so she kept quiet, reciting in her heart the wise proverb, 'If the kings' anger grows hot against you, don't lose your cool.'

Om Mansour jumped up and snatched Amal from her husband's hands.

"Leave her alone, Abu Mansour! She's only a poor orphan. Why do you treat her like this, while she is our guest?"

"I don't want her in my house, as she's lost me my son, and caused division in my house, so she must leave immediately. Let her go and love her enemy!"

Amal's heart fluttered. "Oh, how lovely!" she thought. "Now I can go to my love at last; and make sure Mansour is not hurt."

Nahid and Om Mansour hugged Amal and cried out,

"You can't throw her out. You know the Israelis will be looking for her, as she escaped, and then that'll be her end! Please Baba, don't throw her out!"

"I will throw her out, and I'll be delighted if they catch her again, and take her away!"

Amal smiled in the midst of all the weeping and wailing and softly said,

"Don't worry about me, please. I'll be alright, as I have no enemy, no matter where I go or who I meet, because everyone is my dear friend, and brother and sister; but I must thank you so much for all the love and care you've shown me. I'll pray that our love project will grow and prosper, as you are both excellent in managing everything. I'll try to visit you if I can, and I'm sure that soon the storm will pass away, and the sun of joy and hope will shine for all of us."

"Amal, I'm getting impatient with your preaching! Out, right now! Go out!" shouted Abu Mansour, dragging her from the arms of the women. She stood by the door, and turned round. Her eyes were filled with tears, and she whispered,

"Maa el-salama." ('I leave you with peace', a farewell).

Then she stepped outside the house, shutting the door behind her. As she walked away, her emotions were in a great turmoil, caused by the tears and weeping of her friends whom she had just left behind, her anxiety about Mansour's safety, and her meeting with her love. "Mansour," her heart worried, "I wonder what has happened to him?"

She looked around and saw Shakouri's van in the distance. "Oh, there is Shakouri, and he's been arrested, but where is Mansour?" She saw army vehicles and soldiers all around the area, and, as she kept her gaze directly ahead, she saw Mansour just disappearing from sight, round the bend. "Thankyou, Lord. He is safe. Jonathan must have met him, I'm sure of that. Oh, how happy my heart is, how wonderful to see love winning the battle!"

Jonathan found himself in a dilemma, as he never anticipated that Mansour would have changed into a meek lamb. "How can I get my Natanya out?" he thought, almost panicking.

"We must put pressure on around the house, and warn them over the megaphone, for everyone to come out, or we'll attack," he commanded.

Promptly a number of armoured vehicles began to move slowly towards the house, while Jonathan walked between their cover, for fear of snipers, as the sun was up in the sky and he could easily be shot at.

Suddenly Aaron shouted,

"A young Palestinian woman is coming out!"

"Look carefully," said Jonathan, anxiously.

"It's Natanya! Baruch ha-shem, it's our Natanya!" shouted Aaron in tremendous excitement. "I can see the star of David round her neck, glowing in the sun. She has a lovely smile. She is out; she is coming!"

"Tell her to raise her hands," commanded Jonathan, so he could deal with her equally, in the same way as Mansour.

The officer ordered,

"Hands up, or we shoot."

Shakouri had just recovered from his shock of witnessing Mansour and Jonathan hugging, and Mansour being given a safe passage through the troops of the enemy, when he saw Amal appear out of the house. "What's happened to Abu Mansour, to let our hero go out while the Israelis are all around? They'll take her into captivity again. I know, he's had one of his fits of rage again, and thrown her out." He felt exasperated when he realised what had happened, and lowered his arms.

Suddenly the soldier guarding him loudly ordered,

"Hands up, and face the van."

"That is a poor girl," he pleaded. "She does a lot of work for the poor; please don't harm her."

"We don't harm anyone," answered the young man.

Jonathan walked towards his love, although he felt like running, but he controlled himself to keep pace with the slow moving vehicles. He saw her raised hands, and the magical smile on her lips, as she hurried her steps towards him. "Thou art beautiful, O my love, as Tirzah, comely as Jerusalem, terrible as an army with banners," he said, quoting his favourite verse from the Song of Solomon. "She does look like a princess, a hero, who has conquered the impossible, and helped others to find the elevated path to perfect love and peace."

He opened his arms ready to embrace her, and his eyes shone with tears of joy. "I must be dreaming; it can't be true! Is this really my Natanya, the girl I love so much, the one I thought had been fatally struck? I'll only believe it when I hold her in my arms."

Natanya saw her love walking towards her. "Oh Jonathan, how lovely to see you," she whispered to herself. "My dear love, I want to run to reach him!" Then she steadied her steps. "Better not to run, we don't want an accident!"

"Natanya is only a few yards from Jonathan; she looks marvellous! It's so wonderful; it's a great scene! Oh, they've met, they're embracing! It's great, it's a beautiful moment!" shouted Aaron, and, with his tears streaming down his cheeks, he hugged Peres.

Then the troops started to hug each other, as the atmosphere suddenly changed into a celebration. Shakouri sensed the change in tension, but was unable to see what happened to Amal, as the armoured vehicles hid her from his sight.

As tears ran down both faces, Jonathan embraced his sweetheart, and found himself lost for words to express his feelings. "It is reality. I'm sure it isn't a dream, as she is actually in my arms."

"Natanya, are we dreaming?" he asked, looking into her soft brown eyes that shone with love, hope and joy, and tears of happiness.

"No Jonathan, we are not dreaming, but it's our first dream coming true."

"My dearest love, if this is our first dream coming true, what will it be like when all of those beautiful dreams come to their completion?"

"It will be paradise! It will be heaven!" she said with a victorious smile. Then she continued, holding his arms, "But we need to live forever to see them all, as we have lots of them, hundreds!"

Victor and the officers at the Centre were also caught by the embracing fever, so they too hugged each other, as they felt caught up in a world of dreams.

"I never experienced a raid like this in my whole life," he said, trying to control his emotions, as he felt tearful. "We should call this raid, 'Love Mission'. It will just fit it right."

The men agreed as they shook each other's hands and had some more hugs.

Jonathan announced to his men,

"Withdraw to base. Mission successfully accomplished."

Then he took his love by her waist and they walked side by side between the celebrating army's vehicles, as they withdrew from Abu Mansour's and the Palestinian camp.

"They're pulling out," said Shakouri, looking around him. "I can't see Amal, Jonathan must have taken her with him."

"You can go now," said the Israeli soldier, with a big smile on his face.

When Shakouri saw everyone hugging, he too was infected with joy and hugged the young soldier. "It's a marvellous atmosphere. I wonder what's going on. I can't wait to tell the story to Abu Mansour," he said to himself, as he got into his van and drove to Abu Mansour's house, and away from the withdrawing army.

Natanya and Jonathan walked on, still holding each other tightly by their waists, with their heads held high, as if they were gazing into a magic land.

"How funny," she thought as she walked between the noisy tanks. "This is very similar to my dream which I had earlier today, when I saw a long road, lined with pits and craters caused by bombs and war, and then that wonderful meek man walking along a dark road, singing a most beautiful song that pulled the hearts of the hearers towards him. Then the pull grew stronger from the magic of the song, impelling some of those standing at the roadside to step onto the dangerous road and join in singing the beautiful song as they followed after him. The more who joined in behind the wonderful singer, the better the song sounded, and the more the pull drew others.

"Now here I am, walking side by side with my love on this road, which has suddenly been transformed by the beautiful song of the heart into a dream land. May all who live one day experience the pull of this wonderful love, the love of thy enemy."